Netherworld Fae

Knotted Myths

USA Today Bestselling Author

Lexi C. Foss

Knotted Myths

Editing by: Outthink Editing, LLC

Proofreading by: Katie Schmahl & Jean Bachen

Cover Design: Sanja Balan of Sanja's Covers

Cover Photography: Wander Aguiar

Cover Model: Brandon M.

Title Page, Background Art & Chapter Headers by: Anna Spries

Illustrated Map by: Ricky Gunawan

Published by: Ninja Newt Publishing, LLC

Digital Edition

ISBN: 978-1-68530-410-2

Print Edition

ISBN: 978-1-68530-411-9

AI Disclaimer: This book does not contain any elements of AI content. All art was designed by real artists, and all of the words were written by the author.

To the narrators who bring my voices to life,
and to the readers who give me a reason to write…
Thank you for inspiring me.
This trilogy wouldn't exist without you.
<3

KNOTTED MYTHS

A NETHERWORLD FAE NOVEL

ABOUT KNOTTED MYTHS

I remember everything now.
Every sordid deed.
Every lie.
Every manipulation.

My soul was deceived by the one Alpha I should have been able to trust.
Locked inside a mortal shell.
And anchored to a plane of nonexistence.

I'm determined to free the innocent Mythos Fae tangled up in this ancient web.
Only, I have to figure out how to free my inner Omega first.
Which is proving trickier than I could ever have imagined.

The three dominant fae in my life are determined to help me.
Protect me.
Mate me.

But surviving means working as a mate-circle, something that doesn't feel possible.
Maliki and Morpheus no longer trust Hades's motives.
And Hades isn't a team player.

If we can't find a path forward, we may be forever bound by the myths of our past.
Or I might be forced to make a choice.
One that will break my heart.
And destroy my soul…

Author's Note: *Knotted Myths* is the conclusion to the Netherworld Fae trilogy. It's a Hades & Persephone "why choose" retelling with Omegaverse vibes. Because knotting is always a good time…

WELCOME BACK TO THE NETHERWORLD KINGDOM

Knotted Myths is the conclusion to the Netherworld Fae trilogy.

Secrets are about to be revealed.

New planes of existence are about to be discovered.

And our heroine is about to fully embrace her destiny as an Omega Goddess…

Are you ready to be bred, little dreamer? To create life? To become the Goddess you were meant to be?

Then be a good girl and let us do what we were made to do.

Because you're ours now, sweetheart.

Ours to fuck.

Ours to knot.

Ours to claim…

Below are some themes you may find in *Knotted Myths*:

✓ This is a Hades and Persephone retelling with a "why choose" twist (will our tortured hero learn how to properly share "his mate"?)

✓ No MM, but there are group scenes/play

✓ Consent between the heroine and her mates

✓ Psychotic Hero (Maliki)

✓ Celibate Hero (Hades) — But he likes to watch…

✓ Hero who loves CNC and sleep play (Morpheus)

✓ No Other Woman or Other Man Drama (No Cheating)

✓ Pregnancy/Breeding

✓ Primal Energy

✓ Possessive Over The Top Alpha Males

✓ Touch Her and Die Vibes

✓ Alpha/Omega Dynamics

✓ Knotting, Nesting, Purring & Growling (because yes, please…)

Enjoy! <3

LABYRINTH
Rutting Grounds
Death's Cabin
Ice Cave
Breeding Pit
Nesting Garden

HADES

In the Labyrinth…

This is impossible.

Serapina should be a writhing mess of need. Begging to be touched. Stroked. *Knotted.*

Yet she's staring up at me with clear blue eyes.

And uttering words that I'm… I'm struggling to understand.

"Persephone didn't betray you," she claimed moments ago. "She tried to crawl her way back to you. Delos was there to help. But Demeter was too strong."

The image those statements conjure sends a dagger through my heart.

Persephone crawling… I can picture her long, dark hair dragging along the ground, her brown eyes glowing as she demurely smiles up at me.

It's a position I used to enjoy.

One she liked, too.

Only now, it feels wrong. And not just because of the context underlying Serapina's words.

The visual shifts in my mind to the blonde cradled in my lap, her delicate features replacing the memory and morphing it into a fantasy.

Because I long to see her on her knees.

Beckoning me with her eyes.

But not under the circumstances she just mentioned.

It's confusing. Debilitating. *Infuriating.*

However, she continues speaking before I can comment.

"I remember everything," she confesses, stealing the breath right out of my lungs. "And I think I know how to find the other Omegas."

I study her, torn between demanding more information and questioning whether or not this has all been a game. A twisted fate. *A fucked-up ruse.*

Except all I find is a mix of anger and intent in her alluring eyes.

"She somehow used your power," Serapina adds, her focus on me. "Demeter, I mean. I… I'm trying to understand how it worked. But I think that's the key to locating the others. Persephone manifested life, yet her link to you—to your ability to *resurrect*—allowed her to form a unique state of existence. Or…"

Her brow furrows as she trails off.

I say nothing, waiting. Thinking. *Spiraling.*

Because my mind is spinning with truths. Curiosities. *Fears.*

If Persephone is lying now—

No. I cut off the thought before it can complete itself.

This is Serapina. She's not Persephone. She's…

I struggle with how to finish that last line, my history

mingling with the present. Knowledge interfering with hopes. Past agony threatening to unravel every delicate emotion inside me.

I need to understand what's happening here. What Serapina truly knows. Otherwise… otherwise, I'll give in to my fears.

That I've been tricked.

That Persephone has chosen now to reveal her true plans.

To show she's a queen in this long game of dreadful chess.

Fuck…

"Or, I think, Demeter used that gift to create that plane," Serapina continues, her voice lowering to a whisper.

I study her features as she seems to look inward, her gaze taking on a strange glint.

This isn't an act, I tell myself, needing to believe it.

Only there isn't anything to believe.

Because the truth is right in front of me as Serapina shudders at whatever she sees in her mind. She's reacting to my mate's memories, seeing things I've longed to understand for millennia.

"That's where Demeter imprisoned the Omega souls." She blinks, her frown deepening. "It's… it's how she releases them. How she *re-creates* life forms. Like mine. Like Alina's. Except I'm different. I… I *remember.* Because the power exists in my soul. That's why it has to remain whole. If it doesn't, I think the plane will shatter."

I give in to the urge to touch her, my need to soothe her overriding every other instinct.

She's scared.

Furious.

Upset.

It's on the tip of my tongue to say "Enough." Because

she doesn't deserve this torment. The past isn't hers to own. To understand. *To share.*

But Maliki speaks before I can utter a sound, his voice rough with an emotion that momentarily distracts me. "How do you suddenly know all of this?"

The quiver underlying his tone is unlike anything I've ever heard from my best friend.

He's concerned.

"I don't know… I saw everything when Demeter tried to pull me from this maze, back to that place of stillness—the plane where she holds the Omega souls hostage. But my ties to you…" She looks at Maliki and then at Morpheus and me. "My ties to *all* of you… helped me find my way back here."

I swallow.

We found her lifeless form in the heart of the labyrinth not even twenty minutes ago. Maliki discovered her first, his growl one that reverberated through every inch of my being as I materialized by his side with Morpheus hot on my tail.

The three of us fell to the ground, gathering up our mate, eager to begin a rut. Only to freeze upon realizing she was lost to a comatose state.

Except, a beat later, she opened her eyes in a miraculous breath and began to speak.

Her words still echo around us now.

Revealing a truth I'm struggling to comprehend.

One that leaves me speechless.

Our Omega hunt began on a wave of feral excitement, the heat of it still simmering inside me now. Yet ice coats every inch of my being, threatening to freeze me from the inside out.

"Maliki's mark," Morpheus says, his comment so unexpected that I look at him. "That's what anchored you to your corporeal form." I follow his movements as he lifts a hand to brush his finger along the crescent claim etched into her shoulder.

"What do you mean?" Serapina asks him.

"His claim is real. Visceral. *Here.*" Morpheus continues to stroke the healed bite mark, his tone almost reverent. "Whatever power Demeter has over your soul must have been momentarily disrupted by his tether, which is why you were able to follow that strand back to us."

I stare at him for a beat, analyzing his train of thought.

I felt my Omega *leave*, her soul vanishing from existence just like all those eons ago in our home realm. Only, her body remained behind this time, something that didn't happen back then.

Persephone vanished and never returned.

Yet Serapina is very much here.

And still utterly human.

Except, she has a hold on Persephone's memories now. They haunt her pretty eyes, making my heart ache with a renewed sensation of loss. *And guilt.*

Persephone—the love that I once knew—is gone. Forever. That much is abundantly clear. Her soul remained intact, as did her memories, but the entity that once held her Omega form didn't survive.

"She tried to crawl her way back to you…"

I close my eyes, wincing as a jolt of longing pierces my heart. *I'll never see her again.*

However, that realization is quickly chased by an unexpected emotion. One that has my eyes opening once more and locking on Serapina as my heart skips a beat.

Because the sensation I feel now is light. A breath of fresh air. A weight leaving my shoulders.

Relief.

Because Serapina is still here. She's alive. She's safe. *She's with us.*

And Persephone's essence simply lives inside her as a distant memory, not a true entity.

Serapina won't be erased…

It's a realization that has me inhaling sharply, almost as though I'm finally able to *breathe.*

I suddenly understand Maliki's previous concern. He worried that Serapina knew all of this because Persephone had taken over.

It's a comprehension I confirm when I note the calmness of his features, so at odds with the quivering note of his tone moments ago.

I palm Serapina's face, needing to see her eyes, to confirm again that she's still *her*, not Persephone.

Uncertainty colors her pretty irises, stabbing me in the chest for a completely different reason. She doesn't trust me. Not yet.

"Ask me anything," she tells me. "I can… I can search for answers. For you."

Fuck. She thinks I want to prioritize the past over our present.

I can't even fault her for that assumption, not after everything we've been through.

But rather than tell her that, I decide to show her how I feel by asking something that truly matters. A question I *need* an answer to.

Because the response may help us save Serapina's life.

"Can you remember anything about your time with Demeter?" I ask. "Anything that can help us determine why you're not in heat right now?"

As far as I'm concerned, these details are what we need right now—details to help us reunite Serapina with her soul.

Not Persephone's spirit, but *Serapina's* inner Omega.

We need her to be whole, to ensure our Goddess is strong enough to face the future.

The past will need to wait.

For now.

"Before you make an assumption, I want to add that Hades isn't asking this because he's eager to knot you, sweetheart," Morpheus interjects, his words making my lips curl down.

He's wrong.

I'm absolutely eager to knot my mate.

Though, yes, that's also not why I asked. "She's human again," I tell him. "That can't be good for her soul."

"Yes, I agree," he replies, looking at her, not at me. "And Hades is also not saying that because he only cares about Persephone's soul. He's saying that because he cares about *your* soul, Serapina."

"I can speak for myself, Cousin," I say, irritated now by his interruptions.

"Then speak more clearly, *Cousin*," he returns, giving me a look. "Tell Serapina why you're asking these questions."

"He's right," Maliki murmurs. "You need to be clear right now, Hades. Not issue demands or questions. But tell her how you feel."

I stare at both men, then down at Serapina.

"You don't need to explain anything," she tells me, sounding tired. "I understand you want your mate back. But I'm not sure how to help. I… I don't remember much of Demeter outside of your mate's memories. Unless you mean something that Demeter did to Persephone?"

My brow creases, and I look at Maliki again.

His expression goes flat. "If I need to explain this to you, we're going to have a problem."

My jaw ticks. "I'm not deaf, Maliki. Nor am I blind." Because yeah, I get what's happened here. Serapina sees Persephone as my mate. Not Serapina herself. But her *soul.*

Because I've not made it clear to this female that I want *her*, and not just because of her Omega spirit.

"Now is a good time to prove that," my best friend drawls. "*My lord.*"

"Fuck you," I mutter under my breath.

"It's fine," Serapina whispers. "As I said, I understand. And I already told you that I'm willing to do whatever is needed to… to help. However, Persephone didn't hurt those Omegas. Not intentionally. Demeter did. But I realize you need my soul—*Persephone's*, I mean—to help unravel what's been done. So. I… I accept that."

"I don't," I bite out. "I don't accept that at all."

"Neither do I," Morpheus all but growls.

However, I hold up a hand before he can say more. "This is my issue to address, Cousin."

"Then address it." His blue-green eyes swirl with fury as he glares at me. And Maliki's eyes glitter with a similar shade of violence, too.

It seems I've failed not only our mate but our entire circle as well.

Sighing, I move my hand to Serapina's nape and run my thumb along the column of her throat. This isn't going to be easy to fix. But I'm going to try.

"I think it's time to show you the changes I've made to the labyrinth," I tell her. "But first, you're going to need some clothes. So how about you head back to the cabin with Maliki, take a calming bath, and then dress for an evening out? I'll be back to pick you up in a few hours for a proper tour."

"And where will you be going in the interim?" Maliki asks.

"A better question—where will *I* be in the interim?" Morpheus interjects.

"With me," I answer my cousin. "I think it's time we visit Ares—*together*."

Because I want access to his infamous prison.

So I can meet with Demeter.

Personally.

MORPHEUS

"HOW IS THIS ADDRESSING THE ISSUE, COUSIN?" I DEMAND a second after Maliki disappears with Serapina. I'm torn between following them and remaining here just long enough to punch Hades in the face. "You didn't even try to explain yourself."

My cousin glances at me. "Serapina doesn't need words from me, Morpheus. She needs actions."

I arch a brow. "Actions she can't see?"

"She knows where we're going."

"And that's supposed to be enough?" I ask.

"Yes."

He doesn't expand upon that response. Just expects me to accept his simple reply.

That's not going to happen.

"Hades, I don't even know why we're going to meet with Ares." Well, that's not entirely true. I suspect it has to do with Pandora's Box. But that's not the point. "How will Serapina understand your intentions if you don't voice them?"

"By experiencing the outcome," he answers flatly. "Words mean nothing. Actions mean everything. Shall we go? Or would you like to waste more of my time?"

I stare at him, my jaw clenching.

Calling him infuriating won't help the situation. Neither will introducing my fist to his face. Though, the latter would be utterly enjoyable right now.

But I need a way to make him talk.

Which means I have to approach this from a different angle. "I can't be useful to you if I don't understand your goal, Hades," I inform him. "Give Ares my regards."

Turning away from him, I start through the maze.

Oh, I could simply mist to Death's Cabin and join Maliki and Serapina, but I want to give Hades a chance to evaluate his actions.

His sigh wraps around me as I take my second step, then his voice bellows, "Wait."

I don't. I keep walking. Because that's the only way to push Hades.

"Morpheus," he says, my name clearly being uttered between his teeth.

I glance back at him. "Yes, Hades?" I arch a brow. "Do you need something?"

His gaze narrows. "You know Ares won't speak to me without you there."

I shrug. "I'm sure if you're nice to him, he'll at least tell you to fuck off."

My cousin gives me an exasperated look that would usually amuse me. But right now, I'm far beyond *amusement* where Hades is concerned.

"I want to talk to Demeter," he informs me flatly.

"About?" I press, turning to face him now.

His expression matches his irritated tone as he replies, "Our mate. Obviously."

"What about her?"

"Are you purposely being obtuse to piss me off?" he returns.

"Interesting question, Cousin. I could ask you the same. Because you're demanding I accompany you on a mission without providing a purpose. Meanwhile, our Omega is naked and no doubt about to enjoy Maliki's brand of attention. So I hope you can understand why I would much prefer to indulge in their presence over yours, yes?"

Rather than wait for a reply—the question was rhetorical—I turn again.

And run right into Hades's chest as he materializes in front of me. "We need to find out what Demeter has done so we can better protect our mate," he growls. "If I have to explain that to you, then perhaps I should reconsider your position in the circle."

I smile, but the sensation feels tight against my lips. Forced. *Angry*. "My *position* in the circle isn't up for your consideration," I tell him. "That pleasure goes to Serapina."

This time, I mist.

Only to find my throat in a chokehold as Hades grabs me mid-movement and teleports both of us to the Mythos Fae Realm.

My teeth grind together when the barren landscape unveils before me, the familiar chill stirring goose bumps along my exposed arms. "Arse," I mutter, manifesting a sweater because it's fucking cold here.

Stepping away from Hades, I pull the fabric over my head to cover my bare torso and face him once more.

"Well?" I prompt, waiting for him to take the lead and call for Ares.

Instead, he runs his gaze over my white sweater and gray sweats. "You look ridiculous."

"Fuck you, Hades." I fold my arms, take in Hades's pristine black suit, and shout, "Ares!"

"You don't have to yell," a deep voice drawls as the Mythos Fae in question appears beside me, a cigarette in his hand. He lights it with a bluish-purple flame from his fingertip, then takes a long drag before looking between me and Hades. "Tension. Fury. *Sex*. Smells like my kind of party. Who are we killing, hmm?"

"Each other," I tell him. "Unless Hades starts fucking talking."

A tic starts around Hades's mouth.

I merely stare at him and begin a countdown in my head. If I reach one—

"Take us to Demeter," Hades commands.

Which is precisely the wrong thing to do where Ares is concerned. One does not issue demands of Ares. One asks for favors instead. But Hades has never been known for polite conversation. Always direct and to the point.

Or cryptic as fuck.

Ares takes another pull on his cigarette, his ruby-colored eyes seeming to glitter with unspoken warning.

I sigh, my patience hanging on by a thread, and attempt to defuse the situation before Ares loses his temper. "Serapina was about to go into heat, then reverted back to her mortal state. We're trying to determine what Demeter has done to her."

"So you do know why we're here," Hades says, his sarcastic tone an unnecessary addition to his words.

I ignore my infuriating cousin and focus on Ares. "Would you be able to help facilitate a conversation between us and Demeter?" I ask him. "We may need some ideas on how to be… persuasive."

He cocks his head, his dark horns glinting in the pale glow from above. "I do enjoy being persuasive."

"Your creativity on the matter knows no bounds."

"And now you're flirting with me."

"No, merely stating a fact," I murmur. "I see all your fantasies, as you know."

He smiles, the expression positively wicked. "True. You are a voyeur."

"I am." No point in denying my nature. "So will you help me talk to Demeter?"

"You? Absolutely." He looks at Hades. "He can fuck off."

I shrug. "You'll hear no complaints from me."

"No. I'll be joining you," Hades inserts. "I need to understand what Demeter has done to my mate."

"*Our* mate," I remind him.

"Then treat me as your equal in this and stop making plans without me," Hades replies, his dark eyes glimmering with barely restrained fury.

A harsh laugh escapes me. "That's a bit rich, Cousin. Particularly as you demanded I accompany you without feeling it necessary to explain why."

"Because you already knew why," he returns sharply. "Why are you being purposely obtuse?"

"Because I don't know why *you* want to see Demeter," I tell him. "I only know why *I* want to see her."

He stares at me. "That doesn't make any sense."

Exasperated, I ask, "Are you going to Demeter to talk about Serapina or Persephone?"

His dark eyes burn. "Both. Obviously."

I shake my head. "That's not the right answer, Cousin."

He just continues to look at me, his expression exuding confusion. "I haven't the slightest idea what you mean, Morpheus. And I'm exhausted by this banter. Stop playing games and be blunt with me."

He wants bluntness? After he refused to do the same with me? Typical. Fucking. Hades.

I have half a mind to leave him here to sort this out for himself. Head back to Serapina and indulge her with Maliki. *Please my mate.*

But something Hades said moments ago rings true—Serapina needs actions.

So I'll be *blunt*. Not for Hades. But for our Omega.

"Serapina is under the impression that you want to erase her existence by replacing her presence with Persephone's soul. Yet rather than take an opportunity to correct her, you opted for this field trip, stating you want to prove your intentions through actions, not words."

I pause to evaluate his expression.

Which provides him with the opportunity to say, "All of that is true."

I nod, aware that it's *true*. But I'm glad we're at least on the same page thus far.

"Right. So I'll ask again—why do you want to speak to Demeter? Are you trying to determine how to fulfill Serapina's suspicions? To replace her existence with Persephone's soul? Because that's not what I want, and if that's why we're here, then you can speak to Demeter alone."

Meanwhile, I'll mist back to grab Maliki and Serapina… and *run*.

Hades's nearly black eyes shine with a furious emotion, one that rivals my own. Only, I suspect it's for entirely different reasons. "I—"

A cluster of smoke springs toward us, causing Ares to

flick his cigarette toward the movement. Vibrant blue flames erupt all over the forming mist, followed by a shriek of enraged agony.

"Oops," Ares murmurs, not sounding at all apologetic. "I suppose I need another cigarette." He starts patting his leather jacket, likely searching for a pack.

"That's a horrible habit," Hades tells him.

My gaze lifts to the smog-covered sky before settling on my cousin. "Seriously?"

But it's too late.

Fire erupts along Ares's fingertips, his focus entirely on Hades now. "You want to visit Pandora's Box?" he asks in a silky tone. "That can absolutely be arranged. In fact, how would you like a prolonged—"

More wasps of smoke appear, causing Ares to send fire across the space, only for one of the balls to be caught and thrown into the sky as Orcus materializes in a wave of fury.

"Do not fuck with me, Ar…" He trails off, taking in the scene. "Oh, thank fate you're here. We need to talk." The words appear to be for Hades since his eyes are locked on his brother. "Is Serapina okay?"

"Why?" Hades demands, causing my spine to stiffen.

"Did you sense something?" I add.

Orcus glances at me before refocusing on his brother. "Alina felt—"

A swirl of energy cuts him off, the furious swarm shifting into the shape of several familiar faces. My lips part. These Alphas are ones I haven't seen in many, many ages. And all of their expressions are feral with need.

Fuck.

"Now you've done it," Ares murmurs, flames licking across his hands. "Bringing that sweet aroma of Omega pussy into a realm full of crazed Alphas." He shakes his head, then waves his hand to create a fiery wall between us and the incoming fae. "Better run."

Those two words come out like a taunt.

And I know from experience that he isn't talking to the approaching Alphas, but to us.

"Fuck," Orcus mutters, misting to Hades's side. "Let's go."

I ignore them and focus on Ares. "A door, please?" I ask my old friend, interested in neither leaving nor running right now. "We came here to talk to Demeter, and I would prefer not to have to return in an hour for that same purpose."

Rather than reply, Ares tosses me a key—one that burns my palm as I catch it.

Because it's on fire.

Just like his hands and horns are now.

"Thank you," I say, trying to infuse some gratitude into my tone, which is difficult given my clenched teeth.

I turn just as a doorway appears, the obsidian slate an entryway that I recognize as one of the many entrances into Ares's world.

Except it's no ordinary door. It's a solid sheet of rock boasting a feminine head at the top with stone snakes for hair.

Medusa, I think, familiar with the folklore surrounding her existence. Only, she used to be a real Omega, one I suspect Ares fancied in a past life. I've never asked. Nor has he ever commented on it. But the evidence of his previous infatuation is built into the foundation of Pandora's Box.

I present the fiery key to the guardian of the doorway and wait for the snakes to writhe with life. One slowly slithers down to take the token from my palm, utterly oblivious to the chaos forming at my back. Or perhaps *uncaring* is the better term.

It's not like those Alphas can harm the door.

But they can absolutely hurt me if they get too close.

So when the threshold parts to grant me entry, I don't bother to look back or think twice. I simply step through.

And freeze when I find Hades and Orcus waiting for me on the other side.

My brow furrows as the wall whispers closed behind me. "How?" I ask, not only startled but also curious.

"I'm the one who brought Demeter here," Orcus says. "Remember?"

"I do," I say. "But how did you mist through Ares's wards?"

Orcus shrugs. "He gave me access eons ago."

"Why?" Hades asks before I can.

"Because he likes me," Orcus tells him.

"You mean he likes Reaper," I reply, folding my arms. "Yes?"

Orcus shrugs again. "We're a circle. If he likes one of us, he likes all of us."

I grunt at that. "Yeah, it's Reaper." That makes sense. Ares adores violent fae, and there are very few who are more violent than Reaper. "I'm surprised he doesn't like Maliki."

"Oh, I do," Ares says as he joins us in a flash, his leather jacket soaking wet as he peels it off to let it plop onto the stone floor. Firelight dances through the corridor in the next instant, allowing me to see the red liquid oozing around his discarded coat.

Blood.

Of course.

Sighing, I shift my attention to his face. "How many did you slaughter?"

"Does it matter?" he asks, some of the crimson leaving

his irises and allowing the dark rims to shine through. "They'll regenerate, Morpheus."

That last sentence is spoken in a tone that's very unlike the Ares I know. It carries a hint of regret. Perhaps because it bothers him to see the madness that has overtaken our kind.

Or maybe one of those Alphas out there was a former ally.

Regardless, I don't press.

There are horrors in our world I don't want to discuss or face. Not tonight, anyway.

"What's going on with Serapina?" Orcus asks, his attention on Hades again. "Alina said she…" Orcus clears his throat. "I need to confirm that Serapina is all right."

I frown. "Why wouldn't she be okay?" I ask, inserting myself into the conversation because he's talking about *my* mate. As far as I'm concerned, Hades is no longer in the circle. Not until he decides to put *Serapina* first.

And I honestly doubt that will ever happen.

"Alina said she felt her… disappear." While Orcus appears to be replying to me, his focus is still on his brother. "What happened?"

"She was about to go into heat, then Demeter did something to stop it," Hades replies. "Actually, I think she did something to her before you brought her to the Netherworld Kingdom. That's why we need to talk to Demeter—to understand exactly what she created with Persephone's and my powers, and also to determine how to fix it."

My eyes narrow. "Yes. Hades wants to erase Serapina and restore Persephone's soul."

Orcus glances at me with wide eyes, then back at his brother.

"*What?*" The word comes out stilted. Angry. *Impassioned.* "Have you lost your fucking mind?"

"No, but Morpheus bloody has," Hades returns in a snap. "Not once have I said that I want to *erase* Serapina. Nor have I commented on *restoring* Persephone's soul. Serapina said that, not me. However, the fact that you seem to assume the same only further confirms what I need to do." He looks at Ares. "Take us to Demeter. *Now.*"

A sigh escapes me as flames erupt down the hallway, the candles all flickering to life with red flames that match the crimson rock decorating the corridor.

"Hades," I mutter, pinching the bridge of my nose.

But it's too late.

This is Pandora's Box.

A prison-like labyrinth riddled with violence.

And its warden is now furious with my cousin.

Bloody idiot, I think, looking up at the writhing red snakes now decorating the ceiling. *Welcome to Ares's realm of pain and suffering, Hades.*

What's the infamous mortal phrase? *You reap what you sow?*

Yeah…

Cheers, Cousin. Cheers.

SERA

BACK IN THE LABYRINTH...

MEMORIES WHIRL THROUGH MY MIND, THE RECOLLECTIONS ones that feel so familiar yet foreign at the same time. It's a bizarre juxtaposition. I… I know these memories are not mine. However, very real sensations roll through me with each remembered experience.

"I feel like I was there," I whisper to myself. "But I know I wasn't. It's… it's so *strange*."

"You feel like you were where?" Maliki asks from the kitchen.

He's cooking again. Something about making one of his favorite human dishes. I… I was listening when he spoke. But it seems that I wasn't listening *well*.

Probably because my mind is whirring with a lifetime I never actually experienced.

"I can remember how it felt to crawl," I tell him. "The

pressure on my knees as I… *she*…" I shake my head. "She reminds me of Serapina. Like my former self?"

A palm against my cheek draws my focus to Maliki—who is apparently right in front of me now. I'm not sure when he left the kitchen to join me in the dining area, but he's so close that I can smell the hint of peppermint on his breath.

"Sera?" he whispers, his gaze level with mine.

I frown, the question in his tone confusing me. "Yes?"

He searches my eyes. "You're still you, right?"

I blink. "What do you mean?"

"You're my sweet mystery, yeah?"

I stare at him. "Not sure about sweet, or being a mystery," I tell him. "Why do you call me that, anyway? Not that I mind. It's a lot better than some of the other nicknames, like *little human*." I all but growl that pet phrase. "Or *sugar tits*." I shudder. "Some of those fae at the den were…" I frown. "It's like they've never met a woman before."

Maliki releases a breath against my mouth, his forehead meeting mine as he visibly shudders. "Thank fuck."

"What?" I frown again. "What are you—"

His lips touch mine, silencing my question. A shiver tracks down my spine as he palms my cheek, his body leaning into mine and bathing me in necessary warmth. I moan, loving the way he feels. His strength. His heat. His muscular form.

"Styx, Sera," he breathes.

And suddenly his tongue is dueling with mine, causing every thought to flee my mind. Because all that matters is Maliki. His touch. *His mouth.*

He takes possession of me with his kiss, his embrace borderline desperate. I don't know what brought this on.

When we arrived back at the cabin, he wrapped me up in a robe and took me to the kitchen, determined to feed me.

Now, he seems to be more interested in seducing me.

Which is fine by me. I much prefer this to food.

But before I can truly fall into his touch, he pulls back and presses his forehead to mine again. "Please don't leave me, trouble," he whispers. "I need you to stay."

My lips curl down, my lashes fluttering as I open my eyes to look at him. "What are you talking about?" I ask him. "Why would I leave you? Especially after a kiss like *that.*" My cheeks heat at having blurted that last part aloud. "I mean… I mean…" My brow furrows. *Actually*… "Maybe I should leave. You *stopped*. Why did you stop?"

Maliki's eyes widen, then he releases an abrupt laugh and shakes his head. "Ah, sweet mystery…" He closes the gap between us again, his mouth capturing mine in a long, sensuous kiss.

Then he pulls away from me.

Again.

This time straightening and returning to the kitchen.

I gape at his back. "*Seriously?*"

"You need to eat" is all he says in reply.

I huff at that. "I'll eat you," I mutter.

Another laugh overtakes him, causing his shoulders to shake. "No, that pleasure belongs to me." His gold eyes swirl with wicked promises as he glances back at me. "If you're a good girl for me, I'll indulge you for dessert, yeah?"

His words inspire a new wave of heat, one that creeps up my neck into my cheeks.

But then another thought occurs to me.

One… one I decide to voice aloud. "Maybe I don't want to be a good girl." Because Persephone would have been *good*. Just like the old me. The obedient, meek little girl in the Monsters Night universe.

There are so many similarities in my memories and the ones I seem to possess now from Persephone. So many similar *traits*.

All at odds with the strong, independent woman I was trying to be in the Netherworld Village.

Only, that's the woman who met Maliki.

"I don't want to be *good*," I repeat, locking eyes with the fae in the kitchen. "I want to be *bad*." I push away from the table. "I want to be *Sera*. Not Serapina. Not Persephone. But *Sera*."

He arches a brow. "Yeah?" He cocks his head, sending a dark, unruly strand of hair over his sinful gaze. "Tell me more, trouble." He sets his spatula down and faces me fully. "What sort of bad behavior do you have in mind?"

A flicker of interest dances through his handsome features, the flicker morphing into a golden simmer as he studies me intently.

I'm not quite sure what to do here.

Something bold.

Something reckless.

Something… *memorable*.

Because maybe I'm about to be erased. Replaced by Persephone. *Vanish into the plane of nonexistence*.

My stomach churns with the thought, a bolt of fear flashing through my veins.

No.

I'm not going to entertain the notion. Not going to think about the future. Only going to focus on the now.

With Maliki.

Here in this cabin.

Alone.

His eyebrow inches up a little higher, his expression

daring me to do something. *Anything.* To be bad. To prove my point. To be… *Sera.*

Holding Maliki's gaze, I unfasten my robe and decide to just do what comes naturally to me. His eyes slide downward as the fabric leaves my shoulders, his gaze following the silk all the way to the ground.

Though, rather than move toward me, he leans back against the counter and continues to study me.

This time, my brow arches. "You're not going to touch me?"

His lips curl. "Is that the bad behavior you have in mind? Because I think I have permission to touch you already, Sera. So we wouldn't exactly be breaking any rules now, would we?"

I consider him for a long moment. "I was told to come back here for a calming bath and to dress for an evening out." All while Hades went to meet with Ares. "He expects me to be ready for him. Waiting for him. *Preparing* for him." My jaw clenches. "Well… I'm not going to do any of that."

Maliki's smile grows. "No?"

"No," I echo. "I want to get dirty instead. And you know what else? I don't even want to think about him. Only you. So are you going to help me with that or not?"

"You're asking me to help you defy Hades's orders?" he asks, his tone filled with dark amusement.

"I'm not asking, Maliki," I decide aloud. "Didn't you say I'm your new boss now?" I seem to recall him commenting that to Hades at some point. While we were in bed, maybe? It's all a blur. But I definitely remember hearing those words. So… "Consider this my version of an assignment."

Maliki catches my hip and pulls me toward him, his opposite hand going to my nape. "You should know that

I'm particular about word choices, *boss*," he tells me. "So you're going to have to provide very specific instructions."

"Kiss me," I say bluntly.

His eyebrow wings upward again. "That's it?" He shrugs and leans in to brush his lips against my cheek. "Done."

When he releases me, I reach out to grab his arms. "Kiss me on the mouth."

He grins and does what I request, only chastely, before trying to slip away again.

"*Maliki.*"

"Yes, boss?"

"Stop being coy with me."

"How would you prefer I be?" he asks, obviously amused.

"Rough," I growl at him. "Treat me like I'm unbreakable. Take me against a wall. On the counter. On the floor. Somewhere. I don't care where. I just... I just want to feel *dirty*. Used. The opposite of rested. The opposite of everything he expects me to be. I want to be Sera. I want to be *me*. And I... I want to be *yours*."

I'm rambling. Ranting. Making very little sense. Yet Maliki seems to understand. Because he's no longer smirking. He's staring down at me with an intense look, his irises glittering with savage intent.

At some point in my demand, I awoke his predatory side. The dangerous part of him that I caught sight of in Death's Den that first night.

Only, I know he has no interest in hurting me.

His expression exudes possession. Darkness. *Yearning*.

He claimed me with his bite, yet somehow it feels unfinished. I can't explain it. Can't define how or why I feel that way. All I know is that I want to finalize it. To be worshipped by this dangerous fae and become *his*.

Maliki never had a preexisting claim on my soul.

We are not fated mates.

But the attraction between us *burns*.

And I want to revel in it. Experience more.

"Give me a memory that I'll never forget," I whisper, allowing him to hear some of the raw emotion bubbling up inside. "Give me something… something that's for *us*, Maliki. Not for Persephone. Or the Mythos Fae. Or Morpheus or Hades. Something that is just between you and me."

Any hints of our previous game have fled. This isn't about me being his boss or wanting to be bad. This is about finishing a dance we started days ago. Weeks ago? I don't know. Time no longer matters. All I care about is the feeling growing inside me. The craving. The smoldering desire.

"Sera," he says, his tone completely different from before. It's deeper now. Underlined with intention. *Dominance*. "You remember your safe word?"

I blink at him. "Safe word?"

"Hades," he replies. "You say his name and everything ends."

My brow furrows. "Why?"

"Because that's how a safe word works, Sera. It allows you to be in charge even when you might feel helpless."

A tremble works through me. Not one born of nerves, but one founded on excitement. "Okay."

"Then you agree that *Hades* is your safe word?" he presses.

"I don't want to think about him."

"Which makes it the perfect safe word, yes?"

"I don't need a safe word," I try again, my hands going to his shoulders and then up to clasp his neck. "You won't hurt me, Maliki. And in no universe will I ever want any of this to stop."

I go up onto my toes to kiss him before he can reply, my breasts pushing against his bare chest. He never put on more than a pair of sweatpants, and I'm thankful for that now. Because it'll be so much easier to disrobe him.

Yet he fists my hair and yanks my head back from his, breaking our kiss. The movement is so sharp and harsh that I yelp. "If you want all of me, then you need to acknowledge your safe word. Because I'm going to give you what you want, Sera. And I need to be able to trust you to make me stop if it becomes too much."

"It won't," I tell him.

"You don't know that," he replies, his gaze searching mine. "You have no idea what I want to do to you, trouble. All the dark cravings that live inside me. My love for blood. My need to *bite*."

His gaze roams over my neck and down to my shoulder, to the mark he left there while buried deep inside me.

"I've been kind, Sera," he informs me. "Gentle. But if you want me—*all of me*—then you need to agree to a safe word." His grip in my hair tightens, causing it to sting a bit at the roots. "Now tell me what it's going to be, *mate*."

I shudder, that term one that goes straight to my heart.

Mate.

Maliki claimed me. Mated me. And now… now he's offering an experience I can't even begin to comprehend.

But I know I want it. I want him. I want *more*.

So there isn't a choice to make. It's clear. "Hades," I tell him. "My safe word is *Hades*."

"Mmm, good girl," he praises and leans down to brush his nose against mine. The tender gesture contradicts the way his fist tightens in my hair.

It also conflicts with the hungry gleam in his eyes.

I'm being held by a predator.

A dangerous fae.

An assassin.

Yet he's ensuring that I feel safe. Providing me with an out. Being a good mate.

"I'm going to turn you into a beautiful mess, Sera," he vows, a dark note underlining his tone. "Make you barely recognizable, all while proving that you don't need a knot to satisfy you. Not when you have me as a mate."

My nipples tighten against his chest, my breasts suddenly heavier than before.

A sound escapes me, one that resembles a plea. Because I want everything he's offering and more. I want to lose myself in him. His touch. His kiss. His everything.

A memory that's all mine.

A moment just between us.

An experience that I'll never forget.

"There's somewhere in the maze that I want to show you," he goes on. "I think that's where we should play."

I blink and push back just a little. "You want to go back into the maze?" I ask, suddenly a little nervous about the idea of leaving this cabin. It feels secure here, like I can't be dragged off to that plane of nonexistence again.

However, a rebellious part of me sort of likes the idea of exploring.

Especially since Hades said he was going to show me the changes he's made to the labyrinth when he returns.

Seeing them without him will probably infuriate him.

Why does the thought of angering Hades excite me? I wonder as Maliki's lips curl.

"Don't worry, trouble. The only thing you need to fear here is me," he informs me, then waves a hand toward the kitchen, causing all his food preparations to vanish into thin air.

I ignore the manifestation magic and focus on what he just said about needing to fear him. "What?" I ask, my eyebrows lifting.

"You told me to treat you as unbreakable, Sera," he replies, nipping at my lower lip before lifting me up into his arms. "So let's see how much you can take before you regret that request."

My eyes widen, my heart skipping a beat in my chest.

However, that erratic movement isn't the result of panic so much as arousal.

And it only becomes more chaotic as Maliki engages his shadows. His power swathes me in a sea of black, momentarily blinding me before releasing my vision to a new scene.

We're no longer in the cabin.

"Where…?" I trail off, studying the rocks all around us. "I thought you said we were going somewhere in the maze?"

Maliki's expression holds a feral note to it, one that reminds me of that night in Death's Den when he threatened Jack. Except I trust Maliki not to hurt me, even with his sensual threats.

"We're in the Rutting Grounds," he says as he sets me down.

"R-rutting Grounds?"

His lips curl. "Yeah, sweet mate. Hades showed it to me the other day during one of your naps. I've been dying to explore it ever since."

I swallow. "O-oh. And… and why is that?"

"Because this whole maze was built for endless days and weeks of fucking, Sera. Which means all those boulders out there were manifested with various positions in mind." He leans against the cream-colored wall beside us. It's a sheet of rock, just like all the ones spread out before us. Only the corridor one is smooth, while the others appear to be textured.

They also vary in shapes and sizes.

Creating a labyrinth of a whole different variety.

My throat goes dry, the field before us taking on a whole new meaning as I replay Maliki's words through my mind.

"Those don't look… comfortable," I say slowly, considering the jagged edges.

"I don't think comfort is what Hades had in mind when he built this place. But I'm certain we'll find a way to enjoy ourselves." He folds his arms and props one bare foot up on the rock behind him. "Go ahead and explore. I'll be right behind you."

My lashes flutter as I try to focus on him again. "Explore?" I repeat, the word nearly a croak.

"I'm telling you to run and hide, trouble," he murmurs, his eyes taking on a wicked glint that matches his tone.

"Why?" I whisper.

"Because, sweet mate, I'm in the mood to hunt." He tilts his head down, his gaze seizing mine. "You wanted to feel dirty, yeah? So we're going to play my way." He cants his head a little to the side. "Now remember your safe word, Sera. And *run*."

The growl that underscores that final word has me reconsidering all my choices.

As do our rocky surroundings.

But a memory tingles in my mind, one of Persephone playing a similar game with Hades long, long ago.

Only, she didn't run so much as frolic. And she certainly didn't hide.

She wanted to be caught.

Dominated.

His.

And while I desire the same game with Maliki, I also want to make him work for it.

I won't wait on my knees the way Persephone did with Hades.

I'll keep running.

Force Maliki to catch me.

Make him prove himself worthy of my submission.

Only then will I give him what he craves. *My body. My heart. Maybe even my soul.*

"Ninety seconds," he warns. "That's the only head start I'm going to give you, trouble."

"Sixty," I counter, wanting to feel challenged, not coddled. "And not a second longer."

I take off across the rocks. Let go of all my worries. Forget the past. Ignore all the memories threatening to overtake my mind. Block Demeter from my thoughts. And focus on the present.

On Maliki.

On running through the Rutting Grounds.

And experiencing life—*my life.*

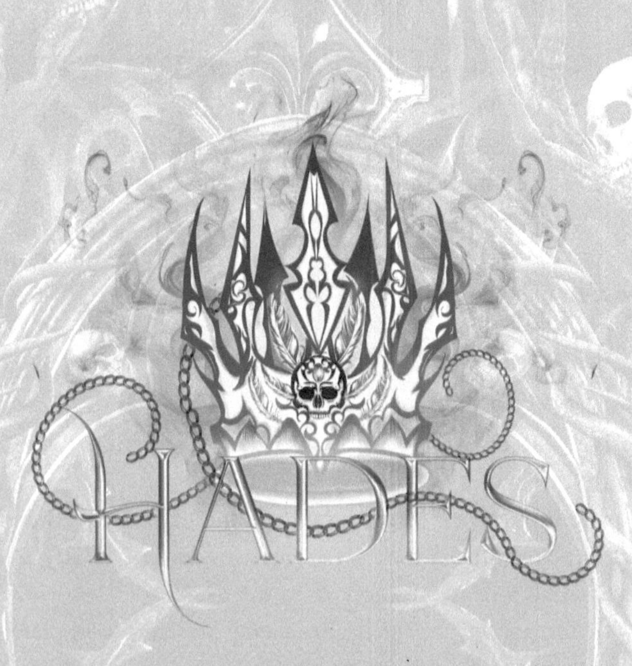

Pandora's Box

I love labyrinths, as evidenced by the little nest of lies I built for Persephone. But Pandora's Box is more than just a maze. It's a prison. A nightmare. A place where powerful souls are held and tortured.

Which makes me want to leave this place as soon as possible.

Everything here feels wrong. The air is too hot. The smells are too potent. And the walls are complex fabrics that shift every few seconds.

Stone one moment.

Fire the next.

My jaw ticks, my patience wearing thin. I want to return to Serapina, to ensure she's all right. My brother's words put me on edge, his concern for her well-being fucking with my head.

Alina felt something.

I don't know what that means. I need more information. But first, I want to talk to Demeter.

And Ares hasn't moved a bloody inch since joining us in his maze of horrors.

All he's doing is staring at me, his irises flickering between black and red.

Exasperated, I look to Morpheus. "Please help me."

My cousin huffs a laugh. "You're beyond help, Hades."

Fuck this, I think. *And fuck him.*

He's acting this way toward me because of his assumptions.

Assumptions I can't exactly fault him for. But it frustrates me that I have to explain myself. I already told him that actions mean more than words.

Unfortunately, though, he seems to have completely misinterpreted my intentions here.

"I don't want to *erase* Serapina, Morpheus," I growl, repeating what I've already said. "That's not how resurrection works. Or not how it should work, anyway. But I won't know what's been done to her until I interrogate Demeter."

I refocus on Ares. Interrogating Demeter requires his assistance. And he hasn't even flinched, his eyes still on me with a mixture of fury and malice.

I've pissed him off.

Well, welcome to the fucking club, I want to tell him. I clearly have a knack for infuriating everyone around me. Perhaps I should have been the God of Irritation and Fury.

Yet, right now, I need to be the God of Patience.

Or perhaps the God of Persuasion, I think, studying Ares's cold features.

"Demeter has created another realm of existence, a

plane of sorts. And she's holding all the Omega souls captive there. Or that's what our mate believes has happened. I'm tired of guessing. Just as I'm exhausted by the state of our realm. We're powerful beings. This reality we've found ourselves in is… depressing."

Ares doesn't reply, just continues to stare at me. But the red gleam is slowly retreating to the blackness of his irises. And his horns are notably missing from his head now.

I'm not sure if that's an indication of his Alpha side remaining calm or if it's related to us being inside his world.

Alas, there isn't time to ponder further.

Either he's going to help us willingly, or he's going to continue making this difficult.

I'm hoping for the former, which is why I add, "If you have any ideas on how to make her talk to us, I would enjoy discussing them. She's your prisoner. I respect that. However, she's used *my* power to create something that should never have existed. Thus, I would appreciate an opportunity to question her."

Ares finally moves. Not a lot. Just a slight tilt of his head. But it's enough to confirm that he's listening.

"I would also appreciate suggestions on how to be persuasive." It's a lie. I know exactly how to make someone talk. But Morpheus commented something similar before entering the prison, and Ares responded favorably.

Unfortunately, he simply remains mute now.

My teeth clench.

If he's going to be an impassable wall, then I'll just—

"I'm curious," Morpheus murmurs. "Are the snakes a tribute to your Medusa? Or is that a coincidence in the choice of decor?"

Crimson flashes in Ares's gaze as his attention slowly moves to Morpheus. "Do not speak her name." The words are measured. Slow. *Deadly*. And very unlike Ares's usual teasing.

My cousin has struck a chord, one that must be ringing angrily inside the other Alpha's head.

I nearly snort. Because I know how that feels. Morpheus is very good at plucking the chords of others.

"Apologies," Morpheus replies, his tone one I recognize instantly. Because he's used it with me countless times.

Which means he doesn't mean the *apology* at all.

"I was studying the intricate design of the ceiling while thinking about Demeter's Omega prison, and the inquiry blossomed in my mind." He shakes his head. "Anyway." He waves between me and Ares. "Continue. I didn't mean to interrupt."

Liar, I think. He absolutely meant to "interrupt." But, for once, I don't mind. Because he's trying to help me. Part of me realizes that this isn't a first, either. Actually, if I'm being honest with myself and our situation, Morpheus has been supporting me for eons.

I just haven't been very receptive to his brand of assistance.

Having it now is… appreciated.

It's also somewhat momentous, given that he's clearly still furious with me over the misunderstanding of my intentions.

Even angry, he's still coming to my aid.

Or perhaps, more specifically, to Serapina's aid.

That's fine. Our mate comes first. Always. And if he's willing to put negative emotions aside to ensure a better outcome for our Omega, then I respect that.

He's a good Alpha, I begrudgingly admit to myself, swallowing. *Much better than I've ever been.*

But now isn't the time to dwell on past mistakes.

I have a future to fix.

A future to *protect.*

"Please, Ares," I say, using a word I rarely ever speak. Yet I've somehow voiced it twice in a matter of minutes.

Fuck. I barely recognize myself. A groveling Alpha. *A desperate fool.*

"You think the Omega souls are being held captive," Ares says slowly. "In a prison?"

"More or less," Morpheus replies before I can speak. "Serapina says it's a place of stillness and mentioned that Demeter is holding the souls hostage. I interpreted that to be… prison-like."

Ares nods. "Yes. Similar to Pandora's Box."

"Exactly," Morpheus says. "Do you think it's possible she's borrowed from your brilliant architecture?"

The God of Wrath cuts him a look. "Don't compliment me, Morpheus. I'm already intrigued. I don't need your simpering statements. Nor am I a fan of your manipulative tactics."

Morpheus merely grins. "I would plead innocence, but you know me too well."

"I do," Ares mutters. "Which is why I hate that you've piqued my interest."

"Some might say I'm rather skilled at the art of understanding fantasies," Morpheus muses. "So it only stands to reason that I may also use such gifts to *intrigue* others, hmm?"

Ares grunts. "I'm about to show you what I'm *skilled* at."

"Persuasion and violence, I hope," Morpheus replies.

"Too fucking right," Ares returns. "Let's go."

The wall beside him morphs into a flaming doorway, one he walks through without a backward glance. I start to move, but Morpheus waves me back with a hand, the gesture near his hip and followed by a pointed look.

A look that resembles a warning.

Frowning, I decide to follow his direction and remain still.

Orcus does as well, the two of us standing shoulder to shoulder as Morpheus follows Ares through the threshold.

When the doorway closes, my frown morphs into a deep scowl.

"Give him a minute," Orcus says softly, no doubt sensing my rising tension. "Having a mate-circle means trusting each other to put your Omega's safety first. He won't do anything to harm Serapina."

"I know," I return shortly. "If only he trusted me to do the same."

"Have you earned his faith, Hades?" Orcus asks, his voice still low and for my ears alone. "Or have several millennia of shutting him out earned you a different sort of reaction from him?"

My jaw ticks. "I'm aware that I've failed my circle, brother. I don't need your commentary on the topic."

"You haven't failed them," he replies, obviously deciding to ignore the second part of my statement. "Failure suggests a permanent outcome. You're… a work in progress."

I look at him. "Are you done critiquing me?"

"Probably not," he admits, meeting my gaze. "I find it rather refreshing to be the one providing advice, *old man*."

I roll my eyes. "Don't get used to it, *baby brother*."

Rather than meet my words with annoyance, he smiles. "I'm the one with mate-circle experience, Hades. I believe that makes me the expert."

"He's not wrong," Morpheus interjects as the doorway opens up again. "I think you could learn a lot about acceptance from Orcus. But right now, we have a Goddess to interrogate. So…" He waves us forward in a "hurry up" gesture.

I have to bite my tongue to keep from lashing out at the infuriating man. However, a look at Ares's serious expression makes it a little easier.

"You have no idea how fortunate you are to have Morpheus in your corner" is all the God of Wrath tells me before turning and leading the way.

My lips curl down once more, my brow furrowing as well. "What does he mean by that?" I ask Morpheus.

My cousin merely shrugs. "One never knows with Ares."

The God of Wrath snorts but doesn't say anything else, just continues down a dark corridor. Violet lights begin to color the walls as purple flames ignite in Ares's wake, the fiery display illuminating their waxlike black candle bases.

I admire the fixtures as I move through the doorway with Orcus behind me, then trail after Ares's steps while observing the shifting walls.

While my labyrinth is encased in stone flowers and skulls, this maze is alive and moving, the corridor writhing with energy and power.

This isn't my first visit. At least, not to Pandora's Box. Though, this may be my first time walking this particular corridor. It's hard to know, as every time I venture into this hellscape, the visage changes.

I suspect it morphs with Ares's moods, which would explain the inky black lines forming along the walls like throbbing veins.

"This isn't where I left Demeter," Orcus comments. "Did you move her cell?"

"Does it matter?" Ares asks, sounding bored.

"Just curious," Orcus replies.

But I know my brother.

He's questioning Ares's intentions. *Is he taking us to Demeter? Or somewhere else?* Valid questions to ponder in regard to Ares.

"This is my burden to manage," the God of Wrath returns, then glances back at my brother. "If you have a critique or a complaint, you're welcome to become the new prison master."

Orcus grunts. "No, thank you."

Ares's resulting grin is tight. "Then don't voice *curious* questions. They're a waste of time."

My lips twitch at that. I'm fairly certain I uttered a similar sentiment to Morpheus shortly before arriving in the Mythos Fae Realm.

A quick look from Morpheus confirms it, his expression darkly amused. That humored glimmer in his vibrant gaze matches his tone as he muses, "You and Hades should have lunch."

Ares pauses. "Why the fuck would I want to eat lunch with him?"

"Because your conversation would be fascinating," Morpheus replies.

"Or end in a bloodbath," my brother adds.

"Which could also be fascinating," Morpheus says.

I shake my head. "What's *fascinating* is your ability to distract everyone from their purposes here," I deadpan.

"See, he can be funny," Morpheus informs Ares.

I'm about to remark on that when Orcus grabs my arm, his eyes flashing red. "*Alina.*"

The world shifts around me in a blink as he takes me out of Pandora's Box and away from the Mythos Fae Realm. His name is a curse that taunts my tongue as the world materializes around us.

Only, that curse ends in an empathic "*Fuck*" when the scene unfolds before me.

Flame is in jaguar form, crouched protectively over Thea.

Reaper is covered in blood with an unconscious Alina in his arms.

And before them is a pile of unconscious Mythos Fae Betas.

I stare at it, then at the world around us.

"You never left the Human Realm," I say, recognizing the Mediterranean coastline.

Orcus frowns. "We did, actually." He steps forward, then jumps back as the vision before us shifts into smoke.

My lips part. *A mirage. It's all a fucking mirage.*

"Where the fuck did they go?" Orcus demands, spinning around. "I can't feel them." His red eyes meet mine, his Alpha fully engaged. "Hades… *I can't feel my mates.*"

MALIKI

Rutting Grounds of the Underworld Labyrinth

Hades is going to kill me.

Not only is this reckless, but it's also dangerous. Especially after everything that's happened with Demeter.

Yet I can feel Sera inside me, our mate-bond thriving with life and knowledge. It's only an initial link, one that marks her as my intended. However, it's a connection that binds our souls together. Unites us as one.

Which allows me to sense her in a unique way.

She's safe. Elated. *Excited.*

I can taste those emotions on my tongue, the sweet flavor causing my veins to burn with the desire to *chase.*

This isn't how it felt before, when she left the cabin while on the vestiges of her heat. Something was wrong then. A darkness lurked in the air, a foreign contagion that tainted the moment.

I don't sense anything like that now.

Just Sera's desire to challenge me. To run. To hide. *To fight.*

I push away from the wall, my dick already hard at the thought.

She has no idea what she's unleashed. *Who* is about to hunt her.

I meant what I said—I've been kind.

That ends now.

She doesn't want to be a good girl. Instead, she wants to break Hades's rules. Create a memory that's just for us.

Fuck yes.

I'll give her that and more. I could sense her uncertainty in the kitchen before, the source of her needs driven by whatever memories she seemed to be experiencing.

She expects to be erased.

But I'm never going to allow that to happen.

She's *mine*. And she just invited me to finish this mating dance.

To take her wherever I want. *However* I want.

Styx, her words nearly undid me. *"Treat me like I'm unbreakable."* Shadows, I'm about to do a lot more than that.

I'm going to bend her in a way that makes her question her grasp on reality. Then introduce her to my version of rapture.

All of this may have started because I was assigned to protect the Bride of Death, but it's going to end with me formally claiming Serapina Everheart as my mate.

I take a step forward, no longer caring about the sixty

or ninety seconds that I promised her. The countdown doesn't matter. The hunt does.

And my female is ready to be *chased*.

The ground feels cool beneath my bare feet, the rocky texture hard yet yielding in an intriguing way. I can almost feel it cushioning my soles as I begin to run, causing my movements to feel buoyant and quick.

Clever, I think, realizing Hades did this on purpose.

He anticipated being naked in this part of the maze and made it comfortable to move around, which is at odds with the harsh-looking landscape.

It's pale, the sandy color different from the bone-white walls of the labyrinth. I can see a bit of those icy corridors in the distance, the Rutting Grounds buried along one edge of the maze.

Hades's brief tour the other day is the only reason I knew how to shadow here. Finding it on foot would have taken too much time. There are only one or two entrances to the Rutting Grounds. Same with all the other surprise areas built into this network of death. I haven't seen them all because Hades is working on some renovations.

Whatever the fuck that means.

I no longer care.

All I want to do is find Sera and show her what it means to be *mine*.

Fire licks through my veins as I pick up my pace, my instincts scanning my surroundings and hunting for any sign of Serapina Everheart.

Our bond throbs inside me, the pulse of it traveling all the way to my groin.

It's a sensation I've never experienced before. A craving I didn't even know existed.

I feel wild. A touch out of control. Borderline *feral*.

Like a beast who has finally been freed from his chain.

She gave me consent to do whatever I want.

A dangerous offer, one I fully intend to accept.

But I can't see Sera anywhere.

The Rutting Grounds are decorated with jagged rocks that jut upward to four or five stories in some places, along with a few shorter spires in others. It's reminiscent of the Fairy Catacombs near the Corpse Fae Crypt.

I can definitely see where Hades found his inspiration, anyway.

So where are you hiding, trouble? I wonder, slowing my pace as I pass through two particularly tall shards of tan-colored stones. It feels like an entrance to another realm, reminding me a bit of a fantastical landscape from one of my favorite science fiction films from the human world.

Hades would love the comparison, I'm sure.

Maybe I'll tell him later, just to further infuriate him.

"I'm impressed," I murmur, focusing on Sera and pushing my thoughts of Hades to the side.

This is about her, not him.

It's about *us*—me and Sera.

"I can feel you," I go on, hoping she can hear me. "But your location is a mystery. Which is rather appropriate, given everything."

She's been an enigma since the moment Hades first mentioned her existence. Not the Omega inside her, but the human—Serapina Everheart.

She's a walking puzzle, one I've been trying to solve for months.

And now she's evaded me in this jagged landscape.

Given her recent disappearance, I should probably be concerned.

But my link to her soul confirms that she's fine.

I don't sense any panic, not like when she vanished before. Instead, the only emotion I sense is her arousal.

It's like a flame, flickering and beckoning me closer. *Stroke me*, it says. *Make me burn.*

Or maybe it's all in my head.

Everything about this is new—our link, these feelings, my instincts.

I've never claimed anyone before. But I suspect these urges are the result of our recent connection.

Every part of me wants to bite, mark, and *fuck*.

I just need to find my hiding female...

She's close, I realize, searching the towering rocks on either side of me. "I can taste your need, mate," I tell Sera quietly, sure she can hear me now. "It's like a sinful chocolate, lingering on my tongue, begging me to swallow."

Except, if I have anything to say about it, Sera will be the one swallowing. Maybe choking, too. *Hmm...*

I take a step to the side and scrutinize the jagged edges surrounding me. Like the ground, they're deceiving in nature, their harsh points soft to the touch. Almost pillowy, actually. I squeeze one particularly savage-looking shard and smirk. "It feels like foam," I marvel aloud.

Which means it's not nearly as inflexible as it looks.

Canting my head, I identify a long crack in the façade and trace it with my fingers.

The material parts beneath my touch, causing me to slide my hand inside and pull it aside, almost like a tent flap.

My eyes widen at the unexpected cave opening.

Then my gaze lands on the prize waiting inside.

"You're not even trying to hide," I say, amused at finding Sera sprawled across a massive bed beneath a series of glittering lights. It's like a million stars, the majestic glow creating an ethereal moment that almost doesn't feel real.

A fantasy come to life.

A fucking wet dream.

I prowl forward, my tattoos writhing along my arms as a myriad of notions spring to life inside my mind.

Notions that darken as Sera says, "I'm not afraid of you, Maliki." She spreads her legs, the invitation all too fucking clear. "You found me. Now take me."

A curse rumbles out of me, my gaze sweeping over the vixen taunting me from the floor. "You really are trouble," I inform her as I unfasten the button on my jeans. "Inviting me to break all the rules…" That last part comes out as a musing thought, one tied to my knowledge that Hades likely built this little love nest as a private place to take his mate.

But I'm about to defile it.

Because I'm going to take Sera so fucking hard that our mingled scents will exist here for eternity. Mark it as *ours*, not *his*, and forever remind him that he has to share Sera.

He told me to please his wife.

Well, I'm about to do a hell of a lot more than that.

Kneeling on the mattress—which is adorned with fresh silk sheets, no doubt from the manifestation magic fueling this whole maze—I scan my prey and evaluate what I want to do to her.

"How do you feel about bondage?" I ask as I stroke her lower calf, my tattoos already moving down to my fingertips. "I mean, since you weren't interested in running, perhaps you would prefer to be tied up instead, yeah?"

Ribbons of smoke leave my skin to weave around hers, the dark strands braiding into a pretty rope pattern along her dainty feet and ankles. She lifts her head off the pillows and inhales sharply, causing my eyebrow to inch upward.

"Scared, mate?" I tilt my head, her aroma swimming around me in a kiss of consent. "Mmm, no, that's excitement, isn't it, sweet mystery?" My shadows continue to circle her like binds, creating an enthralling design against her pale skin—one that resembles delicate knots in strategic locations.

When the strands reach the apex between her thighs, I tell my inky ribbons to skip over her slick folds and weave down her other leg again. Then I tug on the ends and affix them to the mattress. It's not perfect, but it'll hold because my mind is in charge of the energy winding around her.

Her lashes flutter when the smoke reaches her hip again. This time I draw it through her pussy, making sure to apply just enough pressure to her clit to drive her wild before looping it back upward to cross her flat stomach.

"*Oh,*" she moans, her lower half trying to writhe against my ropes.

But I hold her in place with a tug, one that draws a gasp from her lips when she realizes just how well I've secured her with my power.

I start slithering it around her torso, creating a pretty pattern of smoke that emphasizes her breasts. Her needy little nipples jut out, begging to be touched, but I leave them exposed. By the time I'm done teasing her, she'll feel like she's in heat.

"Maliki…" A hint of uncertainty enters her voice as the smoke wraps around her throat.

"Sera," I return.

"Is this…?" She swallows against my binding, the strand splitting to go down her arms at the same time. "Is this how you torture your victims?"

It's a dark question, one that makes my lips curl. There are so many forms of *torture*, some of them cruel, others, well… "Worried, mate?" I ask her. Because I know she's been uneasy about my penchant for death. But I won't apologize for my abilities or how I've chosen to use them.

I'm an assassin.

A good one.

She needs to accept that and accept *me.*

Her blue eyes hold mine as goose bumps pebble along her arms beneath my writhing strands. "I trust you not to hurt me, Maliki."

I tighten the smoky rope against her wrists and yank her hands over her head without touching her. It's all mental. All a show of power. And the way her tight little body squirms beneath my hold says she's enjoying every second.

"Sometimes pain and pleasure are interchangeable," I inform her as I send a subtle jolt of electricity through the strands, the sensation one I strategically place in some of her more sensitive areas.

Her beautiful lips part, her eyes widening.

"But you're right to trust me," I go on, my mind telling the tendrils to soothe the sting left over from the momentary shock. "I would kill anyone who so much as looked at you the wrong way, Sera. Even your other mates."

Her eyebrows lift, surprise turning her cheeks a shade of pink.

But I mean every word.

If Hades returns here with news of how to bring Persephone back or replace Sera or whatever it is he's trying to do… I'll kill him and take my mate somewhere else. *Anywhere* else.

He's not going to destroy her.

"You're mine," I tell Sera, the binds around her tightening with the words. "No one is allowed to hurt you… except for maybe me." I utter that last part as I send another zing through her prone form.

She gasps and tries to arch, but the ropes hold her down.

And the one strategically between her legs begins to subtly rub against her slick flesh.

A moan escapes her, followed by my name on her tongue.

"So you did want to be bound," I muse, my fingers trailing up her thighs as I inspect my handiwork. "Good to know, trouble."

I crawl over her and lean down to lick one puckered nipple, then the other, all while she writhes. My bands of power are humming with need now, eliciting my version of a purr as I lull her into a state of confused bliss.

She relaxes.

Then she stiffens as more sensations pour through her.

Followed by another wave of easing energy.

Back and forth.

Taunting.

Teasing.

Pleasuring.

She starts to pant, her body flushed from my rhythmic torment. "Maliki," she breathes. "*Please.*"

I smile, still hovering over her on my hands and knees.

"I'm not fucking you until you're screaming for mercy, Sera," I tell her. "You wanted me wild and unhinged, which means I need you just as feral. That's the only way you'll truly be able to take me."

I don't give her a chance to reply, instead increasing the frequency of my power into a low rumble that no doubt resembles a growl to her Omega senses.

The way she begins to whimper confirms my suspicions, as does the beautiful display of wetness between her splayed legs. Leaning down, I give her a firm lick, longing for a taste.

"*Oh!*" Sera screams, causing me to chuckle against her spasming pussy. My sweet mystery's body is so overstimulated that a simple stroke from my tongue has sent her flying.

I hum against her slick cunt, then kiss a path up to her hip.

And sink my teeth into her skin.

Which earns me another delicious shriek.

Probably because that hurt a bit.

My tendrils warm around her, seeking to heal the small wound while I lick the blood away with my tongue.

Another link slides into place between us, our bond firming even more.

But it's not complete yet.

I honestly don't know how many times I'll need to bite her to make her truly mine. I've never done this before, and there are not any others out there who are like me. So it's hard to say.

However, I suspect it's three. That's a pretty standard expectation.

Which means my final bite needs to be somewhere special. Somewhere *impactful.*

Because these little crescent scars in her skin will last for eternity.

"Do you have a preference on where I mark you next?" I ask as her breathing begins to settle once more.

I go to my knees on either side of her hips and stare down at her pretty form, all bound and sweaty and *mine.* It makes me so fucking hard that I nearly burst free from my pants, the zipper suddenly excruciatingly painful against my shaft.

"You're going to bite me… again?" she asks, her voice a little hoarse, probably from her screams.

"Yes." There's no point in telling her otherwise. This connection between us has begun. We must finish it. And I need her to know what she means to me.

"To mate me," she adds, not asking but telling me.

"Yes," I repeat.

"But you already initiated the bond, right?"

"Right," I echo, pulling down the zipper of my jeans because I can't take the pressure anymore. "Now you just need one or two more marks to make this connection permanent."

"And what about you?" she questions, her tone regaining some of its strength. "Where do I mark you?"

I arch a brow. "You want to bite me back?"

"Yes." This time it's her using that word and not elaborating. Just a firm response. A longing of a sort. Or, more accurately, a *claim*.

Shifting off of her, I make quick work of my pants, then go to sprawl out beside her, all while my shadows hum along her pretty skin, the ropes still keeping her in a prolonged state of arousal. Only the edge was taken off by my tongue, her body still very much primed and ready for fucking.

But maybe giving her freedom will allow her a chance to join me in my savagery. To embrace her own… decadent cravings.

Grasping her chin, I pull her toward me and use my shadows to move her body as well until she's on her side and pressed up against me.

Then I kiss her.

Long. Hard. Purposefully. Letting her taste the mixture of her arousal and blood on my tongue. Granting her a glimpse of my need. Devouring her thoroughly with a dominant embrace.

By the time I'm done, her nostrils are flaring and her eyes are drowsy with lust.

It's a reaction I stroke with my smoky tendrils as I slowly unravel them from her creamy skin.

After she's mostly free, I push her back into the bed and slide my hard cock between her soaked folds. Not fucking. Just bathing in the sensations created by her *need*.

My tongue slips back into her mouth, memorizing her, adoring her, *indulging* her. With my palm on her cheek, I deepen the embrace even more while pressing against her pussy, demanding that she feel my arousal.

"You can bite me wherever you desire, mate," I say against her mouth. "My body is your canvas to explore, to bloody, to hurt, to do whatever you wish. Just know that when you're done, I'm going to destroy this beautiful cunt of yours. In the best fucking way."

Pandora's Box

"I STILL EXPECT YOU TO UPHOLD YOUR PART OF OUR agreement," Ares says from his position against the wall. "It's not my fault Hades fucked off and didn't return. But I did let him through, just like you requested."

I sigh, my focus leaving my watch to lock gazes with the God of Wrath. "I'll create your little fantasy," I promise. Because he's right—it's not his fault that Orcus and Hades disappeared.

But I'm not sure it's Hades's fault either.

"You're certain you haven't sensed his return?" I ask, wary.

"Isn't he supposed to be your bond-mate?" Ares's expression exudes the same boredom as his tone. "Shouldn't you feel him?"

"I'm bonded to the same Omega, not Hades."

"Sounds like a mate-circle problem," he deadpans. "I'd recommend talking to Hades, but a recommendation would imply that I care. Which I do not." He pushes off the wall. "I also don't care to wait any longer. If you want to talk to Demeter, follow me. Otherwise…"

He turns and walks away, not bothering to finish his statement.

My eyes lift toward the writhing snakes in the ceiling before I start after the impatient Alpha. He's not wrong to respond with impatience. But that doesn't mean I have to enjoy it.

Heaving yet another sigh—a sound I fear I've made a lot lately—I match his pace and join him as we wind through the corridors of his deadly mazelike prison.

If Hades returns, I suspect Ares will feel him and perhaps create a doorway to join us. Or, I hope he will, anyway.

Is Alina all right? I wonder. Orcus uttered her name seconds before vanishing, the disappearance so quick that I wasn't given a chance to speak or react.

Though, I did immediately check on my link to Serapina.

Which I found thriving with intensity.

An intensity that nearly had me returning to her.

I can only imagine what Maliki did to inspire such a sensation in our mate. And that sensation only seems to be strengthening right now.

Fuck. Her arousal is like a beacon I can taste on my tongue, one that beckons me to join in on the fun.

But I need to see this task through first, as I highly doubt Ares will be up for rescheduling this visit. And while I may not trust Hades's intentions with Serapina, I do think there's merit in questioning Demeter. Thus, I'll—

"*Ares*." The guttural hiss precedes the appearance of a door, one that didn't exist in the wall a mere second ago but is wide open and there now.

The God of Wrath pauses before slowly turning toward the dark entryway.

I arch a brow and try to glance inside, but it's pitch black.

"I feel her," the voice says in a rasp. "*She's here*."

Ares's jaw ticks. "You've been saying that for twenty-four years, Levi."

My brow inches higher. "Now there's a nickname I haven't heard in a millennium or two." Leviathan, the God of Havoc, went mad when Medusa disappeared.

I'm not surprised Ares has him locked up in Pandora's Box. Leviathan and Ares were best friends, once upon a time. *Is that friendship why Leviathan can create his own doors in Ares's prison?* I wonder.

"Quiet, dreamer," Levi returns, sounding less raspy now and interestingly sane. "Ares, you need to listen to me. She's *here*. In prison. Or one like this. A cage. They call her Mad Maddie. And—"

"*Enough*. I've told you before that there is no one here by that name."

"Not *here* here, but there," the God of Havoc bites back, sounding a bit more crazed now. "In a cage!"

Ares releases a breath, his shoulders seeming to sink in defeat. "We'll discuss it later, Levi." He waves his hand, causing the door to slam shut before the other Alpha can reply. Then he resumes walking without a word.

"Leviathan senses Medusa?" I ask softly after a few seconds of walking. "Do you sense her, too?"

"What I sense or do not sense is not your business, Morpheus."

"True," I agree. "But if Serapina is right about this

Omega plane, it's possible that Leviathan's ramblings are relevant to the existing situation."

Ares pauses again, this time looking back at me with an expression I haven't seen on his face in a very long time. It's an expression I haven't witnessed on any Alphas in eons, in fact. An expression of *hope.*

Although, it fades in a blink, his nonchalant mask falling over his features as he says, "Levi's ramblings are the curse of a broken bond. His spirit will never recover."

My eyebrow inches upward. Ares speaks about Leviathan like he's one of those husks decorating the barren fields of the Mythos Fae Realm.

Yet the God of Havoc seemed quite competent mere moments ago.

"Is that why he's able to manifest doors at will in your prison?" I ask when Ares resumes walking again.

He doesn't reply.

But I can tell my question irks him by the way his shoulders tense again.

So I casually add, "Because that sort of ability strikes me as not only intentional, but capable. Which is odd because the mad Alphas I've engaged with over the last few centuries don't appear to have enough focus or brainpower to pull off that sort of trick with such flawless ease."

Ares remains silent.

That's fine. I've said what I needed to say.

Just a few brief comments have intrigued Ares enough to ensure he'll be exceptionally helpful during this interrogation. Because he wants to know about the Omega plane almost as much as I do, but for very different reasons.

He'll be extremely interested in learning about Medusa's fate. Is she alive somewhere? Reincarnated as another? Only Demeter can tell us.

Just like only Demeter can explain what the fuck she's done to Serapina.

Even now, I feel her ecstasy spiraling through our connection, yet she's no longer nearing her heat. It's like her Omega side has shut off entirely.

Which isn't good.

A starved Omega is a tortured soul.

And I worry about what that means for Serapina's future. Especially with her commenting on Persephone's memories.

Whatever Demeter has done, I'll fix it.

Serapina Everheart will not be erased.

Not if I have anything to do with it.

"Here," Ares says, turning abruptly toward a solid wall.

I move to his side, my gaze vigilant as the stone begins to shift into a set of stairs that lead down. Cobwebs decorate the interior, as does an array of insects that literally make my skin crawl. Mostly because those "bugs" are the size of my forearm, with multiple legs and eyes, as well as a variety of fiery colors.

"Creative," I mutter.

Ares's lips twitch. "She's the Goddess of Fertility, yeah? So I got creative with fertile animals that replicate."

I'm about to question what he means when the stairs before us start to move.

And I realize there are more than a few bugs on the walls.

Because the walls *are* bugs.

All replicating.

On repeat.

To the point where some are on top of the others because there isn't enough room.

I swallow, my stomach in knots. "Can we pause their

reproductive activities long enough for us to walk through them?"

Ares's smile grows. "I thought you were the God of Fantasies."

"I'm the God of Dreams," I correct him. "*Good* dreams."

"This isn't a good dream?"

"No, I rather think this is a nightmare for some."

He lifts a shoulder, the picture of nonchalance, and steps inside.

Which is when the visage changes to reveal plain stairs.

My lips purse. I strongly suspect he's fucking with me and will just enable the same visual as before the moment I follow him. But I don't have a choice if this is the way to see Demeter.

Fuck.

Gritting my teeth, I shift forward, only for Ares to shove me back with his hand against my chest.

"What—"

"Quiet," he demands, his focus returning to the stairwell that abruptly evaporates into an empty room. His brow comes down, his hand curling into a fist against my chest. "That's not fucking possible. I shackled her this time."

He moves into the space with two long strides, his gaze searching the ceiling, then the walls, and finally the floor.

I watch from the threshold, not wanting to interrupt whatever he's doing. But I fear I already understand what's happened. *Demeter isn't here.*

And given Ares's reaction to that, he never felt her leave.

Which should be impossible, as he's the warden here. No one enters or escapes without his express permission.

Except, this isn't the first time Demeter has managed to find a way out of Pandora's Box.

"How the fuck did she…?" The words leave Ares on a low growl, his horns suddenly glowing with fire. "I've been breached." He spins toward me. "Or this has all been a trick and she was never really here."

My brow furrows, both from his commentary about the breach and, particularly, as a response to his suggestion that Demeter's presence was some sort of a mirage. "Orcus delivered her to your prison," I say slowly.

"I know. I authorized the entry." He looks at me, his eyes twin black flames. "So either Demeter manufactured a millennia-long mirage—which I hear she's skilled at—or she's somehow managed to vanish."

"Just like the Omegas two thousand years ago," I say, following his logic. "Or, as you say, she never actually returned from that original disappearing act."

"Yes." The word is bitten off between his teeth, clearly irritated by both possibilities. Ares does not take deception well.

Neither do I, but it's an art I've mastered over my eternal lifetime. Benefits of being the God of Dreams. "We need to find this Omega plane."

"No. *You* need to find the Omega plane. *I* need to ensure Pandora's Box is secure." With those final words, he vanishes.

In true Alpha nature, he expects me to follow his command.

Usually, I would be irritated by such a presumption and do the exact opposite of what's been demanded of me.

However, on this point, we're agreed.

Because this mysterious existence that Demeter has crafted holds all the answers. Answers Mythos Fae kind has strived to understand for millennia. Answers to what really happened with Persephone. And answers regarding Serapina's fate.

It's time to hunt, I decide, my gaze narrowing at the closing wall before me. *First up on my tracking list—Orcus.*

Because I have questions about Demeter's capture and imprisonment.

So where the fuck did you and Hades go…?

SERA

Every part of me is simmering with hot, tangible *fire*.

Maliki's power elicited responses inside me that I… I can't define or explain. All I know is that this male has claimed me in a manner that makes me feel safe. Exposed. *Owned*.

It's a contradiction.

Confusing.

Overwhelming.

Oh, so amazing.

Yet he's just told me I can do whatever I want to him. I would be a fool to deny the opportunity. Especially after all these dark urges have awoken inside me.

Urges I don't really understand.

But when he bit me, then started talking about marking me elsewhere, I… I grew hot. Angry. *Rabid*. Because how dare he claim me without allowing me to claim him.

I want my scent etched into his skin. My mark forever instilled in his smooth, tan flesh.

It's the strangest need, one I don't fully understand. But I don't want to analyze it. I just want to fulfill the craving. To take my mate and make him mine.

To forever remember this moment.

To feel cherished.

Connected.

Loved.

The needs roll through me in a tornado of insanity, driving my instincts and forcing me to forget everything else.

All that matters is this memory.

This moment.

My Maliki.

He's lounging beside me like a piece of art, his tattoos swimming all over as they settle into a new pattern of skulls along his forearms. I swear those skulls are grinning, their eyes seeming to taunt me into action.

Maliki just used his powers to ignite every nerve inside me, making me long for so much more than just his smoky touch.

Yet all he did was lick me a few times until I exploded.

And now…

Now I want to return the favor.

Biting will have to wait.

I want to torture him like he tortured me. Only, I don't have magical ribbons that evoke sensation. But I do have hands, as well as a mouth.

Grabbing his shoulder, I press against him and push him to his back on the bed. He goes easily, allowing me to move him as I desire, though his hands grasp my hips when I straddle him. I half expect him to take over, but all he does is give me a squeeze and say, "You look good on top of me, mate."

I shiver, that term making my thighs clench.

I like being his mate. It's not something we ever discussed. Not something I ever thought I would be to anyone, let alone this dangerous male. When he bit me, I didn't think much of it. It just seemed natural, like something Maliki would do.

Now I realize that claim went so much deeper than just being a flesh wound.

He connected our souls.

So is he mated to me… or to Persephone? The question gives me pause, causing me to sit up fully on Maliki's lap and stare down at him. "Tell me how this mate-bond works." I have a slight understanding of my fated links to Morpheus and Hades—through my Omega soul.

But Maliki is a mystery.

Which I guess is fitting, given his chosen nickname for me.

"I don't know," he says, his gold eyes glinting off the glow cast by the magic glittering all over this cave. I caught sight of the glowing enchantment while running through the Rutting Grounds, the starlike pattern enthralling me in an instant.

It was as though this space beckoned me into it, the cavern opening and closing without me doing anything other than walking inside.

Now, I feel the energy thriving all around us. See it reflected in Maliki's features. Sense it humming across my naked skin with wicked promises of extreme delight.

Or perhaps that's the mate-bond I'm experiencing.

Except…

My brow furrows as I process Maliki's words. "You don't know how this works?" I ask slowly.

He tucks his hands behind his head, his arms flexing enticingly with the movement. But then he murmurs, "Nope."

"Oh." My nose crinkles, uncertain now.

"I've never taken a mate before," Maliki says, a little softer now. "I'm just following my instincts." His eyes go to my shoulder before traveling down to my hip. "And those instincts are telling me to *bite*." That statement is uttered in a deeper tone than before, his need a palpable presence I feel blistering between us.

I squeeze my thighs again, which has his grip on me tightening in response.

"What are your instincts telling you to do, trouble?" he asks, his silky tone a warm caress to my senses.

"A lot of things," I say, squirming a little. "So many things." The words come out on a breath, my gaze roaming over his rippling physique. His tattoos are calm now, settled into his skin like permanent fixtures. But I know better. Those smoky tendrils of his are decadent. Devious. *Divine*.

My need reignites—the one that urges me to taunt him in the same way he did me—and I lean down to press a kiss to his pec. It jumps beneath my touch, causing me to do it again before dragging my lips to his flat nipple.

He groans when I scrape my teeth against the bud, making me wonder if he would enjoy being bitten there. I nibble him lightly, then grin when he hisses in expectation.

As if I would make it that easy.

No.

I want to explore. Taunt. *Torture*. Just like he's done to me.

He said his body was my canvas to do whatever I wanted to, and I fully intend to indulge myself.

His muscles flex as I begin to explore, his skin hot beneath my fingertips. I swear I see his tattoos writhe, too. But I can't focus on his arms right now, not when I have all the hard planes of his stomach to memorize.

Which I proceed to do with my tongue.

He releases a sound of approval. Or maybe it's a curse. I'm not sure. But the way he tenses beneath me says I'm doing something right.

I think about Morpheus and what I learned to do with my mouth and continue my path lower to Maliki's groin.

Where I meet his cock with my tongue.

There is no hesitation. No second-guessing. Just me following my instincts, similar to what he said.

It's all so natural. So necessary. *So erotic.*

Because *stars*, he tastes good. Like sin. Like… like *forever.*

I can't define it. Can't even make sense of it. And I don't need to. I just need to enjoy this. Enjoy him. Enjoy *us.*

And that's what I do, taking him into my mouth and swallowing deep.

"Fuck, Sera," he groans, his hand suddenly on the back of my head. But rather than pull me away, he threads his fingers through my tangled strands and holds me against him.

I wait for him to guide me, kind of like how Morpheus did.

But Maliki isn't Morpheus.

Maliki wants me to *take.* He wants me to follow my own needs.

Which urge me to go deeper. To take more of him. To swallow around the head and moan as he comes a little on my tongue.

I want to make him do that again. Drive him to the point of no return. Force him to claim me in this intimate way.

It's an animalistic craving, one I don't deny as I grab his base and work him to the point of madness with me.

"If you keep this up, trouble, then you'd better be ready to commit," he pants. "*Fuck…*"

I'm too lost to him to smile at the victory coursing through me. But on some level, I'm aware that I'm mastering him. Reducing this strong male to a puddle of warmth and sensation.

With my mouth wrapped around him, I'm in charge.

And that feeling is liberating. Empowering. *Arousing.*

My thighs clench around nothing, my desire to put him inside me nearly overriding everything else. However, there's a competing craving, one highlighted by the subtle burn radiating from my hip.

Mine, that sting says. *Maliki made me his… but he's also* mine.

I draw my teeth up along his shaft, earning me a deep growl of approval from the fae I want to claim as my mate.

More of that delicious precum enters my mouth, and I know he's close. That knowledge comes from the way he stiffens in my mouth. But also from somewhere deep within. A connection that seems to be blossoming more and more with each passing second.

A connection I long to *strengthen.*

I suck harder, my mind melting beneath this onslaught of sensations. This overwhelming hunger. My dark desire to *bite.*

It's all too much.

Yet not enough.

I'm dizzy with it, my mouth greedy for more. I take Maliki so far into my throat that I nearly gag, but I don't care. He's my oxygen now. My world. And I… I *need* him to feel this intensity with me. To be driven so utterly insane that all he can think about is me.

I want to blow his mind.

Prove I'm worthy of this bond.

Ensure he never doubts this connection between us.

It's insanity. I don't know where this need is coming from or why I've fallen under its spell, but I'm so tired of questioning my fate. For once, I just want to do what feels right.

And that's this—with Maliki. Sucking him. Teasing him. Making him groan my name.

His muscles strain, revealing his sculpted perfection. He's so close that I can feel his orgasm pulsing against my tongue.

Now, I decide, releasing him from my mouth.

"*Sera,*" he growls.

I ignore him, my lips ghosting over his head to the side of his cock.

He starts to come, my hand around his base stroking the release from him.

A release I interrupt by parting my lips against his shaft and biting down.

"*Fuck!*" he shouts, his ecstasy mingling with the pain. It's a sensation I suddenly feel as though it's my own as blood trickles onto my tongue.

I've hurt him.

But the pleasure he's feeling outweighs the sting of my bite. Pleasure born from his orgasm. Pleasure stemming from our enhanced connection. Pleasure heightened by his elation at what I've done.

"You just permanently marked my dick," he breathes, panting through the euphoria. "Shadows, Sera…"

His fist in my hair tightens. I sense what he's about to do a second before he acts, allowing me to release him from my bite right as he yanks me up over him on the bed.

In the next instant, I'm on my back and he slams into me.

It's so seamless. So fantastical. Like his body just knows

mine, knew where to go, how to connect, and exactly what we both needed.

He's still coming.

Yet fucking me.

Creating a mess of us both, but I embrace the sensations. Live for his thrusts. Meet him with equal passion. And kiss him with a desperation I can barely explain.

It's a frenzy of fiery devotion, our existence joining as one.

I can feel you in my mind, I breathe, igniting a mental connection that I didn't know was possible.

Because you just made me your mate, Maliki replies via the same channel, his voice a low purr that has me clenching my legs around him.

He spins us and sits up, my chest to his, our mouths brushing but no longer engaging. Probably because I'm too busy exhaling a gasp at what he just did.

Yet he's still inside me.

Still pulsing.

"Ride me," he demands. "Make me come again in this sweet pussy, Sera. Keep me where I belong for hours."

His mind helps me understand what he's saying—*his cum*. I didn't swallow before. So he's going to ensure he fills me up in a way that forces me to feel his claim for days.

"Not days, mate," he says against my mouth. "For fucking eternity."

His tongue slides between my lips before I can reply, his hips punching into mine and forcing me to accept every inch of him while his cock begins to vibrate.

Stars, those tattoos of his are going to drive me mad.

And I can't wait.

I love the vibrations pulsating between my thighs, the

way his movements make me feel, how beautifully we fit together.

Rather than think about my inexperience or question his wish for me to ride him, I simply follow my instincts and move.

I writhe.

I moan.

I nip at his lips.

I suck on his tongue.

I press my breasts to him, wrap my arms around his shoulders, and show him with my body that I never intend to let him go.

He's mine, just like he said.

But I'm also his.

I feel it deep down, our link solidifying more and more with each stroke inside me.

He's branding me with his energy, swathing me in his scent, and owning me with his touch.

"Maliki," I breathe.

"Sera," he returns. Then sinks his teeth into my neck. There's no notice. No warning. No asking. He simply marks me for a third time.

Because he knows this is who we're meant to be together.

Time is irrelevant.

This is about fate. Our destiny as one. Our unique connection that no one else will ever understand.

Except maybe Morpheus and Hades.

But I don't think about them right now.

This moment is for Maliki. For me. For us.

It's a memory that's all mine. Not tainted by my Omega past. Only my history with Maliki… *as Sera.*

His mouth captures mine once more, the taste of my blood disappearing beneath our mutual arousal.

His hands roam over me, stroking my breasts, my sides, disappearing between my thighs to touch my clit.

All while I ride him. All while our bond firms into an impenetrable link. All while I lose myself in this euphoric embrace.

"Be a good girl and come on my cock, trouble," he tells me. "I want to feel that tight cunt squeeze me while I continue fucking you."

I shudder, his words stoking my inner fire as his tattoos writhe inside me. Thrumming harshly. Demanding… demanding that I…

A scream escapes me as an avalanche of sensation roars through me.

The world goes dark.

My limbs cease to function.

And I swear I've suddenly learned how to fly.

But as my back lands on something soft, I know I'm still with Maliki. Still in the bed in that cave. In the Rutting Grounds. In the maze.

His body is moving almost violently against mine.

My hands suddenly bound over my head.

His shadowy tendrils are everywhere. His body is overpowering mine. His cock feels even larger. So many crazy feelings. So much heat. *So intensely right…*

Maliki drives me over another cliff, one I didn't even realize I was nearing until suddenly I'm falling.

He catches me with his tongue, his kiss anchoring me in reality as his hands guide my hips.

Punishing thrusts have me moaning his name.

I'm torn between wanting him to stop and needing him to keep using me. *Show me everything*, I beg him in my mind. *I want all of you, Maliki.*

His responding rumble is borderline feral. But I

embrace it. Relax beneath him. Let him use me. Take me. Please me. *Fuck me.*

He bites me *again*, this time on my lip.

Except it's more of a nibble, not harsh. It doesn't break the skin. It serves as a way to hold me in the moment. And it's followed by a kiss so overwhelming that I swear I lose time.

His pace begins to slow, his hand on my hip and his other at my throat.

It's tender.

Which makes it that much more intense as he continues to slide in and out of me.

His tattoos seem to be affixing themselves deep inside me now, and I realize with a start that he's engraving his essence into my sensitive flesh.

"They'll feel my mark every time they knot you," Maliki murmurs, a possessive note underlying his tone. "Those Alphas will know you're mine just as much as you're theirs. For-fucking-ever."

Heat lances through me, causing me to clamp down around his cock as the flash of pain quickly morphs into something so much hotter.

I stare up at him, stunned by what he's done.

Yet again, it feels right.

I marked his shaft.

And now, he's tattooed me with his shadows.

What he just did was permanent.

It can't be undone.

I sense in his mind that he never knew this was possible, but he's also not surprised. "You're my mate," he says, stroking his nose against mine. "Mine to pleasure… whenever… I desire."

I jolt as that mark inside me pulses again, the sensation one he's evoking and forcing me to experience.

And oh my stars, does it feel amazing.

Like a vibrator deep inside.

"Right next to your G-spot," he tells me, heightening the pulsation. "Now come again, mate. Come hard. Come fast. And force me to come with you."

It's like his voice resembles a compulsion that I'm forced to follow, because I'm already trembling with the oncoming orgasm before he even finishes speaking.

Or maybe it's the combination of what he just did to me coupled with his own mounting elation.

I feel everything. My arousal. His need. Our joint excitement. Our… our mutual affection.

It's so incredible.

So perfect.

So unbelievable.

And so… so… "*Stars!*" The world erupts, his seed shooting deep inside me in ripples of scorching ecstasy.

I lose myself to the moment, barely aware of Maliki growling against my neck.

He's everywhere at once.

In my core. In my mind. In my *heart.*

Whatever has ignited between us has officially solidified. For good.

For eternity, Maliki tells me. *Now hold on, Sera. Because we're going to do all of that again. But against the wall this time.*

I only have a second to realize my hands are no longer bound and to grab his shoulders before suddenly we're standing and he has me braced against the cavern rocks.

They cushion my back, something I would never have expected when seeing their texture. But I don't have the brainpower to consider how or why they feel this way.

Because Maliki is already fucking me again.

And I hear in his mind that he's only just begun.

This is the mating frenzy, perhaps similar to an Omega's heat.

I accept that.

Accept him.

Accept *this*.

Which I tell him with my mind as he grasps my hips to change his angle.

We're going to spend hours or days here.

That's fine.

I don't mind.

Only… only there's something… hmm.

Whatever that something is doesn't matter.

I just want Maliki. His cock. This oblivion. *This fate.*

Everything else… can wait.

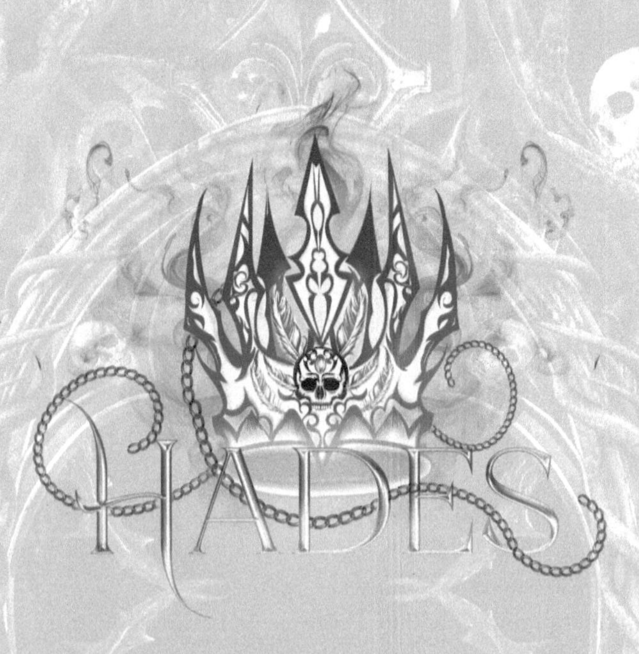

Human Realm

"Orcus." It's my fifth attempt at grabbing my brother's attention. And like the other four times, he ignores me, too lost to his mind to hear me.

Given how I initially responded to his words, I understand. Because my instinct was to check on Serapina, to ensure I still felt her. Which required me to go deep inside my soul to locate our link. Feeling it thrive allowed me to breathe. And sensing she was still safe inside my maze granted me the ability to focus.

At least until I experienced her pleasure.

It was like a blazing sun that nearly yanked me back to the labyrinth, her ecstasy a call to my Alpha instincts.

But my brother's rigid stance and glowing red eyes forced me to remain on this jagged cliff.

It's been… a while since the macabre scene vanished

around us. Thus, I've had time to analyze everything in sight, all while Orcus remained utterly still.

What I can't determine is how a mirage lured my brother here or why the creator of that image would choose this location.

There are numerous Alphas capable of such tricks, Morpheus being one of the best. He's an obvious suspect, given that we were just with him.

But Morpheus isn't cruel.

He might think little of my intentions with Serapina, but he wouldn't drag Orcus into our personal battle.

Though, Morpheus would attempt to distract me if he felt I was a danger to our mate. The notion has me checking on Serapina again, only to feel another blast of energy flood our soul bond.

Energy underlined in a completed mating link.

To Maliki.

"Fuck," I breathe, my palm pressing into my chest as pain lances through my heart. It's not… it's not unpleasant. Just… unexpected.

Born from not being there to witness their connection.

Underscored by the very real likelihood that Maliki and Serapina probably didn't want me to be part of their union.

None of my mate-circle members trust me, and being away from them isn't helping matters.

I thought obtaining answers would prove my objective, but all I've done thus far is disappear. If I could return to Pandora's Box to finish what I started, I would. However, I can't leave Orcus in this state. He's unprotected. Unaware. *Hurt.*

I… I also need to know what's happened. Because while Alina and Serapina may not be related by blood, they're still sisters of the heart. A fact I haven't acknowledged as well as I should have, perhaps. But I'm recognizing it now.

If Serapina learns that her sister went missing and I did nothing to help find her, she may never forgive me. And I really don't need to add to my list of mistakes.

Right. So why here? I think again, scanning the Italian coastline. *And who sent—*

Orcus snaps from his daze with a growl and grabs my arm, much like he did in Pandora's Box. Except, rather than utter his mate's name, he simply mists us once more.

My jaw ticks, my inner Alpha not appreciating the manhandling from my brother. But as the familiar Gothic corridor of my palace is revealed around us, I find my lips curling downward instead.

"Took you long enough," a familiar voice drawls.

My brow furrows as I find Reaper casually leaning against a column etched into the hallway wall, utterly unperturbed by the skull adornment mere inches from his head. Given his Death Fae roots, I suppose that's to be expected.

What isn't expected, however, is his nonchalant presence. "What the fuck is going on?" I demand.

"I would like to know the same," Orcus says.

Reaper frowns at my brother. "You said to meet here if we ever lost contact." He glances at me. "Did he suffer a blow to the head? Lose balance in the sky and hit a tree?" He brightens like he's just found a new favorite weapon. "Oh, no, please tell me you punched him." His focus flies back to Orcus. "And you punched him back?"

"No one has punched anyone," I interject. "Not today, at least." I shake my head. "What are we doing here?" I look at my brother. "And why did you tell me you couldn't feel your mates?"

"Because I can't," he says through his teeth.

"Returning here was our backup plan should we become separated."

"Ah, so you do remember the emergency procedures. Maybe—"

"Why can't I feel you?" Orcus interrupts, cutting off Reaper's words.

"Well, I'm not a genius, but I imagine it's because we're not actively touching," Reaper drawls.

Which causes my brother to growl, "*Where is Alina*?"

"I'm here, Alpha," Alina says, her voice soft yet carrying down the hall.

Orcus takes one look at her and mists to her side, his hands on her face as he pulls her into his much larger form, his wings folding around her to shield her from view. The pair of them engage in whispers that I purposely try not to hear, my attention returning to Reaper. "An Alpha losing touch with his circle isn't a joking matter."

The Death Fae's expression doesn't change.

No remorse.

No guilt.

Not even a hint of fear or resignation.

Just a slightly unhinged look in his silver-blue eyes that never quite leaves.

"There are a lot of rules when referring to Alphas and mate-circles, Hades," he says, his tone uncharacteristically serious and at odds with his insouciant behavior. "Forgive me if I don't look to you for examples of what to do and what not to do."

With that, he disappears into a cloud of smoke that dissipates into the walls.

My jaw ticks.

He acts inappropriately in response to Orcus's valid concerns, yet I'm the one who ends up reprimanded.

"You know, I've always liked Reaper," Morpheus says, appearing beside me. "He's a wise Death Fae."

I pinch the bridge of my nose. "If you're here to chastise me for leaving Pandora's Box, save it." I look at the God of Dreams. "But please tell me you were able to talk to Demeter."

"Sadly, I was not," he replies, his vibrant gaze on Orcus down the hall. "And now I need to speak to your brother about it."

"My brother?" I echo as a question. "Why?"

He lifts a shoulder. "Follow me and find out."

"Morpheus," I begin.

But he's already walking away from me and toward my brother, who is still in full Alpha form with his wings curled around Alina.

"I'm not sure what caused you both to leave without an explanation or why it brought you here. I'm just glad it didn't take me long to find you, because I have questions." Morpheus's voice carries down the hall, ensuring my brother hears him.

"I wouldn't—" I start, trying to warn my cousin not to interrupt.

But he talks right over me.

"Orcus, I need to know every detail surrounding the day you caught and imprisoned Demeter," he says. "Because she's not in Pandora's Box."

I freeze.

And my brother slowly pulls back from Alina. "Ares released her?"

"No. He suspects she was never really there, that her imprisonment was some sort of elaborate mirage." Morpheus stops a few paces away from my brother and slips his hands into the pockets of his pants. "Or she escaped."

One of Orcus's wings remains tucked around Alina as he faces Morpheus. "You're telling me Demeter is no longer in custody. That she somehow managed to escape Pandora's Box… *again*?"

I wince.

Because yes, Demeter was supposedly imprisoned eons ago after the Omegas disappeared. However, her recent antics in the Monsters Night dimension made it clear that she'd escaped Ares's cells long ago.

Or…

"Or that she was never imprisoned, yes," Morpheus replies, finishing my thought. "Which is why I need all the details surrounding her capture."

"Maybe her escaping is what I sensed," Alina says, her focus on Orcus. "Or the mirage was a distraction?"

"Mirage?" Morpheus echoes.

"Orcus felt something from Alina that led him—*us*—to the Human Realm, where we found his mates covered in blood and surrounded by a bunch of unconscious Betas," I reply as I reach his side. "But it wasn't real."

"Alina's call was real," Orcus corrects me. "But then she created a defensive shield around all of us to block Demeter, not realizing it also cut me off from her and the others."

Alina's cheeks blossom with twin patches of red. "I'm sorry. I—"

Orcus yanks her into him with one palm around her nape and silences her words with a kiss, one born of passion and appreciation.

I understand it, as I would react the same way had Serapina manifested such a barrier.

"Never apologize for protecting our circle and our daughter," he says softly against her mouth. "You followed your instincts, just like you should."

"But I made you worry."

"My worry is nothing compared to my pride in you, little one," he whispers. "You're amazing. And I love you with the fury of a million suns." He kisses her again, this time forcing me to look away.

Because I want that—that sense of fulfillment and trust. I used to have something similar with Persephone, but not quite this fierce.

I always feared she would break beneath my touch, her delicate nature what I expected and cherished from her as an Omega.

But Serapina has opened my eyes to what I didn't know I needed—a strong mate, one who could be my equal.

That's what Orcus has in Alina. She didn't need him to come to her aid. She saved herself and her mates.

And from what I understand, she acted similarly in her home realm, too, when battling Demeter.

Orcus helped, but Alina started that fight by shattering Demeter's mirage.

Something tells me that Serapina would attempt to do the same, especially given everything that she now knows.

Unless her flame sizzles out, I think, recalling how meek she became earlier when discussing her expected fate. How she not only assumed that I would replace her fiery spirit with my long-lost mate, but also *accepted* it without a fight.

My lips curl down, not liking the memory at all or how it made me feel.

I don't want to lose Serapina.

She… she isn't Persephone. And while part of me mourns the loss of my past Omega, another part of me is relieved.

It's wrong.

It's confusing.

And it isn't something I have time to ponder now.

Not with what Morpheus just revealed. *Demeter isn't in Pandora's Box.* Which explains how she's been able to reach Serapina in my underworld.

"I need to go resecure the labyrinth," I tell Morpheus, thinking through all the security framework and wards that require attention.

No one should be able to enter my woven world.

However, Demeter has more than proved to be a unique adversary.

A realization that has me locking gazes with my brother. "I know we decided to split up before, but the parameters have changed."

He stares me down for a long moment, then dips his chin once in agreement. "There's safety in numbers."

"Something I've commented on for eons, alas..." Morpheus utters the words as though speaking to himself, his gaze distant. "Anyway," he goes on before I can comment, his blue-green eyes meeting mine in an instant. "The three of us will go together, as I still want details on Demeter's capture. Orcus can elaborate while we work."

"We?" I arch a brow. "It's *my* labyrinth."

"As you said, the parameters have changed," he tells me, his voice resembling steel. "And not just in regard to Demeter."

I suddenly have the urge to growl.

Because I could take that comment a myriad of ways.

But I'm done concerning myself with Morpheus's intentions.

Instead, I simply reply, "Fine."

"Sera will be there, right?" Alina asks, her focus on Orcus. "And she's... she's definitely okay?"

"I haven't seen her myself, but Hades says she's fine."

Alina huffs. "Like he would know."

"She's fine," Morpheus echoes, his voice soft. "I

wouldn't be standing here if I felt she was in danger. I also have complete faith in Maliki to properly protect her."

"Why wouldn't I know?" I ask, ignoring my cousin and focusing on the tiny female Omega. "Serapina is my mate."

"Don't you mean *Persephone*?" she counters.

My eyebrows rise. "Persephone's soul and memories reside within your sister, but that does not make them the same."

Orcus snorts. "Now he gets it."

"Does he, though?" Morpheus inquires.

I shake my head. "Demeter is a direct threat to our mate. Whatever issues remain between us need to be set aside because Serapina's safety is our priority. So either help me or fuck off. Choose. Now."

Morpheus considers me for a moment, his expression sobering. "You're right, Hades. My apologies. Orcus?"

My brother, who also wears a more serious expression now, leans down to kiss Alina on the cheek. "Tell Flame and Reaper that I'll be back for you all soon. Pack warm clothes for yourself and our Thea."

"How warm?" Alina whispers.

"Multiple layers and jackets," I tell her. "Where we're going is as cold as death."

With that, I vanish.

Morpheus knows where I'm going.

He can grab Orcus and meet me in the tunnels.

I have work to do.

MORPHEUS

NETHERWORLD KINGDOM

"AND THAT, MY DARLING, IS HOW YOU PUSH AN ALPHA'S buttons," Reaper announces as he rounds the corner with Thea in his arms. "It's not always advised, but your Uncle Hades is an asshole who—"

"*Reaper*," Alina chastises.

He frowns at her. "What?"

"Language?" she suggests.

He cocks his head. "Ah, right. Sorry." He looks down at the little wide-eyed Omega in his arms. "It's not always advised, but your Uncle Hades is an Alphahole who de—"

"Seriously?" This time the interruption is from Orcus.

"Do you have a better description?" Reaper asks him. "I assume *bastard* and *fucking ignoramus* are—"

"I'll just take Thea back now," Flame interjects, reaching for the tiny brunette.

Reaper's brow furrows, but he doesn't fight Flame as he plucks the sweet beauty from his arms. "You all do realize that she's going to be exposed to various aspects of language, yes?" the Death Fae demands. "Better she learns it from me than from someone else."

He disappears before anyone can reply, leaving Alina to sigh loudly in his wake.

"I'll talk to him," Orcus says.

"No need," Reaper announces, returning with a cupcake that he hands to Alina.

Her cheeks turn a pretty pink that matches the frosting. "Thank you."

He winks, then looks at me. "I assume you know where we're going?"

"To the Underworld Labyrinth," I reply, my lips twitching. "You're going to love it there."

Excitement dances across his features. "Am I?"

"Indeed," I murmur.

He wraps his arm around Alina and pulls her forward, his gaze on me. "Excellent. Lead the way, God of Dreams."

"We haven't packed yet, Reaper," Alina reminds him.

"Why would we pack?" he inquires. "We have an Alpha in our circle who can just manifest whatever shit we need."

Alina scowls at him.

His white eyebrows wing upward, reaching his equally white hairline. "Is the cupcake not to your liking, pet? Shall I fetch another?"

"What?" she asks.

"Your face," he goes on. "You're… you're glaring at me."

"Because… because…" She tilts her head back and sighs. "Never mind."

"You cursed again," Flame says softly from behind him. "In front of Thea."

"Oh." Reaper's nose crinkles. "Sorry, pet. I will try harder to… alter my vocabulary."

"And use better terms than *Alphahole*," Orcus mutters.

"That, I don't promise to do," Reaper returns. "I actually quite like the term. Perhaps I'll make it your new nickname."

"Try it," Orcus dares him.

Flame releases a purr from his chest, the sound seeming to be for Thea. She nuzzles into him with a happy little coo, one that has Alina smiling in response.

"Show-off," Reaper mutters.

And I… I just shake my head. "As entertaining as you all are, I would like to get back to Serapina sooner rather than later. Which means catching up to Hades in his little tunnel of wards." I'm not sure what else to call it. But the terminology feels appropriate.

"You and Orcus go," Alina murmurs. "I need to feed Thea first. Then we'll join you in Hades's version of the underworld."

"We don't have to go," Flame tells her. "We can choose a more neutral location."

Alina presses her palm to his chest, then lowers it to rest on Thea. "I appreciate the notion, Flame. But I need to see Sera. And while I don't like Hades very much right now, I do trust him to keep us safe." She glances at Orcus. "Right?"

"Right," the Alpha agrees. "He may be an ignorant prick on occasion, but he's a master at creating protective wards."

"So *ignorant prick* is allowed?" Reaper asks. When all

three of his mates look at him, he shrugs. "All right, fine. Noted. *Ignorant* and *prick* are now in my vocabulary."

"Shall we go, Orcus?" I press, meaning what I said a bit ago about wanting to return to my mate. She's still secure with Maliki—a fact that thrums through my veins like wildfire as my Omega's pleasure washes through me for the umpteenth time—which allows me to feel both at ease and agitated at the same time.

I want to join them.

Watch as he takes her to oblivion on repeat.

Bare witness to their *mating*.

Because I can feel his connection to her now, the live wire a current I long to stroke. He needs a token of kinship from me, similar to that gold coin Hades bestowed upon him.

I'm just not sure Maliki will accept it.

We're still dancing around this whole situationship.

Learning to trust. Manifesting faith in each other's intentions. Mastering the art of friendship and matehood.

Very unlike the connections Orcus has established with Reaper and Flame. They're as bonded as blood brothers.

And Alina is the center of their world.

As is Thea.

I want that with Serapina more than anything. I think Maliki does, too.

Hades…

Well, Hades is the linchpin in our little circle of chaos. If he hurts our mate and shatters the tenuous links we've formed, then we're all fucked.

"Let's go," Orcus says, walking toward me.

"I hope you're in the mood for storytelling," I say as I hold out my hand. "Because I want every detail of that fated day."

He nods. "Then I'll start from the beginning…"

Death's Cabin

Sera snuggles into my chest as I shadow us back to the cabin, her eyes closed. "You look so well used," I tell her. "So properly fucked." I press my lips to her forehead. "But now I need to make sure you're fed."

She mumbles something incoherent in response. Probably another comment about how I'm always trying to make her eat.

However, in this case, she needs sustenance.

"I worked you hard, Sera." I lay her on the bed. "And now it's my job to take care of you."

Forget that my own legs are still shaking from the intensity of our mating or that my cock is already at half-mast and ready to fuck again.

Sera is still mortal.

Her libido, though, is definitely inhuman.

She came over a dozen times for me, which is exceptionally fae-like. It gives me hope that her Mythos side will rise soon and convert her into the Goddess she's meant to be.

Not Persephone.

But Goddess Sera.

My mate.

I kiss her temple, my lips twitching upward at the soft little mewl she releases in response. Then her body goes completely limp as sleep steals over her.

"That's fine," I decide aloud. "You rest. I'll cook."

Because I'm in the mood to make something from scratch. Not manifest it. Not magic it into existence. But put my hands to work and create something special for my sweet mystery.

Drawing my knuckles down her cheek, I step back and admire her bare skin. There are some bruises. My crescent marks. Streaks of arousal. Sweat. And a little bit of blood.

Definitely a mess, I muse. *Just like she desired.*

Normally, I would bathe her.

But that's not what she requested.

So I'll let her scent these sheets with our intense fucking while I work in the kitchen.

With one more lingering look, I turn and find Pip hovering in the doorway with an uncertain expression. "She's fine," I promise him. "More than fine, actually."

He doesn't look convinced.

"How about you help me make something for her to eat, yeah? Then you can see for yourself that she's okay, just needs a little rest and an energy boost."

His blue robes sway along the floor, his gaze suspicious.

"Hey, remember that I'm the one who tried to help you out with Fleur. We're a team, right?" I press.

He considers me, then looks around me as Sera sighs on the bed, her body curling up in the silky sheets.

"See?" I murmur. "She's taking a nap."

I move around him and down the hall to where my sphinx is resting on the couch.

"Similar to Fleur," I muse.

My cat peeks at me with one bright blue eye. Then goes right back to sleep.

"You must be on guard duty." Not that there's much to protect against right now.

Except Demeter…

With that thought in mind, I ensure I'm connected to Sera—something that's as simple as breathing now that we're fully mated—and monitor her mental state.

When I find her dreaming about me, I grin.

That grin only grows when Morpheus makes an appearance.

Sera spins toward him, her eyes widening. "Oh," she breathes. "Hi."

"Hi, little dreamer," he murmurs, his voice oddly loud in my head. "I see Maliki did his job, hmm? Pleasured you so hard that you've fallen unconscious?"

My brow furrows, my eyes opening to find the God of Dreams leaning against the wall in the hallway that leads to the bedroom. His gaze is unfocused, confirming he's lost to the dream world, yet physically present in the labyrinth.

I feel Sera blush, my connection to her so visceral that I'm nearly pulled back into her dream.

I've never been linked to anyone like this, the mental bond new and very welcome. However, it's a bit strange when her arousal hums through my blood.

A quick glance into her mind tells me Morpheus is now

kissing her. "When you wake up, I want to discuss consensual non-consent activities with you," I hear him say.

"What?" she breathes, making my lips twitch.

"I want permission to knot you while you sleep," he says bluntly. "But I can feel your exhaustion, sweetheart. So rest. We'll talk when you rise again."

Her mind goes quiet, her dream melting into blissful silence.

It's strange but comforting. I can sense that she's here and present, just sleeping. Very different from the times Demeter has taken her.

However, I don't allow that to lull me into a false state of confidence. Instead, I remain firmly anchored in her mind while also paying attention to my surroundings.

Surroundings that are now shifting as Morpheus saunters toward me. Behind him, Pip wanders off back down the hallway, likely to check on Sera again. Or maybe he's chosen to play guard while she sleeps.

It seems Hades's pet—the sentry usually stationed near Sera in this place—has wandered off outside. Perhaps with Morpheus's familiar, Athena.

"I assume you're planning to feed our mate something other than cum now?" Morpheus asks, drawing my focus back to him.

I cant my head, considering my options. "Maybe" is all I say on the topic before turning toward the kitchen, the God of Dreams on my heels. "Did you and Hades have a nice meeting with Demeter?"

"No," he answers. "It seems she's no longer a resident of Pandora's Box, or perhaps never was a resident to begin with."

I freeze near the counter, then slowly face him again. "*What?*"

"Yes, that seems to be everyone's reaction." He opens the fridge and pulls out a bottle of what looks like sparkling water, which I assume he just manifested, and pops the top before taking a long drink.

"Elaborate, Morpheus."

"Careful, Maliki," he returns. "Our Omega might enjoy commands, but I do not."

"You can't mist in here and drop that sort of verbal bomb without further explanation," I bite out. "Tell me what I need to know so I can properly protect my mate."

His silver eyebrow lifts. "Your mate?" This time he cants his head. "I do believe you mean *our* mate."

I fold my arms across my bare chest. I didn't bother with putting on clothes, something that doesn't seem to faze Morpheus at all.

Just like he doesn't appear to be bothered by the scent of ecstasy permeating my skin.

Because he doesn't mind sharing.

I know that.

It's Hades who has always been possessive of his Omega, not Morpheus.

But that does lead me to wonder… "Where's Hades?" I voice the query aloud, curious as to why Morpheus has returned without the other Alpha. "Is he hunting down Demeter?"

"No, he's securing the wards to his labyrinth again, and also altering some of the parameters to allow Orcus's mate-circle to enter." He stares me down. "But on that topic, you do understand the purpose of a mate-circle, yes? That we all have equal claim on our Omega, regardless of who may have secured a bond first?"

"I think it depends on whether everyone in the circle has the same intentions regarding the heart of the circle. That heart being Sera," I return, my gaze narrowing.

"Now cut the cryptic bullshit and talk to me about Demeter."

He sets the glass bottle down. "I have. We don't know anything else yet, aside from Orcus's recounting of the day she was captured. Which, unfortunately, only confirms what we already knew—she's adept at crafting mirages."

Morpheus goes on to tell me about the scene Demeter created just today that depicted a bloodbath in the Human Realm—one that caused Orcus to momentarily panic until Alina intervened and shattered the image.

Only, it was apparently at the expense of their mental link, too.

Which sent him into another spiral of worry when he couldn't feel his mates.

"Long story short, it was decided that we should all reside here, where Hades maintains control of the wards," Morpheus concludes.

"Except Demeter has been able to reach Sera here a few times already," I point out.

"Yes, and both times you were able to bring her back. That's partly due to your bond, but aided by Hades's wards," Morpheus replies. "Or that's my suspicion, anyway. Regardless, we all have the same goal in mind—to protect Serapina."

I consider that as I begin manifesting ingredients for the pasta dish I've decided to make.

The items appear along the counter, all in the precise order of my thoughts. Fortunately, the onions and peppers remain whole, thus granting me the opportunity to chop them. Same with the garlic and basil.

Good.

I need something for my hands to do.

And I really like that it involves playing with a knife.

Going to the sink, I wash up, then begin my preparations while Morpheus sips his bubbling liquid.

I assume it's not actually sparkling water but some sort of alcohol or Mythos Fae drink I've never seen before. *Maybe it's the mythical ambrosia.*

I nearly snort at the thought.

"Can we address the *my mate* comment now?" Morpheus asks as he settles on a stool at the counter. "I'm all for sharing, Maliki. But I won't take lightly to you staking a permanent solo claim on *our* Omega."

Rather than reply, I focus on my blade.

Slicing and dicing.

Such a beautiful sound.

"Maliki." Morpheus is standing beside me now, his Alpha energy wrapping around me in warning. "I sense your claim, which means you can also sense mine."

"Do you know why she asked me to fuck her today?" I voice the question conversationally, my attention moving to the garlic as I begin to mince it with sharp motions. "She said it was because she wanted to defy Hades—to be the opposite of fed and clean, like he originally requested."

Morpheus remains silent for a beat. "Irritating Hades is an enjoyable pastime, so I can see the allure."

"As did I," I agree. "But her request went much deeper than a need to rebel." I push all the garlic to one side with my blade, then set the instrument down and face the God of Dreams. "She wanted an experience with me that she could remember, one that will keep her company when she ends up in that state of nonexistence again."

I overheard that fact after she bit me, the memory of her thoughts drifting in and out of my mind as though those cravings belonged to me, too.

"Basically, she wants to experience mating—and knotting, for that matter—for herself before she disappears," I tell him. I don't add the part about how she assumes she'll *disappear* when Persephone takes over again. That part is implied.

His gaze searches mine. "Then that's what we should give her. *Together*."

I huff a laugh, one that doesn't sound all that amused.

Because I'm not fucking amused.

"Wrong answer, God of Dreams," I inform him.

I expected such a reply from Hades.

But Morpheus? I guess, deep down, I thought he would understand. That he would feel similarly to me.

"How is that the wrong answer?" he demands, facing me full on. "If our Omega wants certain experiences, then we should give her those experiences."

"So she can take those memories with her to the place of nonexistence?" I press. "That's good enough for you, yeah? To know that you gave her a few nights of pleasure in exchange for an eternity of fucking loneliness?"

He frowns at me. "What the fuck are you talking about, Maliki?"

"The fact that you just said we should give her what she wants—which are memories to keep her warm when she's otherwise cold," I fire back at him. "Bringing Persephone back means that much to you that you're willing to subject an innocent woman to a hellish existence so you can have your precious Omega back?"

Morpheus gapes at me. "That is not what I said at all."

"You just said—"

"No, Enforcer." He crowds me against the counter, making me consider grabbing the knife again. "I suggested we fulfill our Omega's wishes. That's it. I did not, in any way, suggest that we fulfill those wishes as a result of her wanting to experience certain things before her potential disappearance. Further, I have no interest in losing Serapina. I simply wish to please her."

I study his face, searching for any hints of a lie or mistrust. But all I find is a sturdy jawline that's clenched in annoyance.

And a pair of eyes that are radiating fury.

"Persephone was my soul's mate," he goes on. "But I was never given the opportunity to properly know her. And while I did care for her deeply, the feelings I've developed for Serapina are far superior to anything I've ever felt before. She's…" He pauses, swallowing. "She's everything I've ever desired and so much more."

His voice is soft at the end, his irritation less evident in his expression and tone.

But he's not done speaking. "I have no wish for her to be erased by Persephone's soul, Maliki. I want Serapina to be who she is, and more importantly, I want her to be *ours*."

I stare at him, our similar heights allowing us to stand gaze to gaze. Everything he's saying rivals how I feel. "So how do we ensure we don't lose her?" I ask him seriously. "How do we protect her from Persephone's soul?"

"You don't," a deep voice says as Hades enters the kitchen, his expression thunderous. "Persephone's soul and Serapina are one and the same. There's no *protection* needed. In fact, the opposite is what needs to happen—the two halves have to fully join."

"You would say that," Morpheus mutters, facing the other Alpha. "It would give you what you desire—your Persephone."

Hades glares at him. "I already have what I desire, Cousin. She resides with Serapina now. And I can't think of a better way to honor her life."

"Right." I don't grab the knife off the counter. I tell the kitchen to manifest a new one. "You grab him and I'll stab him." The words are for Morpheus, something he clearly understands because he mists to Hades's back, his hands already reaching for the other Alpha.

Hades doesn't fight him.

Instead, he flashes a look of surprise my way, the emotion quickly morphing into an expression of betrayal and hurt. It's unlike anything he's ever displayed in front of me.

Which gives me momentary pause.

"I may not understand how Demeter borrowed my gifts, or what exactly she's done with them, but I am the God of Death. Resurrection is *my* power." His words are quiet yet dominant. Filled with emotion. And underlined with frustration.

Morpheus doesn't touch him, just stands behind him, his gaze guarded as he watches Hades.

I don't pick up the knife I created, but I do keep my hand on top of it.

And wait for Hades to continue.

"When a soul is reborn, it doesn't take over the host. It simply grows and flourishes inside the being and lives a new life. Manifests new characteristics. New personality traits. New likes and dislikes. And while fate may ensure that soul finds its way back to a certain mate or lures it down a specific path, that soul does not *erase* the entity. It's impossible."

"Yet Sera has Persephone's memories," I say. "So what does that mean?"

"It means what I already said, Maliki. Persephone resides within Serapina now. Her memories. Her heart. Her feelings. Every part of her is memorialized inside our mate in a unique bond that essentially allows Serapina to see her soul's past life. But she's still her own person, which is exactly what resurrection is about—a second chance at life."

Silence falls between the three of us, Hades's words oddly heavy.

"Why didn't you explain that before?" Morpheus finally asks.

"Because you didn't ask," Hades replies. "Instead, you made assumptions, ones I know I deserved. But the only reason I wanted to talk to Demeter was to find out how she's blocking Serapina from fully embracing her Omega soul." He turns toward his cousin, saying, "I fear…"

He freezes.

And I suddenly realize why.

I was so caught up in the conversation that I didn't feel Sera wake up.

Nor did I sense her leave the bedroom.

Or notice her enter the living area.

Where she's apparently been standing for several minutes.

With a nervous Pip right by her side.

HADES'S DARK EYES FLARE, HIS WORDS ENDING ABRUPTLY AS his gaze meets mine.

All three men were so caught up in discussing me and my soul that they didn't hear me walk down the hallway.

Though, I was purposely quiet. I even lingered behind the wall for a moment when I overheard my name.

"*Persephone's soul and Serapina are one and the same.*"

Hearing Hades's deep tone gave me pause and nearly sent me skipping back into the bedroom.

But curiosity held me captive.

Something I swear Fleur judged me for as she watched me from the couch with knowing eyes.

It was my stare-down with her that eventually forced me to move toward the couch. I was worried she might meow and give away my presence. And I didn't want to be caught eavesdropping.

However, it didn't end up mattering since the men were too deep in conversation to notice me.

But they certainly notice me now.

Morpheus's lips part when he finds me wrapped up in a short robe.

Maliki gives me a sad smile.

And Hades just… stares. Then he clears his throat and says, "Your sister is here."

My eyes widen. "*What*?" I instinctively pull the ties of my robe tighter as I start to look around. "Where?"

Pip disappears, maybe to go find my sister. Or maybe to hide. I'm not sure. But Hades distracts me from trying to figure it out when he replies, "Near Glass Lake."

"The… the what?" I'm so confused. "There's a glass lake?"

"In the Nesting Gardens," he clarifies. Not that it helps. "I can escort you there once she and her circle are better settled."

"I… I would like that." Seeing Alina might be a relief right now, especially with all my competing emotions over everything Hades just said about my soul and resurrection. *Except…* "What are you afraid of?"

He was in the middle of saying he fears something when he met my gaze, and I want to know the end of that sentence.

His brow furrows. "I'm not afraid of anything, Serapina."

"You said, 'I fear,' and didn't finish your statement. I want to know what you were going to say. Please."

He gives me a strange look, one that almost resembles pride. But the expression is short-lived, his features turning somber as he replies, "I fear what will happen if you remain separated from your Omega soul. You should have gone into heat a year ago. I thought you were intentionally suppressing your instincts. But now…"

"Now you realize I'm not," I finish for him.

"Yes," he admits. "And I'm afraid of what that might mean. I wanted to question Demeter so I could provide you with answers, the way an Alpha should be able to in a situation such as this. But I was unable to fulfill my quest. I'm sorry for my failure."

He sounds so contrite, his words and tone suggesting he's apologizing for so much more with that statement.

It's so unlike the Hades in Persephone's memories, his unerring confidence something she adored about him.

But I'm finding his softness to be alluring. It makes me feel… safe.

Which is confusing, as I worried about his intentions not even ten minutes ago.

However, his explanation about resurrection provided a sense of relief that I wasn't expecting.

He seemed pleased to know Persephone's memory lives on inside me. And not because he wants her to take over, or for me to disappear as she inhabits this form. But because he's happy she's been memorialized.

"I can't think of a better way to honor her life."

I completely misunderstood what he meant when he originally said that. I thought he was saying he couldn't think of a better way to honor *my* life by replacing it with Persephone's essence.

However, that's not what he intended at all.

He was saying that he feels I'm worthy of hosting Persephone's soul. Of being the one to carry her memories. Of embodying the Omega who used to be his mate.

It's a strange sort of compliment, one I'm still trying to accept.

Hades clears his throat, his expression seeming to exude discomfort.

A discomfort that matches his tone as he says, "Right,

well, I should go see if Orcus needs my help with anything. Unless you have more questions?" He doesn't sound wary when he asks this, so much as defeated.

It's difficult to reconcile this version of Hades with all the memories in my head. Memories of his arrogance. His confidence. *His lethal sensuality.*

There isn't a single recollection from Persephone's past that matches the version of Hades before me. He's never uneasy or hesitant.

This visage, compared with the ones in my mind, confuses me. It… it also *hurts*. Because I don't enjoy seeing Hades like this.

Some part of me aches in response. That part of me forces me to move toward him, my hands seeming to reach for him as though I have no control over my reaction.

Maybe this is Persephone taking over my form.

Or maybe it's just me.

A second chance at life.

That's what Hades said about resurrection.

But maybe it applies to us as well.

Our soul bond.

A second chance to do this correctly.

Whatever that might mean.

But I know for sure it doesn't mean this—him standing there with his shoulders somewhat curved inward, his eyes exuding uncertainty, his words littered with apologies that are not his to voice.

Whatever Demeter did isn't his fault. And he didn't fail by not being able to obtain answers.

"You're a good Alpha, Hades," I tell him, somehow knowing those are the words he needs to hear. The knowledge comes from deep down. *From my soul.* Persephone might be a memory inside me, but her experience is what's driving my actions now. "Please don't feel otherwise." I press my palm to his chest and go up onto my toes to brush a kiss against his jaw.

It's so natural.

So *intrinsic.*

And it draws a sharp intake of breath from him, like I've struck a nerve of some kind.

Maybe rekindled something inside him.

Persephone used to do this, I realize with a start. *This is how she showed affection.*

The understanding has my stomach twisting with a combination of sensations, ones that leave me feeling both sick and relieved at the same time.

It's… it's confusing.

Yet I can't pull away from him.

I… I want to ensure he's okay. To show that I'm not upset with him. But I want to do it *my* way. Not like Persephone. Not quite, anyway.

Because I'm still me.

Not Persephone.

Not Serapina.

But *Sera.*

The version of me who defied Hades's demands earlier.

The version who chose a village hut and lived alone in a world of deadly fae.

The version who chastised a God for trying to force me to marry him.

That woman is fierce. Independent. And bold.

I've lost sight of her over the last week, I think. Too lost in the need to supplicate and give in to fate. To atone for the sins of my soul. To naively accept a future in a plane of nonexistence when I've done nothing to deserve that.

The Sera who was determined to live alone and

discover herself without anyone else's help is the Sera I want to be.

That journey began again today.

When I told Maliki what I desired.

Accepted his claim.

Returned his bite.

And embraced his dark side.

I'm going to continue down that path now—but with Hades.

Which is why I kiss his jaw again, just like Persephone would have done eons ago. But I grab his nape, too. Go up even more onto my toes. And angle his head toward mine so I can kiss him.

Because I want to.

Because his lips are addictive.

Because it feels like an eternity since we last embraced.

His hand catches my hip, holding me steady as I press my mouth to his. It's soft. A little hesitant. And not at all what I want.

Wrapping my arms around his neck, I kiss him again, this time harder. More demanding. Telling him with my lips that I desire more.

He releases a purr that vibrates through my robe and caresses my bare skin. It's an alluring sound, so beautiful and warm and *mine.*

When his hand shifts to my lower back and his opposite hand goes to my neck, I practically melt into him.

His rumble intensifies as his tongue slips into my mouth, his warmth and masculinity swathing me in a sea of security and bliss.

I moan, utterly captivated and lost to his touch. His strength. His *scent.*

Stars, it's like I'm outside in the snow on a cold wintry night. The aroma of a freshly cut rose in the air. Curling around me. Bathing me in rightness. Making me feel like I've finally come home.

I cling to him as he deepens our embrace, his hand moving along my back as he wraps his arm around me. Holding me. Protecting me. *Cherishing me.*

It's different from Persephone's memories, though. He always held her with more caution, as though he was afraid she might break. But there's a hint of desperation in how he embraces me now, like he's afraid I'll disappear.

His arm turns hard around my back, his mouth urgent, his hand a brand against my nape.

I tighten my hold on his neck, too. Giving him the same treatment. Showing him that I'm not afraid. That I might be human, but that doesn't make me fragile.

I want to be strong.

Powerful.

An equal.

It's an insane notion, one that can never come to fruition. But that doesn't mean I won't try.

Which I proceed to demonstrate with my tongue—sparring with him in a sensual, intimate way and ensuring he knows I'm here. *Sera.* Not a meek human. Not a former Goddess. But *me.*

"Fuck, darling. If you keep kissing me like this, I'm going to drag you back to the bedroom and knot you until you can't walk," he threatens.

"Do it," I dare him, feeling bold. Alive. *Like the woman I want to be.*

"No," Maliki interjects. "She needs to eat first."

My gaze narrows. *Stop trying to feed me, Maliki.* The words go from my mind to his, but Hades speaks before Maliki can respond.

"She hasn't eaten yet?" Hades asks, his lips brushing

mine with each word. "Didn't I task you with feeding her before I left?"

"Oh, he fed her," Morpheus drawls. "Cum, at least."

My eyes widen, heat suddenly suffocating my cheeks. "*Morpheus*."

"I'm not wrong, sweetheart. Just as Maliki isn't wrong to suggest food. If you're eager to take a knot, then you need energy to keep up." He doesn't sound at all apologetic about his bluntness or the fact that he basically just said I'm not in a state where I can properly "keep up."

Which has me releasing Hades to look at the God of Dreams. "I'm more than capable of *keeping up*," I tell him, irritated by the very prospect of him thinking otherwise. "I took your knot in my mouth just fine."

His lips twitch. "I didn't knot your mouth, little dreamer. I merely fucked it."

My brow furrows. I'm aware of the distinction, especially now that I possess Persephone's more intimate memories, but I still feel the need to say, "I took everything you gave me."

"That you did," he agrees. "But I didn't let my knot attach to your throat. That would hurt. Not to mention suffocate you."

Okay.

Right.

Fine.

Still…

"I can handle a knot, Morpheus," I try again, right as my stomach decides to betray me with a loud grumble.

A sound that I promptly follow with an irritated growl.

Which causes Hades to release a rumble of a similar kind, only far more fierce.

My knees instantly shake, my legs threatening to give out before me.

Oh, this is just ridiculous, I think, dizzy as the harsh reverberation grows in his chest.

"I'm disappointed, Maliki," he says. "Her needs come first, not yours."

"She told me to fuck her, Hades," Maliki returns without missing a beat. "So I took her to the Rutting Grounds and satisfied her urges."

"The Rutting Grounds?" Hades releases me so suddenly that I nearly fall. But Morpheus is immediately there to catch me as Hades spins around to face Maliki. "What the fuck were you thinking?"

"That my mate told me not to hold back, so I didn't," he answers simply. "As I said the other day, I no longer report to you, Hades. Only her."

"You never fucking reported to me," he growls at him. "But at least I'm beginning to understand how you viewed me all these centuries—not as a friend, but as a boss."

Morpheus nuzzles my neck, his arms coming around me from behind. "You smell amazing like this, little dreamer," he whispers against my ear. "Freshly fucked with a hint of silky sheets. Like sinful decadence."

I shiver at his words but also frown at what's unfolding before me.

Hades's shoulders are curving again.

"My expressed disappointment isn't because you failed to follow an order, but because you failed to care for our mate," Hades says. "However, if you were following her wishes, then I stand corrected." He takes a step to the side and runs his hands through his hair before glancing back at me. "I…" His dark eyes go to my lips, and he swallows. "I really should check on Orcus."

He vanishes before I can comment.

Maliki stares at the space he just vacated, his brows pinched a little, and I can hear his mind playing over their conversation. *"Not as a friend, but as a boss"* seems to be the loudest comment repeating in his thoughts.

Morpheus presses another kiss to my neck. "How about you and I go take a shower while Maliki cooks, hmm?" He nuzzles me a little. "I'll teach you more about knotting while also taking care of you."

My nipples harden at the offer.

I… I should probably refuse. Talk to Maliki about what Hades said. Or… or go after Hades and fix whatever seemed broken.

But I don't know how to do either.

And I can sense from Maliki's thoughts that he's already considering doing the same—going after Hades for a chat. Or maybe waiting until Hades returns.

Regardless, it seems like an issue between them that needs to be addressed.

So spending time with Morpheus is probably a good idea.

"Here, take this with you," Maliki says, grabbing a glass from the counter as it magically appears. "It's a fruit smoothie. Should give you enough energy to… play." He winks at me. "I'll be here cooking." His gaze goes to Morpheus. "I need forty-five minutes."

"That shouldn't be a problem," the Alpha holding me replies, his accented tone deep and meaningful near my ear. "We'll be at least an hour."

Maliki nods.

And I begin to wonder if they have a mental bond, too. Because they seem to be having more than one conversation between each other.

But I'm suddenly too consumed by the scents coming from Maliki's offered drink to ask any questions.

My stomach grumbles again. However, I don't even mind this time. It's in response to the sweetness caressing my nose. I reach for Maliki's glass, wrap my lips around the straw, suck, and groan when the flavor bursts across my tongue.

Morpheus chuckles behind me. "That reminds me of something."

"A great many things," Maliki murmurs.

I ignore them both, too lost to the drink to care.

I'm only vaguely aware of Morpheus picking me up to carry me to the bedroom.

This drink is drugged, isn't it? I think, hoping Maliki can hear me.

I may have requested an irresistible twist to the mixture, he replies into my mind. *A very special ingredient.*

I try to search his thoughts for the name of said ingredient, but it's like hunting through a flower field for a specific petal.

Giving up, I just enjoy the drink and let Morpheus take me wherever he desires.

To the shower, I remember as we enter the bathroom. *To play with a knot.*

But only after I finish my drink.

Which is… almost gone already.

Wow, I marvel. *Wow.*

Right back at you, trouble, Maliki replies. *Now be a good girl and do what Morpheus tells you to do, yeah?*

I MIST TO THE RUTTING GROUNDS, NOT THE NESTING Gardens, and *growl*.

Apparently, I'm in a punishing mood, not a helpful one. Because I would much rather bask in the scent of sex than the fire lilies surrounding Glass Lake.

Although, ironically, Serapina's arousal reminds me of the fiery flowers. So potent and rich. *So aromatic*.

I inhale, my eyes falling closed as my knot pulses in response.

It doesn't take me long to track the alluring fragrance to one of the artfully hidden cave nests. I slip inside, my gaze taking in the freshly fucked-in sheets and the imprints against some of the walls.

"You certainly figured out the purpose of my designs," I say when I feel Maliki join me in the cavern. "And shouldn't you be cooking?"

"Shouldn't you be helping Orcus?" he counters.

I sigh and face him. "What do you want from me, Maliki? An apology? A concession? Some sort of explanation?" I hold his gaze as I add, "A task?"

"Want to manifest me some pants?" he asks, causing me to glance downward.

I noticed he was naked in the kitchen earlier and didn't think much of it.

But he's starting to get hard now. Probably because he's surrounded by the memories of what he and Serapina did here mere hours ago. Or perhaps even more recently than that. Time has felt more elusive than ever lately.

Shaking my head, I conjure a pair of jeans and toss them at Maliki. He grunts out a "Thanks" and starts dressing himself. Ignoring him, I prowl around the cave and imagine all the ways he fucked my mate.

My Omega.

My Serapina.

Her scent tells me she enjoyed herself. I should be furious. Violent. *Something.* Yet all I feel is a pang in my heart. Because I missed their mating. Missed watching my female come. Missed hearing her moan. Missed her screams. Her cries of pleasure. Her tears.

All I see now is evidence of rough sex.

Blood.

Shared arousal.

Sweat.

And Serapina's sweet slick…

Fuck, my mouth is watering for a taste.

I close my eyes and imagine it—Serapina lying on the bed. Legs spread. Beckoning me with those beautiful blue irises.

She kissed me earlier with a ferocity I've never experienced before.

It was as though she wanted to drag me into battle. Ravage me. Prove her worth as my partner. *Become my equal.*

That's exactly what makes this reincarnation of my mate so very powerful.

The Persephone I knew always relied on me to protect her. She was soft. Sweet. *Easy to command.*

But Serapina defied me.

As evidenced by this cave and the mess she and Maliki made of each other in that bed. I open my eyes to take it all in again, my knot pulsing with need.

I want to punish her for her rebellion.

Then praise her for it with my tongue.

It's a conflict of interest, one I rather enjoy. Because I want to spank her and fuck her at the same time.

"Hades." Maliki's voice pulls my attention to where he's standing by the edge of the mattress.

"Do you want a shirt?" I ask. "Or shoes, perhaps?"

He grunts. "No. But thank you for the pants."

"Consider it payment for a job well done," I mutter, looking at the bed again.

"Hades," he repeats, this time with more stress on my name.

"Maliki," I return, aware that I sound exhausted.

"Morpheus says Demeter isn't in Pandora's Box."

I nod, my gaze still on the silk sheets. "That's why I couldn't question her about what she's done to Serapina." I inhale deeply, noting the scents in the air, the way the sensual undertones almost remind me of an Omega's heat, but not quite. "I've secured all my wards, and I intend to review them frequently."

When Maliki doesn't reply, I look at him and find him staring right at me.

My jaw clenches.

This is ridiculous.

"Right, you may not trust me, but I'll keep Serapina safe," I tell him. "And if that's not enough for you, then consider that she harbors what's left of Persephone. I would never allow anyone or anything to harm her." My need to protect Serapina goes so much deeper than that, but I'm done trying to explain myself.

Especially to him.

The male I thought was my best friend.

Until I realized that friendship was one-sided. Not only does he not trust my intentions with my mate, but he also considers me to be his *boss*.

The term radiates like a bloody curse in my head, making me want to put my fist through the wall.

Or Maliki's face.

Rather than do that, I turn and head toward the cave's exit. Because the last thing I need to do is start a fight with a member of the mate-circle. Not when our bonds are holding on by a thread.

"I trust you implicitly, Hades," Maliki says, giving me pause. "You're like a brother to me. One I frequently want to punch in the face, but I respect you. That hasn't changed. However, my priorities have changed. Perhaps for the first time in my life, I value someone else's life more than my own."

"Serapina's," I say.

"Yes," he replies. "And I'll fight anyone who tries to take her from me. Just as I will argue against being told what to do where my mate is concerned."

"Your mate," I repeat, the words ones I would usually utter with a heavy dose of incredulity. But I don't have it in me to do so now. "She's yours now, not ours. An important distinction." I fold my arms over my chest. "*Your* mate just dared me to knot her."

His lips twitch. "She did. It was cute. I look forward to

watching it happen, hopefully soon. As it is, I've never watched you fuck. Always the other way around. I think I'll make some popcorn for the occasion."

I gape at him. "You anticipate being entertained and not aroused?"

"I can eat popcorn with an erection, Hades."

I roll my eyes. "Your bedroom manners need work."

"My bedroom manners are fine," he counters. "Just ask Sera."

I stare at him. "I fear you're not the only one who frequently desires to punch another in the face, Maliki."

He smiles. "Then we're good, yeah?"

"We were never *not* good," I tell him.

"Sure," he agrees. "We'll pretend like you weren't here to sulk." He cocks his head. "You do realize that I found you on the first try, right? Want to know how I did that?"

"Not really," I admit.

"Too bad," he returns. "I might not always be able to anticipate your movements, or understand them, but I do know you, Hades. And I've never seen you as a boss. I've made some jokes about it because that's what Sera thought in the beginning since I mentioned working for you."

My brow furrows. "You've never worked for me."

"I've done a lot of jobs for you, Hades."

"Because you enjoyed the tasks," I counter. "So I shared opportunities with you."

"Exactly," he replies. "But guarding Sera certainly started as a job, and she knows that. Which is why she thought you were my boss."

"I asked you to guard Serapina because you were the only one I trusted to help keep her safe," I mutter. "Not because it was a *job*."

"I know," he replies. "I referred to it as a job to her, though, because I had to think of her as an assignment. It was too risky to consider her as anything else, not when you made it clear she belonged to you."

My jaw ticks. He's not wrong—I did stake my claim. But… "I would have shared her with you, had you asked."

His eyebrow lifts. "Would you have?" He voices the question with a hint of sarcasm. "Hades, you are one of the most possessive fae I know."

"Yet you spent the last however many hours fucking my Omega in a cave I built specifically for her heat, and I've not reacted negatively," I point out. "I think that proves I can share."

"Now, yes," he agrees. "But a year ago? Not a chance."

I take a deep breath and release it through my teeth. "I would comment on the futility of focusing on the past, but that would clearly make me a hypocrite."

Maliki's lips twitch. "It would, yeah."

I palm my nape and stretch it back a little to look at the glittering ceiling above. The twinkling lights were supposed to resemble glowworms, a phenomenon from the Human Realm that Persephone favored eons ago.

It was supposed to be a boon—a gift to show her I still loved her despite her betrayal.

Everything's changed now.

Serapina knows the truths hidden inside my mate's soul. She told me that Persephone fought to reach me. But Demeter was too strong. She possessed too much control.

Because she groomed her daughter to do her bidding.

I can see that clearly now.

Just as I can see how Demeter has failed to do the same with this reincarnated version of my mate.

Serapina has fought Demeter and won a few times now. In her own way, at least. Via her link to Maliki. By being safeguarded by this labyrinth.

However, deep down, it's because Serapina refuses to submit to Demeter's wishes.

Which is what makes her such an ideal mate. The perfect reincarnation for Persephone.

"I loved my Omega," I tell Maliki quietly. "Fae, I loved her more than anyone or anything in all the dimensions. Spent millennia hunting for her, not only to punish her, but to save her. To rekindle our bond. To…" I trail off, unsure of how to articulate everything I thought I desired.

But what I wanted really isn't the point.

"Serapina has changed everything," I admit, my voice still soft, like I'm confiding a sin. "She's not Persephone. She's… she's so much more. And she's made me realize that I never actually knew what I wanted, or what I truly *needed*, until I met her."

My gaze leaves the ceiling and refocuses on Maliki, who is leaning against a wall now, arms crossed, eyes on me.

"I'm conflicted," I tell him. "Is it wrong to fall for a woman who is nothing like my mate? Am I tarnishing Persephone's memory… or honoring it?"

I shake my head, trying to clear it. I've revealed more than I intended to. Though, that's always been the way with Maliki.

Whether he realizes it or not, I've trusted him with a myriad of secrets.

He said I'm like a brother to him, but I fear he's so much more to me. A soulmate of a sort. Perhaps not romantically, but we're… bonded.

"What would Persephone want?" Maliki asks, his question causing me to frown a little. "Would she want you to love this reincarnated version? Or to forever reside in the past?"

I nearly flinch, the answer hitting me almost instantly.

"She would want me to choose happiness." Because that's who Persephone was—a beacon of sunshine. "She was the light in my darkness, burning so brightly that I often felt blind."

"And Sera?" he asks. "Does she resemble light, too?"

"No," I reply, my lips curling a little. "Serapina is like a flame, her fire blazing so hot that she would probably melt this entire maze, if I let her." I can feel her energy all around me, even now.

Which is insanity, given that she's still very human.

Maybe it's wishful thinking.

Or perhaps it's all just a too-vivid metaphor.

Regardless, I see Maliki's point. "Persephone would be heartbroken if I rejected her reincarnation. She believed love to be pure and ever evolving. She once compared it to a flower, saying no two blooms were the same, which was why she found life to be so fascinating."

Uttering the comment aloud brings back a memory of lounging in a field, talking about life cycles.

"She always loved the rebirth aspect of her gardens, preferring to nurture her perennials more than any other type of plant." I shake my head. "I don't even know why I'm still talking."

"Because you're processing," Maliki murmurs. "But your comment on rebirth is interesting. It sounds as though your gift for resurrection might have had more overlap with Persephone's gift for life than you originally considered."

My brow creases as I consider his words. "Perhaps you're right." I never really thought about it, but there are some similarities.

Similarities that allowed her mother to borrow my ability and use it as her own.

To create a new plane of existence.

Where she nurtures and grows new Omegas.

Like flowers.

"I'm going to need to see how much Serapina can pull from Persephone's memories," I tell Maliki. "See if there's an obvious link that I've missed." Maybe I won't need Demeter's answers after all.

My hand falls from my neck, and I roll my shoulders.

"Not yet," Maliki says before I can mist back to the cabin. "She's… learning about knots."

I frown.

Then remember that we left her with Morpheus.

"Weren't you supposed to feed her?" I say, unable to mask my annoyance. "She's still human."

Maliki chuckles. "I'm aware. And yeah, I gave her a special smoothie. So she'll be good for a bit. But I do need to finish what I imagine will be a late version of dinner at this point."

My eyebrows come together. "A special smoothie?"

His gold eyes glitter with intensity. "It has protein in it. And some vitamins."

I stare at him. "What am I missing, Maliki?" Because I can sense from his tone that he's not telling me something.

"Remember that time you told me about Omegas losing their appetite during their heats? How Alphas have to get creative to ensure they eat?" His lips curl. "Let's just say I was paying attention during that chat."

My eyebrows lift. "You seasoned this smoothie with cum?"

"Not directly. I simply told your magic kitchen that I wanted a protein shake with vitamins that tasted even better than sex, with a fruity twist." He shrugs. "She swallowed it pretty eagerly. So I can only imagine what your manifestation magic did, but it worked."

Words escape me.

And all I can do is join in his amusement. "I imagine the enchantment spelled the drink with all of our essences." Shaking my head again, I add, "Please ensure you explain this to Serapina while I'm present. I'll have popcorn." That last comment comes out as a gibe, one that has Maliki laughing in response.

"It's a date, *my lord*."

I roll my eyes. "I hate it when you call me that."

"I know." He grins again. "Better get used to it, though. I hear mate-circles are for eternity. Oh!" He pushes off the wall. "That reminds me. I need your hand."

"My hand?" I echo, glancing down at the two I own in confusion. "Why?"

"I need to return a favor," he says.

"What favor?" I ask, not following him at all.

"Just give me your hand, Hades," he demands as he stops right in front of me. "Unless you're not intrigued, in which case..."

His words nag at a memory, one I don't waste time chasing.

Because this feels like a dare of sorts.

And I'm not afraid of Maliki or his antics.

"If you stab me, I will be most displeased," I say as I lift my right hand toward him.

"Don't worry. I left the knife in the kitchen," he replies, grabbing my wrist. "Besides, I don't need a blade to make you bleed."

My eyes widen. "Wh—"

He leans down and sinks his teeth into my palm, right by my thumb.

"*Fuck*," I snarl, not enjoying that sensation at all.

When I yank my abused hand away, he allows it but makes a show of licking his lips and swallowing. "You marked me with that damn coin. So now I've returned the favor, just like I said, *mate*."

I gape at him. "I should kill you."

He shrugs. "Maybe. But then you'll have to resurrect me."

"Or leave you to rot," I mutter.

"Sera wouldn't be pleased," he drawls. "And speaking of our mate, we should get back. I have a dinner to finish, and I need you to set the table."

My eyes somehow widen even more. "You need me to set the table?" I repeat, incredulous.

"Yeah, I do. Besides, it's time you start taking on certain mate-circle tasks, and this one feels appropriate. So let's go."

I'm too busy trying to process his words to realize he's reached for me.

When the world shifts, I don't fight it, instead growling as the cabin interior comes into view.

A curse coupled with Maliki's name sits on my tongue as the scent of Serapina's arousal strangles me, making it impossible to speak.

Her scream follows.

As does a groan from Morpheus.

"Don't," Maliki says when I take a step toward the hallway. "We're going to sit down, have a mate-circle dinner, and discuss Demeter. If Serapina wants dessert, we'll give it to her. But until then, all she's enjoying now is an appetizer. Understood?"

I find myself once again gaping at my best friend. "When did you become an Alpha?"

"When an Omega bit my cock," he returns. "Now set the table, Hades. When you're done, you can help me with the garlic bread."

A Few Minutes Earlier…

"Sweetheart, if you keep squeezing my knot like that, I'm going to end this lesson by fucking you against this wall."

Serapina's gaze darts up to mine, her pupils so dilated that her blue irises are thin rims. "Yes, please."

I groan, her eager response making my knot pulse against her palm.

Which, naturally, has her tightening her grip again.

Fuck.

Serapina's petite form is pressed back against the marbled wall, my body crowding hers as I lean over her with my arm braced above her head.

An arm that's now flexing as my fingers curl into a fist.

"Fuck, Serapina," I whisper, my forehead falling to

hers. "This was meant to be a soft lesson and a discussion on consent."

I started by disrobing her and pulling her into the shower. She let me wash her hair and lather up her skin. But as soon as we finished rinsing, she grabbed my cock and gave it a firm stroke.

Which is when I walked her back into the wall.

Such a bold little dreamer. With the way she's acting and how good she smells, it's hard to believe she's not in heat. Because it certainly feels like she is, especially with how insatiable she seems to be.

"Did Maliki not give you enough earlier?" I ask, my hand finding her hip while my opposite arm remains on the wall over her head.

"He marked me," she says, arching into me. "And it's *vibrating*."

I frown. "It's vibrating you?"

She nods, her eyes falling closed as she tightens her grip again. "It's so strange, Morpheus. I… I can remember being knotted, yet I've never actually been knotted… Because it wasn't me who experienced it." She sounds a bit dreamy, which feels appropriate, given everything. "I want it to be me, though. I want… to *feel* it."

Her hand resembles granite around my cock, causing my abs to clench in response. She's not letting me go anytime soon.

And her words…

Her soft voice…

The way she starts to stroke my shaft like she's trying to seduce me into making her every fantasy come true…

"Serapina," I breathe, my eyes closing as I fight the urge to take her up against the wall. "I… I've never been this tempted… Your slick…" Fuck, I can't even form proper sentences. Her scent is everywhere, reminding me of silky sheets sweetened by sin. A hint of chocolate. A note of *need.*

I'm going to lose my mind.

"I wanted to talk about fucking you while you sleep," I manage to say, my voice partly choked. "It's my fantasy—to take you while you dream of me. I want you to wake up with my knot buried so deep inside you that you can taste my seed in your throat."

I can picture it—her coming alive with a scream as her body convulses around mine, the experience making her feral for more.

So we can fuck all day.

Nest.

Cuddle.

Fuck again.

"I've imagined that moment countless times," I confide. "Yet you're making me want to forget all my fantasies and knot you in this shower. Right here. Right now. Make you my first and my last. My mate. *My everything.*"

"Your first and last?" she repeats, sounding breathless.

"Yes," I tell her. "My first and last Omega." I lower my arm and cup her cheek. "I've saved my knot for my mate, Serapina. For *you.*"

"For Persephone, you mean."

But I shake my head. "She was never mine. Not like you."

"Because of Hades," she says slowly, frowning a little. "Because he never let you formally meet her. I don't think Persephone even realized you were a potential mate. I… I can't see any memories of her knowing, anyway."

"I doubt she did, as we never officially met. Hades made his preferences clear, and I did what I could to respect his choice. I used to regret it, as I thought maybe I could have saved Persephone. But I realize now that everything happened for a reason. You're her soul's second chance, which makes this *my* second chance."

I brush my lips against hers, needing to taste her. To feel her. To tell her without words how much this means to me. How much *she* means to me.

She's my world now.

My Omega.

My mate.

"I will forever be yours," I vow against her mouth. "My heart, my soul, my *knot*—every part of me belongs to you. For eternity."

She shivers, the quivering motion at odds with the humid air surrounding us. Warm water trickles down my back, the primary showerhead only a few inches from where I have her cornered.

"You've never knotted an Omega before." She utters the words as a statement, but I suspect she's seeking confirmation and wanting to ensure she understands what I've said.

So I respond with a simple "Yes." Then I think better of it and pull away a little to add, "But I'm not a saint, love. I've been with other fae, just never an Omega. And only Omegas can take a knot."

She shivers again. "So I would be your first, and you would be mine. In this body, I mean. As… as *me*."

My lips curl. "Yes, little dreamer. We would be each other's first, if that's your desire." That last part is voiced out of respect for Hades, as he could technically be her first as well.

Although, she doesn't appear to be thinking about him right now.

Not with the way she's stroking *my* knot.

"But you want to knot me… while I sleep?"

I stroke my thumb along her bottom lip. "I'm the God of Dreams, love. Most of my fantasies involve sleep play."

She stares at me with her beautiful blue eyes, her gaze searching. "I… I was hoping my first time would be, I guess, real? Not a dream. But if that's—"

I silence her with my mouth, understanding exactly what she's going to say next and not wanting to hear it. "Serapina, our first time is about you, not me," I tell her. "So if you want it to be here in this shower while you're very much awake, then this is where I'll knot you."

"But you want to do it while I sleep," she argues, moving when I try to hush her with my lips again. "And it's not just about me, Morpheus. I want this to be special for you, too." She releases my cock to grab my face with both hands. "It's about *us*, not me."

I press my forehead to hers and sigh.

"Little dreamer, when I mentioned my desires, I meant that's what I wanted to discuss with you—*consent*. I was trying to tell you what I want to do to you… eventually. Not now. Not for our first time. But at some point, when you're ready."

"Oh," she whispers.

My hand goes to her hip while the opposite slips to her nape.

"You wanting to be aware for our first time makes sense," I tell her. "More than that, *I* want to watch your eyes widen when you feel my knot explode inside you. Feel your breath catch against my tongue. Observe as you fall apart over and over again, all while I fill you with my seed."

She trembles beneath my touch, her pupils dilating again. "I want that, too. Very, very much."

My lips threaten to curl in amusement, mostly because she sounds a little lust-drunk. *Like an Omega in heat.* Her insatiability, her scent, her boldness when fondling my cock, and her words now… They're all common symptoms of an Omega lost to her estrus.

Yet she's still completely coherent.

And human.

It's so fucking confusing.

What the fuck did you do to this precious soul, Demeter? I want to demand.

But then Serapina kisses me, her tongue laving my bottom lip, and I forget everything.

My thoughts. Our conversation. My own fucking name.

Because she tastes like temptation. Sin. *The future.*

I press her more firmly against the wall, my cock resting against her lower belly.

Which apparently isn't good enough for my Omega because she lifts one leg to wrap around my hip and hops on her opposite foot.

I chuckle as I catch her and hoist her into the air, where she encircles my waist with her long, sexy legs. "Is this what you want?" I ask, my shaft gliding along her slick center. It's the hottest sensation of my life, a sensual welcome that has my chest igniting with a purr.

"Yes," she whispers. "I want you. I want your knot. *I want to fuck.*"

My purr shifts into a growl as I curse in response to her words. "I swear you're in heat," I tell her. "I've heard stories, have witnessed millions of fantasies based on real experiences…" I trail off and swallow. "It's nothing compared to the reality. To you. *To this.*"

I'm not even sure what I'm saying anymore.

This female renders me mindless.

She must know that because she clenches her thighs

around me, grabs my shoulders, and confidently says, "Knot me, Alpha."

I would be a fool to refuse.

Still, I want to ensure her consent. To make sure she truly is aware of what she's asking. Because this is all so fantastical, despite being very clearly real.

Meeting her gaze, I say, "Make me, Omega."

Her eyebrows lift a little, like she's surprised by the challenge. But then her lips curl, and I know I'm fucked.

In the best possible way…

She leans back into the wall, trusting me entirely to hold her, and reaches into the small space that's formed between us.

My eyes are drawn downward, my body incapable of doing anything other than following her lead. She's in charge right now. Telling me what she wants not with words but with actions.

By wrapping her hand around my knot.

Giving it another lethal squeeze.

And angling my cock toward her sweet pussy.

My grip resembles granite around her hips, my body hers to command.

A command she makes fucking clear when the head of my dick kisses her slick entrance.

I don't think; I act, my lower half punching forward and filling her without recourse. Without patience. Without appropriate care.

But her responding scream isn't one of agony so much as pure bliss.

Somehow she moved her hand in time to palm my lower back, like she knew that sensual kiss would be exactly what we both needed for my body to act.

I'm convinced she's woven some sort of spell over me,

her Omega soul very much in charge of my Alpha beast. I feel tamed. Calmed. *Claimed.*

It's… it's unlike anything I could ever have anticipated, and it draws a furious growl from my chest, one that has her arching into me like she wants me to go deeper.

Which I can.

With my knot.

"Fuck, Serapina," I breathe against her mouth. "*Fuck.*"

MORPHEUS

SERAPINA DOESN'T RESPOND WITH WORDS, INSTEAD KISSING me with the heat of a thousand suns. I feel utterly possessed by her. *Owned*.

Which is insanity.

I'm the Alpha.

A natural-born leader.

A Dominant.

Yet her touch makes me want to submit in ways I could never have imagined.

"You're enchanting," I whisper, needing her to know how bewitched I am by her. "More engaging than any fantasy. Better than any dream. A fucking fantastical experience."

I show her how enthralled I am by kissing her deeper than I ever have before, my tongue dancing with hers and sending us to another plane of existence.

The sounds of water dropping no longer fill my ears. Because all I can hear is our hearts beating in unison. Our groans. Growls. Screams. The pounding against the wall as my hips rock into hers.

I'm utterly lost to the moment, no longer in charge of anything other than the pace with which our bodies mate.

She claws at my back, the Omega turning into a wildcat in my arms.

It's ferocious.

Amazing.

Fucking adorable.

My beast growls in kind, my cock straining inside her as a blanket of warmth settles around us.

This is a rut, I think dizzily. Alphas often succumb to those dangerous inclinations during an Omega's heat, the animal inside us driving our instincts and demanding that we *breed.*

My veins burn.

My muscles clench.

And my knot *throbs.*

I can't stop moving. Can't stop taking her against this wall. Can't stop *kissing* her.

It's to the point of savagery, our mouths engaged in a violent dance as we both forget how to breathe.

And suddenly I feel a sting against my lip.

The telltale signs of a *bite.*

Serapina's eyes blow wide, her mouth coming away from mine with blood.

I stare at the dark red liquid painting her kiss-swollen lips, and all I can do is lean forward to lick the essence away with my own tongue.

But doing so has her leaning in to bite me again, this time her nostrils flaring as she makes a show of swallowing.

Our lower halves are no longer moving, just locked

together in an intimate embrace as my cock pulsates with need inside her tight pussy.

"You just claimed me," I marvel, feeling the magic weaving through us as she clenches around my shaft.

She doesn't look startled or regretful. She simply looks… *pleased.*

My fingers thread through her hair as I pull her to me once more. It's like her bite has aroused my inner beast, his strength finally making an appearance.

She moans in response, her nipples tight little buds against my chest. I cup one tit with my free hand, then pinch her aroused point. Her resulting gasp allows me to deepen the kiss, my instincts firing all at once.

My hips start to move again.

My tongue dominates hers.

My grip turns rough in her hair.

My palm *squeezes* her breast.

Then I kiss a path along her slender throat, down to her fleshy mound, and take her erect nipple into my mouth.

She pants, her pretty eyes meeting mine as I sink my teeth into her tender skin.

A scream leaves her, and her slick walls clamp down around my cock.

Fuck, that makes my beast wild. Because my claim made her come.

She's moaning, screaming, *crying* my name, and following it with demands for more.

If she's this feral outside of her heat, I can't fucking wait until she falls into her first estrus.

Because this is unbelievable.

She's a demanding Omega, telling me what she wants with both her words and her body, and taking all of my thrusts like she was fucking built for this. Which she was. I know that. She's… she's my mate for a reason. My other half. *My heart.*

I release her breast and straighten to kiss her again, which she returns with the same fervor that I feel warming every inch of my being.

We're connected now.

Mated.

I can hear her mind. Feel her emotions. Her arousal. *Her pleasure.*

It strokes my desire even hotter, causing my knot to ache. I need to be inside her fully. Claim her pussy just like…

My lips part against hers as a hint of something unexpected vibrates against the tip of my cock.

I suddenly know what she meant about Maliki *marking* her. His shadows tattooed her cunt, leaving behind a string of sensation.

One that I feel against my shaft now.

It's not entirely unwelcome either, which is confusing as fuck.

And I'm too consumed by Serapina to consider it further.

I need to add my own mark inside her, one left behind by my knot.

My balls tighten in response to my yearning, my body seeming to tense as an overwhelming urge to explode rockets through me.

Serapina deepens that need by sinking her teeth into my lip again, the little vixen ensuring her bite is *felt.*

"Fuck, little dreamer," I growl, my hands going to her hips as I slam her into the wall.

She digs her nails into my shoulders, her little body ferocious in the best way as she takes everything I give her.

"So fucking perfect," I tell her. "So fucking *mine.*" My knot swells, the reaction new and overwhelming. "*Serapina…*" The sensation travels through my shaft as my knot shoots out of me and into her sweet heat, attaching to her deep inside.

"Morpheus!" she cries out, her body seeming to freeze against me.

And then she begins to shriek for another reason entirely as rapturous waves of intensity swallow us both.

I shudder. Growl. Whisper her name. Convulse. *And come.*

Fuck, I've never felt myself erupt like this.

I feel myself filling her, owning her womb, claiming her as my mate. My Omega. *Mine.*

And the way she's clenching around me echoes that visceral possession, her body staking a claim, too.

Our tongues duel again, neither of us breathing.

Because who needs air when we're soaring in joined ecstasy?

She clings to me like I'm her world, and I hold on to her with the same fervency.

It's a union unlike any other. A mating of completion. An introduction to *us.*

Our future.

Our bond.

Our love…

I kiss her through the pain created by my internal claim. Kiss her through the pleasure that is my knot. Kiss her through the intensity of being filled with my seed. Kiss her through the joining of our souls.

Tears leak from her eyes.

I lick them away.

Then take her mouth again.

Worshipping her.

Allowing her to hear my every thought. Feel my every emotion. Learn all my truths.

By the time we're done, she's still crying but for entirely different reasons. She's mystified by our connection. Shocked by the vehemence of my feelings for her. And captivated by my steadfast loyalty.

But underneath all of that, she's stunned by my knotting.

Because a mortal can't survive such an experience with a Mythos Fae Alpha. Yet her body acclimated to my intrusion with ease, just as I knew it would.

Had there even been a question, my inner beast wouldn't have released my knot.

However, everything between us was exceptionally natural.

Which leaves Serapina staring up at me with wonder in her gaze as she asks, "When can we do that again?"

A laugh escapes me. "You're not even done coming on my cock, and you already want to begin another round?" I shake my head. "Fuck, love. If you're this hungry on a normal day, your heat might kill me."

"Which is why she has three mates, not one," a voice drawls from the doorway. "We'll keep up with her just fine as a circle."

With my forehead against Serapina's, I slowly turn a little so I can see Maliki standing in the threshold of the bathroom. "Are you wanting to join us, Enforcer? Because I'm not sure I'm in a sharing mood right now."

He leans against the doorframe, his shirtless form flexing as he folds his arms. "You're going to have to share, Morpheus." He punctuates that statement by igniting that spot within Serapina that he's claimed, causing a vibration to hum down my shaft.

I flinch, not because I dislike it, but because it's a lot of sensation to handle right now. "Point taken," I say through my teeth as Serapina squirms in response. "Tone it down, Maliki." It comes out as a demand because I don't want him overwhelming our mate.

The vibration stops, but the male doesn't leave. "We're having a mate-circle dinner in five minutes. You can join with her in your lap if you're still connected. But the countdown has begun."

With those words, which sounded suspiciously like a demand, he leaves.

"Mate-circle dinner?" Serapina repeats to me, her voice holding a dreamy note to it that seems to be caused by our union more than the mentioned activity.

"Apparently," I murmur. "So we have five minutes to… finish. Unless you want me to fuck you over the table in front of Maliki and Hades?"

She blinks a few times, her lips rounding.

It's like she's just begun to understand *whom* a mate-circle dinner might include.

Because I assume Maliki's words were a subtle warning that Hades has returned.

Not that I require the warning.

I told him that if our mate asked for my knot, I would give it to her. Hopefully, him not barging in during our knotting means he's accepted this fate.

Serapina's forehead falls to my shoulder, her inner walls lessening their grip on my cock. "I…" She trails off, clearly unsure of what to say. I can hear the confusion in her mind, her thoughts trying to process how she should feel.

She doesn't regret this union.

However, she is a little worried that Hades will feel betrayed by her asking for my knot first.

"He knows you're mine, too," I tell her. "Accepting it

may be difficult for him, but he'll never hold it against you, Serapina." Of that, I'm sure.

If he blames anyone for this, it'll be me.

And I'm more than ready to handle that fight.

My knot slides out of her then, my body seeming to almost instantly return to normal. Except my cock remains hard.

Because, yeah, I could absolutely go again.

A realization that has my little Omega peeking up at me with interest. Then she shakes her head and reminds herself that Maliki wants to have dinner.

It's like I'm obsessed with sex, she thinks.

You're an Omega, I reply into her mind, causing her eyes to widen. *Omegas love to be fucked.* I kiss her temple. *And Alphas love to fuck, too.*

With my hands on her hips, I take a step back from the wall and bring us under the water again.

As much as I would love for her to walk into that dining room with my seed dripping down her thighs, I suspect it would set Hades off.

So, out of respect for my cousin, I rinse off our Omega.

Then use a towel to dry her.

And manifest a gold silk robe for her to wear.

She resembles a Goddess by the time I'm done, her damp hair combed and hanging over one shoulder. Her blue eyes shining. Her full lips swollen from my affections.

I pull the fabric back to take in the mark I left on her nipple, the crescent bite already healing to form a permanent scar. It's similar to the one on her neck and shoulder, making my lips twitch.

"How many times did Maliki bite you?" I wonder, recalling the indent on her hip, too.

"Three times," she says, shivering. "But you only needed one bite to claim me."

"Different types of fae require different bonding techniques," I tell her, shrugging. "That doesn't mean I can't bite you again, though."

However, those future blemishes should heal.

Unlike the one on her tit.

That will forever mark her as mine.

"Maybe in my dreams?" she offers, causing me to meet her gaze. "You can bite me again, like it's the first time, anywhere you want, then wake me up with your knot inside me."

Her cheeks pinken with the words, but her mind instantly starts to unravel the fantasy for me, causing my dick to throb beneath my towel.

"Hmm," I hum, manifesting a robe for myself since pants will be extremely uncomfortable now.

Serapina watches as I trade the fluffy cotton for the golden silk, her gaze running appreciatively over my form.

"I very much like this fantasy unfolding in your thoughts," I murmur. "If you're a good girl and eat your food tonight, maybe I'll make your dreams come true later."

The pun isn't lost on her.

"I think you've already made my dreams come true," she says softly, then goes to her toes and kisses my cheek. "Thank you for knotting me, Alpha."

My eyes close, her line delivered so flawlessly that I'm ready to forget what I said about her eating and drag her to bed instead.

"You're so fucking perfect, Serapina," I tell her. "My absolutely amazing Omega." I pull her in for a kiss, and she melts into me.

"You're my absolutely amazing Alpha, too," she whispers.

A throat clears from the doorway, and I know without looking that it's Hades. His aura is all around us in an instant, his dominance nearly suffocating.

Serapina looks at him, her cheeks still flushed, and I hear a hint of concern cross her thoughts. "Hades," she breathes.

"Sorry to interrupt," he says, his voice as stoic as ever. "Maliki sent me in here to say that dinner is served."

With that, he mists out of the room.

And I suspect he's no longer joining us for the "mate-circle dinner" now.

Oh, Cousin, I think, mentally shaking my head. *It's time for you to either agree to share… or fuck off entirely.*

SERA

My stomach churns as Morpheus leads me out of the bedroom, my thoughts mingling with his.

He suspects Hades has left again.

And I… I'm irritated by the prospect.

Because I'm tired of him *leaving*.

He would never have done that to Persephone. So why does he keep abandoning me?

It leaves me feeling inferior. Less important. *Unwanted*.

"Serapina," Morpheus starts, his palm on my lower back as he moves to block my path down the hallway.

"I'm okay," I tell him, aware that he can hear my inner monologue. "I just need to think… for a bit."

Which is something I didn't want to do five minutes ago.

I wanted him to knot me again instead.

To lose my mind to the euphoria inspired by his thrusts and reside in a sea of orgasmic bliss.

Alas, my stomach is grumbling again, and I really can't remember the last time I ate or properly slept.

How much sex have I had today? I wonder, my brow furrowing. *Why do I feel so… needy?*

Morpheus frowns down at me, and I shake my head to clear it. "Really, I'm fine," I try again. "Just a little… confused?" Yeah, that's not the right term at all. Or maybe it is. I—

"Confused about what?" a deep voice asks, one I was not expecting to hear.

I look around Morpheus to find Hades waiting at the end of the hallway with his hands tucked into the pockets of his black slacks. His button-down shirt is undone at the neck, and his sleeves are rolled to the elbows, too, giving him a more casual appearance than usual.

One that's enhanced by him not wearing any shoes.

He was dressed like this in the bathroom as well. Yet somehow I'm more aware of it now. I blink, almost certain he's an illusion.

But he's still standing there when I open my eyes again.

Only, he's frowning now. "Are you all right, Serapina?"

"You're here," I whisper.

His brow furrows even more. "Am I not meant to be here?"

"No," I say slowly, which has him flinching. I shake my head and move around Morpheus toward Hades. "No, no, I mean, you're supposed to be here. I just…" I narrow my gaze at him. "When you misted out of the bathroom, I assumed you left again. And I'm really tired of you doing that."

The words just sort of leave me in a rush, my annoyance piquing again.

"You would never have done that to Persephone," I go

on, then slap a hand over my mouth. Because I really need to stop talking now. "Sorry," I mumble.

Only, my brow pulls down again when I realize I'm not the one who should be apologizing.

Dropping my hand, I say, "Actually, no, I'm not sorry. You keep leaving. If you don't want to be here, that's fine. Just admit it. Otherwise, stop abandoning me."

Great. Now I sound like a pouty female.

"That's not what I meant," I rush to add. "I…" I clamp my jaw shut. Because I don't really know what I'm trying to say, only that I'm exhausted by his hot and cold presence. And having Persephone's memories doesn't help in this situation.

All the recollections from her point of view showcase a doting Alpha, one who gave her everything she desired and loved her beyond reason.

I'll probably never see that side of Hades, which… which hurts.

But I have to accept who he is, just as he has to accept the reincarnation of his mate's soul.

I close my eyes and shake my head. "Okay, ignore me," I mutter. "I'm not feeling like myself right now." Which isn't entirely true. And yet not a lie, either.

I've been on a journey of self-discovery since arriving in the Netherworld Kingdom. So I'm not even sure I know who I am at all.

"I could never ignore you, Serapina," Hades tells me softly, his wintry scent surrounding me.

When I open my eyes again, I realize he's standing less than a foot from me.

"And I'm sorry for leaving," he adds. "You're right. I need to be near you, and not just because of your potential heat, but because the only way to solve Demeter's puzzle is if we work together."

I nearly wince at his response.

He's not saying he wants to be near me because he likes me, but because it's practical.

That shouldn't hurt.

But it does.

Because I'm feeling foolishly sensitive, I think. Then I look at Maliki and remember he can hear me.

Just like Morpheus can, too.

No commentary from either of you, I mentally say to both of them. *This is between me and Hades.*

Morpheus steps into my side and presses a kiss to my neck. "I wouldn't dream of helping him clean up his mess, little dreamer," he says, then winks at Hades. "Good luck."

Hades frowns at him. "Good luck with what?"

Morpheus merely shrugs, then goes to join Maliki by the dining table. "You made enough to feed an army," he murmurs. "Good. I'm famished. And I know our mate is, too."

"Can't imagine why," Maliki drawls.

"Oh, I'm sure you could, actually," Morpheus muses. "Quite well, too."

Maliki replies with something I don't hear because Hades is suddenly in my space, and all I can focus on is his broad chest and soft purr coming from beneath his black dress shirt. It's a familiar sound, one he's emitted in my presence before. But it also evokes a slew of memories that don't actually belong to me.

Which is mystifying and a tad misleading. Because I'm instantly calmed, like my body is trained to respond to his enchanting rumble.

"You can't magic your way out of this," I mumble, already leaning toward him.

"I'm not trying to magic my way out of anything, darling," he says, his palm wrapping around my nape as he pulls me into him. "I simply want to hold you for a moment."

"Why?" I ask as I nuzzle into his chest, needing more of his purr and his scent.

"Because I need you to know that I respect your choices, Serapina." The words are a breath against my ear. "And now that I realize space isn't what you desire from me, I'm going to give you closeness instead."

"Why would I want space?" I wonder out loud. "All I want is to know you." *Like Persephone did*, I almost add. But I manage to swallow that part of my desire.

"I haven't been a good enough Alpha for you," he replies. "So I've been trying to find a way to fix things, only you've made me realize I've worsened your faith in me by leaving. I never meant to abandon you, Serapina. I was trying to find ways to prove my worth through actions rather than words."

His thumb strokes the column of my neck, stirring a tingling sensation inside me that seems to travel down my spine. Or maybe it's his purr that's making me feel this way.

Regardless, I like it.

"As for me never leaving Persephone, it's not because I valued her in a different way to you. It's because I was never given the opportunity. She always left me. Not the other way around."

My lips curl downward as I consider his words, my mind rifling through dozens of memories at once to determine the veracity of his claim.

And I realize quickly that he's right. "She left you every few months." The truth leaves me quietly as I try to process why she chose to be away from him. "To visit Demeter," I recall aloud. "Her mother required her to visit for six months a year."

My frown deepens.

Persephone was essentially treated like property. Particularly by her mother.

"Demeter said it was to ensure her daughter received enough life to counter my deadly influence," Hades tells me. "I hated it but agreed to do what was best for Persephone."

"I'm not sure it was best for her," I reply as I continue processing her memories. "Demeter was… not a good influence." I'm not sure how else to define her presence. "She cared about Persephone, but she hurt her, too."

However, it seems as though Demeter's actions were grounded in a need to protect Persephone. Which makes sense with everything I've learned about the infamous Alpha.

"Persephone never confided anything to me about her mother," Hades says, his voice thick with emotion. "But that wasn't our relationship. She never spoke about anything uncomfortable, always choosing to follow my lead and submit to the Alphas in her life."

I nod because I can feel that history in Persephone's essence. "She reminds me of who I used to be in the Nightingale Village," I admit in a whisper. "I followed all the rules and did what I was told. Very unlike Alina."

But it was her influence that helped me choose to become Sera.

That, coupled with everything I went through in Demeter's Gardens. Not having memories of her manipulation or what I even did there made me realize that I didn't want to be a mindless puppet. I wanted to *live*.

I share some of that self-discovery out loud, mostly talking to myself rather than to Hades.

But he reminds me of his presence by moving his hand away from my nape and cupping my jaw. "That's what makes this new and refreshing," he informs me. "You tell me what you need. You're not afraid to challenge me, either. And I find that enthralling, Serapina."

His lips brush mine.

"I'm sorry for leaving you when I should have stayed. It won't happen again, okay?"

I shudder, his words seeming to seep into me to stir warmth from deep within. "Okay. Thank you."

"Don't thank me for doing what's right," he replies. "But *thank you* for voicing your feelings. Please don't ever stop." He kisses me again, this time with a little more pressure, then lifts me into the air to carry me to the table.

I don't fully understand his intent until he sits down with me in his lap.

My eyes widen at finding both Maliki and Morpheus already seated, their gazes fixed on Hades.

"That was actually not bad," Maliki says. "Good job, *my lord.*"

Hades grunts. "Fuck off, *subordinate.*"

"Subordinate?" Maliki repeats, then barks out a laugh. "Touché, *my lord.* Touché."

Hades ignores him, instead reaching around me to start fixing a plate of food from the dishes spread out on the table. I blink, confused by… well, everything.

But mostly by Hades choosing to hold me like this at the table. Particularly as there is a perfectly good chair right beside us.

Nibbling my lip, I try to casually slide off of him.

And find myself suddenly trapped by a strong arm around my waist. "Let me hold you, please," he says softly against my ear. "I want an opportunity to take care of you, Serapina. In my own way."

I swallow, my mind instantly sifting through Persephone's memories for information that will help me understand Hades's motives. However, I can't find a single instance of him saying those words to her.

Actually, it seems they didn't often say much to each other. Just let their bodies do all the communicating. Not just with sex, though. With simply being near one another.

I shake my head, wanting to clear it.

And Hades drops his arm. "I understand," he murmurs, leaning back. No hint of annoyance or hurt. Just… a stoic comment.

"Understand what?" I ask, confused again.

"Your refusal. I'll never make you do anything, Serapina."

It's on the tip of my tongue to remark on how he almost made me marry him, but I realize he's misunderstood my reason for shaking my head. "I wasn't refusing you," I tell him as I glance back to meet his dark gaze. "I was just… trying to clear my head. There's a lot going on up there right now."

He studies me for a moment. "Because of your new bonds?"

I frown. "Actually, no." I shift my attention to Morpheus and Maliki, then back to Hades. "I meant with Persephone's memories."

Why can't I hear you? I think at my two mates.

Because you're naturally shielding, Morpheus replies into my mind. *We're not closed off to you, sweetheart. You can access our minds at any time; you just have to think about it.*

And you? I ask, looking at him. "Are you able to hear my thoughts anytime you wish?" I switch to speaking aloud because Maliki was also trying to mentally talk to me and I didn't want him to think I was ignoring him. It's just that there's only so much room in my mind right now.

"Yes," Morpheus confirms. "But I know how to respect

your boundaries, Serapina. That's just as natural to me as it is to you."

"What he said," Maliki echoes. "Or that last part, anyway. Not sure what he said in your head."

Morpheus's blue-green eyes go to Maliki. "I just told her that we'll never shut our minds off from her; she just has to want to reach us to be able to talk to us or hear us."

Maliki nods. "Okay, then yes, what he said." He folds his arms. "I've never been mentally connected to anyone before today, but I don't feel all that different. Just closer to you." He looks at Hades. "Both of you."

My eyebrow lifts. "You can hear Hades?"

"Yep," Maliki replies, his lips popping on the *p*. "Much to his chagrin, I'm sure."

Hades scoffs at that. "You can't *hear* me, just *sense* certain things."

"Pretty much the same thing," Maliki drawls. "All a bunch of brooding air." He waves his hands around in a careless motion. "Now, are we going to eat or let the food continue to cool?"

Hades's arm encircles me again as he shifts forward to resume filling a plate. "Maliki fancies himself an Alpha," he murmurs. I'm not sure if the words are for me or for Morpheus. "Seems to think he can command the entire mate-circle now, too."

"Someone has to do it," Maliki returns, though he doesn't sound annoyed so much as amused.

"Hmm," Hades hums, then focuses entirely on sorting through all the various food items.

I'm not sure what half of them are, but I recognize the Italian cuisine. Reaper introduced me to several over the last year, mostly because he seems to favor pizza. But Orcus likes a variety of other dishes—including a spicy tomato dish like the one Hades scoops onto the plate now.

"Shrimp fra diavolo?" Morpheus asks.

"With a twist," Maliki replies. "I added some sausage crumbles."

"And this one?" Morpheus points to a pan with circular white noodles—or… or I think it's a noodle?—and no sauce.

"Decided to add a garlic butter option for the scallops. Will pair nicely with the angel hair."

Morpheus nods. "Excellent."

"Do you want to try a scallop?" Hades asks me, perhaps noting that I'm still staring at the sauceless item.

"What's a scallop?" I question, uncertain if I want to try it or not.

"A bivalve mollusk," Maliki answers, making me blink. "It's similar to the shrimp. A meat from the Human Realm."

"Yes, Maliki is obsessed with Human Realm foods and culture and movies," Hades drawls. "Don't ask him to make anything from the Elemental Fae Kingdom. He'll fail."

"I would not fail," Maliki argues. "But I would hate every minute of it."

"Then perhaps you should make a shroom loaf tomorrow," Hades suggests. "Maybe Serapina would like it."

"Why do you hate me?" Maliki asks him, sounding wounded.

Hades chuckles. "It's not like I requested troll fat."

"Troll fat?" I repeat, my nose scrunching.

"It tastes like bacon," Hades tells me, sounding amused.

Maliki gags. "It's disgusting."

"Dragonsteak, then?" Hades offers.

My eyes go wide. "Elemental Fae eat dragons?"

"No, sweetheart. It's just a type of food. It's not even meat, if I recall correctly," Morpheus says. "Elemental Fae are a strange breed with peculiar cuisine tastes."

"Oh." My nose crinkles again. "I don't think… I don't think I want to go there."

"Their realm is actually quite beautiful." Hades repositions me in his lap, bringing my legs over his opposite thigh so that I'm sitting with my shoulder against his chest as his one arm braces his back. "Now open. I've cut a scallop in half for you to try it."

I have half a mind to refuse him, mostly because it sounds very strange. But the garlic notes wafting off the fork have me parting my lips instead.

The moment the flavor touches my tongue, I'm very glad my body acted on my behalf and didn't allow my reservations to stop this experience from happening. Because wow. *Wow*. "That's really good," I mumble around the mouthful of food.

"Try chewing," Maliki suggests. "I hear it's good for you."

I really want to roll my eyes at him, but I'm enjoying his *scallops* too much to bother.

Chewing, though, does end up being an excellent idea because it spreads the flavor out through my senses.

As soon as I'm done, another bite appears. But this one is from the tomato dish—the *shrimp fra diavolo*.

It's equally as delicious as the other, but so different in taste. I'm not sure which one I like more. Fortunately, I don't have to decide because Hades continues to feed me both options.

Along with a garlic roll—the bread is warm and so, so *good*.

Plus some sort of fruity drink.

A salad of greens flavored by a spicy vinaigrette.

Another vegetable that Maliki calls *asparagus*, which I'm not as keen on, but the lemon flavor helps.

More pasta.

More shrimp.

More scallops.

I just keep eating.

Because Hades doesn't stop feeding me.

His purr seems to be the only sound anchoring me to the present as he brings the fork up to my mouth, my body doing the rest. I'm vaguely aware that he's holding a conversation with Maliki and Morpheus. Something about the maze. Alterations. I don't really know or care. I'm consumed by sensations of rightness. Calmness. *Security*.

It's… it's like the food has drugged me.

Or maybe it's my exhaustion finally catching up to me.

I'm pretty sure I've been awake for more than twenty-four hours. Other than my nap, anyway. Maybe even more time has passed.

I also had a lot of sex.

Which… which was very good. Amazing, actually. *I want more*, I think, sighing. *But sleep… sleep would be good, too.*

I'm only partly aware that I've stopped eating. Even less aware that I've curled myself up on Hades's lap, my head against his chest.

Perhaps it's his purr that drugged me, not the food, I consider, yawning. *Hmm, doesn't matter.* Because I'm comfortable. Warm. And very, *very* tired. *I'll just close my eyes for a min… hmm, like this… yeah… 'kay.*

I BRUSH A STRAND OF SERAPINA'S HAIR BEHIND HER EAR AND place a kiss on her forehead.

She sighs in response, then nuzzles my chest in her sleep. The action makes me wish I were shirtless like Maliki or in a robe like Morpheus.

Alas, I chose to wear a button-down shirt and slacks.

"Do you think it's possible that she's currently in heat?" Morpheus asks, his gaze on Serapina.

I frown at him. "If she were in heat, my knot would currently be inside her."

Assuming she accepted me as a mate, anyway. But that part isn't entirely relevant to our current discussion.

"She just ate about five meals' worth of food and passed out in your lap," Morpheus says. "She was also quite demanding in the shower. And that was after whatever Maliki did to her earlier, plus what happened overnight between the four of us. I realize she's an Omega, but she's still mortal. However…"

He leaves that final word to dangle between us while I gaze down at the sleeping beauty in my lap. I did notice her voracious appetite both for food and sex today. It was very heat-like. And she was about to go into estrus before whatever Demeter did to her.

"Do you think she's in heat and just isn't emitting a signal?" Maliki asks, causing me to glance up at him because that exact question was forming in my mind.

Well, not *exactly* the same. "It's not a signal but a scent," I tell him. "One that acts as a beacon."

He looks at me. "You knew what I meant."

"I did," I admit. "But correcting you entertains me."

He rolls his eyes and reaches for a bottle just as it manifests on the table. Apparently, he's figured out that the magic that exists in the kitchen actually permeates the entire cabin. Knowing Maliki, he's also likely aware that it fuels every inch of this maze, too.

Though, if that were true, he wouldn't have asked me to manifest those jeans in the cave; he would have just done it himself.

So maybe he doesn't know.

Or he was playing with me.

Typical Maliki, I think, watching as he pours himself a healthy serving of red wine.

Holding my gaze, he leans back and takes a long sip, his expression unreadable.

"You really do fancy human inventions," Morpheus muses. "I myself am more drawn to ambrosia." He creates a glass that's filled with something pink, the scent of it hitting me almost instantly and drawing a growl from my throat.

Because it's *slick*.

And not just any slick—it's from our mate. "*Morpheus*."

He shrugs and brings the glass to his mouth, his gaze daring me to do something about it as he makes a show of swallowing some of the divine liquid.

"Was knotting her first not enough?" I demand. "Now you want to flaunt your knowledge of how she tastes?"

"I actually haven't experienced that for myself yet," he murmurs. "I believe Maliki is the only one who has feasted between her thighs, yes?"

"Yeah, and she's fucking delicious." He grabs Morpheus's cup to steal a sip, causing his gold irises to glitter. "That's very close, but not quite right."

"Hmm." Morpheus takes the glass back and causes it to vanish with a quick move of his hand. "Maybe I'll find out the true taste while she dreams." His eyes are on Serapina now. "She gave me permission to knot her while she sleeps."

"You will not be doing that while she's asleep in my lap," I tell him flatly.

He chuckles. "No, I imagine not." He looks at me again. "Is that what's keeping you calm, Cousin? Holding our mate?"

My jaw ticks. "I'm not sure *calm* is the correct term to describe how I'm feeling right now, Morpheus."

One of his silver brows lifts. "Then what term would you use?"

"*Jealous*," I admit, not afraid to voice the emotion. "Very. Fucking. Jealous."

Morpheus doesn't respond the way I expect him to—with an amused expression. Instead, he seems to sober as he replies with a simple "I understand."

I wince. Because of course he understands. How many times did he feel me knot Persephone, all while knowing he could never have her?

I've only endured a hint of what I forced him to experience. And there is a huge difference in our situations as well—he's willing to share, whereas I was not.

"You're my absolutely amazing Alpha."

Serapina's comment plays through my mind, the emotion beneath it making my heart ache. Because she meant every word.

It hurt to hear, even though I knew she was right. Morpheus is a good Alpha. While I still have a lot to prove to her.

However, I will show her that I can be good to her, too.

"I want to apologize, but I can't," Morpheus adds, surprising me again. "It would be a betrayal to our mate to feel sorry about what's happened. Which is why I can't entirely fault you for taking care of Persephone the way you did for all those years. You were doing what you felt was right for her."

"I was being selfish," I mutter.

"That, too," he agrees. "Alas, we can't change the past." He gives me a long, serious look, then says, "Fortunately for you, I'm much more focused on the present and our future."

"Cheers to that," Maliki drawls, lifting his glass of wine in the air. "The first item on our future agenda involves Hades doing the dishes."

I stare at him, then wish away all the items on the table—and include the glass in his hand.

His eyes narrow, and he manifests another drink, this time a glass filled with spider ale. I'm about to cause it to vanish as well, but a pint of blood ale appears in front of me.

Maliki arches a brow, daring me to make my move.

"Hmm," I hum, reaching carefully for the goblet. Serapina snuggles into my chest as I move, then sighs when

I settle back into the chair, the glass in one hand as I cradle her with my opposite arm. "Cheers," I say, purposely mimicking Maliki.

Then I take a drink and nearly groan as an unexpected sweetness bursts across my tongue.

"This is not blood ale." The words come out choked, my cock suddenly throbbing between my legs. Because that sinfully decadent flavor can only belong to one female. *My mate.*

"Oh, it's blood ale," Maliki drawls. "I just added an ingredient."

Morpheus snorts beside him, obviously amused.

I do not share the sentiment. "You're taunting me."

"No, I'm introducing you to the future, *my lord*," Maliki murmurs. "And trust me when I say it's fucking exquisite."

I close my eyes and inhale, striving for patience.

But it's the wrong response.

Because Serapina's delicious fragrance is all I can smell.

I set the glass down with a low growl, one that has my Omega whimpering in response. That small sound forces me to find patience—*for her*—and morphs my deep rumble into a purr.

She snuggles deeper into my chest on a sigh, instantly at ease once more.

"It is not wise to torture me with a taste when I've been abstinent for over two thousand years, Maliki." The words are smooth. Clear. Utterly calm. Yet inside, a storm is raging. My beast is hungry. Demanding. *Yearning*. And I ensure Maliki can feel every ounce of that weight.

By the time I open my eyes, he's no longer smiling.

"I'm not trying to torture you, Hades," he says. "But I won't deny that you deserve to feel a little tormented after how you treated Sera."

I stare at him. "Do you think I'm unaware of how I've wronged her?"

"No, I think you're very aware. Which is why I'm letting you hold her right now," he informs me. "If I thought you were going to hurt her again, I wouldn't let you touch her."

I arch a brow, the irony of our situation playing through my mind. "Just a week ago, she was *my* mate, and only *my* mate. Now you're the one telling me what to do. Does that make you the boss of our mate-circle?"

He smirks. "Would you kneel if I demanded it?"

I cock my head, considering the question. "Depends on why I'm being told to kneel."

His gold eyes glitter with amusement as he enjoys his spider ale. "Hear that, Morpheus?" he drawls as he sets down the now-empty glass. "The God of Death is saying he'll kneel under the right circumstances."

"I imagine the right circumstances involve the Omega in his lap," Morpheus murmurs. "I would kneel for her, too."

Rather than comment, I just stroke Serapina's arm again, enjoying her nearness and the soft little sighs she releases when I touch her. She's very clearly seeking safety and warmth right now.

As Omegas do when in heat, I think, my brow furrowing a little as I reconsider what Morpheus said a few minutes ago about her estrus.

My gaze drifts down to her delicate features, taking in the flush of her cheeks. She's still mortal, just like Morpheus mentioned. And only an Omega can go into a true heat.

But maybe… maybe that has something to do with whatever Demeter has done to her.

Is Serapina experiencing a cycle right now? I wonder, studying her even more intently. *As a… human?*

"She took your knot," I say slowly, interrupting whatever Maliki just said to Morpheus. I wasn't paying attention. If it was important, he'll repeat it after I finish questioning my cousin. "Did it hurt her at all?"

His blue-green eyes meet mine, a hint of challenge in his depths. "You think I would have allowed myself to harm her?"

"That's not my question," I reply. "I'm asking if she even flinched. She's mortal. Taking a knot should have been impossible. But she took your knot. So did she even flinch? Because a human…" I trail off, not wanting to think about what a knot could do to a true human. It would rip one apart in the most excruciating of ways.

That's why Mythos Fae playing with mortals was frowned upon eons ago.

Does it still happen? Yes.

But not for knotting purposes.

Just sex.

"Your knot attached to her," I press, no longer questioning him but processing what I already know. "And she… enjoyed it."

"You're wondering about her heat now," Morpheus says, clearly following my train of thought. "Realizing I might be right."

"Yes," I admit, holding his intense gaze. "I'm trying to… to understand if that's possible." Resurrection can take on so many forms, but Mythos Fae should never be subjected to the process because our souls are immortal.

However, Demeter did something with my gift to… to *manipulate* eternal life.

"Omegas are not meant to be mortal," I utter aloud

now, looking between Maliki and Morpheus. "Serapina is human, and yet…"

"She accepted every part of me today," Maliki says. "My bites. My aggression. A human would not have survived what I did to her."

Morpheus nods. "An Alpha can't knot a human, Hades."

"I know."

"Yet my knot didn't hesitate," he adds. "Not only that, but she bit me. Just like an Omega should when wanting to claim her Alpha."

"Not just when she wants to claim an Alpha, but her mate," Maliki tells him. "You should have seen her bite my cock earlier."

I wince, not because it sounds painful, but because his words… *hurt.*

He doesn't notice, though, because his focus is on Morpheus as he muses, "Maybe she'll offer a repeat performance later."

"Styx, I hope so," Maliki groans, leaning back in his chair. "She can mark me whenever and wherever the fuck she wants."

Morpheus touches his lip, highlighting the crescent scar there. "We are in agreement on that, Enforcer."

"I wonder where she'll bite Hades," Maliki murmurs, glancing back at me. "Any ideas or desires?"

His questions render me speechless as a deep-seated ache echoes inside my soul, one I've ignored for thousands of years. "I would just be pleased to be bitten," I admit quietly.

Maliki frowns at that. Or maybe he frowns because he can sense the agony I'm failing to suppress.

"Persephone never bit you," Morpheus whispers, his words not a guess but a statement.

I'm not sure how he came to that conclusion. Maybe because he can relate to the pain of an unestablished bond and recognized something in my tone. Or perhaps I don't give him enough credit for his observational skills.

Regardless, I confirm his assessment by saying, "It wasn't in her nature to bite." She let me claim her and, in fact, encouraged me to as well. But she never marked me in response. "Our bond was complete in our own way." I could hear her, and she could hear me. Our souls were always fated, too. So I just… never pressed the issue.

But deep down, I mourned the lack of a mark.

So for Serapina to claim Maliki and Morpheus in this way, it… it gives me a sense of hope and dread. Hope that she'll choose me like she's chosen them. Dread that she'll reject me because of everything we've been through.

I clear my throat. "Anyway, as Morpheus said, the past is… not what we need to focus on."

"That's not exactly what I said," he replies softly. "But the sentiment is shared." He leans forward. "So what should we do if she's actually in heat right now? Other than knot her, of course."

I shake my head. "I wish I knew, Cousin." Because nothing about this is standard or expected. "My only suggestion is to try to discover what Demeter did and perhaps use Persephone's memories to do that."

"You could also try replicating whatever she's done," Maliki says, his expression thoughtful. "By working with Sera, I mean. Because maybe it's not just her heat instincts that are buried right now, but her soul's powers, too."

I consider his words as I study Serapina again, wondering if he could be right. "You're suggesting that her human shell is some sort of façade." I frown. "Demeter does appear to possess a penchant for illusions."

"When I took Serapina to the Mythos Fae Realm, no

one recognized her as an Omega," Morpheus replies in a slow, measured tone. "I found it strange at the time but assumed it was related to whatever suppressant Demeter had crafted. So what if it isn't a suppressant at all, but, as you said, an illusion of some kind?"

"One we can only partially see through because our souls are fated," I add, meeting Morpheus's gaze. "So how do we shatter the mirage? Because both of you mating her didn't work, which suggests my bite won't fix it either."

Silence falls between us for several beats. I comb my fingers through Serapina's golden hair, my purr strengthening as my inner Alpha fights to solve this puzzle.

But I don't know what to do or how to fix this.

"I think Maliki is right," Morpheus finally says, voice soft. "You need to spend some quality time with Serapina and see what the two of you can re-create in terms of power. The answers are somewhere inside her soul, but you're going to have to help her search."

Maliki nods. "Yep. But try not to piss her off in the process, yeah?"

I look at him. "That's helpful advice, thank you," I deadpan.

He grins. "Just let me know when you start so I can make popcorn."

"Maybe I'll start by showing her how a soul gains access to the Death World," I tell him.

"You do that in the way I think you're suggesting, and you'll piss her off," he drawls back at me. "Which would be against my advice, by the way."

I roll my eyes. "I know how to please an Omega, Maliki."

"With your knot, sure. With your personality?" He pauses. "That'll be a bit more work, I think."

"He proved earlier that he knows how to make jokes,"

Morpheus says conversationally. "Maybe he can make Serapina laugh?"

I push away from the table and stand with Serapina in my arms. "This mate-circle-meeting bullshit is done," I inform them both. "Next time, I'm in charge of the discourse."

"So we'll all brood in silence, then?" Maliki asks.

My jaw ticks. "You're lucky our Omega likes you," I inform him quietly, allowing him to hear the lethal threat underlying my words.

But all he does is smile. "Luck has nothing to do with it, *my lord*. It's all skill on my part. I mean, as you once told me, I'm good with women."

"Men, too, from what I hear," Morpheus comments.

Maliki glances at him. "Piqued your interest, have I?"

I don't stay to hear the response, very much over this inane bonding session, and instead mist Serapina to the bedroom.

She's still lost to her dreams, her deep sleep very heat-like. If Morpheus's hypothesis is right, she'll probably wake in a few hours and be ready to fuck again.

Or maybe not.

Nothing about this situation is typical or expected.

Which makes what Maliki and Morpheus said valid—I need to spend more time with Serapina. Get to know her mind. And solve this mystery… *as a team.*

A Few Days Later...

My eyes feel heavy. It's that deep-slumber sensation. The one that makes movement difficult upon waking. An indicator of a good, long night of rest.

When did I fall asleep? I wonder, my mental voice slow and dreamlike. *Mmm, and what is that amazing scent?*

I inhale deeply, then sigh.

It's a winter morning. I can feel it in every ounce of my being. Only there's a hint of cotton freshness, too.

My bedding, I realize.

Except, there's a note of smoke in the air. Not an intense, terrifying kind, though. Which is strange. All smoke should inspire fear. But this smoky tendril is twined with leather.

My nose scrunches as I try to determine where I am.

Shouldn't I be more concerned or panicked?

Mmm, no, I think in the next breath. *Definitely not*.

Because I'm surrounded by masculine warmth.

Not… not directly, though. More like an imprint left behind by their presence.

My brow furrows, and my eyes slit open to survey the black and gold sheets surrounding me. The colors seem slightly different from before. Like maybe someone changed the bedding.

Why? I wonder, taking in the otherwise familiar surroundings of the cabin bedroom.

Dark decor. Death etched into the walls. Frozen flowers. Deep blue tones mingling with obsidian rock.

I stretch and roll in the silk, only to discover that some of it is attached to me.

A robe.

Ohhh, that's the source of the gold.

Wow, I must have slept for a long time.

I feel almost dizzy from oversleeping. Except, I also feel extremely rested. Like, better than ever.

Sighing, I go to my knees to take in the bed again. *The sheets definitely were not changed,* I realize now. For some delirious reason, that pleases me. I like the scents here.

It's like enjoying a bonfire on a crisp winter morning while wearing something decadent and silky.

Oddly specific, I suppose.

But the combination of aromas pleases me. And I'm not in the mood to question my preferences.

Instead, I analyze the massive bed. It's… it's beautiful. Which is a strange thing to notice, but I can't help feeling enamored with the shape and size of the space.

Going to my knees, I also admire the posts decorating each corner.

There are skulls etched into the black wood, along with more timeless fire lilies. Timeless because they're forever frozen in a blooming position.

The only missing quality is the floral scent, a fact that nearly makes me sigh.

However, I distract myself by examining the mattress and the sheets and the…

I frown. "We need more pillows." I utter the words aloud even though I'm the only one in the room. "We need another comforter, too. A charcoal one. Like smoke."

All the items appear around me in a flourish of magic, causing my eyes to widen as I scan the room for the source of the gifts.

But I'm alone.

It's the manifestation enchantment, I realize, my lips curling.

"More pillows," I say. "All silky decadence, like Morpheus."

The pillows that appear are gold, not black.

"Now a few that have a leathery cologne but a smoky texture," I murmur.

A bundle forms beside me, deepening my smile.

"How about some scarves for wintry mornings?" I suggest. "But wrap them around the poles."

The magic does what I ask, the strands a pretty black color edged in gold and silver frays.

"Perfect." This decorating game is fun.

However, now I need to figure out where all the pillows are going to go. The comforter is easy since it goes in the center of the bed—*obviously*.

Hmm, but the other items need to be strategically placed.

Remaining on my knees, I crawl around the bed and follow my instincts—which seem to be tied to my nose because I keep inhaling the mingling scents and deciding where things go based on how they smell.

By the time I'm done, I've created a pillowy haven of amazingness that I never want to leave.

But my stomach has other ideas.

"How are you already rumbling?" I mutter, irritated. "Hades fed us a lot of food just… just…" My brow furrows. "Last night?"

"Three nights ago," a deep voice says softly, causing my gaze to jump up to where Hades is standing beside one of the posts. His assessing gaze is on the scarves, causing my cheeks to heat.

I just… I just redecorated his bed.

Oh, thorns.

What if he hates it?

Was I even allowed to do this?

"I…" I trail off, an apology lingering on my tongue that refuses to escape me.

But I should say "Sorry," right? He built this place for Persephone, not me. And I basically defiled the bed he planned to knot her in.

Except… except she would have hated *this place.* My brow furrows. I already knew she would dislike it here—Hades mentioned it—but now I *understand* how she would feel because I can see her memories.

"This place would have tortured Persephone," I whisper, my heart breaking a little on her behalf.

Hades's dark eyes find mine. "I know."

"You wanted to hurt her…" I can't finish the statement, the sudden understanding stirring a convoluted mix of emotions inside me. Sadness. Fear. *Anger.*

"I thought she used me to destroy Omega kind," he says, sounding more broken than defensive. "It's yet another failure on my part as her Alpha. I see that now, but I can't change the past. I can only learn from my mistakes and try to do better."

The anger inside me simmers as I consider his words. I want to demand that he explain how he could think so poorly of Persephone's intentions. He was her mate. He should have known her better.

Only… only as I learn more about her and her bond with Hades, I realize it… it wasn't as deep as it should have been.

They rarely spoke to each other.

I mean, they… they talked every day, but they rarely engaged in deep conversations. Just about Hades satisfying Persephone's needs and doting on her.

However, she never really opened up to him. There simply hadn't been a need to because she trusted him implicitly.

Demeter also taught her that a good Omega doesn't burden an Alpha with concerns.

A manipulation, I register now. A way to control her daughter and ensure she didn't confide too much to Hades.

He should have pried more, asked questions, *something*.

Only, how could he have known it was needed when Persephone didn't give him any indication of her inner struggles?

"Serapina." Hades voices my name with a hint of regret. "I could apologize for a century, and it still won't right the sins of my past. All I can do is promise to do right by you going forward."

"I know," I tell him quietly, still processing everything I've come to understand over the last few minutes about his relationship with Persephone. "We need to ensure that we talk to each other, Hades. Always. No matter what."

He slips his hands into his pressed slacks, his forearms—revealed by the rolled sleeves of his black dress shirt—flexing with the movement. "What would you like to discuss?"

"Everything," I say, not bothering to ponder what that means. I just need him to understand that we can't experience the same downfall. "There will be no secrets between us."

He stares at me, his dark brow drawing downward. "You think I'm hiding something from you?"

I shake my head. "No, that's not what I'm trying to say. I just want us to be open with each other. Share our burdens. Our worries. Every detail. So we don't make the same mistakes…"

Understanding seems to cross his features. "The same mistakes as I made with Persephone."

"As you made with each other," I correct him. "She should have told you more about Demeter, but she was taught not to." My nose scrunches. "Kind of like how I was raised not to speak out against authority and to just accept my fate with the monsters, should I be chosen as a bride."

He studies me. "Demeter taught her not to talk to me?"

I consider the statement and nod, then shake my head. "Not with you specifically, but all Alphas." I go on to explain how she was instructed to be meek and sweet and quiet.

Just like me in the Nightingale Village.

Hades listens as I tell him about my experiences, how the Nightingale Viscount essentially groomed all the humans to worship monsterkind. "Alina and I were taught to bow and accept our place in the world." Which ended in me being chosen for Monsters Night and taken to a mystical garden in some alternate reality.

Meanwhile, Alina rebelled.

And met her mate-circle as a result.

Now, I'm here with my own mate-circle, too. "There are benefits to breaking the mold," I conclude quietly, my cheeks heating again.

"There are benefits to being who you want to be," Hades replies, his arms moving to cross against his chest as he leans on the bedpost. "It's not about rebellion so much as finding yourself. You're a strong woman, Serapina. You may feel that's a new trait, one you've been trying to master, but the truth is, you've always been this way."

I frown at him. "If you knew me in my home world, you wouldn't be saying that."

"The fact that you survived that world with your mind intact only proves my point, Serapina. That you were taken to the Netherworld Kingdom and so quickly acclimated to a brand-new dimension of possibilities serves to further that point. And the mere desire to live alone in the village, to find yourself, punctuates the point."

"But Persephone did the same by living in your underworld."

"Part-time," he replies. "She couldn't remain there indefinitely. She had to visit her mother because at no point was she ever truly separated from Demeter. Never independent enough to make her own choices. Never strong enough to voice her wants and needs."

He straightens again, his arms falling to his sides.

"I don't say all that to tarnish her memory. I love Persephone with all my being, and I accept blame for not recognizing what she truly needed until now. But fate has given our souls a second chance. And I won't let myself make the same mistake twice. Not with you, Serapina."

His words sound like a vow, one that's underscored by his intense gaze.

I swallow, unsure of how to respond.

He just said he loves Persephone—present tense. It makes me wonder if he can ever love me, too.

The concern festers in my mind for only a few seconds before I give voice to it, because I just told him that there can be no secrets between us. That we need to discuss *everything.*

And that includes this—his feelings for Persephone. For my *soul.*

"I know you'll always love her," I say, swallowing again. "I understand and accept that. But I need to know if there's room in your heart to love me, too."

His nostrils flare, his expression morphing into something I can't define. Pain, maybe? Fear? *Anger*?

He's suddenly on the bed in front of me, both of us kneeling, his palms on my face. He's not touching me harshly, but gently. *Reverently.*

"Serapina, part of me already loves you because our souls are fated," he says. "But as for there being room for more?"

He presses his forehead to mine, his eyes falling closed, and I'm suddenly terrified to hear more.

Worried he's going to say that's all he can give me.

Sad that I… I'll be forced to *accept* it.

Because how can I not? Hades—

"I'm afraid," Hades whispers, his confession jarring me from my thoughts.

"Afraid?" I echo, confused.

He nods slowly, his forehead still against mine. "I asked Maliki the other day if it's wrong to fall for a woman who is nothing like my mate," he confides, his voice still soft. "I wondered if I was tarnishing Persephone's memory or honoring it."

I blink a little, unsure of how to respond to that. "I… I'm not that different from Persephone. Not really."

"You are," he says, pulling back to look at me. "This conversation is proof of that, Serapina. Persephone and I never spoke like this, yet you and I…" His thumb caresses my cheek, his focus sliding down to my mouth. "We're not even fully bonded. However, I'm already telling you more than I would ever have said to her."

"Because neither of you had reason to question your connection," I tell him. "There was no need to have this conversation."

"Maybe, but it's not what we're discussing, Serapina, that makes us different. It's the fact that we're sharing our feelings at all." His gaze meets mine again. "I'm at risk of falling for you in a way I never fell for her. That's my truth. And it both enthralls and terrifies me."

A shiver traverses my spine. "Hades, I…"

I don't know what else to say.

So I don't say anything at all and just press my lips to his. It's tentative. Seeking. Full of hope. And a tad fearful.

This relationship between us is complicated.

I can remember Persephone's love for him, her adoration, her *worship*.

Yet my feelings are more… intense.

He infuriates me. Bewitches me. Scares me. *Seduces me.*

All those dreams I've had of him were my own, which is so insane to realize. They were born of Persephone's connection to him, but all my fantasies were crafted by my mind, not from her memories.

Fate, I marvel. *Fate is… fascinating.*

And so is Hades.

He's complex. Strong. An Alpha in his prime. *A God.*

Yet he's handling me with a softness right now that belies his inner strength. His lips brush mine, his palm remains on my cheek, and his eyes fall closed.

It's gentle.

Sweet.

So at odds with the power I know this male possesses.

Except this is how he handled Persephone. With the utmost care. Like she could shatter at any second.

I want more than that. I want his beast. His dominance. *His virility*. "Hades," I breathe, ready to demand more.

But he ends our embrace instead, his gaze once more capturing mine. "I want to show you something," he murmurs. "Something I made for *you*. Not Persephone. But *you*."

I blink a few times, startled by the boyishness in his tone. He sounds… excited? "Oh. I… okay." My brow crinkles. "Here?"

He gives a little nod. "Yes, in the maze."

"Oh," I repeat, then glance down at my robe, the fabric of which is hanging off me and not actually covering my nudity at all.

Hades follows my gaze, his focus seeming to sharpen. "You have no idea how alluring you are like this," he tells me. "Kneeling in the middle of your new nest, mostly naked. But you said you wanted us to talk, and I agree that it's important for us to know each other."

He brushes his lips against mine, then slips off the bed.

A pillow tumbles after him, the action making my lips curl down.

Wincing, he picks it up and tries to place it back where it was on the bed.

"Sorry," he murmurs. "I didn't mean to disturb your nest. I also should have asked before entering it." He winces again. "You would think I know nothing about women and Omegas."

"That's what I've been saying for months," Maliki drawls as he enters a room with a tray. "Good to hear you acknowledge it."

My eyes widen at seeing the food approaching me. "Do *not* put that in here," I growl, the sharpness in my tone surprising both me and Maliki. But the idea of him placing that tray anywhere near this bed has something savage inside me roaring to life. "Food goes in the dining room, not the bedroom."

Maliki gapes at me.

And Hades chuckles. "Our Omega has made a nest." He claps Maliki on the back. "Offending her will ensure you're never invited into the safe haven."

"How is me walking in here an offense?" Maliki demands.

"You brought food near her secure space," Morpheus says from the doorway. "I was in the middle of warning you not to do that when you insisted on checking in on her and Hades."

"I did not insist."

"You insisted," Morpheus repeats. "But they're fine. So bring the food back out here before the Omega growls again. Because otherwise, I'm going to request she make that sound while I fuck her mouth."

My eyes widen at his crass words. "*Morpheus.*"

"Ah, see, my little dreamer is already trying to make the fantasy become a reality," he all but purrs, and starts toward the bed.

But Hades steps into his path. "No. We agreed she's mine today."

"We didn't actually agree on anything," Morpheus returns. "You simply stated a demand and expected us to comply."

"Morpheus," Hades says, a hint of patience underlying his tone, one that conflicts with his rigid posture.

The two Alphas lock gazes for a long moment, then the God of Dreams inclines his head. "Fine."

"Thank you," Hades murmurs, causing Morpheus's eyebrows to shoot upward.

"Oh, don't thank me. We're only giving you sixty minutes."

"We?" Maliki echoes.

"We," Morpheus repeats. Then he grabs Maliki, and the pair of them vanish from the room. Fortunately, the food disappears with them.

But I'm left utterly confused by my actions.

And also the word *nest* is now repeating in my head.

Hades has voiced the term a few times. However, it didn't permeate the fog in my mind until now. Which has me glancing around the massive bed of fluffy pillows and the comforter I magically manifested earlier. "A nest," I whisper.

"A nest," Hades murmurs. "A very pretty one at that."

I look up at him. "I made a nest."

His lips twitch. "You did, yes."

"And you… like it?" I'm not sure why I feel hesitant, or why I suddenly need his approval, but I do. Maybe because it's his space. His bed. His cabin. His maze. Or… or perhaps I just want to impress him.

"I more than like it, Serapina," he says, his dark eyes finding mine. "I love it." He gives me a small smile, then says, "I'll be waiting for you in the living area. Wear whatever you want."

He disappears before I can reply.

Not that I have anything to say.

I'm too busy smiling.

Because my Alpha just said he *loves* my nest.

A nest I hadn't even meant to create.

Yet it's mine now. My space. My sanctuary. *Mine.*

SERAPINA MADE A NEST.

That knowledge has my chest warming with pride.

Not only did she feel safe enough to create her haven, but she also made it in my maze.

I try not to let her see how I'm feeling, then remember that she requested we talk to each other.

Hmm. She's walking silently beside me while sipping on the fruity protein shake Maliki manifested for her. It was his compromise after Morpheus made the tray of food vanish.

"She needs to eat," Maliki told me, a hint of desperation in his tone. "It's been *three days*."

"Proving that she's indeed not human at all," Morpheus inserted.

"I'll make sure she gets it" was my reply, though I fully agreed with Morpheus's statement, too. However, I also wanted to placate Maliki.

Which was a strange need, as I've never much cared to placate anyone before.

Yet I felt obligated to try this morning. Hence the reason I handed Serapina the drink when she joined me in the living area, and why I encouraged her to take it with us on our stroll through the maze.

She says nothing as her gaze traces over the icy walls, skull adornments, and frozen flowers. It makes me wonder what she's thinking.

So I speak my mind first, hoping to inspire her to do the same. "I'm very pleased that you built a nest," I tell her, feeling slightly foolish for admitting that aloud, but wanting to share my pride nonetheless. "It means you feel safe here."

Her blue eyes meet mine, her straw perched daintily between her lips. "I didn't realize that was what I was doing," she says around the straw. "It just… happened."

I nod. "That's normal. Although, an Omega usually creates a nest during a heat."

Her nose scrunches.

"Morpheus hypothesized that you might actually be in heat right now," I go on, wanting to inform her of what we discussed while she slept. "He thinks your human shell might be a façade of sorts. Like a mirage."

Serapina stops walking near one of the many false exits in the maze. If she were to try to run in that direction, she would find herself deep in a labyrinth of walls that all lead back to this main corridor—the one that takes her back to the cabin.

Though, she doesn't even look at the false exit.

Instead, she faces me and lowers the straw from her mouth. "A mirage? But I was born human."

"So was Alina," I point out. "However, both of your souls are Mythos Fae Omegas."

She frowns. "True. But shouldn't I feel different?"

"Don't you?" I ask, my head canting a bit to the side. "You just slept for three days, Serapina. Humans only do that under extreme circumstances. Yet you woke up rested and glowing." She resembled a Goddess whilst kneeling in those sheets earlier.

And she resembles a Goddess now in her black pants and flowy sweater—two items she clearly manifested for herself in the closet. Along with the sexy boots she's wearing. No heels, which is fine. I rather enjoy her smaller stature.

"You also took Morpheus's knot," I add, grimacing a little with the concept. However, the more I acknowledge it, the more I acc—

No. Fuck. I don't accept it. I fucking loathe it.

But, for Serapina, I'll try to… respect it.

Clearing my throat, I move on to a more *acceptable* mating topic. "And Maliki mentioned he wasn't exactly gentle with you in the Rutting Grounds. A human likely would have been hurt or worse. By both encounters, I mean. Thus, Morpheus's hypothesis holds merit."

Not to mention the fact that she just created a nest.

"Regardless, we'll figure it out," I promise her, my palm instantly seeking her cheek. "Morpheus and Maliki said we—you and I—need to work together to determine what Demeter has done. And I agree."

Which naturally brings us full circle.

"So I want to start by showing you some of the changes I made to the maze." I brush my thumb across her plump lower lip. "I want your opinion on the modifications."

"My opinion?"

I nod. "Yes." I draw my touch away from her cheek, down her neck to her arm, and gently shift my palm to her lower back. "Part of communicating is learning more about one another. That's why I told you I'm pleased you made a nest in the maze. And now, I would like to hear your thoughts on my labyrinth designs."

I give her a little nudge to begin walking, and she does, but I can tell by her hesitant steps that she's trying to understand what I've said.

"There's no motive," I promise. "This is solely about us getting to know each other, okay?"

"Like a… a date?" she asks.

My lips twist at the term, my inner Alpha huffing at the inconsequential notion. What I want to do with her is a soul-bonding exercise, not something as simplistic as a *date.* That's such a mortal concept.

But rather than comment all of that aloud, I reply, "Let's call it a courting exercise." I glance down at her. "This is me trying to prove my worth as a mate."

"Then it's kind of going to suck for you if I don't like any of the changes you've made," she replies, her candid response giving me pause.

A chuckle escapes me after a beat, the sound both nervous and humored. "You're not wrong, Serapina. But, if that's the case, I'll just use your input to alter the design again."

She cocks her head. "That probably would have been a more efficient approach in the beginning—to ask my opinion before making alterations."

"True."

My response must embolden her because she adds, "Much better than running off to hide and doing it yourself."

"Yes, you've made your feelings on that quite clear."

"Good," she says, her confidence coming through in

the straightening of her shoulders. "Now show me what kept you from me."

I can't help but smile at her sassiness. It's so… *unique.* No one ever sasses me.

Well, apart from Maliki, anyway.

But I rather like that my Omega feels comfortable enough to put me in my place. Especially when I've earned her castigation.

Because she's right. I thought my actions would speak louder than words, and they did. Only, those actions told her the wrong things about my intentions.

"Thank you for being honest with me," I tell her, meaning it. "I appreciate your candor, Serapina."

She finishes her smoothie and leans into me as we walk. My palm shifts so I can encircle her lower back, and I give her a tentative squeeze. When she snuggles in a little more, a purr ignites in my chest, and she sighs, "I love that sound."

I'm about to say *I know.*

However, she continues with "But that's not going to save you from my critique. If I hate what you've done, I'll tell you."

I chuckle again. "Noted, darling."

"Good. So tell me why you messed with perfection," she says. "Because as far as I…" She trails off as we reach a bend in the maze, one that angles us toward the first stop on our journey.

Her feet stop moving, and her lips part, the shake slipping from her grip. I wave my hand, making it disappear before it can hit the ground. Then I pick her up and carry her through the field of flowers—which are all blooming around us—toward the trench ahead. It's not that deep, maybe five feet. But it sort of looks like a pond from here.

Except it's not a pond. In fact, it's not made of any water at all.

"*Hades*!" she shrieks as I toss her into the sea of pillows.

My lips twitch as I jump down to follow her, my feet landing on the ledge of the pit. I bounce a little, the ground beneath me reminiscent of a mattress, not ice and stone like the rest of the maze.

"Where did my sassy little Omega go?" I ask as I watch her trying to swim in the cushiony refuge.

She comes up sputtering, her blonde hair wild around her face, when she realizes I didn't toss her into water, but into silky cotton. "What in the thorns is this?" Her eyes take in the massive bed around her.

"The Breeding Pit."

Her lips part. "T-the…"

"Breeding Pit," I say again. "Since Maliki already showed you the Rutting Grounds, I thought you'd enjoy seeing the Breeding Pit." Gesturing to the flowers behind me, I add, "I planted all of those flowers for you, by hand. They're not fire lilies, though. They're Autumn Damask roses."

I chose those since she had seeds for them back in the Netherworld Kingdom.

But that's not all I did…

Looking up, I give the sky a nod and hear Serapina gasp as sun rays peek through the gloom to highlight the flowery field.

"I changed the atmosphere over here, so it'll rain, too," I tell her. "But only enough to water and nurture the roses. The temperature varies now in this area as well, making the air warm enough to ensure your flowers survive."

I purposely didn't use magic to immortalize her flowers, as I wanted to leave them for her to tend to as she wishes.

Or I'll add that enchantment, if that's her desire.

I explain all of this to her as well while she gapes at me.

Her lack of a comment seems positive at first, but the longer the time stretches, the more uncertain I become.

"Do you… dislike it?" I finally ask. "Should I get rid of the flowers and make the pit colder again?" Because it was surrounded by ice statues before—similar to the frigid garden back at my palace in the Netherworld Kingdom.

"N-no," she stammers. "This is…" Her brow comes down. "This is *beautiful*, Hades. It's… it's…" She trails off as a bird flies by, reminding me that I also added some wildlife to this area of the labyrinth.

Serapina stands up, her eyes glued to the winged creature as she tries to maneuver through the Breeding Pit. Holding out my hand, I help her, then she follows the bird along the edge to where a set of stairs leads back up to the garden. I could have traversed down those but chose to toss her in for effect instead.

However, I trail after her now and catch up to her when she pauses by a tree.

"Uh, yeah, I added a few of these, too. Seemed needed for the birds." When I glance up, I find Morpheus's owl up on a high branch. "Seems Athena approves."

She follows my gaze upward, then returns her focus to me. "I love it," she whispers, tears sprouting in her eyes. "It reminds me of home. Or what used to be home."

"The Human Realm," I murmur, understanding what she means.

"Yeah," she says as a bird lands on my wrist. The wings flutter a little, the feathers flickering blue before turning black again.

"These are not from the mortal world," I admit. "They wouldn't survive here. So I adopted some stygians from the Midnight Fae Realm."

The bird's wings flare again, this time turning a burnt orange before shifting to obsidian once more.

"I think the sun is confusing for her," I admit. "There are only moons in her home realm. But maybe you can create some life that's more appropriate here, once we figure out how to tap into your Omega powers."

Serapina frowns, her focus on the bird as it flies over to settle in her now-open hand. "You think I have powers?" she asks as she kneels in the grass—something else I manifested for her—beneath the tree.

I follow her down and pull her into my lap. She settles against me while petting the bird. Every time she strokes the feathers, they change colors.

"I do, yes," I confirm as I kick off my dress shoes.

Then I lean around Serapina to slip off her boots and socks so she can feel the grass. It's a natural instinct on my part, one that proves to be right as she sinks her toes into the plush ground.

"That's part of us getting to know each other so I can help you navigate your gifts," I go on.

She relaxes into me again, then releases the bird to fly up into the tree. Her eyes drift upward to watch as Athena ruffles her feathers, the animal clearly taking over guard duty for Serapina.

Part of me wonders if Morpheus sent her or if Athena chose to be here out of distrust for my intentions.

I'm not concerned. She can report back whatever she wants to my cousin. All I care about is Serapina's contentment.

"Where should we start?" Serapina asks.

I assume she means with getting to know each other, since that's what I just said. Or maybe she's talking about my helping her navigate her gifts.

Either way, my answer is the same.

"Let's begin by discussing your thoughts about this space," I suggest. "Maybe think of an enhancement you would like to make, then we can figure out how to work on it together."

Her lips twist a little as she considers me and then the field around us. She even glances up into the sky for a moment to admire the sun before giving me her attention once more. "It's perfect as is, Hades."

My heart warms at her praise, mostly because it means I guessed correctly. "There has to be something you would like to add," I murmur. "Another kind of flower, perhaps?"

She shakes her head. "No, I love the field you created. But maybe… maybe some snow?"

I frown. "Won't that kill the flowers?"

"Not if you use magic to isolate the snowflakes," she replies. "Perhaps just a few can fall right here where we're sitting."

She sounds hopeful.

However, her request confuses me. Persephone hated cold weather. And while I realize Serapina isn't Persephone, it's fascinating to me that Serapina seems to favor the winter.

Because I, too, enjoy a good snowfall.

"Let's see what we can manifest together," I murmur. "Give me your hand…"

"WHAT IN THE STYX ARE YOU DOING?"

Morpheus doesn't respond, his focus on the swirling black hole forming before us.

I recognize this magic.

It's what earned me a prolonged stay in the Hell Fae King's interrogation room last year.

"No." It's an emphatic statement. A solitary word. An absolute denial.

Yet the Mythos Fae pretends like he can't hear me at all and grabs my wrist.

"Mor—"

The world dissolves around us, causing me to curse into the void. *Shadows*. Lucifer is going to fucking kill me when we return. My familial relation to his mate Az won't save me this time.

"Have you lost your fucking mind?" I demand the moment we step into a new dimension.

Morpheus touches his head, frowning. "No. No, I believe my mind is still fully intact."

I glare at him. "That's not what I bloody meant."

He smiles. "Then be more specific, Enforcer."

"You just opened a portal to another dimension, something Typhos Lucifer made pretty fucking clear that he didn't want us to do again," I say through my teeth. "Not to mention the fact that you didn't even ask me to go with you; you simply took me."

"You didn't tell him about our chat?" a familiar voice asks, drawing my attention to Orcus.

Reaper is standing beside him, twirling a blade, his gaze bouncing between me and Morpheus. "Want to borrow a toy?" he asks me.

"Yes," I reply without hesitation.

He tosses it to me, but Morpheus mists and catches it before I can move. "If I told you we were heading to the Monsters Night universe, you would have alerted Hades."

"So my brother doesn't know either?" Orcus demands.

Morpheus sighs. "Not everything needs to involve the God of Death."

"No, but it should involve *me*." A cultured tone rings through the air as an imposing male with glass-like eyes steps into view.

One blink confirms his human appearance is a mask. Though, his unexpected arrival also confirms him to be something *other* because his approach was silent. I'm not even sure where he came from. It's like he stepped out of the lake behind him. Only, his suit is dry, as is his dark hair.

However, there's a hint of a shadow around him, like he just finished morphing into this humanoid façade.

Fucking Morpheus. Visiting a dimension like this is

dangerous. He could have at least let me grab a jacket. *And some knives…*

"Hello, Cain," Morpheus greets, the name making me wince.

Because I recognize it instantly.

Cain. The Elite City King.

Just. Fucking. Great.

"I'm trying to decide if I prefer your human appearance or the one I've seen lurking in my dream world," Morpheus goes on.

"*Your* dream world?" Cain echoes, eyebrow arching.

Morpheus glances down and pats his pristine suit. "Hmm, yes, I'm still the God of Dreams, even in your dimension. So yes, *my* dream world."

Cain's jaw visibly ticks. "Are you here to challenge me, *God of Dreams*?"

"Morpheus, please," he returns, smiling. "And no, not at all. That would be quite unfortunate for us both, I believe."

"Morpheus," Cain repeats, one eyebrow arching. "You do realize we have portal protocols, yes?" His focus shifts to Orcus. "I am certain that *you* are aware of them, Orcus."

"Yes. Our visit won't be a prolonged one. I promise," Orcus replies.

"Prolonged or not, rules must be obeyed," Cain states flatly.

"Well, if that's the case, then I suppose Sabre and Cage will need to return to my kingdom," Morpheus interjects, his tone underlined in an authority I rarely hear from him. He almost sounds like Hades.

However, I'm more interested in him mentioning Sabre and Cage. They slipped through the portal into the Monsters Night universe last year, and I haven't seen them since.

Sabre and I are friends.

Which is why I helped him and Cage escape into this new world. Their love was a forbidden one, and from what I understand, they found their mate-circle here—with Cain and a female named Scarlett.

"Is that why you're here, God of Dreams?" Cain's inquiry is a soft one, yet it's underscored with lethal intent.

So now he also sounds like Hades. *Awesome.*

I look at Reaper and note the way his blade is no longer twirling between his fingers. He's clearly picked up on the tension, too.

"No," Morpheus says. "But if you continue talking to me about rules and the need to enforce them, it could become my reason for being here. Because, if I recall correctly, I bent the rules for your mate-circle once. So I would hope that you could return the favor now. However, if that's not possible..."

Cain's jaw ticks. Then he cants his head and assesses Morpheus with a quick glance over his suit-clad form. Their similar attire and stature mark them as equals. But those aren't the only characteristics they share—they're both connected to the Dream Realm as well. Except in different dimensions.

It's confusing.

But it also sort of makes them rivals.

Or allies.

Depends on the situation, I suppose.

So what's it going to be today? I wonder, wishing now more than ever that Morpheus had allowed me to properly suit up before dragging me into this dimension.

Sera, I whisper, wanting to let her know where we are and what's happening in case Hades is needed.

She doesn't reply.

Which has my blood icing over.

"I can't hear Sera," I tell Morpheus, not caring at all that he and this other dream God are in a standoff. Sera is much more important. "Open another portal. I'm going back."

"Not hearing our mates when in an alternate dimension is unfortunately normal," Orcus tells me, though his focus is entirely on Cain. "That's why we're going to make this a very quick trip."

"To do what?" I demand.

Orcus finally looks at me. "To evaluate the site where Sera was held in this dimension."

"We're hunting for clues on what Demeter may have done, or perhaps information that will help us understand her mirage abilities," Morpheus adds. "Flame and Alina know we're here. If Hades or Serapina expresses concern, they'll inform them of our intentions."

"Yes, because unlike your circle, our mate-circle actually communicates plans prior to acting on them," Reaper drawls.

"What's that like?" I deadpan, irritated as fuck with Morpheus right now. While I agree this is a good use of our time, we should have at least told Sera we were leaving the fucking dimension.

"I can allow this one-time visit," Cain says before Reaper can reply. "But I require payment in the form of a future favor."

"No," Orcus replies immediately.

"I believe I already granted you a favor," Morpheus murmurs. "*Two*, to be precise."

"Then it's a good thing I don't want a favor from you, God of Dreams," Cain returns, his focus shifting to Reaper. "*You* are the one I want a favor from."

"No," Orcus repeats. "Absolutely not."

"Now wait a minute," Reaper says, holding up a hand. "I might be intrigued."

"Which is exactly why I'm saying no," Orcus says through his teeth.

"But the last time Cain invited me out to play, it was to attend a bloody wedding, and that was so much fun." Reaper gives Orcus a wistful smile. "The souls were delicious."

Orcus rolls his eyes. "*No*."

Reaper shrugs. "You're not the one I answer to, *Alpha*. I'll just ask Alina if I can come back here to play." He flashes Cain a smile. "I'm sure I can persuade her."

Orcus folds his arms and shakes his head. "As Morpheus stated, you've already been given favors, Cain. This trip should cost us nothing."

Cain stares at him. "We have rules for a reason, Orcus. Without them, other kingdoms and realms might choose to visit on a whim rather than adhere to our Monsters Night protocols. If I give you leeway, others will expect it as well. And I cannot run this region in such a manner."

"Unless it benefits you in some way," Morpheus muses. "Such as receiving a favor as payment, thereby explaining why an exception was made."

Cain meets his gaze. "I see why Cage and Sabre admire you."

"They fear me as well," Morpheus points out.

"Perhaps. But I do not." The shadows surrounding Cain seem to move. I'm not sure if it's a trick of the light or his inner monster making his presence known.

However, all Morpheus does is smile. "There is very little I fear, too, Elite City King." His expression sobers. "Unfortunately, whatever Demeter has done to my mate is one of those few things. So, if you're done emphasizing your importance here, I would appreciate you either assisting us or fucking off."

Cain's glacial gaze narrows. "Careful, God of Dreams. You're in my world now."

"Perhaps, but the two Strigoi I've *allowed* to remain here are still from *my* world."

I shake my head. "This posturing is never going to end," I mutter, stepping in front of Morpheus to face Cain. "Call Sabre."

The Elite City King arches a brow. "And you are?"

"The reason you met your mates," I tell him. "The one who created the portal to your world. The one who told Sabre about it. The one who helped Sabre and Cage enter *your* world. Good enough yet?"

His lips twitch. "Maliki."

"Maliki," I confirm. "Now ask Sabre if he thinks you should give us a pass."

"You can't command me to do anything, fae," he returns. "That said..." He slides his hand into his pocket, which causes Reaper to step up to my side.

"I like you, Dream King," Reaper says. "Don't do anything to make me *dislike* you."

"Dream King?" Cain sounds amused by the nickname—one I assume Reaper assigned to him on a whim—and finishes pulling the item from his pocket. He flashes it toward Reaper. "A mirror."

"Which is a weapon for your kind," Reaper says. "I'm aware."

Cain snorts. "If you consider handheld portals to be a weapon, then yes, I suppose so." He holds the mirror in front of him and says, "Sabre."

"This had better be important, Cain," a deep voice returns, irritation coloring his tone. "You know we were busy."

"I know Cage is currently busy," Cain replies, a hint of humor in his tone. "I believe you were… watching."

Sabre mutters something in response, causing Cain to chuckle as he holds the mirror out to his side.

My eyebrow inches upward when smoke comes through the glass, then takes shape and reveals Sabre's large, muscular form.

The Strigoi Prince looks at me in surprise, then stares pointedly over my shoulder. "My lord," he grinds out before inclining his chin in subtle respect.

"I'm rather certain Cain is your lord now," Morpheus replies. "Unless he keeps wasting my time. Then I may require you to call me that for eternity."

"Try to take what's mine and see what happens, God of Dreams," Cain says, his voice iced over.

I shake my head. "Enough. You're both powerful. You're both dream Gods or whatever. Can we please stop measuring our magical cocks now and do whatever it is we came here to do? Because I do not like being cut off from my mate."

"*Our* mate," Morpheus corrects me.

I move to the side so I can stare him down. "She's going to be *my* mate after I kill you for dragging me here without consent."

"Oh, there's a fight I want to watch." Reaper nudges Orcus. "Wanna place bets?"

"You and God Morpheus share a mate…?" Sabre asks, ignoring Reaper's side commentary and focusing his black eyes on me. "Since when?"

"There are a great many important developments you've missed over the last year or so, Sabre," Morpheus replies before I have a chance to speak, his attention shifting from me to the Strigoi Prince. "Which reminds me, we should discuss your father. And soon."

My old friend frowns. "Has Xanthus…?" Sabre doesn't finish the question, just leaves it hanging after uttering the name of Cage's brother.

"Xanthus is alive and well," Morpheus tells him, his tone serious. "Your father, however… let's just say fate has finally caught up with him."

The Strigoi Prince bows his dark head for a moment, then nods. "Whatever happened, I'm just glad Xanthus wasn't involved."

"Well, I didn't exactly say that," Morpheus replies. "Only that he's alive and well. If you want to know more, you'll need to reach out."

Sabre swallows. "I may do that." He looks at Cain and falls silent, the two of them seeming to communicate without spoken words, or perhaps even mentally.

Thank Styx I don't have that ability with Morpheus. His voice in my head would drive me mad. Hades, too, for that matter.

I fold my arms. Definitely *not* going to request any sort of bond that allows us to communicate, as I strongly doubt it would ever be efficient. Morpheus would just speak in riddles, and Hades would bark orders.

No. Fucking. Thank you.

"Fine," Cain says after a beat, holding up his hands. "We'll assist."

"I believe I said *you*," Sabre mutters.

"And I translated it aloud as *we*," he returns, flashing a quick smile. "If I have to suffer, you might as well join me. These are *your fae*, after all."

Sabre sighs. "Right. Fine." He waves a hand. "What do you need?" He directs the question at me.

"Oh, I wish I could answer that," I reply. "But this was Morpheus's idea, not mine."

"Actually, that honor goes to Orcus," Morpheus corrects me.

I roll my eyes. "Just explain what you want to do, God of Dreams."

The Mythos Fae smiles. "I thought you'd never ask, Enforcer. So let's travel to the Nightingale Village, where Serapina was chosen for Monsters Night and her story truly began…"

SERA

Back in the Labyrinth…

A chill stirs across my palm as Hades draws a star pattern along my skin. I shiver, his warmth and nearness a blanket of protectiveness that elicits little quivers deep inside me.

The way I feel for him is… confusing. It's dreamlike. Mythical. Founded on memories that are not truly mine and fantasies inspired by a past life.

Yet I can't ignore the way I feel in his arms.

I also can't deny the chemistry between us.

Being fated isn't a foreign concept. But I never thought this could happen to me. Even with my sister being entangled in a mate-circle, I just… I just never considered this to be possible.

However, despite the dreamlike quality of the moment, I know it's real.

Hades's purr is a soft rumble against my back, the

sound seeping deep into my bones and adding to that sense of security thriving within me.

"Do you feel that?" he asks against my ear.

"I feel a lot of things right now," I admit. "So you're going to have to be more specific."

He chuckles, the sound a welcome caress. "The magic, darling." He strokes my palm again. "*This*."

Another tremble tickles my spine, making me shudder against him. "I feel a slight chill?" It comes out like a question because I'm not sure which sensation I should highlight. "My hand is a little cold, but inside… I'm warm."

Hot, actually. But I… I don't admit that part.

"Focus on the chill." He traces another line against my skin. "See if you can replicate it."

I stare down at where our hands are touching, my brow crinkling. "I have no idea how to do that."

"You do," he promises me. "You manifested items for the nest a few hours ago."

"Using your magic," I point out.

"Yes, so do it again now." His voice is so soft that it's almost a whisper. "My power is your power, Serapina. It exists all around us, and most importantly, it's yours to wield whenever you so choose. Just like this morning in the bedroom."

My lips twist to the side. "All I did was say what I wanted out loud."

"Then try it again now," he encourages, his hand leaving mine to rest in my lap against my thigh.

That subtle shift in touch has me shivering for a very different reason from before.

Or maybe a similar one.

I… I really don't know. The way Hades makes me feel is unique and unparalleled by anyone else in my life.

Which I guess could also be said about Maliki and Morpheus, too.

All three males are so unique. Yet equally mine.

It's such an extraordinary claim, one I don't want to define. One I refuse to give up. One I will not question.

Maliki is my dangerous fae. My guard. My feral lover.

Morpheus is too perfect for words. He listens to me. Talks to me. Acts as a confidant and a teacher.

And Hades… Hades is intensity personified. He's possessive. He's intimidating. He's the other half of my soul.

The three of them together create a powerful experience that's all mine to enjoy. So all I want to do is lose myself in them and this life.

To kiss Hades right now instead of playing with magic.

To let him feel my need. My acceptance. *My heart.*

"Serapina," he murmurs, drawing my gaze to his lips. "You seem distracted."

"Because I am." I blink, my mind trying to focus. "All I want to do is kiss you, Hades."

He smiles. "I'll let you kiss me anywhere you desire—after you create some snow."

I frown, the sensation provoked by a petulant feeling brewing deep within me. "That doesn't sound nearly as fun as kissing you."

His smile deepens. "You underestimate how intriguing things can become with a little magic, mate." His hand leaves my thigh to trace up my arm, his term—*mate*—and his touch stirring a fluttering sensation in my stomach.

I like the possessive quality underscoring the word *mate.*

But it's more than that.

His fingertips are electrifying, his power almost palpable as he glides his hand back down to encircle my wrist.

"Make it snow, Serapina," he says, his lips at my ear again. "Make it snow, and I'll reward you with my mouth."

This time my shiver is more of a violent tremor, which I know he feels because his pupils pulsate in response. "I really want it to snow now," I whisper, staring deep into his eyes. "Please snow."

Nothing appears on my palm.

But something icy kisses my cheek, causing me to glance upward into the sky above. It's still sunny, at least in this flowery field. However, tiny white crystals begin to form all around us, the snowflakes glittering in the orange and yellow rays.

My lips part at the sight, the enchantment swirling around us in a dusting of impossible fantasy.

Only, nothing is impossible here.

Because this whole maze is grounded in Hades's essence.

I can taste it on my tongue, the hum of intensity seeming to slide down my throat like a warm, addictive dessert. A moan escapes me, the power an unexpected aphrodisiac.

"You're starting to understand the intrigue," Hades murmurs, his lips ghosting along my now-throbbing pulse. "Our souls are meant to dance, Serapina. This is just the beginning of what we'll become together."

"I'm not even sure what I'm doing," I admit, lifting my hand to catch a snowflake. "All I did was ask for snow. And I'm pretty sure this is your power, not mine."

"It's mine, yes. But you're wielding it the way only an Omega can—specifically, the way only *my* Omega can." His lips return to my ear. "And you can feel it, can't you? The energy roaming all over your body, caressing every inch of you while marking you as *mine*."

I swallow, my eyes falling closed as I absorb his deep

tenor, revel in his purr, and lose myself to the sensation he just commented on.

Because yes, I feel it all.

His claim.

His energy.

His soul…

It's everywhere. *He* is everywhere. And I—

"Sera!"

My lashes flutter, the feminine voice yanking me from the moment. *Alina.* My eyes spring wide, my gaze searching the field for her presence.

I completely forgot that she and her mate-circle were here. Hades told me… *several days ago?* I think, recalling what he said about sleeping for three nights.

I was so caught up in this dreamy state that I didn't truly process what that meant. His commentary focused on my mortality—or lack thereof. Which I heard and understood, but didn't fully consider.

Just like I failed to remember that he mentioned my sister being in the maze, too.

"Where is she?" Alina demands, her voice seeming to come from my left.

"I'm over here!" I call out to her, then wince when I realize I just yelled in Hades's face. "Sorry."

He leans in to brush his lips against mine. "I'm the one who will be apologizing for eternity, not you, darling." His hands find my hips as he lifts me off his lap.

I frown at him as he stands up with me. "You don't need to apologize either, Hades. I understand you now. More than you may realize."

"Understanding my actions helps. But that doesn't mean my actions are forgivable." He brushes a kiss against my temple, then looks over my head. "Hello, Alina. Flame." His lips curl a little, his gaze softening. "Thea."

My breath catches, the adoration in his features so… so… *new*. I've never seen him look like this. Not even in Persephone's memories. But the doting expression he's wearing now is… it's heartwarming. So unlike the arrogant God I'm used to seeing. And different from the tender Alpha he's been these last few days, too.

He's looking at Thea like she's the most precious gift in the universe.

My heart warms in response, my insides seeming to melt. *He wants a child,* I realize, studying his features. *He's wanted one for eternity*.

However, Persephone never desired one.

No. That's not quite right.

The memory springs into my mind, the day she told Hades she couldn't risk bringing an Omega into this cruel world. Her heart broke inside at the admission, but she meant every word.

Except… except they weren't *her* words. They were ones Demeter instilled in her, warning her that creating a life in this troubled universe would be a sin to all of Omega kind.

Persephone never explained that to Hades, never gathered his input, never *confided* her wants or needs to him. Because Demeter convinced her not to.

And Hades…

Oh, Hades…

"I'll respect and honor your wishes, Persephone" was his response that day. "Always." But he uttered the words in a flat tone, his expression giving nothing away.

Because he didn't confide in her either.

I nearly shake my head now at them both. However, the incident exists in the past. And the past cannot be changed.

Only the future.

I press my palm to Hades's cheek, which draws his gaze down to me. I don't say anything, just go up onto my toes and brush a kiss against his cheek. His arm encircles my waist as he holds me to him, his forehead touching mine.

There is something powerful happening between us.

An awakening.

A rekindling.

A reunion between our souls.

It's enlightening and terrifying. Mostly because nothing about this feels *human* at all.

Which has me thinking about what he said earlier. *"Morpheus hypothesized that you might actually be in heat right now. He thinks your human shell might be a façade of sorts. Like a mirage."*

What if he's right? What if I've never been truly human?

Did Demeter do something to mask my instincts? To hide who I am, even from myself?

A cooing sounds behind me, reminding me that Hades and I are not alone. I pull away, but not too far since Hades doesn't release me from his embrace. Instead, he guides me into his side and smiles indulgently at Thea again.

"We didn't mean to ignore you, little angel," he murmurs to Thea.

My niece—who I suppose is more *his* niece than mine since they're actually related by blood—gives him a sweet little grin before nuzzling into Flame's chest. I can't hear it, but I assume he's purring, as he seems to do that often when holding Thea.

"Sera?" Alina asks, her gaze skating over me like she's trying to ensure that I'm real.

"Yeah?" I reply, frowning. "Are you okay?"

"Am *I* okay?" She huffs a laugh. "Pretty sure that's *my* line for you."

"I told you she was fine," Hades mutters.

"Like I would ever take your word for it," my sister spits at him.

Hades merely sighs in response, his defeat palpable.

Which… which irritates me. Because he doesn't deserve to feel that way.

Or maybe he does.

But *I* will be the one to exact judgment here. No one else.

"Please don't speak to Hades that way, Alina," I say quietly. It's not a snap or a command, just a stern request. One I follow up with "Hades is my mate. If I'm upset with him, he'll know it. So I don't need you to castigate him on my behalf."

Her dark eyes—so very different from my own—widen. "I…" She glances between us. "But he…"

"I realize his methods haven't been the easiest to understand or accept. However, I have faith in his intentions. Because I trust him."

Maybe that's naive after everything we've experienced together.

Or maybe I've forgiven him too easily.

But my instincts are all urging me to move forward, not backward. Persephone's memories provide perspective, too. And Hades has explained himself in a way that helps me understand our situation.

He might not be my mate in the same way as Morpheus and Maliki are now, but our souls are still intertwined. I accept that, just as I accept him.

His purr ignites in his chest, the rhythm different from the soothing rumble from before. This reverberation has a unique cadence to it, one that almost sounds… *pleased.*

Startled, I meet Hades's gaze and find him smiling down at me.

And then he's kissing me.

It happens so quickly that I don't even have a chance to breathe.

But I don't really need to. Hades gives me all the oxygen I need, his presence a lifeline I cling to as he pulls me flush against him.

"Um." Alina clears her throat. "We should probably, er, go…"

"Yeah," Flame replies. "Yeah, we should."

Hades releases me almost as quickly as he grabbed me, his eyes holding mine. "Did you want to talk more with your sister?"

I blink, a little dazed. "I…"

"It's okay," Alina says. "You two seem like you, uh, need some alone time?" She glances around, her brow furrowing. "Which I guess I should have realized since you're near a nesting pit."

"Breeding Pit," I correct her without thinking. Then I slap a hand over my mouth as Hades flashes a somewhat amused grin.

"You told her it's a *breeding pit?*" my sister demands.

"At least he's honest," Flame murmurs.

I release a giggle, one that just seems to come from nowhere and everywhere at once. All of this is… well, it's a lot. It's not what I expected my life to be. It's still like a dream. And I… I'm done trying to fight whatever I was fighting.

This is my world.

It's Alina's world.

It's fate.

Except, it's also *contrived.*

Not because of Hades or this labyrinth. But because of Demeter.

And that… that realization has me no longer laughing or smiling.

Thinking about her sends ice shooting through my veins. Because I suddenly remember the plane of nonexistence. The Omegas. The horrible sensation of *nothingness*.

"Do you remember it at all?" I ask, looking at Alina. "The plane of nonexistence?" I'm not even sure if that's a formal name or not, but it's what I call it. "That feeling where you exist without a corporeal form?"

Alina blinks at me. "I… I don't know what you're talking about. Do you mean Monsters Night? Like, all the things that happened on the train?"

I shake my head. "No, those were tangible." They groomed us. Fed us. Prepared us to *run*. Only I was never given the chance to flee. The Viscount took me into a room, and the rest… the rest is blurry. At least until my sister arrived in that garden.

But that's not what's important.

It's that *place*. "I'm talking about the plane where the Omegas are being kept. We have to save them." I look at Hades. "We have to *find* them."

Thorns, how could I forget? It's like I fell into a strange fog the last few days. Or a coma, I guess, since I slept for so long.

"Hades, their souls are being held there in captivity. They can't feel or speak or even breathe, but their minds… their essences…" I trail off, struggling to explain. To *understand*. "Maybe they're unaware. Maybe only I feel while there? Or rather, *Persephone*, since she has to remain whole. Regardless, we need to *find* them."

"We'll hunt for them," he tells me, his palm on my

cheek. "But we need to solve the mystery surrounding your human mask first."

"Okay, hold on," my sister interjects. "There's a lot of information going back and forth here. I know Orcus and Reaper are in the Monsters Night dimension hunting for clues with Morpheus and Maliki, but they didn't mention anything about a *human mask* or a *plane of nonexistence.*"

Confused, I look at her, but she's shifted her focus to Flame.

"Morpheus and Maliki are in another dimension?" I repeat, my voice barely audible as my mind tries to connect to my mates.

"Did you know any of that?" Alina asks, her voice only barely registering above my own as I mentally whisper, *Maliki? Morpheus?*

"Only the human mask part," Flame replies while my mind remains silent. *Too* silent. "Nothing about a plane of nonexistence."

"I think we have a few things to discuss," Hades says, a note of irritation in his tone. A note I understand because I feel the same way.

You left the labyrinth—this dimension—*without so much as a warning?* I think at Maliki and Morpheus.

No response.

Not even an inkling of feeling.

I suddenly feel… bereft. Forgotten. *Abandoned…*

"You tell us what you know about our mates going to another dimension"—Hades utters the words through his teeth—"and we'll explain the plane of nonexistence."

Why would you leave without talking to us? I wonder at my mates. *Did you hear nothing that I said to Hades? Nothing at all?*

Hurt pricks my chest.

Followed by annoyance.

An annoyance that grows as Flame says, "Orcus

suggested going to the Monsters Night dimension to search for any hints regarding what Demeter might have done to Sera while in the Nightingale Viscount Manor, or even before that in the village."

"And he didn't think to run that notion by me?" Hades inquires, his voice taking on that lethal calmness that tells me he's furious.

"You were busy with Sera, so he spoke with Morpheus," Flame replies. "And Morpheus said it would be wise to go as soon as possible."

Hades arches a brow, his expression one that indicates he does not approve of any of this. It's a sentiment we share. "And Maliki?" he asks, his tone so quiet that I almost don't hear him.

"I don't think he knew what Morpheus intended to do," Alina informs us, her nose crinkling. "That's actually why we came looking for you and Sera—we wanted to tell you where they went."

"I see." Hades's arm is like granite around me. "My cousin, the one who favors communication, seems to have forgotten all of his *teachings*."

"Pretty sure Maliki felt similarly, as his last words before they disappeared were something along the lines of *What in the Styx are you doing?*" Flame says. "Or that's what I overheard from Reaper's mind—he was amused by Maliki's surprise."

Well, that makes me feel mildly better. Not that Maliki was surprised, but that he didn't leave me on purpose.

But I'm not all that pleased with Morpheus right now. "Why would he not consult us before leaving?"

"I think he wanted to give you and Hades bonding time." Alina's expression and voice are slightly contrite. "That's what Orcus assumed, anyway."

"Morpheus did mention that he didn't want to

interrupt you and Hades, yeah," Flame adds. "But when we realized Maliki didn't know the plan, we thought it might be a good idea to let you know where they went."

"*I* thought it would be a good idea," Alina corrects him. "*You* said to stay out of it."

"I suggested we let Morpheus confess his sins to Hades," Flame murmurs. "Then you mentioned being worried about Sera and how we hadn't seen her in the maze yet, so it became *our* idea to venture over here."

Alina purses her lips. "True."

Flame flashes her a smile. "I will always do whatever you need me to do, little panther." He leans in to brush a kiss against her temple, which causes Thea to giggle and reach for my sister.

Alina's expression melts as she takes her from Flame's arms. She bumps noses with the little one, then holds her close and starts whispering sweet words to her.

Thea responds with more coos and giggles, the sounds causing Flame to pull them both into a big hug.

"She has them wrapped around her finger," I muse, loving their familial embrace.

"As she should," Hades murmurs. "Thea is a miracle."

"Yes, she is," my sister agrees, giving Hades a small smile. It's not a token of love or acceptance, but it's a gesture I appreciate nonetheless.

Because it shows that she might come around. Perhaps not quickly, but eventually. Which is important since we're all… family.

Clearing my throat, I look at Hades. "We need to discuss the plane of nonexistence. Those Omegas need us."

He nods. "They do. But we need to prioritize freeing your inner Omega first, Serapina. I think that's the key to all of this."

Frustrated, I nearly sigh.

However, that won't help or solve anything.

So instead, I face him completely and demand, "Where do we begin?"

His lips curl. "We already have." He glances upward and then back at me. "We started with the snow. So let's see what else you can manifest, *mate*."

Monsters Night Dimension

"I hope Sera bites your fucking knot," Maliki mutters as we wander through the silent Nightingale Village.

I cast a sleeping net over all the humans, dragging them into the dream world—something Cain seemed both impressed and disturbed by. I even lulled the Village Protectors into a sleep state, desiring a peaceful stroll through Serapina's hometown.

Which, as it turns out, is quite small.

And very outdated.

It reminds me of Victorian England from the Human Realm, only with a dystopian twist.

And monsters.

Because, in this dimension, monsters are known and

worshipped. Very different from the mortal world of my universe, where all supernatural beings are considered to be myths.

"Not for foreplay or enjoyment," Maliki goes on, still talking about our mate biting my knot. "But to make you bleed."

I glance at him, amused by his desire. "Are you hoping this happens while you're fucking her? Because I'm sure that can be arranged."

"No, you bloody idiot," he snarls. "Did you not hear her when she was talking to Hades about feeling abandoned?"

Some of my amusement dies, my steps slowing. "Yes, I heard her. That's why I left her and Hades to bond."

Maliki stops walking and faces me. "By *abandoning* her without warning or explanation, Morpheus."

My brow furrows. "I..." *Oh.* "I didn't think that through."

"Obviously," he returns flatly. "Which makes you a bloody idiot."

"Hmm." I don't necessarily appreciate his insult—particularly as he issued it *twice*—but it does seem to be warranted.

Maliki and I had chosen to familiarize ourselves with the village while Reaper and Orcus went to investigate the train station and the stage where the infamous Day of the Choosing occurs. We're supposed to regroup in the town square in about five minutes.

Which means I have some time.

Waving my hand through the air, I create a portal window that peeks into our home dimension. Specifically, Hades's labyrinth. Maliki folds his arms beside me. "Can you make it a little bigger? I'd like to go back now."

"Shh," I hush him, my gaze scanning the interior of

the cabin. "I'm looking for Serapina." Having the window open allows me to sense her, but she doesn't appear to be in this part of the maze. I suppose that means Hades took her on that tour he kept mentioning.

Little dreamer? I whisper into her mind.

Morpheus, she hisses back at me. *Where are you?*

In your home dimension, I tell her. *I've manifested a win—*

"Perhaps you didn't hear me earlier about illegal portals," Cain says, interrupting my mental conversation.

Sighing, I glance away from the window to look at him. "I heard you just fine, Elite City King. I just chose not to care."

Ignoring his responding growl, I focus on my mate. *Sorry, love, Cain is displeased that I opened a window to talk to you. But I wanted to apologize for leaving you without explanation. We're looking for clues regarding Demeter's penchant for—*

"I wouldn't." Maliki's deadly tone and sudden proximity jar me from my mental discussion once more, causing me to blink. I stare at the enforcer's back, then look around him to see that he's squaring off against Cain. "Give him a moment and he'll close the portal."

"Or I'll close it right now by ripping his heart out."

"While I would enjoy watching you try, it would upset my mate," Maliki replies evenly. "So I'm going to advise you to take a step back, let him finish whatever he's doing, and then—after the portal is closed—you can go all monster on him."

I roll my eyes. "I'm not afraid of a dream monster." I can easily become one, too. Just not in a physical form like Cain.

Dismissing both of them without further words, I return to my mate-link and wince when I hear Serapina panicking. *Shh,* I hush her. *Everything is fine. We're just looking for—*

You mentioned Cain, like the Elite City King?

The very same, I mutter. *He's an arrogant prick. Utterly ungrateful, too. Particularly as—*

He's a monster, Morpheus.

Well, yes. Most supernaturals in this dimension are, I suppose. But you should know that in our—

No, I mean, he's terrifying, she stresses, interrupting me again. *Alina told me that he's the one all the monsters in that world fear. He's powerful. He's like a… a…*

God? I suggest, smiling. *So am I, Serapina. And the monsters of your home world don't scare me. That's also not why I opened this window—I wanted to apologize for leaving and to tell you that we'll return soon. Hopefully, with some information that can help break whatever mirage Demeter has cast over you.*

You need to come back now, she says. *You don't want to mess with Cain.*

Oh, I think I won't have a choice there, love. He's wanted a dose of my power since we arrived. I might have to give it before he lets us leave. But don't worry about me and Maliki. We're okay. I try to find her again via the window, but doing that draws my focus to where Reaper and Orcus have joined the line with Maliki to form a protective shield between me and Cain.

Sighing, I say, *Serapina, darling, we'll be back soon, but I need to close the portal now. I'll check in again in an hour, either in person or via another window.*

Because fuck Cain's rules.

I gave him his Strigoi when I could have easily forced them to return to my kingdom. That decision could change in an instant, something Cain needs to respect and understand if he wants to maintain this tentative alliance with our dimension.

Morpheus, Serapina whispers.

Maliki and I will return to you, love, I promise. *I should have told you that before we left. I wanted you to have time with Hades alone, but Maliki made me see that not communicating was a mistake. I'll do whatever you need me to do to earn your forgiveness—once we're back.*

With that, I close the portal because I suspect her request would be for us to come home right now. But we're not done hunting for any traces of the mirage Demeter left behind here.

Blinking, I focus on my surroundings once more. "I would apologize, Cain, but I'm not sorry. My mate's needs supersede your rules." I shift my gaze to Orcus. "Find anything interesting at the train station?"

"Just the new Viscount," he mutters. "She was asleep at a desk in the station. Seemed to be a new office, not one Demeter used."

"A lot has changed in the Nightingale Village over the last year and a half," Cain states flatly. "I would elaborate, but I don't want to."

I smile. "As I'm uninterested in these changes, that's fine by me." Looking at Orcus, I ask, "Shall we move on to the Viscount's former home in the mountains?"

That's where the showdown happened with Demeter after Alina shattered the Alpha's mirage. We probably should have started there, but seeing where Serapina was raised made sense, too. Especially since Demeter lurked here for decades while disguised as the Village Viscount.

"We'll need to—"

Magic seems to hum around Cain, cutting off his statement. My eyebrow inches upward as he curses and pulls the mirror from his pocket again. It's the same one Sabre came out of, the device piquing my curiosity. I've never seen a mirror used in such a manner.

Cain sighs, his gaze flicking up to mine with murderous intent, then he focuses on the device in his palm.

"Zael," he says, his tone bored.

"Cain," a deep voice returns. "Anything you want to explain?"

The Elite City King cocks his head. "Depends. There are so many things I could discuss. Do you have a specific topic in mind?"

"Portals?" Zael suggests. "Illegal ones, perhaps?"

Cain pretends to consider that for a long moment and slowly shakes his head. "Not sure I have much to say on that topic at present. But if there were any that popped up in my territory, we both know that I would handle it personally."

"And if any appear on my islands?" A hint of a silky accent caresses those words, the origin sounding almost Australian in nature, but not quite.

"Then I would expect you to drown it," Cain answers flatly. "That is what you sea lords do, yes?"

A grunt sounds from the mirror. "Perhaps I'll show you what we *sea lords* do the next time I see you, Dream Eater."

The line goes dead with a flash, causing Cain to mutter something foreign before pocketing his device. "Your presence here is already alerting nearby territory kings. I suggest you quickly visit the Viscount's former home, then disappear. For good."

I shrug. "As I already told my mate, I'm not worried about your world's monsters." I smile then, wanting to offer him a subtle placating comment. "Of course, she replied that most monsters in your world fear you. So I'm intrigued by this Zael and why he does not."

"Because he's the Elite Island King and has his own monsters to terrify." Cain stares me down, unflinching. "Do what you came here to do, God of Dreams. Or I'll take you to Zael for a visit, see if he's as amused by your antics as I am."

I arch a brow. "Need I remind you about those favors

you owe me? I believe you refer to them as Sabre and Cage?" The former of which disappeared with Cain after entering the village and hasn't rejoined our party yet in the town square.

Part of me wonders if Cain discreetly sent him back to the Elite City to hide.

Or if he has Sabre coming up with a backup plan should it be needed.

Stepping around Maliki—who is still acting as a shield, despite being clearly irritated with me mere minutes ago—I move within arm's reach of Cain.

"I'm not your enemy, Elite City King," I tell him in all seriousness. "I've always liked Sabre and Cage, and I have no interest in removing them from your mate-circle. However, as a recently mated male, you should understand why I am willing to risk everything for my own mate."

He searches my gaze, his posture remaining defensive. I suspect that might just be his usual stance. He has a world to protect, one frequently visited by monsters from various realms, and I appreciate the difficulty he faces in managing his unique territory.

But we're not here to cause problems, something I know he's figured out by now.

"It would help if I understood what you were searching for here," he finally says. "Perhaps it's something I can assist you in finding."

"That's the problem," I tell him. "We're not sure what we're looking for exactly." Glancing around, I add, "I can attempt to elaborate while we walk?"

"We're going to drive," he replies. "The Viscount's home was up in the mountains, a good several miles from here. And I'm not letting either of you *mist* me up there."

My lips twitch.

Orcus offered to do that earlier, but Cain refused and

used his fancy little device instead. I'm not quite sure how it works, but I've gathered it's linked to a portal of mirrors and glass-like surfaces—such as lakes—that he uses to move freely around his territory.

"I already sent Sabre to get a car," he adds. "He's parked behind the train station." Cain glances around. "It'll fit four of us comfortably. The rest can..." He lifts a hand, his fingers dancing a little in the air. It's like he said *mist* once and can't repeat it.

"Maliki and I will join you," I say. Reaper and Orcus can meet us up there since they know where to go already.

Orcus nods, disappearing.

Reaper glances between us and shrugs, then follows his Alpha.

"Once we're a safe distance from the village, I'll release my hold on your humans," I tell Cain before he can ask. "Now, about Demeter..."

Back in the Underworld Labyrinth...

Alina walks beside me through the field, her appreciative gaze on the blossoming flowers around us. "This really is beautiful."

"I know," I say softly before casting a furtive glance backward at Hades. He's still sitting beneath the tree, only Thea is in his lap now. Her pretty brown eyes are focused upward to where Flame is lounging in jaguar form on a branch above their heads. He bats playfully in the air at one of the birds, causing Thea to giggle excitedly.

"He won't… hurt the bird, right?" I ask my sister, my brow furrowing a bit in concern. "I rather like the—"

A chirp sounds as Flame grabs the winged creature with his claws.

My feet stumble, my trajectory changing in a second as I start to head back toward the tree. But a burst of light has me freezing mid-step, then an array of feathers appears in burnt gold colors as the bird materializes above Flame's head.

His green eyes dart upward just as the bird pecks him square on his big black head.

With a chastising chirp, the creature flies up higher to perch on a branch just out of reach.

The jaguar grumbles in response.

And Thea bursts out in another fit of giggles.

I blink, confused.

What did Hades call these? *Stygians*? From the Midnight Fae Realm? He said Human Realm birds wouldn't survive here. So maybe these fascinating creatures are immortal?

I hope that's the case.

I don't like the idea of anything dying here, or anywhere else for that matter.

"Looks like he can't hurt the bird," my sister says, sounding amused. "His jaguar is annoyed."

"Well, *I* will be annoyed with his jaguar if he hurts Hades's gift," I mutter.

Alina glances at me. "The bird is a gift?"

"This whole field is, I think," I say, resuming our walk. "He said he created it for me."

"Didn't he technically make this whole maze for you?"

My lips twist to the side. "For Persephone, yeah." I glance around, my heart beating a little faster as I take in the rows of endless roses. "But these flowers are mine." I look at Alina, see her souring expression, and add, "I think this was his way of apologizing to me. Or maybe trying to make this place feel more welcoming."

What I don't tell her is that I already liked the labyrinth before he made these changes. The timeless quality of the icy walls, frozen flowers, and deadly skulls is intricate and unique.

This world he's created doesn't scare me so much as enthrall me.

I can't say why. Nor can I explain the comfort I sense here. It just feels right to me.

The chill. The complexity. The cruel visage.

I like all the details that went into its manifestation, even if the motivations were founded on darkness. But this place depicts the fractures of Hades's broken heart, the pain he experienced when he thought his Omega betrayed him. And that history is one I respect. One I understand. One I long to make right.

Not by seeking forgiveness on Persephone's behalf, but by freeing her memory from the burden of blame.

We need to find those Omegas, I think. *Which means I have to somehow set my soul free.*

Clearing my throat, I focus on Alina. "How did you access your creation gifts?"

Her lashes flutter, her eyebrows curling down a little. Then she shakes her head like she's clearing it.

"Sorry, did you say something else?" I wonder out loud, noting her startled reaction. "If you did, I… I wasn't listening. My head is kind of cloudy right now, trying to understand everything that's happened and also figure out what I'm supposed to do next." I swallow and add, "It's all really confusing."

"I just said Hades has a lot to apologize for and that I hope he does more than make you a garden." She winces. "Which… is probably not helpful."

"It's not," I admit, giving her a small smile. "But I think you're just being protective of me… like always."

"I am," she agrees. "However, you were right when you told me it's not my place to, er, *castigate* Hades. He's your, uh, mate, and it's wrong of me to try to… tell him what to do. Though, I won't apologize for wanting to kill him at certain points."

"Lina," I sigh.

She holds up her hands. "I'm not going to interfere, Sera. It's your mate-circle. Just know that if he ever hurts you, I'm going to give Reaper permission to rip off Hades's head."

I cut her a look.

But her expression tells me she's serious.

"You've always been protective of me."

"As is my duty as the older sister," she replies. "I suppose it's also my duty to try to teach you about being an Omega, too. But I have to be honest—it just sort of happened. I'm not sure what advice I can give. I mean, Orcus bit me, I went into heat, made a nest, and just… Well, I woke up and everything felt as natural as breathing."

"Hmm," I hum, thinking through her response as I move closer to some rose bushes to examine the red color. "None of this feels natural to me, something I suppose you already guessed after watching me try and fail to manifest things with Hades's power."

I was able to create some snow. And then… nothing.

That's when Hades recommended I take a walk around the flower field. "See what comes naturally to you," he told me. "You could garden a little, if you want. I'll manifest whatever you need. Or you can simply enjoy the scenery. But try not to think too much, and just… indulge your senses."

Obviously, I wasn't doing a good job with the *try not to think too much* part.

Because that's all I seem to be doing.

Alina coming with me didn't help, either. Though, I do appreciate the company. And I rather like seeing Hades spending time with Thea. It's not something I've seen him do before.

Actually… "Has Hades spent any time with Thea before today?" I ask Alina softly.

She blinks at me, her face doing the same thing as a minute or two ago, making me wince.

"Sorry, you said something else, didn't you?" I shake my head, trying to clear it. "Sorry, Lina. I… I'm struggling to focus on anything right now."

She stops walking and grabs my shoulders, her dark eyes meeting my blue ones. "Stop apologizing, Sera. I know you're going through a lot, okay?"

I bite my lower lip and nod. "Okay."

"Now I'm going to answer your question about Thea first because it's an easy one to address—yes, he's spent time with her before. Usually with Orcus, though. For all of Hades's faults where his behavior with you is concerned, he's…" She looks over at him, drawing my focus there, too.

His cheeks are currently puffed out as he makes a silly expression at Thea. Her little hand pats the side of his face, causing the air to escape. Or I assume that's what happens because his cheeks go back to normal and she giggles so loudly the sound carries across the field.

"He's pretty good with his niece," Alina says, a begrudging note in her tone. "Very good, actually." Those three words seem to be underlined in admiration. "She loves playing with his wings, probably because they remind her of Orcus's wings."

That comment has me looking sharply at Alina. "You've seen Hades's wings?"

She frowns back at me. "You haven't?"

"No." For some reason, that admission makes me feel warm all over. And not in a good way.

I'm about to march over to Hades to demand that he show me his feathers.

But Alina stops me by saying, "Before you get distracted again, I want to repeat my comment about you trying to manifest Hades's power since I don't think you heard me before. However, I said that I didn't know how to use Orcus's gifts. So I'm not quite sure why Hades is trying to teach you how to use his abilities, and therefore I can't really give you advice on that."

Hades looks over, maybe because he keeps hearing his name.

Or perhaps because he felt my intense gaze on him.

His lips move, the words too quiet for me to hear, but they appear to be for Flame because the jaguar jumps from the tree and begins to transform.

I focus on my sister, not wanting to see her mate in the nude. "You don't use Orcus's powers?"

She shakes her head. "No. I… I only use my own. And I'm not sure I would actually call it a power. Omegas create life. It's… it's…" Her brow furrows, and she walks over to touch one of the flowers.

My eyes widen as another stem begins to sprout off of the same stalk, the bud forming far more rapidly than should be possible until the ends are blossoming with red petals.

It happens in a few seconds.

The entire life cycle of a plant unfolding before my eyes in an impossible way. Because it shouldn't even work like that, but as I approach and touch the rose, I realize it's very real.

"How…?"

She shrugs. "I don't know. I willed it to exist… and now it does. Anything I wish to give life to does the same thing."

"And you've been able to do this since…?"

"Since my heat," she murmurs. "Maybe even before that, but I never tried."

I stroke the same stem, my mind telling it to create life like Alina just did. However, nothing happens. I grit my teeth in annoyance. "I don't understand why I can't access this part of my soul. I… I don't feel any different. Not really."

"How did you feel when you made your nest earlier?" Hades asks, his smooth tone wrapping around me in a cloak of comfort as he joins us in the field. "Did you feel normal then? Human?"

My brow crinkles. "I… I don't know. I didn't really think about it. I just wanted to fix the bedding. So I… I thought of things I wanted for the bed, and they appeared because of your magic. Kind of like manifesting food in the kitchen."

His hands slide into the pockets of his slacks, his exposed forearms flexing with the motion. "An Alpha can wish any inanimate object into existence, but we can't create life. That's the primary difference between an Alpha's skill and an Omega's gift. Further, Alphas also tend to have an affinity for a specific plane of existence."

I swallow. "Like a state of nothingness?" I ask, thinking of the dreaded place Demeter seems to have crafted for Omega kind.

He cants his head. "Yes, I suppose. But usually our worlds are tangible, not vacant."

"So maybe that plane of nonexistence isn't a true Alpha creation," I say slowly. "Which I suppose we already know since Persephone's soul is linked to it somehow. Like an… an anchor, I guess."

Hades's dark eyes hold mine. "A mixture of life and

resurrection, underscored by the gift of controlling life cycles and fertility."

I frown at him. "That sounds complicated."

"Yes," he agrees, stepping closer to me. "But we're going to figure it out, Serapina." He lifts his hands to my face and pulls me in for a soft kiss. "The key, I think, is to let your instincts lead you—like you did with your nest."

"But I don't seem to have any instincts for creating life," I tell him.

"Perhaps none that you're aware of," he murmurs, his forehead falling to mine. "But I think those inclinations are being dimmed by whatever Demeter has done to your soul."

"The mirage," I whisper.

"Hmm," he hums, the sound one of agreement. However, he pulls away a little and looks at Alina. "Do you sense anything around your sister? A façade of any kind? Like the one you thwarted whilst Orcus and I were in Pandora's Box the other day?"

"You thwarted a façade?" I interrupt, alarmed. "What does that even mean?"

Alina glances between us, then chooses to answer me instead of Hades. "I sensed something weird happening to my vision, almost like a veil was being pulled over my eyes. It freaked me out, so I… I more or less pushed it away? But with my mind. And it, uh, cut me off from Orcus…"

I gape at her. "This happened the other day?" I look at Hades. "Why did no one tell me?"

"I intended to when I mentioned that Alina was here with her mates. But our conversation shifted course."

To his fears about my soul, I think, recalling the discussion and the dinner that followed. We never returned to the topic of my sister because I… I kind of forgot about her being in the maze.

"Everything feels so fuzzy," I confide in a low voice, irritated by the heavy sensation weighing in my mind. "It's like I'm struggling to focus."

"That's a side effect of being in an Omega heat," he says, his voice equally soft. "Yet another indication that Morpheus's mirage theory holds merit."

"So I might still be in heat… right now?" I wonder aloud.

"Possibly. Or you're in the after stages, which are still typically *fuzzy*, as you said."

"Oh." It's such an underwhelming word for how I'm feeling. But I don't really know what else to say. All of this is just… *a lot.*

"Did you tell her that Demeter escaped?" my sister asks, causing my eyes to widen once more, the fog sensation lifting instantly.

"*What?*"

"I'll translate that as a no," Alina says, drawing out the "o" of "no."

"Demeter *escaped?*" I gawk at her and then at Hades.

But it's Flame who says, "Or was never actually imprisoned to begin with." He joins our circle with a sleeping Thea tucked up against his rumbling chest.

Normally, I would admire the adorable view.

However, I'm a bit distracted by his words.

"That's why Orcus wanted to go back to your home dimension—to check the site where we ensnared her. Morpheus suggested it could have been a mirage," he goes on. "Orcus doesn't agree, but he wanted to be certain. So… they, uh, went on a field trip."

"Field trip," Hades repeats under his breath.

Flame shrugs. "That's what Reaper called it."

"Of that, I have no doubt," Hades drawls.

"Can we go back to Demeter, please?" I snap. "She's not in Pandora's Box. And I'm just finding this out…?"

Hades only sounds mildly contrite as he replies, "Because you've been asleep for the better part of the last four days, Serapina."

"So you should have told me the moment I woke up!" I sputter. "Or you should have woken me up to tell me." That last part is said through my clenched teeth.

"Disturbing an Omega's rest during her heat is unhealthy and can introduce unnecessary risks," he tells me patiently. "We already don't know what Demeter has done to you. Interrupting your cycle… I'm sorry, Serapina, but it wasn't an option. Your safety comes first. Always."

He presses his finger to my lips before I can even begin to formulate a retort. Not that I actually have one; his words are underlined in an authority that has me instinctively quieting.

Which is probably insane.

And just my "inner Omega" bowing to her Alpha.

But I can't deny the way his tone and presence make me feel.

"Aside from that," he continues, "if Demeter has, in fact, never truly been captured, then her *escape* is a moot point. She has been and continues to be a threat. Thus, our objective remains the same—we need to free your inner Omega. And then, we need to work together to undo whatever Demeter has done."

Okay, he's not wrong, but… "One of you should have told me about Demeter," I mutter against his finger.

"Yes," he says. "And we fully intended to discuss it during dinner the other night, but…"

"But I fell asleep." It comes out as a grumble because I'm annoyed by the situation and he's still touching my mouth. "I don't even know why I did that."

"It's common for an Omega to sleep soundly before and after a heat cycle." He removes his finger and cups my cheek. "Serapina, we did not intentionally keep this information from you. There just hasn't been a good moment to discuss it."

"You could have mentioned it when showing me the flowers," I tell him. "Or before making snow with me."

He nods. "Yes, that's true. I'm sorry I didn't think to bring it up earlier; I was focused on teaching you how to use my energy. But you're safe here, Serapina. Demeter can't pass through my wards."

"Except she already has," I argue. "*Twice*. Or she's done something in this labyrinth, anyway." This time I cover his mouth before he can reply so I can add, "Regardless, you can't keep me in the dark. I understand things have been weird these last few days, but I can't defend myself if I'm unaware of potential dangers."

His midnight irises swirl with understanding as he gazes down at me.

"I know you want to guard me, Hades, and I appreciate you for doing so. However, the best way to protect me is to ensure I'm informed and prepared for whatever may or may not be coming." I slowly remove my hand and press it to his chest. "I want to be strong. And to do that, I need your support."

He draws his thumb along my cheek and leans in to press his lips to mine. It's a tender kiss, one that sends tingles down my spine. But I don't let it distract me from our conversation.

And thankfully, he doesn't either.

"You're right," he murmurs. "I will not keep anything from you, Serapina. You have my word."

I study his expression, staring deep into his eyes. "I believe you."

He smiles. "And I believe in you, mate." He kisses me again, his praise playing through my mind and drugging my senses. However, before I can lose myself in his touch, he pulls back and looks to the left.

Which draws my attention to my blushing sister.

Oh.

I… I forgot she was here. Er, well, I didn't *forget*—more… I was caught up in my conversation with Hades.

"Alina," he says.

"No." Her response is immediate, the emphatic nature of it startling me.

"What do you mean, *no*?" I ask, confused by her refusal. I'm not even sure what she's refusing.

"Sorry, I…" She clears her throat and seems to visibly shake herself. "I'm responding to his question—the one about mirages. And the answer is no, I don't sense anything around you at all. However, I really wish I did."

"It's not your fault, little panther," Flame says, wrapping an arm around her while holding Thea with the other.

"Maybe not. But that doesn't make it any less frustrating," she grumbles back to him. "That is what you were going to ask me, right?" The question seems to be for Hades.

"Yes," he confirms, his palm drifting down my neck to my back as he steps to my side. "So you don't sense any sort of *veil* around Serapina, but what about… life? Does she feel human to you?"

Alina's brow furrows. "I'm not sure how to answer that."

"Can you sense her soul?" he tries again.

"I…" She looks from him to me, her frown seeming to deepen.

But she doesn't speak again.

Instead, she moves away from Flame and into my space. Her hand lifts, then she pauses. "Can I…?"

"Are you going to ask if you can touch me?" I inquire, somewhat humored.

I wrap my arms around her in a hug before she can respond, and bury my face in her brown hair.

She instantly returns the embrace, her grip strong around me, like she's afraid she might lose me.

"We might not be blood, but we're still sisters," she says against my ear. "Always."

"Always," I agree, relieved that she's here. Relieved that we're creating a new balance together. And relieved that… that this is my existence.

It's a strange realization, one I don't think I've ever experienced.

For far too long, I've questioned my fate. Fought to be someone else. Desired to be stronger, more independent, to be *Sera*.

And I… I think I'm finally *her*—that woman I've aspired to become.

It makes me feel light. Proud. *Fulfilled.* Like I've—

Alina gasps, interrupting my moment, and pulls away to place her hand on my belly. "Oh my monsters…"

My brow crinkles. "What?" I ask, confused by her reaction and the way she's touching me now.

"Sera…" She looks down and then back up. "You're… you're…"

"I'm what?" I demand, not liking this at all. "I'm *what*, Lina?"

Her eyes are wide, her mouth working without making a sound. Until finally she forces out, "*Life.*"

"Life?" I look down, see where her hand is resting

against my abdomen, then look back up at her. "N-no… No, that… That's not…"

"Life," she repeats in a breath. "A baby, Sera. You're… you're with child."

MALIKI

Nightingale Viscount Manor

This is a complete waste of fucking time.

Well, mostly.

Morpheus's conversation with Cain in the car actually proved interesting. Hades has told me about Demeter a few times, but never in quite as much depth as Morpheus went into when elaborating on her history to Cain.

"In our version of the Human Realm, we have something referred to as *Greek mythology*. Demeter is known as the Goddess of the Harvest. Not sure if you have that here or not, but if you do, some of the myths are founded on truth. At least in our dimension."

Morpheus went on to explain that Mythos Fae once mingled with humans in our world, which created many of those stories that have been passed down from generation to generation. But, unlike Cain's dimension, ours opted to erase the evidence of a fae presence from the Human Realm and to essentially encourage our mortals to think we're just figments of their vast imagination.

Those were all details I already knew.

However, then Morpheus started talking about the downfall of Alpha kind and the twelve who went insane.

"It started after we severed ties with the Human Realm," Morpheus began. "I'm not sure if that's a coincidence or not, but that's how far back in history we're going—roughly two thousand five hundred years ago…"

He talked about how the insane Alphas tried to enslave Omega kind.

"Demeter was one of them," he continued, that information shocking the hell out of me since the Demeter I've heard all about loathed Alphas for hurting Omegas. "But something changed when she had Persephone."

Morpheus goes on, talking about how Demeter essentially became a refuge for many of the Omegas.

"She's the Goddess of Fertility in the Mythos Fae Realm, which includes agriculture and plant life, but her gift goes much deeper than a simple harvest. Her powers are grounded in reproduction cycles, which almost makes her Omega-like since our Omegas are the ones who create life."

This was all new information to me, so I listened intently as he continued talking about her taking on a sanctuary role for Omegas.

"They would go to her when in heat, begging for protection," Morpheus said. "Oftentimes in the spring since that's when a lot of Mythos Fae Omegas once experienced their first estrous cycles."

I consider that comment again now as I move through

the dusty manor, my mind spinning with the concept of *spring*.

There is no *spring* in the Netherworld. No summer or fall either. It's basically winter year-round, just without the snow.

All the plants are dead.

All the wildlife is dead.

There is no seasonal influence whatsoever.

Could that be why Sera never went into heat? It's a question I want to voice to Morpheus, but I haven't seen him since exiting the vehicle. He misted off to investigate something he sensed, thus leaving me behind with Sabre and Cain.

The pair of them are somewhere outside, waiting for the rest of us to conclude our visit.

Or I assume that's where they are, as I haven't seen them enter the manor.

I kick some fist-sized stones with my boot, the dark color at odds with the white marble floor. But it's the jagged edges I focus on, particularly as they appear sharp.

Fortunately, I dressed this morning with the intention of walking through the maze. Otherwise, I would have been completely unprepared for this dimension. As it is, I'm in jeans and a T-shirt. But I really miss my weapons right now.

I also miss Hades's manifestation magic.

It would be rather useful right about now, as I'd really like to create some knives laced with slug venom. Ones I could keep hidden until the journey home.

Then, the moment we returned to the labyrinth, I could stab Morpheus with them.

Alas, I'm weaponless. Bored. And utterly pissed off.

I may understand why Morpheus dragged us to this world, but thus far, it has proved futile. While I appreciate the Demeter history lesson, he could have provided that back in the maze.

Sera would probably be interested in the information as well.

Learn more about the power her mother wields over plants and other manners of life.

"She can't create life," Morpheus reiterated at one point. "But she can manipulate the life cycle via reproduction and fertility. Which is a very powerful skill. It impacts so many things. Like the seasons. To alter a plant's reproductive patterns, one must control all elements of weather—sun, rain, heat, cold—and she has access to all those life-altering components."

I consider all that now, my mind working through what *components* Demeter would need to alter around Sera to essentially control her reproductive cycle. To mask her true nature. To make her seem *human*.

And how is she manipulating those facts in Hades's labyrinth? I wonder, frowning.

It implies that her power can not only traverse dimensions, but penetrate Hades's wards, too. Otherwise, Sera would be her true self in that maze, right?

"No, that's not how it happened," Orcus says, his deep voice drawing me from my perch on the second floor and luring me to the balcony railing.

Glancing over it, I find him and Reaper in the main room below, the entertaining space covered in archaic-looking furniture—some of which has blood on it.

And feathers.

I noticed it when I first entered, already aware that this was the location of the battle between Demeter and everyone else.

But now I'm intrigued by what Reaper and Orcus are discussing.

"Yes, it is," Reaper says, weapons forming in his hand. "Sera stabbed Demeter like this"—he uses a blade to demonstrate in the air—"and then..." His scythe appears, and he heaves it through the air as well. "I did that, Flame pounced, and we sent the bitch into your portal."

Orcus frowns. "I remember Sera stabbing her and Flame pouncing, but not your scythe."

Reaper gapes at him. "The Goddess bitch had it lodged in her stomach when she fell into Pandora's Box, Orcus. I put it there."

"But it wasn't there when I handed her off to Ares," Orcus stresses as I start down the grand staircase toward them. "Only Sera's knife. And I remember that because I pulled it out to bring it back to you."

Reaper shakes his head. "You never gave it back to me."

"I did. I portaled back here and handed it to you before venturing outside to talk to Helia and Cain."

"No, you stepped out of the portal, checked on Alina and Sera, then told me to follow you for some fresh air—which was code for needing to wrap up loose ends with the administrators of this realm." Reaper glances over at the door where Cain and Sabre have just entered. "Then I told the Dream King that this dimension sucks."

Cain grunts. "I believe your exact commentary was in regard to our lack of pizza options."

"Yes, that." Reaper faces Orcus again. "They also have really stupid rules here. *Stop stealing cupcakes. Stop torturing the humans in the dungeon.*" Reaper glances at me as I approach. "Seriously, Mal, be glad this experience is short-lived. They don't even let you eat the dark souls."

"I don't eat souls, Reaper," I remind him.

He sighs and shakes his head. "None of you know how to have a good time."

"Focus, Reaper," Orcus says, his voice serious. "You really don't remember me returning the knife to you?"

"No. Because it didn't happen." Reaper rolls up his sleeves to show off his ink, the dark lines writhing and changing just like mine. Only, his power is quite different. I inspire sensation; he manifests weapons. "I would be able to craft the exact same one Sera used if you gave it back to me, blood and all. But…"

Dark ribbons of smoke curl out from his fingertips, drawing my gaze to the glint of metal as it forms into a dagger.

"Is that like the one Sera used?" I ask, my voice a little deeper than seconds ago. Mostly because I'm now envisioning my mate holding that pretty little toy.

"Yeah, just like this," Reaper says. "Only, it would have been smeared with blood after she used it, and as you can see, it's clean."

"You can remanufacture weapons that have been used?" Cain asks, sounding intrigued. "Like the exact same one?"

Reaper looks at him. "If it's one I created and reabsorbed"—he glances pointedly at Orcus before returning his attention to Cain—"yes."

Cain folds his arms over his chest, his immaculate suit reminding me of Hades's preferred attire. "So you're able to create weapons at will and feast on souls."

Reaper stares him down. "I can't tell if you're about to hit on me or offer me a job."

The Elite City King grins. "I'm merely expressing a *professional* interest. Nothing more."

"Good. Because Alina doesn't like to share. That's why her name is tattooed on my cock."

"You did that to yourself," Orcus mutters.

Reaper smiles dreamily. "Yeah, I did, while Alina—"

Orcus clears his throat. "We're getting off topic."

"Indeed," Morpheus agrees, appearing in the center of the room. "If I overheard everything correctly, you both have different recollections about Demeter's capture, which would make sense if she was forced to quickly craft a mirage. We should ask Sera, Alina, and Flame what they remember."

"Where have you been?" I ask him, suspicious of his sudden appearance and obvious eavesdropping.

"Attempting to re-create the garden," he says before tossing a jagged stone onto the ground.

I frown because the color resembles the rocks I kicked upstairs with my boot. I didn't think much of it—this place is a bit of a mess from being left to rot for the last year or so—but rocks are an interesting adornment.

Glass, I would understand. Several of the windows are decorated with jagged edges and open to the outside world.

Animals have also obviously been burrowing in here, too.

But that doesn't explain the fist-sized rocks.

Kneeling, I take a closer look and frown. "I don't understand, Morpheus." Everything about the rock looks normal to me. Just out of place against the marble. However, he's the one who just tossed it there.

"It's not from this world," Morpheus says before slipping his hands back into his pockets. "It's starmud."

I stare at him. "What?"

"Starmud," he repeats, like that's going to clear everything up. "It's from the Mythos Fae Realm."

My brow furrows. "I… I trust your expertise on that, but it looks like a regular Earth rock to me, Morpheus."

"Sure," he agrees. "Until you shine light on it."

"You know, I failed to bring a *light* with me," I tell him.

"Because I didn't know we were leaving our fucking dimension."

"Too bad you don't have access to an Alpha who can manifest items for you," he returns. "Oh, wait…" A bloody lantern appears in his hand, one that has me raising both my eyebrows because it looks like something used in the Human Realm centuries ago.

But the moment the fire shines upon the stone, it begins to sparkle like a cluster of stars.

"You found that here?" Orcus asks as the glittering stone begins to shift into a new shape and color.

One that resembles… *grass*?

I'm so confused by what I'm seeing that I can't take my gaze away from the sight. Because the grass is expanding. Growing along the floor. Then stops when it reaches the edge of the glow cast by Morpheus's lantern.

When the light disappears, the magical substance turns inward, rolling up tightly into a bundle of rock again.

"Well, that was… interesting," Cain comments.

"Yes, because it means the garden mirage was anchored to a tangible substance," Morpheus says, meeting my gaze. "We should return to the maze. Now."

My brow furrows a little at Morpheus's stern tone. It suggests he found something else that he doesn't want to share here, but back in the labyrinth.

Considering that going home is exactly what I want to do, I don't argue and just say, "Then make a portal, God of Dreams."

"I will. But please don't stab me with a slug venom dagger, Enforcer. You're going to want me awake and aware when we arrive."

My eyebrow inches upward. "Playing in my head?"

"Fantasies are my realm, Maliki," he replies, stepping toward me until we're chest to chest. "And the one you were daydreaming about whilst wandering the manor tonight was quite loud."

I stare at him, unwilling to deny his claim or make any promises. "Take me back to Sera, and we'll see what happens."

"Hmm," he hums, grabbing my arm. "I suppose we will." Without glancing backward, he adds, "Take care of my Strigoi, Elite City King. And sweet dreams, Sabre…"

Ominous energy swirls in the air, but I'm not given a chance to react to it because Morpheus shoves me backward.

And suddenly I'm falling through space.

Only to land with a sharp thud outside a familiar door.

Death's Cabin.

Thank Styx.

I don't think for a second more, instead manifesting a knife and throwing it right at Morpheus the moment he steps into view.

The bastard catches it, not by the sharp end but by the handle, and quickly tosses it onto the ground.

Tsking, he says, "Now, Mali…" His voice trails off, and he coughs a little.

I jump to my feet just as his knees give out.

"I switched it up. Not slug venom this time, just some spider ale. Or rather, the *raw* ingredient of spider ale that causes numbing." Leaning down until we're eye level, I add, "And I coated the handle with it, not the blade."

I don't wait to see what happens.

I simply walk inside and leave him to suffer. Assuming the blade manifested correctly, it shouldn't be for long. If it didn't manifest correctly, well… I shrug.

Morpheus deserves a little discomfort.

Sweet dreams, indeed…

The Labyrinth Breeding Pit

Serapina is pregnant.

Yet I can't sense a damn thing.

Not a soul. Not the scent of life. Not even an Omega designation from my own fucking mate.

When I find Demeter—and I will—I'm going to take her into the death pits and let the souls feast on her for eons.

But my hunt will need to wait because Serapina's skin has taken on an ashen quality.

"That's not possible," she says to Alina. "I… Can it even happen that fast? I don't… But I just… Lina, *that's impossible.*"

"I can sense it," her sister replies, both of her palms against Serapina's belly now. "A thriving soul. Can you not feel the life inside you? The beautiful creation?"

Tears form in her blue eyes, the reaction one that has my heart freezing in my chest. Because she looks horrified. "Oh, stars," she breathes, looking at me. "Hades, I… I'm so sorry… I…"

A tear falls, the path down her cheek catching my focus as a frown tugs at my mouth. "Why are you sorry?" I ask, utterly confused by her reaction.

Omegas love children. They exist to create life. Why would Serapina apologize for such an amazing gift?

"I'm supposed to be yours. And I… I…" Her face falls as she palms her stomach. "I'm sorry, Hades. It's… I didn't realize…"

I stare at her for a beat, trying to understand her sorrow. But it doesn't make any sense. "Why are you apologizing for creating a life?"

"Because I… I feel like I failed you?" She jolts backward like I slapped her, but I haven't even moved. "Stars, what's wrong with me? I'm pregnant. I'm… I…" She blinks rapidly. "I shouldn't feel bad. I shouldn't be apologizing. I… This is *my* child. Why am I apologizing?"

She sounds almost angry. And when she looks up again, her eyes are narrowed at me.

"I take it back. I'm not sorry," she tells me, her voice stronger now. "I mean, I… I feel bad that it's not yours, but I—"

"Not mine?" I repeat, my brow coming down.

Then suddenly her words all click into place.

Her statement about how she is supposed to be mine.

Her commentary about *failing* me.

Stating the child isn't mine.

Because of course I'm not the biological father, as I haven't knotted her yet.

But she's very clearly not understanding a key dynamic

of our relationship. Which highlights a significant failure on my part.

"Oh, Serapina," I say, pulling her into my arms. "Your child is very much mine. Just as you are mine."

Confusion pulls her brows down, but I kiss her before she can give voice to the emotion.

"We're a mate-circle, darling," I say softly against her mouth. "That means the life inside you is *ours*, as a circle. Your child. My child. Maliki's child. Morpheus's child. We will all love him or her equally, just as Alina's circle adores Thea."

Serapina blinks. Then she looks at her sister, who is snuggled into Flame's side and taking comfort from his purr. I imagine she felt distressed at seeing Serapina upset. I experienced a similar feeling of distress, so I understand her needing her mate.

However, the situation is clear to me now.

And I'm oddly a little amused by it.

Which is rather ridiculous considering the circumstances.

Serapina thought I would be displeased because she doesn't trust my intentions when it comes to our circle.

I can't fault her concerns. But it is my responsibility to fix them.

"Do you mind if I spend some time alone with Serapina?" I ask, my query for Alina. "It's clear we need to discuss a few things."

Alina stares at me, then looks at Serapina. "That's up to Sera. Do you want to be alone with him?"

"You're right," I interject, my focus returning to my mate. "I should have asked you first, Serapina. Can we have a few minutes alone?"

She stares up at me. "You're not mad?"

I smile. "No, mate. I'm very much the opposite of mad."

"But you and Persephone never…"

My smile wanes a bit. "She never desired children." And now my smile dies completely. "Do you desire children?"

"I… I didn't before. Or I don't think I did. It's not something I considered too deeply, though. But I…" She blows out a breath. "A lot has changed in a very short amount of time. I didn't think a mate-circle was even possible for me. I also didn't want to be bred. Or taken by monsters. Or… or…"

She trails off and buries her head in my chest.

My purr rumbles to life in response, my arms tightening around her as I meet Alina's gaze.

She glances at her sister, then shifts her attention to Flame and their sleeping daughter. "Let's go tuck Thea into the nest."

His lips curl. "That sounds like a good plan. Especially since Reaper and Orcus are back and looking for us."

I blink. "They're back?"

He nods.

"Did they find anything?"

"Orcus says to talk to Morpheus" is the only information he provides. Well, at least until he adds, "And work on your mate-circle."

I nearly snort. "Solid advice." The words come out in a deadpan tone, one that has Flame chuckling as he steers Alina down the path through the rose garden.

She glances backward near the exit to the labyrinth, her gaze on Serapina. Flame kisses his mate's head, his eyes meeting mine. Then he pulls her and Thea into the labyrinth.

I stare after them, a pang hitting my heart.

What is it like to have a complete circle? One that allows all the mates to speak mentally and constantly be in tune with one another?

As it is, I didn't realize Morpheus and Maliki had returned until Flame's commentary about heading back to the nest.

I frown then, a thought occurring to me. *Flame actually only mentioned Orcus and Reaper.* I assumed his words meant everyone came back together. However…

"Can you sense Maliki and Morpheus?" I ask Serapina, a little frustrated that I can't automatically do that myself. My link to Maliki is subdued, our bond more of a surface-level connection since we've only initially marked one another.

A single bite from me would change that.

Which appears to be what Orcus did with Reaper and Flame. I'm not sure when that happened, or if my suspicion is correct. I just know that their circle deepened their bonds when Alina joined them, and furthered their connections once Thea arrived.

Perhaps they did it as a form of security to ensure they could properly guard their Omega and their child.

Or maybe it's something more.

But I can definitely understand furthering a connection in the name of protection.

I'll need to discuss it with Maliki later.

And Morpheus, too.

"Maliki says they're at the cabin and Morpheus is taking a nap," Serapina mumbles against my chest.

"Morpheus is taking a nap?" I repeat, confused.

"Maliki used another venom-laced knife on him."

My eyebrows lift. "Another venom-laced knife? When did he use the first one?"

"In the Netherworld Village." She's starting to sound

sleepy, perhaps because of my purr. Or maybe it's a result of her residual heat.

Regardless of the cause, I lift her into the air with my hands on her hips, not wanting to risk her collapsing at my feet.

"Morpheus sent Maliki into a nightmare or something," she goes on as her arms weave around my neck. "So Maliki got him back by throwing a knife at him. Morpheus caught it, thinking it was just a dagger. But it was laced with slug venom."

My lips curl. "That sounds like our clever Maliki."

"He used ingredients from his favorite drink today," she tells me, her nose scrunching. "I can't believe I've been pouring those spider ales. I had no idea what they were made of. Not sure I do now, either. But if it was strong enough to knock out Morpheus, I shouldn't have been allowed to serve it."

"You shouldn't have been serving anyone or anything at all," I correct her. "But that's my fault. I should have talked to you."

"I'm glad you didn't," she says, her words hurting a bit.

"You're glad I didn't talk to you?" I phrase it as a question because I'm not sure how to interpret that. "You don't want me?"

She laughs a little. "No, Hades."

I wince.

"No, I mean, I'm glad I had some time to be independent," she clarifies, her palm against my cheek as she clings to me with her opposite arm.

I readjust my hold on her, lifting her even more and slipping one arm under her knees as my opposite braces her back.

A bridal carrying position.

How appropriate.

"I've spent my life always living by someone else's rules," she adds. "It was nice to do something just for me. And while it may have been short-lived, I'm grateful I had the opportunity to prove that I can survive on my own." Her lips twist. "Sort of, anyway."

"You can still make your own choices," I promise her. "But now you have three mates who will fully support those choices, too."

"Three mates," she repeats, her expression turning dreamy. But the look is gone in a blink. "Hey, I want to see your wings. It's not fair that Alina has seen them and I haven't."

I startle, her abrupt conversation change almost as unexpected as her request. "You want to see my wings?"

"Well, yes. You showed them off for another Omega. Two, actually. Alina and Thea. But I haven't seen them. And I… I don't like that."

I blink at her, then start to digest her words and the little petulant pout now forming in her features. "You're jealous."

"No, I'm annoyed."

"And feeling possessive," I add, too pleased by this development to acknowledge her comment. "How very Omega of you, darling mate. I approve."

"You approve of what?" she demands. "Showing me your wings?"

"How about I take you flying?" I suggest. "Would that appease your possessive needs?"

"I didn't say anything about *possessive needs*, Hades."

"You could see the maze from above," I go on, intentionally ignoring her rebuttal. "I've never taken Thea or Alina flying before."

She doesn't immediately respond, her mouth

appearing to be frozen in slight awe. "You won't take them flying, will you?"

"Thea, maybe," I admit. "But only if she asks. Alina, no. Orcus would kill me."

"But you want to take her flying?" my proprietorial little mate demands. "She's my sister!"

"I didn't say I want to take anyone flying other than you, *wife*," I say, ensuring she hears my claim with that single word. "You're the only one I want. The only one I'll ever desire. The only one I *need*. So if you tell me my wings are yours and yours alone, then no one else will ever see them again."

Her full lips part on a sweet gasp, her eyes seeming to glaze over. "Okay."

"Okay?"

"Okay," she says again. "Take me flying, Hades. Please."

MORPHEUS

Maliki…

My head is throbbing, and there's a stinging sensation radiating up through my wrist that will not cease.

All because of a knife.

Fuck. Maliki's antics make me feel almost mortal.

Except a mortal wouldn't have survived such a trick.

Pushing up from the ground, I clench my teeth and force myself to my feet. Brushing the debris from my dress pants, I fix my shirt and reroll the sleeves to my elbows.

It's all a stalling tactic while I attempt to tame the ringing in my ears. Alas, it's still there as I start up the path to the cabin door.

My fingers curl and uncurl, the fists seeming to form of their own accord. Because I really, *really* want to punch Maliki in the face.

Then drag him into a nightmare to teach him just what I can do as his God.

The rebellious fae is waiting for me when I enter, his damp hair and shirtless state suggesting he just exited the shower.

"How long was I out?" I demand.

He lifts a muscular shoulder, then holds out a cup of coffee like it's some sort of peace offering. "Longer than I expected, but also not long enough."

My jaw ticks.

He must notice because his lips curl into a playful grin. "It's not fun feeling helpless to our fate, is it, God of Dreams?"

"You've never been *helpless*, Enforcer."

"Not being able to shadow home makes me *feel* helpless, Morpheus. Just as I assume being paralyzed by venom does the same to you." He steps into my personal space and presses the mug against my chest. "So the next time you want to mist me somewhere without asking, remember that I will *always* return the favor."

I grab the hand holding the coffee cup, then wrap my palm around his nape before he can leave my space. "You're lucky we share a mate, Maliki. Or I would drag you into a nightmare right now and never let you fucking wake up."

He doesn't try to escape me, just stares me down with his intense golden irises. "I'm not afraid of you, God of Dreams."

"You should be," I say, voice low. "But I like that you're not. It'll make this far more fun."

One of his dark brows arches. "Yeah?"

I pull him closer, my grip on the back of his neck causing his head to bow just enough for his messy hair to fall across his forehead. "*Yes.*"

His nostrils flare, his chest seeming to puff upward. "If you kiss me—"

I thread my fingers through his thick hair and yank his head back, cutting off his words, and sink my teeth into his fucking neck.

A growl reverberates from his chest, the sound doing pleasant things to my senses. I suspect our mate would enjoy hearing him do that while choking on my cock.

Perhaps I'll see if that's a fantasy she would enjoy.

Give her the option to dictate what we do to each other.

Force Maliki to *submit.*

Or I would kneel, if that's her preference.

Regardless, playing as a threesome could be fun.

And made even better now that I've *claimed* him.

"*Fuck,*" Maliki snarls. "*What the fuck?*"

I release him with a shove and lick his blood from my bottom lip. "You're mine now, Enforcer." I give him a "Cheers!" motion with the mug, then take a sip of the coffee, the warm liquid pairing nicely with his essence on my tongue.

"*Morpheus.*" I'm not sure if he says my name out loud or in his head. Perhaps both.

Maliki, I return mentally.

And he clutches his head. "Oh, fuck this."

Can't undo an Alpha bite, I'm afraid, I inform him, amused by his sudden fury. I can both feel it and taste it, which is a great combination. "I warned you not to play with knives when we returned, *mate.*"

"I'm going to fucking kill you," he says, coming toward me.

So I mist to the kitchen and set the coffee cup down. "Now, now..."

He shadows to my side, his hand going for the butcher

block that just appeared on the counter. I wish it away with a wave of my hand, already aware of his moves since we're now linked mentally. And I am very much paying attention to his thoughts.

Maliki growls again, the sound feral in nature.

I mist before he can grab me, only to find my throat in a chokehold and my back pressed up against the wall.

Maliki's teeth are suddenly in my fucking neck.

My eyes widen, my mind struggling to understand how he got the upper hand, when I realize that he quickly figured out how to hear *my* motives, too.

Which makes us more or less evenly matched.

And now doubly mated, thanks to his vicious claim.

I go to shove him away when he bites me on the shoulder through my shirt.

"*Fuck.*" I mist, but the fucker comes with me and bites me a third time—this time on the side of my neck—before punching me in the face.

My nose instantly smarts, causing me to gag as my vision blinks in and out.

It's like he hit me with a hammer.

And maybe he did.

Because I've somehow ended up on the floor with him standing over me.

I glare up at him, then note the hand he's holding out for me as a show of a truce.

I blink, startled. He's holding another fresh cup of coffee, and I have no idea when or how he grabbed it.

Then I hear his mental commentary—his *pride*—about giving me another dose of slug venom.

Part of me wants to kill him.

Yet amusement washes over me in the next wave, and all I can do is huff out a laugh. "I'm impressed," I concede.

"As you should be," he drawls, his palm still hovering above me in that peace-offering gesture.

With a shake of my head, I grab it and let him yank me up to my feet. Then he shoves that new cup at me.

"Drink this. It'll help the headache."

I frown, not sure what he means.

But not a second later, the pounding starts, and I become conscious of the fact that he hit me with more than slug venom. He mingled about five or six poisons together.

In his original coffee cup, I realize. "You tricked me."

"I anticipated the need" is all he says in reply. "But don't worry, that cup has the antidote."

There's a retort on my tongue about not believing a word he says. However, I don't bother voicing it since I can hear in his mind that he's telling the truth.

So rather than fight him, I just accept the coffee and finish it completely.

The throbbing eventually subsides, allowing me to see more clearly. "You've been busy," I mutter, taking in all the food on the counter.

"Not really. Just manifesting every food I can think of to see what will tempt Sera when she returns from her flight."

"Flight?" I repeat, lost.

"Hades took her flying," he murmurs. "And our mate is very much enjoying herself."

Blinking, I allow my mind to connect to hers and hear her dreamy sighs and wonder as Hades shows her around Glass Lake. My lips curl a little, pleased to hear that Hades is taking proper care of our Omega. "She's happy."

"She is," Maliki agrees, picking up a croissant. "Wonder how she'll feel about our new bond, *mate*."

I shrug. "It strengthens our circle, which is centered around her. I imagine she'll approve."

"Still wish I had been given a chance to ask her," he drawls, his golden eyes intense once more. "Which brings us to our first order of *mate* business—fucking ask for permission first, Morpheus."

I sigh. "Are you really going to create a rule book?"

"For you? Yeah, I am. Because it's clearly needed." He gives me a look that dares me to argue. "Now grab something to eat and meet me in the dining room. I want to discuss what you found in the other dimension. Then I'll decide if I can forgive you for dragging me there."

It was a worthwhile trip, I nearly tell him.

But hearing his mind, I know that won't be good enough.

So I nod.

Then manifest myself a stiff drink instead of taking any food.

And join him at the table.

"You have a very strange obsession with food," I inform him, amused by his penchant for feeding everyone around him. "You realize we're all immortal, yes?"

"Food provides comfort." He leans back in his chair. "But I honestly get just as much enjoyment from stabbing people. So if you would prefer that activity"—a blade appears, and he twirls it between his fingers—"I would be happy to oblige you, God of Dreams."

"Always so violent," I murmur. "I like you, Maliki."

"Is that why you almost kissed me earlier?"

My lips curl. "When I kiss you, it will be for our mate's enjoyment."

One of his dark brows lifts. "*When*?" He huffs out a laugh. "I will fucking bite you if you try."

"Something Serapina might also enjoy," I muse, letting

my eyes track over his muscled form. "There are a lot of intriguing things we could do with her between us. Things that would very likely enhance the experience for our Omega."

He picks up a glass as it manifests on the table, the liquid amber in color. "I'm not opposed to that."

"I know." I tap my head. "I can hear your intrigue, Enforcer."

"Then you know I'll never submit to you."

"To me? No. To Serapina? Perhaps."

He leans back in his chair. "Sera's pleasure is all that matters to me."

"Then we're in agreement that we'll play if it benefits her," I say. "Or if she asks us to."

One of his muscular shoulders lifts in a partial shrug. "I've always enjoyed group play. My limits are… nonexistent."

"Which makes the experience all the more intriguing," I muse, taking a sip of my ambrosia. Then I set it aside and lean forward. "So, about our field trip…"

HADES'S OBSIDIAN FEATHERS ARE THE SOFTEST TEXTURE IN all the dimensions. I can't stop stroking his wings, my focus on him more than the maze below us.

Though, I did somewhat pay attention as he pointed out all the various areas throughout our flight.

Glass Lake isn't made of glass, but of chunks of ice. And it's surrounded by a park littered with fire lilies and frozen trees. It's such a unique landscape that I absolutely wanted to explore.

However, it's currently being inhabited by my sister and her mates, so I didn't ask Hades to pause our flight for a walkabout.

Instead, I held on as he continued to fly and admired the intricate weave of frigid vines and fiery flowers. The trees were also covered in bright blue leaves, their limbs as frozen as the rest of the maze.

It was a gorgeous area to observe.

As was the heart-shaped Ice Cave—a place Hades said

we would need to return to, as the inside is apparently crystallized in a myriad of azure and sapphire shades.

The rest of the labyrinth consists of corridors and false ends and winding paths. But it's all so intricate and beautiful.

"I can't believe you manifested all of this," I say as he sets us both down outside of Death's Cabin. "And it's all under the Netherworld Kingdom?"

He considers that for a moment. "Yes and no. It's connected in a unique way that no one other than our mate-circle can access. Well, and Orcus's circle now. But no one else in the Netherworld Kingdom can enter, nor do they even know it exists. It had to be that way to keep certain Hell Fae out."

"Hell Fae?" I echo.

"Primarily Typhos Lucifer," he mutters. "As the Hell Fae King, he reigns over the Hell Fae Realm. And the Netherworld Kingdom is part of that realm; ergo, it's technically under his jurisdiction. However, this labyrinth is all my creation and therefore not a space he can enter."

"That sounds very complicated."

"It is," he admits as he combs his fingers through my hair. "He's the ruler of the Hell Fae, which includes all of the Netherworld Fae. However, I'm the one the Netherworld Fae worship. They think my presence provides them protection."

"Does it?" I wonder out loud, my brow furrowing a little. "Do you guard them?"

"No." It's a flat answer. "And yes."

I stare at him. "Because that's not confusing at all."

His lips twitch. "I don't actively do anything, but my presence scares off potential threats. Most faedoms fear Mythos Fae Alphas. We're powerful."

"So what would you do if someone attacked the

Netherworld Kingdom?" I ask as his palm finds my lower back.

He doesn't immediately reply, just guides me toward the door, his wings vanishing from sight.

I'm about to protest, but he says, "It would depend on the reason for their assault."

I frown. "So you would potentially let an external force attack the Netherworld Fae?" I stop walking and face him. "Would you let your fae get hurt?"

"That's not what I said," he murmurs. "You asked what I would do, and I stated that it would depend on the motive. There is a wide array of punishments at my disposal, Serapina. I would not allow harm to befall the fae under my dominion. But my *reaction* to the attack would absolutely vary by situation."

"Oh." My lips twist. "So you do… care about your fae?"

"My domain and the inhabitants within it are a responsibility," he tells me. "As far as me caring for anyone… I care about *you*." He leans down to brush his lips against mine. "I care about the life inside you." His hand caresses my belly. "And I care about our mate-circle." He opens the door.

And Maliki is waiting on the other side, his arms folded across his bare chest and a scowl on his face.

"I realize Persephone is your soulmate, but you cannot continue to refer to her as the *life inside* of Sera. Yeah, she has access to your *dead mate's* memories, but she's not a fucking sarcophagus, Hades. She's our female. Our Omega. Our *mate*. And you will respect her as a person, not as a bloody cenotaph."

My eyes are wide by the end of his rant, his fury a whip to my senses. "Uh, Maliki—"

"No, trouble. Don't you dare tell me that what he said

is okay. I understand that you've embraced your former life, but he needs to start focusing on the future, not the past. Or we will *never* move forward."

"Okay, but—"

"No," Maliki says again, his hand wrapping around my hip as he pulls me away from Hades. "No making excuses for him, Sera. You are more than just your soul."

Hades clears his throat. "That's true. She's so much more than her *soul*."

Maliki grunts and starts guiding me toward the dining area.

Because of course he has more food.

But Morpheus is waiting there in a suit, his blue-green eyes dancing over me appreciatively. "Did you enjoy your flight, little dreamer?"

"Yes," I tell him, then realize that he must have wings, too. "Are your feathers as dark as Hades's?"

His lips curl. "No, not in the slightest. Want to see them?"

I nod, eager. "Yes. Please. Now."

One silver brow inches upward, but he pushes away from the table. "All right." He starts toward me just as a gorgeous display of white plumes appears behind him, the wings somehow forming despite his dress shirt.

The same happened with Hades earlier. "I just alter the clothing with a thought," he told me. "It's… instinctual."

That word is one I'm starting to loathe since nothing feels *instinctual* to me, thanks to whatever Demeter has done to my Omega soul.

But I ignore my irritation and focus on Morpheus's wings instead. "Wow," I breathe, reaching for him. Then I pause and whisper, "Can I touch you?"

His smile is the definition of dazzling, his handsome

features almost too alluring to be real. *He truly is the God of Dreams.*

That I am, love, he replies into my mind.

Out loud, he says, "You can always touch me, Serapina. I'm yours entirely."

Between his comment and Hades's words outside, I'm starting to feel really warm.

That warmth increases as Morpheus wraps his white wings around me, forming a cocoon with just the two of us inside. I shiver, my gaze drawn to the hints of gold decorating the tips of his feathers. His majestic plumes are… hypnotizing. Dreamlike. *Otherworldly.*

I almost feel like we should be lost in some sort of fantasy, with Morpheus wearing royal robes of some kind and me… in a white dress to match his wings.

My eyes fall closed as I imagine it, my fingers gliding through his feathers and shivering at the tingles the soft texture provokes within me.

So similar to Hades's wings.

Yet different, too.

And they're both mine, I marvel, dizzy with the realization. *I'm mated to two…* Gods.

Three, Morpheus whispers back into my mind. *Maliki might not be a Mythos Fae, but he's just as much of an Alpha as Hades and me.*

I swallow, nodding as an enchantment swirls over my skin. I sense it kissing the hairs along my arms, stirring static electricity through my being.

It leaves me feeling dizzy and overwhelmed, my eyes opening to identify the source.

And I gasp when I find Morpheus dressed in the same blue robes as my mental fantasy.

He's shirtless beneath the robe, his muscles flexing in clear welcome. Or that's the way my hands translate his attire because I'm no longer stroking his wings; I'm tracing the ridges of his abs as his feathers continue to hold us in a soft cocoon.

"I like this dress on you," he murmurs, luring my gaze down to the white gown he's somehow dressed me in.

I can't even remember what I was wearing before. But it certainly wasn't *this*. It's white with gold adornments—the flash of it catching my attention and causing me to glance at my shoulder. "Am I dreaming?" I ask him, wondering when we left reality.

Not that I even know what reality is anymore.

I just went flying with Hades.

And I'm pregnant.

"You're pregnant?" Maliki asks, shattering my fantasy bubble.

"That's what I meant when I said I cared about the soul inside her," Hades says conversationally. "In case you were wondering."

Morpheus draws his wings back, his hands on my cheeks to hold my attention on him. "You're pregnant?" His voice is a lot less startled than Maliki's, more... more *hopeful*, I think.

"That's what Alina senses, yes." The words come out a bit hoarse, my mind struggling to keep up with the changing events. The shift in sensations. *The very real need to nestle into Morpheus's embrace...*

He smells like sin.

Silk sheets.

Sensual chocolate.

Thorns, I don't know if this is a result of his wings—maybe they possess some sort of magical aphrodisiac—but all I want to do right now is *climb him*.

His blue-green eyes widen, his hands suddenly on my

hips. "I can make that dream come true, too. Just say the words."

"Hold on," Maliki interjects. "Can we talk about this? Are we sure she's pregnant?"

"I can't sense it," Hades tells him. "But Alina seems to have a knack for seeing around Demeter's mirages. And she said she can sense a new life inside of Serapina."

"It would make sense," Morpheus murmurs, his eyes still holding mine, his hands hot against my hips. "If she's been in heat… she could very well be pregnant from the other day."

"Or still in heat," I whisper, pressing my nose into his chest.

His purr ignites, causing my legs to shake.

I have no idea what's come over me.

But all three of my men suddenly smell *amazing*.

Maliki's smoke and leather.

Hades's wintry kiss.

Morpheus's decadence.

He traces my spine, his palm securing my nape as his opposite hand remains on my hip. "Hmm," he hums, leaning down to kiss me.

It's not a soft touch or a whisper of lips.

It's… it's *hungry*.

Domineering.

Exactly what I need. What I crave. What I *demand*.

He holds me to him as he takes my mouth with abandon, destroying me with his tongue, owning me with his growls, and mastering me with his strength.

I'm practically weeping in his arms by the time he releases me, tears gracing my eyes as I nearly beg him to do more.

I barely recognize myself.

I'm not this person. I don't… I don't just *collapse* for a man.

But I feel like I'm going to die if he stops touching me.

"Morpheus…"

"Shh," he hushes, the world moving around us. "I've got you, little dreamer."

"We've got you," another voice says.

Hades.

I feel him behind me, his dominance seeping into my being and making me turn toward him on instinct. He's waiting for me, his arms catching me as I fall into his embrace.

And then he's kissing me like Morpheus did, his taste so different yet equally as addictive.

I claw at his shoulders, hating that he's clothed. Hating that I don't have access to more of him.

He growls, his commanding presence wrapping around me in a tight hold, demanding that I submit.

But I don't want to bow.

I want to *strip.*

So I rip at his jacket and dress shirt, not caring at all that I'm acting like a feral beast. He's mine, and he's denied me access to his Alpha form.

"Fuck," Maliki breathes.

And I realize he's right next to me, too.

His hand is on my hip.

I don't know when he started touching me, but I suddenly need to feel him. My Maliki. *My mate.*

He rumbles in response, his mental voice a kiss to my senses as I lean toward him to give him my mouth. There isn't an ounce of hesitation as he returns my need, his tongue dancing with mine while I continue to divest Hades of his clothes.

"When did our Omega become the Dominant?" Morpheus asks, sounding amused.

"Pretty sure she has us all by our cocks," Maliki says against my mouth.

Cocks.

Yes.

I try to find Hades's *knot*, to free him from his pants. But his hand catches my wrist, and he pushes me back. "No."

That single word has me pulling away from Maliki, my mind fracturing beneath the rejection. "*No?*"

Everything around me… trembles.

The world no longer feels right.

My heart stops beating.

"Serapina," Hades breathes, his hands on my face.

But I don't want to look at him. I don't want to be near him. I can't handle his… his…

A purr wraps around me, the sound so intense that my knees buckle.

Or maybe it's a growl.

I… I can't tell the difference.

My entire being is lost to that rumble. Submitting without thought. Falling… into a cloud…

Air infuses my lungs, reminding me to breathe.

My lips are occupied by the taste of a familiar male. The peppermint bite of winter. Encased in a field of roses. *A winter wonderland…*

There's leather, too.

And silk.

All around me. Holding me. Touching me. Stroking my bare skin.

I'm no longer clothed. It's a beautiful realization, one that lets me feel *free*. And there's a heaviness on top of me, one that I've not experienced before.

Masculine and strong.

My Alpha.

He's still kissing me, loving me with his tongue, caressing me with his hands. "Hades," I whisper, aware that it's him. "Please don't reject me."

"I would never reject you, Serapina," he says against my mouth. "But I want you properly prepared to take me."

My brow furrows. "I'm prepared."

"You're not," he tells me, and I'm pretty sure there's a chuckle underlining those two words. "But Maliki is going to ensure that you are."

I'm about to ask what he means when I feel something wet between my legs. A kiss. *A tongue.* "Ohhh…" And I'm pulsing deep inside, too.

Maliki's mark.

It's vibrating.

Driving me to a point of no return.

Causing me to see stars as his mouth seals around my clit.

I scream, the sensation enough to clear my vision and mind for a long, necessary moment.

I'm in the bedroom, surrounded by my fae. Morpheus is lounging alongside me, his hand on his cock as he slowly strokes it. Maliki is drawing out my orgasm with his expert touch. And Hades is on my opposite side, his palm on my throat as he coaxes my gaze up to his.

"Serapina."

"Hades." I blink at him. "I don't understand what's happening."

"I think your inner Omega is trying to break free," he tells me. "Remember what I said about following your instincts?"

There's that word again.

I nearly growl at it.

But instead, I clench my jaw and nod.

Because if this is what I need to do… well, I can think of worse ways to free my Omega.

"Knot me, Alpha," I tell Hades, feeling bold. Feeling needy. Feeling *ready*. "*That* is what my instincts are telling me I need. So give me your knot."

His dark eyes hold mine, his expression giving nothing away.

And for one horrifying second, I worry he's going to say *no* again.

However, he leans down and presses his lips to mine instead. Then brings his mouth to my ear and whispers, "Be a good girl and suck Maliki's cock. Then I'll consider giving you my knot."

I'M BEING HARD ON SERAPINA, BUT IT'S WHAT SHE NEEDS. IF we're going to shatter this mirage—this *curse*—then I need her inner Omega pissed off and ready to fight for her claim.

I told Serapina to follow her instincts, and this is me following mine.

There's a hint of challenge in her gaze now, one that tells me I've said something unexpected… and *right*.

Because now she wants to prove herself worthy of my knot.

Which is the opposite of what should be happening here. Alphas prove their worth to Omegas, not the other way around.

However, nothing about this situation is ordinary.

Omegas run. Alphas chase. Then we breed. A life is created. And the Omega nests.

That's how our mating process works.

Though, with Persephone, I took a suppressant to ensure we never created a life. Which definitely went against the norm. So I suppose it's only fate that her reincarnation would be different, too.

But this goes so much deeper than an abnormality.

This is the result of another Alpha tampering with the fertility cycle of an Omega.

And that Omega is now fighting back.

I can see it in her fiery sapphire eyes. She's glaring at me with a determination that promises revenge.

My lips curl, intrigued.

Because she's going to take that frustration out on Maliki.

Serves him right for how he treated us upon our return. Oh, he may have muttered an apology my way—one I don't think Serapina heard—but that doesn't mean I've completely forgiven him.

Serapina is going to help me punish him.

With her sweet fucking mouth.

She slides her long fingers into Maliki's hair and pulls him away from her pussy. His mouth is glistening with the evidence of her arousal, his gold irises swirling with his own need.

He looks only at her, his focus clear.

She's his.

And she captivates his every move.

"Tell me where you want me, sweet mystery," he says.

"In my mouth," she replies. "So come up here and feed me your cock."

Fuck, her filthy words make my knot pulse.

I don't know who taught her to say that or if she just picked up the language from Morpheus's or Maliki's mind, but it's exactly the right thing to say.

Maliki crawls over her to kiss her dirty mouth, his

praise coming through with his tongue as he presses his groin against her slick heat.

"Don't you dare fuck her cunt," I tell him. "I want to watch you *feed* her, just like she demanded."

Morpheus hums in approval, his hand on his knot as he watches Maliki and Serapina.

"See how tight her ass is while you're down there," he says.

I arch a brow at him.

And he arches one right back. "Don't tell me you've never wanted to double knot an Omega before, Hades."

It's not a concept I've ever allowed myself to entertain. But his words absolutely have me pondering it now. "Do what Morpheus says, Maliki."

"I don't answer to either of you" is Maliki's response as he thrusts into Serapina. "Sera is my boss now, remember?" His gold eyes glance up at me, the look one that dares me to fight him.

It's a dare he emboldens with another punch of his hips, the motion causing Serapina to moan deeply.

"Hmm." I lean down to press my lips to Serapina's ear. "Make him fuck your mouth, darling. Or I won't give you my knot."

Serapina ignores me for a moment, but I know she heard me. So I let her decide how to proceed, and lean back to watch as Maliki continues to take her with abandon.

His tattoos writhe with the movements, his body sleek and powerful against hers, and stir the most delicious of moans from our mate's mouth.

But after a few more enthusiastic seconds, she pulls Maliki's lips away from hers and says, "I want your cock in my mouth. Please."

"Mmm…" He nuzzles her cheek, the sweet gesture at

odds with how roughly he was just taking her pussy. "If I put my dick in your mouth, I'm going to expect you to swallow everything I give you, trouble. Think you can handle that?"

The challenge in his tone suggests he understands the assignment—we need to push her Omega. Either he sensed that in my intentions via our tentative bond or…

Or Morpheus told him, I realize, locking gazes with my cousin. "You mated Maliki." I didn't pick up on it when Serapina and I returned, my best friend's angry welcome having distracted me entirely.

However, I feel it now, the live-wire current running between him and Morpheus.

They're not just initially joined, but also fully connected.

"Jealous?" Maliki asks me, a wicked glint in his gaze. "Want me to bite you again, *my lord*?"

My jaw ticks. I have no idea what has transpired between my cousin and my best friend, but three of them—Serapina, Maliki, and Morpheus—have all bitten one another, forming the perfect mate-circle.

And I've only been bitten once—by Maliki.

So, yes, I'm very fucking jealous.

It's an emotion I ensure my best friend feels as he stares me down. Triumph glitters in his gaze for a beat, then he starts kissing a path down our Omega's body to resume feasting on her cunt. Only, he pivots over her so he's upside down and slides his slick cock right into her waiting mouth.

There is no mercy.

He fucks her lips like he did her pussy, causing our mate to gag. She grabs his ass, her nails biting into his flesh as she tries to force him off of her.

"Remember your safe motion, Serapina," I tell her. "A fist in the air. Do that and he'll stop."

She responds by changing the position of her hands to push him downward instead of trying to yank him off, her determination evident.

Fuck, she's tenacious.

Skilled.

Strong.

I love seeing her like this, taking Maliki's brutality while urging him to go harder.

I can almost taste her slick, her own climax already rising.

Because she was made for this—made for *us*.

And we are finally going to free her inner Omega.

Morpheus draws his fingers along her cheek, his gaze admiring as he says, "You're taking him perfectly, little dreamer. I can't wait to watch you swallow his seed."

She shudders, and I swear I hear a little mewl escape her, but then it's all groans and suction and wet sounds.

Maliki is practically vibrating, his smoky tendrils swirling all over as he taunts Serapina with his sensual touch.

It's amazing to watch, the two of them well matched in every way.

And then he's coming down her throat, his growl one that resonates deep within me.

Serapina flounders a little, his cock choking her as he comes with a ferocity I can almost feel.

Morpheus watches closely, his expression telling me he'll yank Maliki off of her the moment this becomes too much.

But our Omega sucks down every drop, just like she should.

"Keep going," I tell them both. "I want Serapina to come again."

Because she hasn't exploded a second time, and I'd like her to fall apart at least one more time before I take over.

Maliki doesn't fight me this time, his mind set on her pleasure.

However, he flips them on the bed, his shadows writhing all over with the movement since he shifted her with his power rather than with his hands.

Her eyes are wide, her mind trying to compute what just happened, so I fist her hair and hold her in place. "Suck his cock, wife. I want to see him come down your throat again."

Her gaze darts over to me, her nostrils flaring as she tries to breathe.

"Show me you can swallow more than a single load so I know you can handle my knot," I tell her, my voice deep with intent. "It's been two thousand years since I've fucked anyone. Two thousand years of building up my seed. If you want it, you'll have to prove you can take what I have to give."

I release her hair, curious to see what she'll do.

She stares me down, her expression darkening as she stops trying to breathe and takes more of Maliki in her mouth.

I smile, letting her see my admiration. "Such a good wife," I praise her. "Now come all over his face for me."

"For us," Morpheus inserts, his hand trailing down her spine to her ass. "I need some of your sweet slick, little dreamer. It'll help us stretch you."

Serapina trembles, her eyes falling closed as Morpheus's fingers slide lower to where Maliki is feasting. She jolts, then groans at Morpheus's touch.

I can't see it from this angle, but it's clear he just penetrated her cunt. Because in the next moment, she's falling apart and gushing all over Maliki, just like I desired.

"Fuck, you're beautiful," I say, admiring her fight as she tries to keep pleasuring Maliki while losing herself to the bliss of her own climax. "Just scream around his cock, darling. He'll love it."

She does, the sound almost a growl as his shaft vibrates in her mouth.

He groans between her legs, his body strung tight as he unloads again, the euphoric moment clearly having tipped him over the edge. And unexpectedly, too, if his curse is any indication.

I smirk, amused by his unintended explosion. "That was new, Maliki."

"Fuck you," he grinds out, utterly lost to his oblivion.

Serapina manages to swallow despite her own rapture, her throat working as she forgets how to breathe and focuses solely on taking his seed.

"Exquisite," I say, combing my fingers through her hair. "You're incredible, wife. Coming all over his face while sucking out every available drop." I draw my touch to her neck and trace a line downward as she swallows again. "Fucking glorious, darling."

She quivers, her nails digging into Maliki's hips. A deep groan escapes her as Morpheus's touch shifts backward, his finger finding her little rosebud and pushing through the tight ring to begin stretching her.

"What do you think, Omega?" I ask, my lips at her ear again. "Can you take two knots?"

It'll feel different for her from behind, the bulb not actually attaching inside her back there. But the copious amounts of cum will be the same, our inner Alpha beasts longing to drench our mate inside and out with our heated claims.

Serapina releases Maliki's cock with a pop, her blue

eyes radiating challenge as she looks at me. "Knot me and find out."

Her sultry voice has my inner Alpha growling in response, the slight rasp of her tone a fucking aphrodisiac that I can't ignore.

She sounds like sex.

And she's radiating need.

I grab her and kiss her, my control seeming to snap.

All I want is to feel her. Worship her. *Claim her.*

But I won't force this. She has to choose me first. And I won't demand that it happen tonight.

What I truly want is for her Omega soul to be freed, for Serapina to finally be able to embrace her fae nature.

I can see hints of her Mythos Fae immortality already shining through, her body proving to be capable of taking far more than her human mirage.

Because I don't think she inhaled properly the entire time she sucked Maliki off.

Serapina moans into my mouth, her body twisting in response to Morpheus's touch and Maliki's tongue.

They're preparing her the way a mate-circle should, ensuring she'll be able to take what her Alphas are about to give her. I can't be gentle. Not after waiting eons for this reunion. It might not be the way I always pictured it would be, but I could never have fathomed Serapina's existence.

And I'm glad for that.

Because if I had known this gorgeous female was my future, the last two thousand years would have been that much more agonizing.

Serapina is perfection. She's the Omega I never knew I needed. The epitome of my deepest desires. The queen to my king. A partner. An equal. *My everything.*

I tell her all of this with my tongue, my fingers weaving

through her hair as I anchor her to me for an even deeper kiss.

I've lost sight of my plans. Given up my control to my beast. Forgotten what I originally intended. And simply exist with her in this moment.

Swallowing her cries of pleasure. Her whimpers. Her *pleas*.

When she reaches for my knot, I don't stop her. I let her stroke me, feel the heat of her touch searing me to my very soul.

"Fuck, Serapina," I breathe against her lips. I stretch out alongside her and Maliki, my grip in her hair forcing her to lean toward me.

She takes it a step further by sliding off of Maliki and pressing her body into mine. I go to my back, curious to see what my Omega has in mind, and hiss when she straddles my hips.

Her slick pussy kisses my shaft, making my knot throb with want. "Serapina…" Her name sounds like a prayer.

I feel enslaved to her wants and needs. Utterly consumed by her presence.

Her hand is still between us, her fingers around my knot.

She sits up and lifts her hips to angle my cock upward.

I know what she's going to do.

Can see the desire in her pretty eyes.

I want to grab her, shove her into the bed beneath me, and thrust into her dripping heat. But I can barely breathe, let alone move.

She's a Goddess. *My* Goddess. And all I can do is bow to her command. Let her lead. Give her what she desires.

A growl rumbles through my chest as my head meets her entrance.

Serapina stills, her eyes holding mine. "I need a new safe word."

My eyebrow wings upward. That's not at all what I expected her to say.

"I want to be able to scream your name," she adds, still hovering there, taunting me with her weeping heat. "Please."

The final word does something to me. It makes me snap out of this enchanted daze and sit up with her in my lap, my hands on her face as I pull her closer.

Her tits are fucking perfection against my bare chest, her body molding to mine in a way that confirms we're destined for one another.

"Tell us your new safe word, wife." I lace my voice with the command I know she needs, my hand moving to her nape. "Then put my cock in your pussy and lean into me so Morpheus can take your ass."

SERA

I HAVE NO IDEA WHAT I'M DOING OR HOW WE ALL ENDED UP here. But I can't fight the need clawing at my insides.

It's suffocating my mind, overwhelming my body, and lighting me on fire from within.

My mates want a safe word. Only, I don't think I need one. They won't hurt me. I know that deep inside my soul.

However, they want me to have this power, to be able to make them stop should I need to.

So I pick a word that I know well, one that describes what I expected from my future.

A word that no longer applies to my situation or *us*.

"Alone."

Hades stares at me, his dark eyes searching my features. "You'll never be alone, Serapina."

"I know," I whisper. "That's what makes it the perfect safe word. Because I'll never feel alone when I'm with all of you."

Understanding deepens the midnight color of his irises,

his expression shifting into something beautiful. Intense. *Loving.*

And then he's kissing me again, his tongue whispering words I can almost taste in my mind.

Only, we're not fully mated yet.

Not like me and Morpheus.

Or even Morpheus and Maliki—a fact I've just begun to wrap my head around. I heard Hades say it, listened to Maliki's reply, but haven't had a moment to fully process it.

Except, now isn't the time. I'm too busy being consumed by Hades's mouth to think about much else.

Oh, and Morpheus's touch… He's tracing my spine again, slipping down my backside to the forbidden place he prodded before.

I'm not sure how many fingers he inserted into me, maybe two or three, but it made me feel full. Especially with Maliki teasing my core with his tongue.

However, now I'm in Hades's lap, and it's his cock that I'm holding against my heated center. His thick head that I long to slip inside me.

"Tell us your new safe word, wife," he said moments ago. "Then put my cock in your pussy…"

Yes, I think, angling him toward my entrance. *Yes…*

He's thicker than Morpheus and Maliki, his girth stretching me in a way I've not experienced since losing my virginity to Maliki.

But I accept the slight pinch and force myself to take Hades, to slide him into my waiting heat, and slowly lower myself more firmly in his lap.

"*Hades,*" I hiss, feeling so incredibly full that I almost pull away from him.

Except, I *know* we fit.

I've felt it in my dreams. Experienced the pain followed by the inexplicable pleasure.

It may have been my mind mixing past memories with a renewed reality, but I have faith in my imagination.

This is right.

Hades is mine.

And his knot…

Ohhhh, I'm going to accept every inch.

Then experience an oblivion unlike any other.

All my mates are different.

Maliki with his vibrations—which I feel starting inside me right now.

Morpheus with his tender touches and wicked thoughts—ones that are humming through our bond as he kneels behind me.

And Hades, with his deep-seated passion and overwhelming desire.

They're all taking me to new heights, lighting me on fire from within, and introducing me to a future that I never knew could be possible.

"Distract her," Morpheus murmurs, his words causing Hades to release me from his kiss.

A protest begins to form on my lips, but Maliki swallows it with his tongue, his mouth suddenly consuming mine with blinding passion.

I moan, lost to his embrace as Hades licks a path down my chest to taunt my nipples with his teeth.

Bite me, I long to beg him. *Bite me right there.*

Only, instead, he traces the mark Morpheus left on my breast. I want to ask him if he's okay, if it bothers him, but the way he's laving the scar suggests he likes it. Or maybe he can tell that it tingles when he licks me there and he's trying to inspire more of that sensation.

My insides vibrate, causing Hades to freeze against me. "What the *fuck* is that?"

"A gift from Maliki," Morpheus replies, his lips against

my neck as his hands roam up and down my spine. "It's delightful, isn't it?"

"You marked her cunt?" Hades demands, no longer licking my breast.

"I did." The two words brush my lips. "She bit my cock, which immensely pleased me. And now, I can please her whenever I desire."

"Hmm." The sound that leaves Hades isn't angry so much as thoughtful. He thrusts up into me, his full size making me gasp as I accept every single inch.

The thrumming deep inside intensifies, almost making me feel Maliki and Hades together in the most unique way.

I nearly fall back into Morpheus, but Maliki's fist in my hair forces me back into his embrace, and his mouth demands my focus.

It's so intense.

So insane.

So good…

Hades plays with my breasts, his hands molding to them, his lips tracing my skin, his tongue *teasing*.

Maliki kisses me with a passion that stokes the already burning fire within me, his mark humming rhythmically.

And Morpheus… *Oh, Morpheus…*

Little dreamer, he whispers back into my mind, his lips caressing my neck. *This is going to hurt, but I promise we'll make it good for you. Trust me, Serapina. Trust* us.

I'm not sure how any of this could hurt at all. He's applying pressure in a delicious way, his fingers working inside me as his other hand roams along my side, down to my hips, to my behind.

I pout when he removes his touch, but Maliki is having none of that. He nips at my bottom lip, reprimanding me for losing focus. His tongue demands entry, his mouth captivating me all over again as Hades nibbles the mark on my nipple.

Electricity zips along my spine, my insides clenching around Hades's shaft.

It's overwhelming.

It's extraordinary.

It's intoxicating.

I moan, my body alive in a way I've never—

Pain rips through me, causing my eyes to widen as Morpheus enters me in a single thrust. His lips are against my ear, his purr a soothing rumble at my back.

"Shh, little dreamer," he hushes me before I can even scream. "I know it's a lot to take, love. But your body was made for this—for us. Just try to relax, okay?"

Tears spring to my eyes, my mind fracturing beneath the shock of agony. Only for Morpheus's purr to lull me into a state of… of *comfort.*

Hades adds his own reverberation, as does Maliki with his mark deep inside me, and I'm instantly conflicted about how I feel.

It hurts.

It's pleasure personified.

I'm scared.

But I'm also… *safe.*

And so full.

Oh, thorns, I'm about to explode.

Hades is all the way inside me, and so is Morpheus, their cocks far too large to be in me at the same time. Panic steals over me, followed by a wave of quiet as more of that delicious thrumming warms my blood.

"I'm so confused," I moan, my lips still against Maliki. "I… I don't know… I… I'm not sure…"

"You can take it," Hades assures me, his mouth leaving my breast as his hips punch upward another impossible inch. "You're an Omega, Serapina. Fucking embrace it." He punctuates his words by grabbing my nape and pulling me in for a domineering kiss.

It isn't gentle.

It isn't a request.

It's a *demand.*

As is the way he starts moving inside me, not giving me time to acclimate or to accept what's happened. He wants me to know I can handle this. That my body was built for an Alpha. For *him.*

No, not just him… *them.*

Because Morpheus is moving now, too. Proving with each thrust that I'm okay. That the sting was only temporary. That this… this is… *Oh, stars…*

I…

I don't…

I arch back into Morpheus, trying to writhe.

Because I feel *alive.*

Like I'm on fire in the best way.

A Goddess trapped between two Gods.

An Omega being taken by her Alphas.

It's *amazing.* So empowering. So right. *So euphoric.*

"There's our Goddess," Hades murmurs, his lips against my throat now. "Come out and play with your Gods, mate. Let us worship you the way you were intended to be worshipped."

"Fuck, this is the hottest thing I've ever seen," Maliki breathes.

"We're only just getting started," Hades promises. "Scream for us, Serapina. Scream for all the dimensions to hear."

A dark part of me wants to deny him. To test him. To make him *work for it.*

I don't recognize that part of me, but I let her free.

Because yeah, I want him to fuck me harder. To *knot me.*

If he wants my voice, he'll have to force me to use it.

A chuckle rumbles through him, amusement curling his cruel lips. "You feel that, Cousin? That defiance?"

"Yes," Morpheus responds, his fingers threading through my hair as he pulls my mouth toward his. "Let's give our Goddess what she needs."

Ice and heat mingle across my skin, the sensation stirring goose bumps all over my arms and down my legs. Somewhere there is fire. Somewhere there is snow. I… I can't see it. But I can feel it.

And my Alphas are fucking me *hard.*

I can feel them meeting in the middle, their cocks stretching me in a way that shouldn't be possible.

"Join us, Maliki," Morpheus says, his fingers still in my hair. "Feed our Omega more cum."

"Fucking gladly," he replies as Morpheus pushes me sideways toward Maliki's waiting groin.

Thorns, the way I'm bending should hurt. And I think… I think it does. But it also feels good, especially as Maliki's cock slides between my lips.

I'm straddling Hades, feeling him so deep inside me.

Morpheus is kneeling behind me, taking my ass while pushing my head down onto Maliki.

I'm no longer in control of my body. Just being taken by my mates. Driving me into a plane of insanity. An existence full of sensation and sinful pleasures.

I let them take me.

Let them own me.

Let them *possess* me.

Because I'm the heart of all this. The star in their circle. The light they all crave to deprave with their inner darkness.

I'm panting.

Crying.

Dying to scream.

But I can't because I'm so full of *them.*

They're in charge now, and I'm submitting. Giving them everything. Trusting them to take me flying. To make me fall apart. To meet me in the world of oblivion.

It's sensational.

It's unbelievable.

It's *freeing.*

Thorns, yes…

I'm free.

I'm who I'm meant to be—their Omega. Their mate. *Their Goddess.*

Words fill my mind and my ears, my mates praising me for this gift. For this experience. *For accepting them…*

"Fuck, you feel so good, little dreamer." *Morpheus.*

"You're taking all of us, just like I knew you could, wife." *Hades.*

"I think I'm addicted to your throat, trouble." *Maliki.*

"Keep writhing, just like that. Milk us, mate." *Hades.*

"Shh, we're almost there." *Morpheus.*

"*Shadows*, I'm about to drown you, Sera…" *Maliki.*

"Swallow, wife."

"I'm about to fill your ass."

"Styx, your throat…"

"My knot is going to destroy your cunt, darling."

"I'm not going to be able to hold back for much longer, little dreamer. Once I start…"

"*Fuck,*" all three of them say in unison, and my world explodes in an array of color. Golds. Silvers. Whites. Blacks. I… I can't see. It's blinding. It's profound. *It's soul-destroying.*

My world detonates.

My soul *screams*.

My heart shatters.

My lungs cease to function.

The world around me is ripped away in a tidal wave of intense sensation that blinds my senses to a point of numbness.

And my grip on reality fades.

I'm no longer human.

I'm no longer alive.

I'm no longer anything at all.

Just pleasure.

A dancing spirit.

Lost in a sea of nothingness.

Until everything comes crashing back to me, my body spasming to life as echoes of intensity ricochet through my limbs. I can't stop trembling.

Someone hums.

Another purrs.

A knot pulses inside me on repeat. No. *Two.*

Thorns, Morpheus is… is connected…

Sorry, little dreamer, he whispers. *I didn't know that would happen…*

I'm not upset. I'm not in pain. I'm just… I'm attached to him and Hades. Forced to writhe. To experience an unending sensation as their knots hold me captive in a spiral of ecstasy.

The world wavers again.

Colors.

More blinding lights.

Another orgasm, or the continuation of the first one. I don't… I don't know. It's all rolling into a rapturous loop of impossibility.

More quakes.

More *shattering*.

More… more…

I…

There's something… a snapping. My heart beating too fast. My soul screaming in agony.

No. Not my soul.

It's…

I can't figure out what I'm feeling. What I'm sensing. But the moment I almost understand, I'm taken under by another wave of excruciating pleasure.

I can't breathe. I'm drowning. There's too much seed. Too much masculinity. Too much…

Thornsss…

I'm whirling again, crying out this time at the unending sensations. I need it to stop. To focus on the… on the…

"*Hades,*" I pant. "*Hades, please…*" I can't figure out how to explain what's happening. It feels amazing, and yet something is breaking. Something has my soul in a chokehold.

I fight against the invisible entity, begging for my spirit to be *mine*. To be *whole*. To be *right*.

But the hook…

"The plane," I whisper, my eyes widening as the room comes back into view. "*The Omegas.*"

I feel them now.

Their souls.

Reaching for mine.

Yanking me back.

It's the plane of nonexistence.

The place Demeter made.

I'm the heart. The soul. *The anchor*.

A gasp escapes me, and I grab Hades's shoulders. "*Bite me.*"

No, that's not right.

I meant to say… I meant to say…

My eyes widen, understanding grasping me by the throat. "Wait—"

Blackness overtakes me.

My soul yanked back to that place.

To restore. To rebuild. *To balance.*

"Welcome home, daughter," a cold voice says, the bitter note sending an invisible chill down my spine. "I see I made a mistake in allowing your reincarnation, but at least I was able to use it to my advantage. This new link to Hades is exactly what we need to bolster our world. And the best part of all? He finally gets to *rot.*"

I try to blink, to bring myself back to the real world.

But I can't feel anything.

Can't hear anything.

Only Demeter's mad laugh as she repeats "rot" like it's some kind of joke.

"Such a fitting end, hmm? Perfect for our life cycle, as it will supply us with an endless array of souls to empower our plane." She sounds positively giddy, her giggles echoing all around my mind.

There's a triumphant undertone to them that makes this feel even more final.

Even more real.

Even more… *terrifying.*

"Enjoy your pit of despair, Hades," she says, the words swirling through my consciousness in a wave of unmistakable agony. "May you rot… *for eternity.*"

MORPHEUS

A Few Minutes Earlier…

Serapina is fucking a Goddess.

Her skin is flushed with excitement, her full lips parted on an endless moan, her eyes closed as oblivion echoes through her spent form all over again.

Hades has her hair in his fist, his eyes glued to her beautiful face as I hold her hips to keep her steady.

Our knots are pulsing inside her, the intensity leaving me breathless at her back.

I didn't mean to claim her like this. I didn't even know it was possible for an Omega to take a knot in the ass.

Yet here we are.

Thankfully, she doesn't seem to mind too much.

I apologized into her mind, but she didn't reply, her mental state swathed in pleasure once more.

Still, I purr for her, longing to provide comfort while I continue to fill her with my seed.

Hades rumbles as well, though his is underlined in a possessive growl, the Alpha inside him basking in the glow of connecting to his long-lost Omega mate.

It doesn't matter that this is the reincarnation; I can sense how pleased his soul is right now.

A reunion of ecstasy.

One grounded in the exquisite nature of the awakening Goddess between us.

"She's fucking unbelievable," Maliki says from the pillows, one arm tucked behind his head as his other hand strokes his already re-hardening cock.

His libido rivals my own, something I'm very fucking impressed by.

Once Serapina returns from her submissive high, we'll all take her again. Perhaps in different ways.

I wouldn't mind experiencing her throat again.

And I'm sure Maliki would love her ass—something I hear him thinking about right now.

She's tight, I think at him. *And squeezing my knot with a vigor—*

A sharp cry leaves Serapina, causing my focus to snap to her contorting expression. "*Hades,*" she pants, suddenly very much awake. "*Hades, please…*"

She goes limp in the next second, causing my cousin to look sharply at me and then at Serapina as he tries to rouse her.

Maliki is instantly on his knees, his brow furrowing. "What's happening?"

"I don't know," Hades says quietly, his palm against her face. "Something's wrong."

The moment he utters the words, I know he's right. Because I can *feel* the change. She was writhing in oblivion just moments ago, moaning and screaming and passing out from the pleasure.

But now…

I can feel her fighting. Her mind. Her body. *Her soul.*

"The plane." The words leave her on a tremble, her eyes opening once more. "*The Omegas…*"

She starts to panic, her fear causing my knot to subside without my command. "Serapina," I whisper.

But she doesn't seem to hear me.

So I try speaking into her mind. However, it's a mess of chaos and sensation. "Can you understand her?" My question is for Maliki.

His answer is lost as Serapina straightens, her hands clamping down on Hades's shoulders. I can't tell if he's still inside her because I'm no longer knotted to her.

"Serapina, talk—" he starts.

"*Bite me,*" she demands, talking over him like she can't hear him.

And given her tumultuous mental state, I'm not surprised. It's as though she's not truly here, too lost to the mayhem unfolding inside her. "Hades," I start. "I wouldn't—"

But his palm is already on her nape, his gaze locked on her throat.

He's lost to her command, giving in to her need without thought.

Which I understand, but something—

"Wait—" Serapina's words are cut off as Hades sinks his teeth into her neck.

Electricity hums through the air, the zap causing me to release Serapina as I fall back to my haunches on the bed.

And then she's gone.

With Hades.

Maliki dives into the spot where they were just seated,

like he can somehow catch them and bring them back. Then his eyes widen. "What in the Styx…?"

"*Fuck.*" I'm on my feet in an instant, the world around us seeming to quake beneath a shock wave of unprecedented power. I can feel it whirring through the air like an invisible energy net, the presence too lively to exist in this labyrinth.

It's going to crumble.

The thought is immediate, my Alpha senses firing on high alert.

Manifesting a pair of jeans and boots, I throw them at Maliki. "Get dressed." I don't pause to hear his acceptance, just create a pair of black trousers for myself and add some shoes. "We need to get back to the Netherworld Kingdom. *Now.*"

"Took the words right out of my mouth," Reaper drawls as he appears in the bedroom. "Meet you… Where's Sera?"

"With Hades," I reply, hoping that I'm right. Hoping that he saw what was coming and took her somewhere safe.

All while worrying that I'm wrong.

But I can't think about that right now.

"We need to go before this plane collapses." I can already feel the chill seeping into my bones, the runes fractur—

A loud screech rings through my ears.

I don't think; I mist, and find Athena outside the cabin with Hades's unconscious familiar.

Ice floods my veins.

Maliki joins me in a shadow of energy, his eyes on the fallen animal. He doesn't hesitate, bending down toward Ossa's big head. "Hey, baby girl," he whispers. "Look at me."

Her silver eyes slowly blink up at him, her body otherwise still.

"Come on now, little beast. Don't do that." His fingers run through her fur, his attention quickly fixating on me. "Morpheus…"

"Shadow them back," I tell him, trying to sound confident when I don't feel that way at all. Because this… this is unprecedented. *Wrong*. Ossa, Howl, and Mort are Hades's familiar. If they're dying…

No.

I can't think about it. Not right now. Not here. Not like this.

"Athena and I will meet you at Death's Palace," I tell Maliki. "Go. *Now.*"

He doesn't argue, just wraps his inky strands around the burly beast and disappears from view.

"You, too," I tell Athena, referring to my command to *go*.

But she doesn't move, her focus on a blue cloak lying prone on the ground.

Pip.

I start forward, only to freeze as the bundle moves.

And Fleur peeks out from beneath the robes, her big blue eyes telling me everything I need to know.

Pip's gone.

What? Maliki demands into my mind. *What do you mean, "Pip's gone"?*

I can't respond to him. I didn't even mean to voice that to him to begin with.

Instead, I hunker down and open my arms for Fleur. "Come here, sweetheart."

She doesn't immediately obey, but as the maze wall behind her begins to split, she jumps out of the cloak and right into my chest. Athena grabs my shoulder next, both familiars terrified as sounds of ice cracking echo all around us.

Holding Fleur close, I mist her and Athena to Death's Palace.

Only for the sound of shattering to follow us.

My eyes widen at the demolition happening right before us—the walls splitting into jagged pieces of obsidian rock.

"Fuck," I breathe, misting once more to the center of the Netherworld Kingdom—to the courtyard. Dozens of Death Fae and Corpse Fae have gathered here, all of them obviously terrified as the skeletal trees shake in an invisible breeze.

"*Morpheus*," a loud voice booms from across the courtyard, drawing my gaze to the Hell Fae King.

My jaw clenches. I do not have time to deal with him right now. This entire kingdom is going to collapse if someone doesn't bolster it.

"Go and hide in Serapina's old hut," I tell Athena and Fleur.

The pair of them fly off together as I look around for a source of power. Anything I can use to fix this mess. To… to serve as a boulder. A way to—

"Morpheus," Typhos repeats, sounding furious.

"I'm not currently capable of explaining this to you" is all I say before misting back up into the Netherworld Mountains that frame the kingdom below.

The Soul Yards are sputtering in the distance, the constant flow of death seeming to be… *dying*. Which is a ridiculous concept, but those geysers serve as a source of resurrection energy.

The Blood River is no longer flowing.

And the Fairy Catacombs are all… *crumbling*.

Orcus appears at my side in a flurry of black feathers,

his eyes red. He doesn't speak, just lifts his arms and sends a shock wave of deadly power cascading across the valley before us.

Everything freezes in an instant, his chilling energy creating a temporary reprieve from the collapsing infrastructure.

It won't hold for long.

He's basically inserted himself beneath an avalanche, the weight of it crushing down on his shoulders and back.

This is Hades's kingdom. His world. It's his power that keeps everything thriving.

Orcus is a God of the Afterlife, his ties to death similar, but not the same.

And it shows as his expression turns to fine lines of granite.

He needs help. A net. More power. But I… I'm the God of Dreams. This isn't my realm of expertise.

Still, I dig deep, trying to find a way to bolster his strength, give him more of a backbone, and help him bear this impossible force.

Where are you? Maliki demands.

In the mountains.

Helpful, he mutters back at me.

Near—

A fierce stream of light comes from Orcus's palm, his bellow carrying across the valley in an icy wave of deadly energy. *He's shattering*, I realize. *He can't—*

Reaper and Alina appear, the Omega instantly wrapping her arms around Orcus's middle, her head resting against his heart.

The light morphs into snowflakes, raining down softly into the kingdom as Alina calms her Alpha. Reaper stands beside them, scythe in hand, like he's ready to fight anyone who dares to interrupt Orcus and his Omega mate.

Moments pass.

The frigid state of the kingdom remains.

And Orcus's shoulders slowly relax.

Balance, I realize, utterly in awe of the demonstration of their bond.

Because it's not just the Alpha-Omega connection, but that of the entire mate-circle.

Reaper's tattoos writhe in response, the air chilled around him to the point that ice has formed on his metal blade. And I have no doubt Flame is radiating the same intensity from somewhere in this kingdom. Maybe even Thea, too.

"Thank you, Alina," Orcus whispers against his mate's ear. "I love you more than words can express." He kisses her soundly, causing my heart to ache.

Where are you, Serapina? I whisper, hating that I can't feel her. Our connection is fully severed, her soul nonexistent. Like she's been taken to another dimension. Or worse…

"Someone had better start talking," Typhos Lucifer says as he joins us on top of the mountain with the Hell Fae Commander, Azazel, right beside him. "And where the fuck is Hades?"

"I wish I knew," I admit aloud. "I really fucking wish I knew…"

SERA

Nothing.

I feel *nothing.*

No warmth. No chill. No sensation at all.

And it's silent.

Like death.

Only, my mind is very much alive.

Did Persephone live like this? I wonder. *Is she… here?* I can still sense her memories. But she's not *present.* Which is really confusing.

Does that mean I'm my own person, just… with her history?

If I had a head, I would shake it.

Actually, no. If I had a head, I would *scream.*

Instead, I'm left to simply think. For hours. Days. *Weeks.* I have no concept of time here. No understanding of where I even am.

The anchor I once felt to Maliki is gone. I can't hear him or feel him. Same with Morpheus and Hades.

My mates.

My fae.

My future…

Demeter has taken everything from me. My sight. My senses. My taste. My touch. But not my soul.

And not my mind.

That thought continues to linger and repeat. Mostly because I can't find a single memory of Persephone existing in this state. Her recollections cease the moment she was sucked into the void with Demeter, shortly after losing her deer, Delos.

So did she not truly experience the state of no existence? Does that mean the other Omegas are oblivious as well?

Is this just some unique torture for my reincarnated soul?

Or does Demeter not realize that I'm still mentally here? I wonder. She spoke to me earlier like she knew I could hear her.

But she also spoke to me like I was *Persephone*, like I remembered her as my mother.

Perhaps she always speaks to her daughter's entity, not realizing that she isn't truly here anymore. Just a memory.

Except, Persephone's essence is more than that. Her link to Hades is what fuels this plane. I felt that when I escaped it before—the connection between Persephone's soul and the prison Demeter created.

Only, it's stronger now. Inescapable and impenetrable.

"This new link to Hades is exactly what we need to bolster our world."

Her words spoken… I'm not sure when… reverberate through my consciousness now.

The "new link" must be the one he has to me—*Sera*—not Persephone.

However, Demeter never acknowledged *my* name or *my* presence here. Only her daughter's.

Because she thinks I'm her.

But I'm not.

I'm Sera.

Mate of Maliki, Morpheus, and Hades.

Although, I never bit Hades back. So our link isn't quite complete.

Just like his connection to Persephone.

It's enough that his power thrives through my being, but it's not on the same level as what I felt with Morpheus and Maliki.

No, that's not quite right.

It's not on the same level as what I *feel* with Morpheus and Maliki.

Wait…

Am I sensing them?

Or something else?

I tug on the strand of energy, curious. It's… it's cold, I think. Which means I'm *feeling* something. Much better than nothing. I would welcome a bucket of ice cubes at this point.

The icy tendril tugs back, causing my mind to blank for a moment. It's surreal. Unexpected. *Utterly welcome.*

But is it truly happening? Or have I finally lost my mind?

Another yank has my awareness blinking in alarm. *That's real.*

I think, anyway.

When the essence pulls even harder, I simply… follow. Which is such a strange realization, as I didn't feel connected to anything before, but I swear I just released my hold on something. Like I mentally untied myself from a tether, thus allowing my being to be guided elsewhere.

So strange…

And I'm starting to feel even colder, a sensation that would normally concern me. However, I greet it with an internal smile, willing myself to freeze. Whatever it takes to *feel* again.

Who knows how long it's been since I last experienced life?

This place is timeless.

A horrible plane of nonexistence.

A web I long to free myself from…

The presence clutches me closer, dragging me faster.

I can almost feel my feet moving, except I have no legs.

It's… it's bizarre.

It's amazing.

It's *terrifying.*

Because what if it stops? What if I suddenly lose this feeling?

I almost freeze. However, the tendril propels me forward with a chilling blast, and colors begin to form. I could almost weep at the sight. The blistering blues. Silvers. *Golds.*

It's a swirl, one that has me wondering if this is it—if I've officially fallen into a permanent state of lunacy.

Being trapped with only my mind is the worst kind of punishment. A horrible way to spend eternity.

That word, that word… hmm…

Yes, Demeter mentioned it.

"May you rot… for eternity*."*

She uttered those words to Hades, telling him to… to *rot.*

Rot where? Rot how?

And what did she mean by "pit"?

She mentioned that as well, something about his *pit of despair.*

I'm still thinking about that as more images begin to form, which is interesting, as I don't think I have eyes.

Or rather, maybe I do… How else would I be able to see right now?

I try to move my head but can't truly feel anything. No neck. Not even eyelashes to bat.

Oooookay, I think. *Maybe… maybe I really have lost it. But at least it's pretty here? Kind of like the stars in that cave with Maliki…*

The empty hollow inside me pangs, my heart… missing… broken… *shattered.*

Why can't I sense my mates?

That chilling touch pulsates, making me focus on the sensation once more. *Maliki?* I try to whisper to it. *Is that you? Or… or is it Morpheus? Hades?*

No one answers.

However, the frigid strand continues to throb, sending pulses of icy energy into me as we move.

Where are we going? I wonder, dizzy from all the blurring blues and silvers.

The gold is blistering in the distance, seeming to be like an orb of some kind. So bright and intense.

I wish I had eyes to shield. A hand. *Something*. Because it's really starting to *hurt.*

But that's good, right? I want to feel.

Pain… pain is welcome.

Just like the chill.

Who are you? I wonder at the tendril, a shape seeming to form.

Only it's more of a blob.

Translucent, too. Blue? Silver? I can't… *hmm.*

Another yank almost makes me stumble. I glance down, searching for legs, then release a mental gasp at realizing I can control my sight. Er, or my viewpoint? I… I don't think I have legs, though. Or a neck. But definitely seem to have eyes?

This is so weird…

Wind whistles by me, alerting me to the reawakened sense. *Hearing.*

It's loud.

A terrifying swirl, one that reminds me of a harsh winter storm.

I nearly wince.

But shapes begin to form in my vision, distracting me from the violent whooshing sounds. The colors don't change, all blues and silvers swirling around that blistering golden sun.

Only… only, I think… I try to blink, but I can't. I have no eyelids. No lashes. Just… just *eyes.*

Is this how Pip feels? I wonder dizzily. I never saw him blink. But he could narrow his gaze. Maybe he… *Wait.*

I glance down at where the strand is pulling me, the ghostly hand making me gasp inside. *Pip!*

The essence doesn't acknowledge my mental shout, just keeps pulling me toward the light.

But now that I've thought of him, I'm certain that's the being guiding me now. It's Pip. My Pip. My familiar.

Only… only… *I'm translucent, too…*

I realize that with a start, seeing my own tendrils connecting to his.

Oh, stars… Oh!

This is bad. So bad. So weird. So… I…

Another breeze nearly knocks me sideways, but Pip is determined, his movements erratic as he pulls me toward the glowing orb.

The silvers and blues around it are other spirits, their translucent essences similar to Pip's and my semitransparent forms.

It's like a terrifying dream.

Only, Morpheus would never let me fall into a nightmare.

I try to call for him. For Maliki. For… *Hades.*

If I possessed lips, they would part.

Because I sense *Hades*. His agony. His fury. His terror.

He's close…

I attempt to look for him, to find my mate lost in this glittering cave.

Or, I think it's a cave, anyway. Maybe a tunnel is more accurate. Everything appears to be spiraling, causing the source of the wind.

It's like a swirl of color, violent and beautiful and chaotic.

And cold.

Death.

I shiver inside, the juxtaposition to my inner energy making me dizzy. Because I… I'm a creature of rebirth. A resurrected spirit. A *Goddess*.

My eyes seem to widen, taking in more of the sights around us as realizations settle deep within my being. *I'm pulsing with* life…

The baby.

Stars, I feel the creation thriving within me.

Which is… impossible. I'm a soul now. No corporeal form. But I'm carrying *two* heartbeats. Or, maybe that's not accurate. However, I sense two thriving vitalities inside me.

One belongs to me.

The other is the life I created with one of my mates.

My thoughts begin to spin, making me dizzy as Pip drags me closer to that blistering cyclone.

Everything feels so alive. So complex. So *consuming.*

I'm trying to understand my surroundings, comprehend what I'm feeling, determine *how* I arrived here. Pip… Pip found me. But how? I was in the plane of nonexistence. How did Pip save me?

And where is he taking me?

His movements are frantic, his energy pulsing through me in waves of anxiety. He's hurrying, and he's afraid of something.

No. Not something. *Someone.*

Demeter.

She's here. Talking. Humming. Throwing her energy around. Acting as a conduit of some kind. I… I can sense her. Yet I can't.

It's all so complicated and unbelievable.

However, the song she's singing… I… I *know* that tune.

From the garden, I think, dizzy again. *She sang it every day.*

A song about the harvest. About gardens. A lullaby of a sort.

Persephone knew it, too. Used to hear it during every visit. It was what Demeter sang to calm her nerves, to nurse her into a state of compliance.

Only… only that wasn't the true intention. Demeter was a nurturer. A mother. *A protector.*

But the last time Persephone heard that tune, it was used to sing her to sleep. For eternity.

Everything inside me seems to stop.

The world… the world unfolding beneath a new light.

A new memory.

Of the day Persephone experienced the deepest of betrayals.

By the Alpha she trusted most…

Over Two Thousand Years Ago...

"Delos?" I call, confused as to why my familiar ran off into the hedge maze. He usually accompanies me on my stroll through the eternal gardens, but he caught sight of something in the distance and bolted after it on his cloven hooves. For a deer, he's rather predatory.

I'm not sure that's what Diana had in mind when she created him for me.

Or maybe she did.

She works in mysterious ways, just like most of Alpha kind.

I exhale slowly, thinking of *my* Alpha and how I miss him. My mother called me home for the harvest, claiming the realms need my gift for life. But something feels different about this visit.

I can't quite determine the cause of my concern, and I didn't dare voice it to Hades. He would have insisted on accompanying me. However, now I'm kind of wishing I had said something, perhaps asked him to spend the first week or so here with me.

Only, that would have been selfish. It's too sunny in this place for him. Too *alive*.

Sighing, I pause by one of the blossoming fire lilies, this area of the park one I created to honor my love for Hades.

Because we have a myriad of these in our palace gardens. I tend to them often, always ensuring they'll survive in his otherwise cold environment.

I planted a seed shortly after our mating.

And that seed multiplied into hundreds of sprouts, one for each kiss. Each touch. *Each kno—*

A chattering noise echoes in the distance, causing me

to freeze. It's… it's not a common sound for this peaceful garden.

We're all about nurturing and life here. A soft environment. Gentle and loving.

But that—

Delos appears, a panicked look on his face as he charges toward me.

"What's wrong?" I ask my familiar, his terror hitting me straight in the heart. "What's happ—"

I fall onto my rump, yanked backward by some inexplicable force.

And suddenly I'm being dragged by an unseen source. "Oh!" I scream, trying to claw at the invisible entity tugging me against my will.

Delos is instantly there, his teeth clamping down around my skirt to try to pull me in the opposite direction.

Only, an arrow sails into his side in the next instant, ceasing his movements.

My eyes widen.

A silent scream parts my lips.

And Delos… Delos goes impossibly still.

No, I think. *No!*

He's mine. My familiar. My soul's entity.

How is this possible?

Why?

I… I feel his last breath as though it's my own. Which makes no sense. He's not… *He's immortal!*

Tears flood my vision.

This has to be a nightmare. A horrible dream. I just need to wake up. To… to… *Hades!* I scream, wishing our mental bond worked here.

But part of the agreement between him and my mother required me to be completely isolated in this garden. "Your deadly touch cannot infiltrate our lively essence," she once told him.

That's the other reason I didn't tell him about the strangeness I felt for this trip. Because even if he could join me, he would've been forced to tamper his energy and suffocate his deadly aura.

My Hades deserves to thrive. To live in his own way. *To be the Alpha he's meant to be…*

But oh, I wish I could reach him now.

Delos, I whisper, my deer vanishing before my eyes as I claw at the earth around me, fighting the invisible entity at my back. *What's been done to my Delos?*

"This is for your own good, child," my mother says against my ear.

I still. *Mother?*

The world vanishes from view, my vision turning unexpectedly black.

And then white.

Too white.

Blinding white…

"Oh, Persephone," my mother whispers, her voice breaking. "I wish I could have warned you, but I knew… I just knew *he* would hear. That monster and his bite. His forced bond to my precious jewel. So many of you have suffered. But nevermore…"

I don't… I don't understand, Mother, I long to say. But I… I can't feel my mouth. Or my hands. Or even my heart. It's all… it's all gone.

Every link. Every fiber of my essence. My very form.

What have you done? I ask my mother. The Goddess of Fertility. The one I've trusted all my life. The one who birthed me. Raised me. *Vowed to protect me…*

"Oh, sweetheart, I'm not doing this to be cruel. I promise this is for the betterment of Omega kind. You won't hurt here. You'll be safe. Forever encased in a sanctuary the Alphas can never breach." Something passes through me, the energy both familiar and foreign. "None of you will ever have to suffer again, Persephone."

I shudder inside, unable to speak or to demand that my mother think about what she's doing. What she's *done*.

I can't feel Hades at all.

At least in the garden, I could sense our bond via the mark on my neck.

But now…

Now I feel nothing.

Hear only my mother's voice.

See… see an unending white light.

"One day, when it's safe, I'll try to resurrect you," my mother tells me, a choked sob underlining that final word. "But until then, I'll… I'll be here to watch over all of you. Protect Omega kind. Ensure no Alphas ever enter this space. I'll do whatever it takes to save you, just as I've always vowed. Since Jove—"

She cuts off, the emotion thick in her voice, just as it always is when she mentions my Omega father. I've never met him, as he's being kept by some of the cruelest Alphas in existence.

He's a rare male Omega, his power vast and unworldly.

My mother used to help him through his heat. Or… or perhaps engaged in some of the wicked games with the others.

I've heard she was once in league with those horrible Alphas.

But my existence changed everything.

And I think a part of her mourns what has been done to Jove and other imprisoned Omegas.

She's always spoken about wanting to free all Mythos Fae Omegas, telling me that Alphas don't deserve my kind and never will.

It was her biggest argument against Hades. I've tried for years to tell her he's not like the others, but she's never listened. Never wanted to believe me. I… I thought time would prove his intentions to her, make her realize that not all Alphas are created equal.

But it seems I was wrong.

She's been planning this for a while.

I can see that now. Realize all the poisonous thoughts she's expressed over my decades of life. Her desire to create a safe haven for Omega kind.

However, what she's done is create a different sort of prison. A plane where our souls will forever reside unless she allows us to be reborn.

Using Hades's power, I suddenly grasp, my mind threatening to fracture with the thought. *Oh, Goddess above… she's using* my *link to* my *mate… to his resurrection… This can't… Mother, you can't!*

She clears her throat, her emotion palpable and surrounding me in a sea of sadness.

"I love you, Persephone. I'll make sure you can't feel anything. It'll be… it'll be like you're sleeping, all right? And when you're reborn, you'll only remember your former life, none of the stillness. Not even this moment. We'll start anew. Live somewhere safe. Build our own garden of happiness."

I can tell she's crying, her grief evident in her voice and her aura.

"This is what I have to do to protect you all. To save Omega kind. Deep down, I know you understand. And one day, you'll thank me. When we've built a dimension or a plane where Omegas thrive without Alpha interference… you'll be pleased. I know it."

Another sniffle.

Then she clears her throat, and I suddenly know there is nothing I can do to stop this. Nothing I can do to change her mind.

Hades, I think, wishing he could hear me while knowing he can't. *I'm so sorry, Hades. I'm not strong enough to fight her. To stop her. But I should have… I should have known.*

Now I'm pretty sure I'm crying, too.

But for a very different reason from that of my mother.

Fates, if you hear me, and if I may, I ask for one gift. Even though I'm undeserving, I ask… I ask that when I'm reborn, you give me the strength I need… to fix this. To be a better mate to Hades. An equal. A worthy Omega. A being capable of fixing what my mother has done. That's all I desire. Another chance… to right this wrong.

It's a broken prayer, one I doubt will ever be heard.

However, all I can do is hope.

Because there's nothing left for me to do. My vision is darkening now, the plane taking hold of my soul.

I'm the anchor, I think, understanding my mother's sorrow. Her apologies. Her promises to keep me in a forever oblivious state.

Because my soul must remain whole for this plane to thrive.

In an instant, I grasp every pivotal aspect of what's happened. Every nuance. The way my mother was able to use my power and my link to Hades to create this "sanctuary." How she wove it all together in a unique life cycle… underscored by *death.*

Hades is the key.

He'll forever sense me. Know that I'm alive somewhere. Because I will be… in spirit.

Maybe he'll find me.
Maybe he'll save us all.
Or maybe… maybe fate will give me that chance.
When my mother… one day… resurrects my soul.

SERA

PERSEPHONE'S MEMORY SWIRLS THROUGH MY MIND, SO fresh and *tangible*.

It's like the incident just occurred, as though my soul is recalling it as "now" instead of "then." But I know it happened ages ago.

And it's Persephone's last true recollection.

After that is simple darkness, akin to death. Yet it's peaceful, too, suggesting her mother kept her word—that she put Persephone in some sort of stasis that protected her daughter's spirit.

Then she resurrected her… into *me*.

Only, I don't think Demeter understands that I'm not her daughter in any way, shape, or form. She raised Persephone in a very specific manner, and while Nightingale Village may have demanded I adopt similar submissive tendencies, I was also influenced by Alina.

And more recently, my experience in the Netherworld Kingdom.

Maliki, Morpheus, and Hades have played their parts in my life as well, thus helping me to discover my inner spirit. Not the one tied to Persephone and her past, but the spirit that is all mine.

A spirit that is currently being led by Pip to that golden glow.

We're close enough now that I can see the source of it is a swirl of souls, all of them swimming upward into a blinding light above.

It's like a cyclone, which explains the wind.

Except... except that roaring sound also might be coming from the souls, as they appear to be screaming. Their mouths are open in a way that expresses agony, making me wonder what this funnel is doing.

When Pip pauses right beside it, he looks at me with his big blue orbs, his features somewhat recognizable now that I seem to be able to properly see again.

Only, he's not wearing his trademark cloak.

And he's translucent instead of being made of bone.

He's also touching me, I realize with a start.

I... I should have considered that before.

But I was too overwhelmed by everything else to contemplate the meaning of his tendrils touching mine.

We're both dead.

Er, sort of.

I... I can sense that I'm still me in a strange sort of way. Just as I can feel another life source inside me. *The baby,* I think, startled. I can actually sense the being inside me, something I couldn't do before. *I'm still carrying my child.*

I look down, wishing I could see the little spirit inside me. But all I find are smokelike strands of blues and silvers.

This is so weird.

As is the swirling stream of souls beside me.

What are we doing here, Pip? I want to ask him. *How do we escape?*

Because I assume he's trying to help me in some way.

Only, he's looking at me with the saddest eyes right now, which gives me pause.

I wish I could ask him what's wrong. But he pulls me into a hug in the next moment, his transparent arms surprisingly strong.

His head touches mine for a brief moment, like he's giving me a kiss.

While it's amazing to finally feel him, I… I'm scared of what this means. *Pip…*

He squeezes me even tighter, like he can hear me.

Then he jolts to the side and sends us both into the swirling pit.

I try to scream, but I can't. Because, unlike the others, I don't appear to have a mouth.

Pip holds me close, his head still against mine, then he gives me a final squeeze before shoving me away with a force that has me going against the violent storm.

I flail inside, whirling invisible arms as I try to understand what's happening. I have no control over my trajectory. I'm falling instead of flying upward, my spiritual form seeming to leave the cluster of souls to go sideways to plummet faster.

Thorns!

I gape up at Pip, horrified by his betrayal.

But the sadness in his expression nearly kills me.

He lifts a little hand in a waving gesture.

And then he vanishes into the swirl of souls.

Pip! I scream in my mind, confused and hurt. And… and *worried.*

Because that felt like a goodbye.

He *waved.*

Why did he wave?

Why did he push me down here?

Wh-why did he *disappear?*

I palm my chest, my heart aching inside. Because I feel disconnected. Like I just lost my friend. My familiar. *My Pip…*

My fingers curl into a fist as pain spirals through me, my soul splintering inside as something irrevocable occurs.

He's gone.

Not just visually, but… but *gone.*

I can feel it, the loss, the separation, the *finality*. He's… he's not coming back. He's lost in that spiral and I'm… I'm…

I blink, then gasp when I realize I have *hands* again.

Not just hands, but also arms. A chest. Legs. *I'm corporeal again.*

I run my palms over my bare skin, startled by the discovery.

How? I wonder.

Then I look sharply up at the spiral and realize Pip did this. He pushed me down here to… to rejoin my body.

But he sacrificed himself in the process.

"No," I whisper, my voice a rasp of sound. "*No*!"

I fall to my knees, the scrape against my bare skin confirming I'm very much *me* again. But I don't care. I want Pip back.

This… this can't be…

Pip! It's a scream in my mind, one I want to release through my lips, but I can't seem to vocalize his name. I can't speak. I can barely breathe.

The pain spearing through me is unlike anything I've ever experienced before.

It's harsh. It's cold. *It's devastating.*

Like I've lost a piece of my soul.

And I did.

I… I lost *Pip*.

My vision blurs behind a sheen of tears, and I don't even have the energy to blink them away.

I'm broken.

I'm overwhelmed.

I'm confused.

I'm *mad*.

I'm…

Why? I want to demand. *Why would you…?*

I bite my cheek, unable to finish the sentence.

Pip… His name sounds like a prayer. A whispering plea.

But the voice that responds isn't one I expect. *Sera?*

He's gone, I whisper. *Pip's gone…*

Sera, where are you?

My forehead touches the ground, my heart in tatters. I know I need to stand up and figure out what Pip meant for me to do. But I… I…

Sera, that voice says again, the masculine undertone demanding my attention.

Maliki, I breathe. *Pip is…* I can't finish the statement. Because I refuse to believe it. *I have to find him. He's in the spirit tunnel thing. I…. There has to be a way, right?*

Sera, I need you to take a deep inhale for me, okay?

Wh-what? I ask, confused by his request. *I don't need to* inhale, *Maliki. I need to find Pip!*

And I want to help you do that, sweet mystery. The first step is breathing with me, yeah?

I nearly growl. Because his request is ridiculous. *Maliki—*

Sera, he says, his dominance washing over me in a wave of fiery heat. *Inhale.*

I want to fight him.

To argue.

To tell him he's being impossible.

Yet I need him to help me find Pip. To help me… help me figure out… *Stars, what am I even doing?* I have no idea where I am or how I'm suddenly corporeal.

But it's clear that Pip… Pip is the reason.

And I… *I didn't even get to say goodbye,* I think, breaking again. *He waved, and I just stared at him, horrified by what I thought was a betrayal, Maliki. Stars, I… I… I don't…* I swallow, my eyes falling closed. *Oh, Pip…*

Breathe, trouble, Maliki tells me. *I need you to breathe, yeah?*

I shake my head. *He can't be gone. He… He just…*

No.

No, I refuse to believe he's gone.

I… I have to…

Dampness touches my cheek.

I hate that I'm crying. I hate that I don't know what happened. I hate that I… that I couldn't *stop* him from whatever he's done.

Serapina Everheart, Maliki growls into my head, his use of my full name startling me a little. *I know it hurts, trouble. But Pip needs you to be* Sera *right now.* I *need you to be Sera, too. Understand?*

I blink, his words chilling me to my core.

It's… it's a jolting moment. An unexpected one. Yet it awakens me to my surroundings.

I'm lying on a slab of obsidian rock.

Souls scream in torment way above me, the swirl of energy the same one that stole Pip from me.

But beneath it all—where I am now—is a pit of skulls.

Talk to us, little dreamer, a soft voice murmurs into my thoughts. *Tell us what you're seeing so we can find you.*

Morpheus, I whisper, my heart skipping a beat in my chest. *Oh, stars, is this even real?*

I was lost in stasis. Feeling nothing. Hearing nothing. Seeing nothing. Only thinking.

Then Pip… Pip tugged me out of that state of nonexistence.

And he… he…

I swallow, my eyes closing as I curl into the cold ground. It certainly feels real. But what if I've lost my mind? What if I've entered some sort of fantasy state?

Do you think I would ever allow you to dream of such nonsense? Morpheus asks me. *You're my heart, Serapina. My love. My Omega. If you were to enter my realm of fantasies, you would not be weeping alone in some unknown place. You would be experiencing pleasure, not sadness. So this is most assuredly real, sweetheart. Which is why I need you to focus.*

If it's real, then Pip…

We'll find him, love, Morpheus assures me. *However, I need you to help me and Maliki find you first.*

A shiver traverses my spine, one born of fear. Maybe despair. But also… also something else.

Something akin to annoyance.

Or anger.

Because Pip *sacrificed* himself for me. Might be in pain right now. Or gone. I… I don't know.

Yet I'm on the floor… weeping?

That's not what he would have wanted. Not who I want to be. Not what I should be doing.

It's all been so much. So overwhelming. So… *infuriating.*

Because of Demeter.

And while I understand her desire to save all of Omega kind, she's no better than the Alphas who treated Omegas like property.

She never gave any of us a choice.

Not even her own daughter.

Definitely not *me.*

My fingers curl into fists against the chilled marble, my bare skin pebbled with goose bumps from the icy air around me. But I barely sense the wintry elements.

I'm too incensed to feel anything other than *heat.*

Shoving away from the floor, I go to my knees and look around the cylinder-shaped room I've landed within. *It's like a cavern of skulls*, I mutter to myself. *Similar to the maze, only a lot creepier.*

This place feels more like a dungeon.

A pit, I think. My brow furrows. *Wait…*

"Enjoy your pit of despair, Hades."

Demeter's words play through my head.

Followed swiftly by a memory of Maliki telling me about the death pits. He said it was a place where judgment occurs. And Pip made it clear he didn't go there.

Yet…

My throat works, my insides aching once more.

I can't…

I close my eyes, take a deep breath, and whisper, *Maliki, what do the death pits look like?*

Because wallowing in my aching loss isn't going to help me right now. It's not going to fix this. *It won't allow me to find Pip.*

They're linked to the Soul Yards, Maliki replies without asking questions. *Basically, it's a cavernous hole where spirits come and go in the afterlife.*

I look around. *I don't see any souls coming… just… just leaving…* This place is more like a geyser than a revolving door; all the spirits seem to be flying upward at a rapid, swirling pace.

Are there any runes on the walls? Morpheus asks, suddenly in my mind.

I suspect he's with Maliki right now.

Rather than inquire, I answer with *I don't know.* Because

I have no idea what a rune looks like. *Can you describe one to me? I can… search.*

They'll resemble glowing symbols etched into the walls, Morpheus murmurs. *You may need to touch the stone to ignite them.*

I nibble my lower lip as I glance around again, determining which stone to touch and how. *This still feels like a weird dream, Morpheus.*

Trust me, Serapina, when you dream, it will be a lot more exciting than the death pits.

His words are punctuated by the eerie howling above. *I guess this is more like a nightmare.*

Which I would never allow you to have, love, Morpheus promises me. *Now, can you reach one of the walls without touching any of the floating souls?*

The souls are all above my head, I inform him. *Like, fifty feet above my head.*

He doesn't immediately reply but eventually says, *Move very slowly in that pit, just in case some of the spirits venture that way.*

I don't think they can. They seem to have a one-way ticket upward. I try to tell him what I experienced when I fell down here—when Pip *pushed* me—but I'm not sure I'm conveying the information correctly. *I was still, er, translucent, when it happened.*

Morpheus falls quiet again, and I wonder if he's talking to Maliki.

I swallow, not liking the silence. Although, it's not entirely quiet. The screaming souls tell me I'm still corporeal, that I still have ears, that I'm still *here*.

Assuming this is real…

Little dreamer, Morpheus says, his tone holding a light admonishment to it. *Once we've resolved the Demeter issue, I'm going to teach you a thorough lesson on how fantasies work.*

Morpheus says you're questioning if this is real or not, Maliki adds. *My worry for you is very fucking real, Sera. So do what the God of Dreams tells you to do so I can bloody find you.*

The hint of desperation in Maliki's tone has my heart kick-starting in my chest. *Okay,* I reply, pushing upward to my feet. *I'll go… touch the wall.*

Because it just looks like black rock right now.

No glowing symbols or anything else.

Careful not to touch any souls, Morpheus reminds me.

I glance around the empty cavern. *That won't be hard.* I already told him there weren't any down here. However, he must not understand what I mean. Maybe I'm not in the death pits at all, but somewhere else entirely.

My lips curl down as I raise my palm toward the wall, a hum of electricity rolling across my skin. *This feels weird,* I tell Morpheus and Maliki. *I—*

Power rips up my arm, causing me to jolt back away from the rock.

Ow. I try to shake out the static residual, but it rumbles through me, causing my insides to pulse with intensity.

Then everything goes quiet.

The souls.

The whoosh of air.

My mind.

And the world… *shifts.*

I part my lips, ready to scream.

However, no sound escapes me.

Other than a breath.

As I find myself suddenly airborne, the ground no longer existent.

I'm falling, I realize, my mental voice a shriek of terror. *I'm falling into… into a* void…

MALIKI

Netherworld Kingdom

My fingers are still in Ossa's fur, my heart suddenly in my throat. "Morpheus…"

"Give it a minute," he says, his tone and expression exuding a seriousness I feel to my very core.

The last few hours have been agonizing, the lack of a connection to Sera nearly driving me insane.

All I could do was sit here and try to comfort Ossa, her soft whimpers long gone.

Because she isn't breathing.

Neither is Mort or Howl.

I have no idea how any of this is possible, how an immortal beast just… *dies*.

But I refuse to let them be alone.

Not after how scared Ossa appeared to be in her final moments of consciousness.

Fuck, her silver eyes looking up at me will forever haunt my dreams.

Hades's beast had better not be fucking dead.

That statement applies to the God of Death, too. Which I realize has a fucked-up sort of irony to it. But I don't bloody care about that Styx right now.

I need Sera to start talking into my head again.

I need Ossa to breathe.

I need Hades to *fucking appear.*

The Netherworld Kingdom is in chaos, the fae not knowing how to handle the fall of their God.

Because *everyone* felt his disappearance.

The mountains fucking shook in response to whatever happened to Hades. Then everything began to crumble.

Orcus and his mate-circle saved the kingdom from utter destruction, but Morpheus doesn't know if it's going to hold—something I've heard in the God of Dreams's thoughts, not from his mouth.

He only recently returned from his prolonged meeting with Typhos Lucifer.

I chose to stay in the hut I once borrowed from Tank, mostly because I couldn't leave Ossa alone in her suffering. The moment I brought her here, she collapsed her big head in my lap while her two brothers fell unconscious. None of us have moved since.

Sera? I whisper, hating that she feels separated from me again. *Talk to me, trouble. Please.*

I don't think Morpheus's idea of touching the wall was a good one is her reply. *In fact, I think it was a very bad idea.*

Why? What's happening?

I'm falling, she mutters. *Into a void. Or a vortex. Or… Wait… I see something glowing… I…*

She goes silent.

Sera?

Nothing.

I repeat what she said to Morpheus and note the way his pupils pulse. "Start talking, or I'm going to introduce you to another blade, God of Dreams."

"You really should work on your patience, Enforcer," he returns. "She can only speak to one of us at a time."

I narrow my gaze. "So she's talking to you?"

"She's trying to," he growls. "But a knife-happy fae keeps interrupting my thought process."

"Then you should ignore him and focus on the more important person in the conversation," I tell him, my fingers resuming their path along Ossa's head and nape.

It's a nervous tic at this point—the petting. The motion makes me feel grounded in a way I can't explain, like I'm somehow connected to Hades even though he isn't here. Which is confusing, as I'm not sure why I even need to feel connected to him. Perhaps because of our initial bond. Or, more likely, because of our mutual ties to Sera.

Sighing, I close my eyes and try to feel her. To hear her. To *anything*. But it's still quiet. Still *vacant*. And I fucking hate feeling this way.

"Maliki," Morpheus says, jolting me with not only his words but also his touch.

I frown, not sure when he grabbed my shoulder.

His eyes are assessing as I focus on him, like he's trying to discern something. "Why are you looking at me like that?" I ask, somewhat surprised to hear the exhaustion in my voice.

"Because I've been trying to talk to you for five minutes," he tells me, his brow furrowing. "Hades must be tugging on your life source, just like he's doing to his familiar." His grip on my shoulder tightens. "We need to find him and Serapina."

"No shadows," I slur, feeling suddenly far too tired. "This is…"

Morpheus grabs my face, his palms burning against my cheeks as his energy pulses between us.

I flinch, then try to move away, because *fuck*. "What the Styx is that?"

"My life essence." The God of Dreams sends another jolt into me that seems to rocket down my spine. "Now get up and help me, Enforcer."

"Get up and help you do what?" I demand, feeling both stronger and more pissed off now. "You have to actually *communicate* for me to know what the fuck to do, Morpheus."

"Just as I need you awake and moving for me to be able to communicate," Morpheus bites back. "So *stand up*."

I hate that his demand makes my legs twitch, almost as though he's commanding me like a puppet.

But my hands flex, too, and my shadows begin to writhe.

So I'm clearly still me because that reaction was driven by my sudden desire to punch the Alpha in the face.

However, hearing Sera suddenly in my mind again helps, her voice steady as she asks, *Are you okay?*

Am I okay? I nearly laugh the words back at her. *Sweet mystery, you're the one who disappeared.*

Yes, but I'm corporeal again.

And thank Styx for that, I mutter, carefully moving Ossa's head from my lap.

"You're going to be okay," I promise the beast, bending down to kiss her on her big, fluffy head. Giving her floppy black ears a little scratch, I adjust her to where I hope she's comfortable and slide out of the bed.

Morpheus observes me with interest. "She's going to attack you the moment she wakes up."

"Yeah," I say, agreeing with that assessment. "And I'll welcome her version of love bites." Because it'll mean she's fucking alive.

Fleur heaves a sigh nearby, clearly feeling the same way as I do. I can see it in her blue eyes and feel it in her aura that she's worried. Though, as I investigate deeper, I realize she's more concerned about Hades than anything or anyone else.

"He's siphoning my energy," I realize, that link to Fleur awakening me to what I should have already discerned. Shifting my attention to Morpheus, I add, "That's why you just gave me a dose of your godly power."

"Obviously," he deadpans. "I wouldn't offer such a gift to anyone, Maliki. Consider yourself fortunate."

"To have your essence inside of me?"

His lips quirk. "I'll give you my true *essence* later, if you'd like. While our mate watches."

I'm not sure if he's talking about his knot or something else. But the euphemism is clear. "Are you really choosing now to flirt with me?"

"If it makes you move faster, then yes," he replies. "As it is, I've already spent ten minutes attempting to rouse you, and I would like to head over to the Soul Yards to start hunting for Serapina."

I still. "You know where she is?"

"Not precisely, no. But I have an idea."

"And you wasted time on me instead of going to get her?" I demand, irritated as fuck. "What if she—"

"You're about to waste more time with unnecessary speculations, Enforcer," he interjects. "So let me just state this plainly for you—we are stronger as a circle. Therefore, I need you alive and aware to assist me in finding our mate. Now stop asking unhelpful questions and follow me."

Rather than comment further, he turns toward the door and strides out of the hut.

I stare at his back for a moment, my hands wishing for a knife.

But then his voice is suddenly in my head, reiterating, *We're stronger as a circle, Maliki.*

My jaw ticks. *I fucking hate that you can read my mind.*

Shall I also point out how that strengthens our ability to function as a circle? Morpheus asks. *Or are you as stubborn as my cousin?*

I grunt and grab a pair of boots to shove my feet into. Then I steal a dark shirt from the dresser—which is still full of my clothes—and meet Morpheus outside. "No one is as stubborn as Hades."

"Hmm, that's true," he says slowly. "But there's a reason he chose you for our circle, Maliki. And it has everything to do with compatibility."

"I'm not like Hades," I tell him as we head toward the Soul Yards.

Morpheus grins. "I think you're more like my cousin than you care to admit."

"Are you trying to insult me or motivate me?"

He bats his long lashes at me. "Oh, I thought we were flirting, Maliki."

I shove him away from my side, and he laughs. "I'm starting to see why Hades *did not* choose you for his circle."

"It's *our* circle," Morpheus corrects me. "And my cousin wasn't given a choice in the matter. Which is good because I provide balance."

"Balance." I scoff at that. "Right."

"You're about to retract that skepticism," he informs me as we wander through the Netherworld Village in the direction of the Blood River Bridge.

Ignoring him, I connect to Sera again, as I haven't heard her voice in far too long. *Everything okay, trouble?*

I'm surrounded by symbols I can't read or understand, and I'm pretty sure Hades is… nearby. She sounds distracted.

Are the symbols runes? I wonder.

Yes, that's what Morpheus says, anyway. He thinks I'm at the bottom of one of the geyser-like things in the Soul Yards, she tells me. *Or something about tunnels?*

I look beyond the Blood River to the open tombstones surrounding the Death Fae Castle. Normally, spirits swirl up into the air from the various cracks along the ground between the grave sites, hence the *Soul Yards* name. But everything is all dried up and, well, *dead* in appearance.

Some of the annoyance Morpheus provoked in me dies at the sight. I could feel the world falling apart, the impact of Hades's fall echoing throughout the Netherworld Kingdom, but seeing it… makes it far too real.

"If she's at the bottom of one of those crypts, then how do we reach her?" I ask him.

Morpheus's wings appear in a sudden swoosh of energy, the gold-tipped plumes brushing my shoulder. "We're going to fly, Maliki."

"Is that what you meant about providing balance? Because I'm fairly certain Hades can fly, too."

He slants me a look, his blue-green irises swirling. "My balance is currently thriving through your blood, Enforcer. Without me and our connection, you would be as dead as Hades's familiar right now."

I flex my hands, feeling the life energy flaring at my fingertips. "What did you do to keep me alive?" It's a serious question, not a sarcastic one. Because I'm tired of banter. Tired of *flirting*. Or whatever the fuck this is between us. I just want to understand what the Styx is happening right now.

"Honestly, I'm not sure how to explain it. My soul sensed the depletion in yours, so I… I bolstered it. But the power is draining faster than I anticipated, meaning we need to hurry. Whatever Demeter has done to Hades is…" He trails off, his brow coming down. "I fear that it's causing irrevocable damage."

"What does that mean?"

"He's becoming one with death," Morpheus says softly, pausing in the middle of the skull-adorned bridge to look at me. "If she manages to kill him, he might take you with him, Maliki."

I stare at him. "He's immortal."

"He should be, yes. But Demeter also shouldn't possess this kind of power either. So at this point, anything is possible." Morpheus sounds uneasy, an emotion that trickles through our connection. "The only way we stand a chance is as a circle. Which makes it time for you to decide—do you trust me or not?"

After everything we've been through, it would be very easy to choose the latter option in that inquiry.

However, oddly, all of our chaotic experiences have had an opposite impact.

Perhaps because I enjoy danger.

I also thrive on the unknown.

And Morpheus has packaged both qualities rather spectacularly.

"I assume you have a plan," I tell him, my arms folding across my chest. "And it doesn't involve lingering on this bridge?"

His lips curl. "Actually… it does."

I frown. "Morph—"

He grabs me by the arms and lifts me into the air, his wings spread wide. A curse echoes in my mind—which I'm sure he can hear—as he takes us over the Blood River toward the dried-up waterfall. It's chilling to see the crimson flow frozen along the jagged rocks, the evidence of this kingdom's trauma staring me straight in the face.

But Morpheus doesn't give me time to ponder it as he angles us directly downward toward a wicked-looking crack.

I thought we were going to the Soul Yards, I say into his mind.

We are, he replies. *I just didn't tell you how I intended to enter them.* His arms tighten around me. *Better hold on, Enforcer. I think we're about to experience a rather bumpy ride.*

SERA

MALIKI'S GROWLS FILL MY HEAD, HIS ANNOYANCE WITH Morpheus palpable. *Is everything okay?* I hedge, frozen inside this circular room—the one I ended up in after free-falling for several minutes before magically landing on my feet. Unlike the last cylinder-shaped pit, this one has a ceiling.

About twelve inches over my head.

So I'm basically in a circular box, something I'm trying not to lose my mind about.

I've already scanned every inch of the glowing rocks around me for a way out, and nope. I'm trapped in here.

It's something that would have bothered me before losing all of my senses in the plane of nonexistence. Now, I'm just thankful to have my hands.

And my connections to Maliki and Morpheus.

Their banter is keeping me sane, their thoughts filled with a lightness I desperately need right now.

I'm not ignorant as to *why* they're bantering, though. Morpheus is purposely goading Maliki in order to keep the situation positive. But deep down, I hear the concern in his thoughts. He's trying to mask them, and I appreciate the effort. However, we all know something is clearly very wrong.

We need to find Hades.

Yes, Morpheus agrees. *And we need to find you, little dreamer.*

We'll, I'm stuck in a box, I remind him. *So good luck.*

Luck isn't needed, he promises me. *You're our mate. We can feel you, Serapina.*

I frown. *You can?*

Mm-hmm, he hums in confirmation. *Can you feel us?*

I… I try to determine *how* to feel them, to garner any sort of sense of my mates. But all I can do is hear their thoughts. *No… But I should be able to, right?*

Morpheus doesn't answer me right away. However, he doesn't need to. Because I find the knowledge in his mind, the very real connection that we should have, which I seem to lack.

Why? I wonder, searching my head for an answer. *Why can't I sense my mates?*

Using the information I gathered from Morpheus's thoughts, I follow the same channels within myself and hunt for my fae.

Only, I don't seem to have access to that part of myself. *It's… it's blocked,* I realize, finding the darkness clouding my mind. *What…?*

Morpheus says something I don't quite hear. I'm too consumed by this shadow lurking in my head. It's… it's familiar. Pulsing. *Hypnotic.*

I try to mentally trace it, seeking to interact with the essence.

So strange and… Why do I recognize it?

Morpheus responds.

I should probably listen.

But I'm… I'm too lost to the enigma inside my mind. It shifts and molds as I mentally prod the substance, the inky membrane clearly concealing something important.

Something linked to my mates, I decide, frowning.

I don't appreciate the cerebral block. I want to be able to sense my males just as well as they sense me.

It'll help us find Hades…

Morpheus speaks again, his tenor a rumble in my head as I psychically punch through the dark smog in my mind.

And suddenly I'm falling. *Again.* Just like before with the endless void.

Only this time… this time I feel a cord pulling me along. *Pip?* I wonder, my eyes scanning the darkness as hope fills my heart. *Are you here, Pip?*

But as glittering lights begin to form, it becomes clear that Pip is nowhere in sight.

I was never truly falling.

I… I never fell in the first place.

The two thoughts hit me at once as I stare up at the swirling souls above me.

I'm still in the same pit.

Or… or I somehow ended up here again.

Blinking around the cylinder room, I note the runes flashing along the obsidian walls. They're more organized than before, their pattern seeming to unfold right before me.

But I find more than just runes. More than a vacant space with a hovering cloud of souls above.

I find *Hades.*

He's on a throne made of decaying bones, his arms and legs tied down by the roots of a thriving tree.

What…?

I gape at the sight of my unconscious mate. He's naked. Ashen in color. *Not breathing…*

And that… that *tree* is the cause.

I push off of the ground. Or I try to, anyway. My arms resemble lead, like I haven't used them in a long time.

My eyelashes flutter, my mind suddenly foggy.

The black substance…

No!

I shove the inky cloud away and propel myself upward until I'm sitting upright.

Hades is less than a foot away, his head hanging at an angle that sends all his dark hair across his features.

But I know he's unaware, at least in the physical sense, because his bare chest isn't moving.

And I can't hear his heartbeat.

Not that I should be able to hear it… However, my instincts tell me he's… he's *dead*.

Except not.

His soul is there, his spirit so closely tied to mine. It's pulsing slowly, absorbing energy from everywhere it can in order to stay alive.

What is that tree doing to you? I wonder, noting the way the limbs are moving and pulsating around him. It's not a normal creation, which isn't surprising. Nothing about this place is *normal*.

Although, that tree also shouldn't exist here.

How I know that is irrelevant. I simply know. And I trust that knowledge.

Just like I trust the instinct that has me going to my knees beside Hades. The instinct that has me reaching for his hand. The instinct that refuses to let go even when his touch sends a shocking wave of ice through my system.

He's trying to push me away, I realize. *That dark essence in my mind belongs to Hades.*

Tightening my hold on his hand, I demand to know *why*.

And I'm immediately hit with the truth—Hades is protecting my essence from his. He doesn't want to hurt me.

But he needs me.

He needs my bond. My soul. *Our connection.*

Don't cut me off, I tell my stubborn Alpha. *Let me help you.*

His dark touch grows in my head again, trying desperately to drown me out. To force me away. *To guard me.*

Because that tree is destroying his soul.

Which puts me at risk. Maliki, too.

I find all of that information in Hades's quiet mind, his focus resolute. All he's thinking about is shielding his circle. His mates. *Me.*

It's almost as though he fell unconscious with that desire in mind and just… never resurfaced.

Maybe what I'm hearing is an echo of his intention, the goal one he considered right before collapsing beneath the power of this foreign plant matter. These roots. *This tree.*

Narrowing my gaze, I release Hades and reach for one of the branches.

"*Thorns,*" I gasp as electricity shoots up my arm. I yank my hand away to shake it through the air. No wonder Hades isn't lucid or alive. That… that *thing* is sucking the literal life out of him.

Or rather… *death.*

It's taking his gift for resurrection and…

I glance upward, my eyes widening as everything clicks into place. Every puzzle piece. Every word said by Demeter. All of Persephone's memories. My own experiences in the plane of nonexistence.

Stars. I palm my belly. *Omegas create life.*

Except Demeter—an *Alpha*—birthed Persephone.

That has to be rare. Maybe even impossible. I… I don't know. But Jove was an Omega. Which means his seed gifted Demeter a dose of life—*in the form of a daughter.*

And that gave Demeter a unique connection—an *anchor* of sorts. Almost like a mate-circle, only vastly different as mother and child.

The way I'll be tied to the life growing inside me, I realize, feeling the pulsing bead of energy.

The bond between mother and child is sacred. A bond not meant to be abused or harmed in any way.

An Omega would know that, I think.

However, Demeter wasn't an Omega. She was an Alpha. Used to being in charge. Used to being the dominant one in a room. Used to making all the decisions, especially in regard to the protection of others.

Having Persephone changed her irrevocably.

She became a mother to all Omegas, choosing to take on our souls as her burden to guard. That care, that *responsibility*, drove her to break the biggest covenant of all.

She betrayed her daughter's soul. Her mind. *Her heart.* She tapped into the mate-bond between Persephone and Hades, something I already suspected, but now I understand *how.*

She took control of her daughter's life force and bent it to her will, created a world, and used Persephone's essence as the anchor.

Only, it wasn't strong enough.

That's why it became a state of nonexistence.

The Omega souls were safe but couldn't manifest a physical presence. Demeter knew that would be the case. But now…

Now with *my* corporeal link to Hades…

I look up again at the spirits writhing in agony above,

their former lives being forced in a direction they're not meant to go.

They're populating the world Demeter created.

She's using Hades's control over death to… to *perfect* her manifestation.

Mingling life and death. Weaving together a new form of resurrection with ties to fertility. It's… it's convoluted. It's a web of confusion that shouldn't be feasible.

But Persephone is the heart of it all.

Her memory.

Her soul.

Her roots.

There's only one way to fix this. To free the Omegas. To save Hades. To *end* this once and for all.

Demeter's ties to her daughter have to be severed.

Which means the anchor must be released.

And Persephone's soul… *needs to be truly resurrected.*

My stomach drops.

The only way for that to happen is if Hades agrees to let Persephone go.

I… I'm not sure he's capable of doing that. His first mate. His *true* mate. His… his *heart.*

My eyes fall closed, my hands dropping to my sides.

Can I convince him to kill her memories? To send her soul to rest in a traditional resurrection cycle?

And what will happen to me in the process? I wonder.

Except, I can't think about that right now. I'll… I'll probably disappear entirely… since her soul is my soul.

I'll die. I wince. *I'm absolutely going to die.*

But what choice do I have? It's the only way to free the Omegas and to stop Demeter from killing Hades. And if he dies, I'll die anyway. So better just me than him, too, right?

And Maliki, I realize. *He has ties to Hades, too.*

If Demeter manages to reallocate all of Hades's power by using it to fuel her new world, then everyone Hades is connected to will be harmed as well.

Maybe Hades won't actually be killed. But he's already being hurt. And it's only a matter of time before I feel that, too.

That was the point of the cloud in my mind—the fog he used to *protect* me.

He knows I'm going to be impacted by Demeter's rerouting of power. By this… this *tree* and its branches that are strangling Hades.

I shake my head.

The first step is freeing him from this monstrosity.

The second step is rousing him.

And the third step… the third step is convincing him to do what needs to be done.

He'll hate it. But there is no other choice. I'll make him see that. Or I'll… I'll find a way to do it myself.

I glance upward. *Unless there's already a way…*

My head cants to the side, a new idea taking form.

What if I join Pip in that swirling mass of souls? I think. *Will I simply go back to the plane of nonexistence as a nonentity again? Or will it be different since I'm in my corporeal form?*

Maliki told me that touching a soul could kill me.

That was when he thought I was human, but I still feel mortal.

Aside from the life pulsing inside me, I realize, my hand falling to my belly again.

My brow furrows. *If I join that swarm of spirits, I'll be taking the one inside me with me, too.* My shoulders straighten. *No. Not that… That, I can't do.*

Sacrificing myself for Hades and the Omegas is one thing.

But the innocent energy inside me?

My gaze narrows. There has to be another way, then. Another way to sever Demeter's ties to her daughter and free Persephone's anchored soul.

Wait…

If Hades's power can be manipulated in this way to empower a new plane, thereby rendering him one with death… can't the same happen to Demeter?

Is there a way to reverse the energy flow?

She's using Persephone to reach Hades.

And I'm… I'm a conduit, too.

"This new link to Hades is exactly what we need to bolster our world." Those were her words when discussing my *resurrection* and how it was a mistake, yet a benefit.

A benefit she's currently using.

Only, I'm *not* her daughter.

So there has to be a way for me to cut her off. *Or shift the exchange of power.*

I'm going to need you to wake up, I think at Hades, once more evaluating the tree wrapped around him. *And I think I'll start by freeing you from these branches…*

MORPHEUS

I HALT MY STEPS IN THE UNDERGROUND TUNNEL, MY EYES narrowed as Serapina's scent calls to my beast.

"She's close," I tell Maliki, my voice soft but not a whisper.

Because there's no point in masking our presence down here.

The souls are well aware of our arrival, but they're too preoccupied with the chaos happening throughout the death pits to care about our intentions. All the spirits are funneling into an unknown orbit, which explains why the Soul Yards have dried up, as well as the Blood River.

Nothing is working as it should in the Netherworld Kingdom. However, Orcus and his mates are still holding things together above ground.

Mostly, anyway.

Still, whatever Demeter has done to Hades has caused catastrophic damage to death's ecosystem.

Which makes finding him—*and* Serapina—paramount.

If only I could still hear my mate. Her mental voice disappeared shortly after she started addressing the fog in her mind.

I determined the cause of that intrusion almost immediately, my instincts firing the moment I heard her investigating the darkness. But she couldn't hear my protests or my warnings that Hades was clearly trying to protect her.

Instead, she faced his magic and dismantled it. *Like a Goddess.* I'm both proud and terrified by what she's done.

Because if Hades is no longer protecting her from his pain, then it's possible she's lost consciousness like Mort, Howl, and Ossa.

"Do you feel Hades at all?" I ask Maliki, needing to distract myself from considering Serapina's current state. Worrying only leads to impulsive decisions, and I cannot afford to be impulsive right now.

I need to be strategic.

Thorough.

And most of all, *lethal.*

"Everything just feels cold," Maliki replies, his tone deadly serious. "And very bloody wrong."

I consider his words. "That's the power vacuum you're sensing." I face him. "Can you trace it? The heart of the wrongness?"

He stares at me, and I half expect him to issue a snarky retort. But instead, he narrows his gaze and says, "Maybe."

I arch a brow. "Then you should lead." Because while I know Serapina is nearby, I can't seem to pinpoint her location. But she's with Hades. And Hades is at the heart of the wrongness Maliki is picking up on.

"You actually know how to follow?" Maliki asks, some of that trademark wit making an appearance.

"I know how to do a great many things, Maliki. Lead us to Hades and our mate, and perhaps I'll introduce you to some of my talents later."

"Always flirting," he drawls, amusement shining in his gold eyes. But a visible shiver rolling through him has him sobering in a blink. "This way."

I don't comment, not wanting to interrupt whatever hint he just picked up on. His mind goes quiet, his thoughts singularly focused on something I can't hear. Not because he's intentionally keeping me out, but because he appears to be engaging one of the other mate-links in his head.

Which is basically what Serapina did when she dismantled Hades's protective energy—she homed all her attention on his essence and tuned out her other mates.

Only, that ended in a complete disruption for reasons I'm not fully aware of yet. Unconsciousness is the obvious explanation.

But I again ignore that potential and instead focus on Maliki's prowling form.

He moves like he's on a mission, something I appreciate as I trail behind him.

Neither of us knows this tunnel system. I only recently learned it existed after Hades brought me down here to show me the protective runes around his labyrinth. But there's a full network of an underground to explore, all laced in and through the death pits.

It's basically a different kind of maze, one with secret passageways masked as obsidian walls.

Maliki walks through one now, not flinching at all when he moves face-first through a visual blockade. He doesn't even put up his hand, suggesting he's either seeing something I can't or simply following his instincts.

No, not instincts, I realize, Maliki's mind still fuzzy from him connecting to another mate. *Directions.*

Someone is talking to him.

And given that I still can't hear Serapina at all, I assume it's Hades.

I don't know if he's actually voicing words into Maliki's head or if he's… he's guiding him in some other way. But it's clear that Maliki is on a mission.

Questions filter through my head, but I keep them to myself. They can be addressed later.

We need to find Serapina and Hades.

And then we need to complete this mate-circle. We'll be stronger as a unit with a shared connection across all of us.

Which means Hades is going to have to accept me as his equal.

He'll need to permanently mate Maliki, too.

But one step at a time.

The Enforcer steps through another solid black wall, then pauses just as I follow him into a similar-looking corridor.

"We're close," he informs me, voice quiet. "The dead should be coming through here to populate the Soul Yards and feed their lethal energy into the Netherworld Kingdom. But they're being driven into another… plane."

"The one Serapina has mentioned?" I guess.

"I think so," he says, not sounding certain. "Only, I think it's changing…" His brow furrows with the words, his gaze narrowing.

Without elaborating, he starts forward once more, this time heading down the hallway instead of through a different wall, only to freeze again on the threshold of another open area. His attention shifts upward, drawing my gaze up with his, and my lips part at the swirl of souls above.

It's like what Serapina kept thinking about, only… only worse.

"They're in agony," I whisper.

"Yes," Maliki agrees. "It's like they're being ripped apart."

I wince as a spirit splinters right above us, its lips parted in a silent scream.

Orcus's control above ground is not going to hold. Not with the chaos unfolding down here. He has to feel this imbalance. While he's an Alpha tied to the death world, he's not the one who manifested it. And all that energy is what feeds the Netherworld Kingdom, what emboldens the Death Fae and the Corpse Fae.

I understand because my dream world is what provides energy to my kingdom. The Ghouls and the Strigoi require dreams to feed. And I am the lord of that domain. If my manifestation were to suddenly be ripped apart by another entity—another *Alpha*—it would alter the stability of my domain.

Just as Demeter is altering the stability here.

She's taking Hades's manifestation and using it to fuel her own creation.

The Netherworld Kingdom will collapse if she completes this transition.

And there's nothing Orcus or his mate-circle will be able to do to stop it.

Because Orcus isn't the God of Death. He didn't manifest the death world. While he could, in theory, create his own version, it would take time.

Time, of which we do not have.

Maliki growls, likely hearing my analysis. Or perhaps

he comes to the same conclusion. It could also have to do with the souls above, as three more were just ripped apart over our heads. Regardless, he's moving again, his strides radiating purpose.

When he breaks into a run, I don't question him; I just follow.

He ducks as a new stream of souls shoots out of a nearby wall, their horrified eyes rounded and exuding pain.

Death is supposed to be peaceful, yet this is anything but.

He moves faster.

Harder.

His boots pounding against the stone floor.

Serapina's presence is all around us, her scent taunting my senses. *Where are you, little dreamer?* I demand, tired of this labyrinth. Tired of not hearing her. Tired of not *holding* her.

This is a nightmare.

And I much prefer fantasies to this insanity.

When Maliki jumps, I pause, my eyes widening at the cavern he's just carelessly leapt into.

"I have wings!" I remind him, furious.

But I jump after him, trusting him implicitly.

When we land with a thud—about twenty or thirty feet down—I wince. I'm immortal, as is he, but that doesn't mean we're unbreakable.

Fortunately, my genetics allow me to heal quickly.

Unfortunately, it's a fucking painful process.

I'm about to demand an explanation when a geyser of souls has me jumping sideways—which hurts, thanks to my still-injured lower limbs.

A curse escapes me.

And Maliki pants, his own torment evident in those

puffs of air, as well as his leaning form against a nearby wall.

"You knew that cyclone was coming," I realize aloud, my voice a low mutter that reveals my own agony from that jump.

"It's not going to stop either," Maliki mutters back to me, his hand on his side as he tries to steady his breathing. "There." He jerks his chin at a glowing rune. "Hades and…" He pushes off the wall and stumbles toward the symbol. "*Sera*."

I join him in stumbling toward the blue mark, my mind already analyzing the familiar sequence. "It's a concealment rune." One that's typically used when trying to hide something of value—like a secret room. "It shouldn't be flashing," I add, frowning at the enchantment. "The whole point is to *conceal*."

I don't touch the blaring rune, instead looking around it for some sort of hint. Some sort of *trigger*.

This has to be a mistake.

A *ruse*.

I'm about to say as much when a burst of swirling energy comes up from the ground and causes Maliki to jump toward the wall.

My eyes widen as his shoulder hits the rune, and he begins to fall *through* the wall.

I go to yank him backward, only to find myself tumbling forward with him into another cavern of sorts.

Fuck. I instantly try to retreat, my hold on Maliki resolute.

But it's too late.

I come up against a solid rock.

And darkness descends.

My instincts fire, my misting ability attempting to free us from this trap. But it's too fucking late. Inky bands are already surrounding us, the limbs reminding me of branches on a tree.

Demeter.

Her influence is everywhere.

Life.

Plants.

A garden… of fucking death.

Maliki tries to shadow, the desire one I sense running through his mind. When it doesn't work, he mentally curses. *Now what?* he demands into my mind.

I don't know, I admit. *I don't fucking know.*

Because none of this should be possible.

Yet here we are, being strung up in a flytrap like one of Demeter's garden pests.

In Death's domain…

SERA

A Few Seconds Earlier…

"Ugh," I mutter, hating this damn magic tree. I've been ripping off pieces of bark and breaking twigs, but it just regenerates in a flash.

And each time it regenerates, it *zaps* me. Like a punishment.

"I need a kn—"

The air shimmers around me, cutting off my grumbled statement.

I swallow and look up, expecting to see more souls. But movement from my left has me snapping my gaze toward a truly unexpected sight. "*Maliki.*"

I stand, so beyond pleased to see him that I might weep.

But he stumbles forward with Morpheus right behind him.

"Oh, good, you're—"

Morpheus turns around and runs right into the wall the pair of them just magically fell through. Only now the wall is made of rock again, apparently, so he collides with the solid surface and releases an irritated grunt.

I frown at him. "What are you doing?"

He grabs Maliki as panic settles over his features, the expression not one I've ever seen the God of Dreams make before.

Energy swirls and pulses, causing my frown to deepen.

Then Maliki and Morpheus lock gazes with one another. And… and freeze.

I stare at them. "Umm…" I creep forward, half expecting my mates to vanish. This all feels like a strange mirage. But I can feel the heat coming off my fae as I near them, their virile auras a welcome caress to my senses.

Only, they don't appear to see me at all.

I wave a hand between their faces, trying to grab their attention.

Nothing.

"Are you even real?" I wonder out loud.

I grab Morpheus's arm, wanting to see if I can feel him, and yank my touch away as electricity zips along my skin.

"What…?" That sensation reminds me of the tree suffocating Hades.

Narrowing my gaze, I poke Maliki and feel the same reaction.

Shaking out my hand, I evaluate their still forms. They're very much aware, yet focused on each other. "You can't see me or hear me," I say, glancing back at Hades. "And you're rooted to that treelike throne."

None of it makes sense.

Like it can't be real.

Only, it is.

I… I *know* this is happening.

Just like I can sense the life blossoming inside me—a life I couldn't sense before… *But Alina sensed it.*

Because she saw through the mirage.

Does that mean I can see through mirages now, too?

Did I finally fracture whatever hold Demeter had on my Omega soul?

Is it because of Pip? I wonder, glancing up again. *Does it have something to do with being reunited with my corporeal form?*

I have so many questions and not nearly enough answers.

But if I am seeing through this mirage, then maybe there are other talents I can access. Talents like Alina's.

She saved her mates from the illusions Demeter wove around them. Can I do the same now? Wake them all up to the reality around us?

Am I even seeing the full reality, though?

Hmm.

The tree seems to regenerate every time I try to pull it apart. But what if that's all mental? What if there is no tree and Hades just needs to be woken up somehow?

I close my eyes, irritated by this game. Frustrated by Demeter's tricks. *Tired* of being constantly used as a conduit for her plane of nonexistence.

I didn't *choose* this path. I didn't *choose* to be Persephone's host. I didn't *choose* to be Demeter's link to Hades.

However, I did choose my mates.

I chose Maliki. I chose Morpheus. I…

My brow furrows. *I didn't choose Hades…*

He was already linked to my soul, our fate intertwined without my consent. Although, I'm not disappointed in our destiny.

Well, I'm disappointed in how that destiny involves Demeter and this very twisted situation.

But when it comes to Hades, I'm not disappointed at all. In fact, I'm *enthralled.* He was a lot to take at first, especially with his marriage demands and the misunderstandings between us.

Then I saw the real him.

I saw the Alpha inside my fated mate.

The man who cares about his niece. Who is tender with me. Dominant, too. Yet oh so careful.

I walk back over to him and rest my palm against his cheek. "We still have so much more to explore together, Hades," I tell him. "So much more life to *live.*"

I want that with all my mates. I want the child inside me to be born, to be raised by me and my mate-circle. To… to have our own experiences. To be Sera, not Persephone, not Serapina, not Demeter's tool or daughter, just… just *me.*

No, not quite.

I want to experience *us.*

I want a future.

I want to build something fantastic.

But to do that, I need my mates to snap out of this daze, to be free from Demeter's tricks, and to… to dismantle what she's created.

She's using my soul to reach Hades. And she's also using *me.*

Because he reclaimed me.

So what happens if I claim him? Persephone never did that. She never engaged a bond-link of her own. And in searching her memories, I really can't determine why. It's like the consideration never crossed her mind.

Alphas claim.

Omegas submit.

Except, I know Omegas can claim, too.

Is that something Demeter never told her? *Is there a reason the desire didn't even occur to Persephone?*

I stare down at Hades's beautiful features. His cheekbones are so pronounced that they almost appear to be carved from stone. And his square jaw is equally as hard. But there's a softness I've seen in his eyes, a softness I miss right now.

"I need you," I tell him, my thumb tracing his lips. "You're my mate, Hades. And I need you to come back to me… to help me *fight*."

Because if Demeter can pull from his power by using me as a go-between, then he should be able to do the same to her.

Or maybe I can access them both, I think, looking inward at all the bonds inside me. The connections I possess with Maliki, Morpheus, and Hades. But also the links anchored into my soul—into *Persephone's* essence.

My palm remains against Hades's cheek as I hunt for Demeter's mental hook.

It's easy to find. Now I just have to figure out how to use the connection in reverse.

She's the epitome of a life cycle, the mother of fertility, a creator of the harvest. Yet she's poisoning her own power with death, weaving together a strand that shouldn't exist.

It defies the laws of order.

The laws of life.

The laws of *resurrection.*

I can taste the wrongness on my tongue, the very tangible nature of it drawing me deeper into the web of her creation.

My heart hurts when I discover the plane of Omegas, the way they're all housed in a prison that shouldn't exist.

And my heart aches at the reason behind it, too.

Because Demeter's intentions are not… infallible. She's protecting lives in the way an Alpha feels she should—by seizing all control for the betterment of others.

However, that's not what Omegas need or crave.

We want Alphas who respect our rights to choose our fates.

Alphas like Morpheus and Hades.

They've valued my consent. Respected my boundaries. Nurtured my desires.

And I've learned that Alphas have a goodness to them, too.

Demeter isn't evil. She's just… lost. Trying to make amends for a lifetime of atrocities. Trying to be a good mother to her daughter.

She's failed, a fact that saddens my soul.

But I understand her, too. I understand that she never meant to cause pain. She just… never understood the point of a sanctuary.

All that knowledge comes to me on a whirlwind of energy as I slowly pull myself away from her manifestation and return to the present. To my Hades. My Morpheus. My Maliki.

"It's time to wake up now," I tell them. "To see the truth and help me fix the wrongs of the past."

I'm not sure where these words are coming from; they seem to be a product of my inner being, of Persephone merging with my own psyche.

Or maybe I'm finally awake myself.

Finally embracing my inner Omega. My fate. *My purpose.*

I don't question it. Instead, I lean down and kiss Hades softly on the lips, then lower my face to his neck.

"*Persephone.*" Demeter's voice echoes through the

chamber, her sudden presence not surprising me in the slightest.

Because she felt my mental prodding, my exploration, my *knowledge.*

She's been in charge of my being from the moment I was reborn.

But it's time to clip her wings. To dismantle her control. *To free my soul.*

A hand clasps my shoulder as a wave of dominance rolls through me, one that tries to force me to submit. My knees shake beneath the weight of it, my spirit screaming inside.

I don't want to obey.

I don't want to *supplicate.*

However, that presence is… it's… it's overwhelming. It's harsh. *It's demanding.*

"Stop this nonsense," Demeter commands, her words echoing through my mind as she asserts even more power over me.

Morpheus and Hades have *never* made me feel this way. Have never throttled me with their Alpha auras. Have never *growled* in this manner.

Yet Demeter does so now, her presence suffocating.

Like the roots around Hades, I think dizzily.

My eyes are no longer open, my body succumbing to the will of another. A will I don't want to bow to. A will that should *never* be asserted over me.

In all of Persephone's memories, I can't find a time when Demeter did this to her daughter.

But I realize now that there are patches of missing recollections, like the one I only recently recalled of what happened *after* Demeter put Persephone in the plane of nonexistence.

Has Demeter altered her daughter's mind? That would make

sense, given everything that happened. Given what Hades never knew.

The relationship between mother and daughter is so toxic. So *wrong.*

But she isn't my *mother.*

Even if she forced my reincarnation, she's not the one who raised me.

Alina was more of a mother figure to me than anyone else.

And Alina taught me how to be strong. She may have been a bit overprotective at times, too. But she understood the importance of thinking for herself and ensured I comprehended that importance as well.

It's a trait my mates admire in me. A trait they've praised me for and fostered in their own unique ways.

A trait I refuse to ignore now, I think as my knees touch the ground. *I will not bow. I… I* dissent. That word echoes through my mind as I force my eyes to open once more.

I'm clutching Hades's leg, his dress pants in tatters from the tree's abusive hold around him. His hip is mostly bare, too, which is where I realize I've rested my head after kneeling on the cold stone floor.

But that's not all I notice.

The roots… they seem to be less rigid than before. Almost like they've lost their hold due to Demeter being distracted.

By me, I think. *She's focused on me now, not him…*

Her hand has shifted from my shoulder to my nape, her power swimming over every inch of my being.

But as I stare up at the Alpha who has shown me compassion, the Alpha who groveled after admitting his mistakes, the Alpha who never truly gave up on his mate… I realize that I want him to be mine. So very much mine.

He may have belonged to Persephone first.

However, he's *my* Alpha now.

Part of *my* circle.

With Morpheus and Maliki.

All three of *my* fae. My mates. *Mine.*

Demeter isn't part of our connection. She's a foreign entity. A being of the past. The catalyst for our future.

I exist because of her.

But I've survived because of *my* decisions. My determination. My inner *strength.*

"I choose *this,*" I say, my voice barely audible due to the crushing presence behind me. "*I choose my own path.*"

Demeter growls, the sound harsh and clamorous against my senses.

However, a purr inside my mind helps battle the intensity.

A purr I love.

A purr I'm not sure I'm hearing in the present time or from the past.

Though, it doesn't matter.

Because it's enough to help free me from the proverbial noose around my neck. Enough to force me to *act.* I press my face into Hades's hip, feel his bare skin touch my lips. And do the only thing I can think to do—I open my mouth and *bite.*

A Few Seconds Earlier...

Serapina, I think, in awe of her resilience. Her *strength*.

I've only recently become aware of where we are and what's happening, but I feel her pushing back against Demeter. *Hear* every thought. Sense her determination and alluring spirit.

She's so much more powerful than she realizes.

Not only is she standing up to an oppressive Alpha, but she's… she's also battling an ancient familial bond. The one between mother and child.

She's severing her soul from Demeter's, and with each passing instant, she's yanking me back into consciousness.

My beautiful, amazing Omega…

My purr is automatic, my pleasure radiating through our bond just as Demeter releases a dominant growl. I nearly release a rumble of my own, but Serapina melts into my side, her lips caressing my skin.

You can hear me, I realize. *Sera—*

Her teeth sink into my hip, the bite so utterly unexpected that I lose all conscious thought. All feeling. *All everything.* And simply exist in the sensation of being claimed by my Omega.

A brightness unlike anything I've ever experienced blossoms inside me. My heart beats as though for the first time. My veins flood with warmth. *Life.*

My Serapina…

I feel *alive* in a way I could never have anticipated. Empowered. Cherished. *Owned* in the best way imaginable.

Hades? she whispers into my mind.

Demeter unleashes a violent growl before I can respond, and Serapina's touch disappears as she releases a pained whimper.

My eyes open, the world coming into focus around me as I see my mate's body fly across the room into a wall as a result of Demeter's vicious throw.

The blonde strands in Demeter's fist tell me she grabbed my mate by the hair, too.

Fury unlike any other boils inside me as I burst free from my restraints—the tree disintegrating in my wake.

Demeter startles then, looking at me in surprise.

My chest rumbles in response, my power wrapping around me in a blanket of intense energy that feels more potent than ever. More deadly. *Lethal.*

Because it's riddled with vitality, too.

Vitality from Serapina.

Our gifts are mingling in a unique manner, one that emboldens my steps as I mist to Demeter and wrap my hand around her throat.

Her bright blue eyes widen, and she grabs my wrist.

Energy hums from her touch, but it doesn't affect me. Because it's less potent than before. *Weakened.*

Serapina's bite seems to have impacted Demeter's control, our fresh bond superseding the one Demeter claimed over her daughter before.

Or maybe Serapina has simply learned how to block it.

Demeter renews her effort, some of her shock dying off as ire fills her features.

She's always loathed me, simply for being the Alpha who mated her daughter. I was never good enough. Never *right.* "Death and life are not compatible," she told me once.

I suppose she was right.

But now I know what is "compatible."

Death and a *reincarnated* mate.

Serapina is my equal. My other half. *My heart.*

I feel her pulse as though it's my own, her essence continuing to mingle with mine to manifest a bold entity. An unyielding power.

Only, some pieces are missing.

We need more than just the two of us, more than just an Alpha and his Omega. *We need our—*

A punch to my chest sends me soaring backward as a fucking tree root seems to drive right through my heart. Everything spins. The air… the air wheezes from my lungs.

And a furious sound erupts from somewhere in the room.

From Serapina…

It was a scream, but filled with anger, not fear.

So strong, my mate, I think at her as I wrap my hands around the item lodged in my torso. The bark digs into my palms, my vision darkening with each passing second.

This won't kill me.

However, it… it *fucking hurts*.

Electricity floods my insides, the foreign energy belonging to the Goddess of Fertility. She's trying to drown me in life.

I shove back with a bolt of icy death, causing the root to wilt and die before me, the bark turning to ash in an instant and relieving the pressure on my chest once more.

But without it anchoring me to the wall, I fall to my knees, only to be caught with a strong arm around my torso.

Maliki. I recognize the writhing sensation against my skin, his tattoos exuding a healing essence that instantly calms my insides.

He forces me back up, his golden eyes catching mine. Then he leans in to bite my fucking shoulder.

I'm about to demand that he explain himself when he strikes at my neck, and I suddenly realize what he's doing as his claim snaps into place.

It's dizzying and different, and not quite right.

I reach for him and yank him to me, but he's already coming willingly, his head canted to the side to expose his throat.

Any other day, I might have tried to be more creative.

But this needs to happen quickly.

So I sink my teeth into the thick tendons of his neck.

That fucking hurt, he growls into my head.

Likewise, I say, releasing him as power floods through me. *Mate* power. But it's still incomplete. *Where's Morpheus?*

However, I already sense my cousin before I even finish the question, my eyes finding the God of Dreams standing between Demeter and our mate. His arms are stretched out at his sides, his hands open, his shoulders tense.

I can't see what he's doing, but I assume he's thrown Demeter into a sleep state.

However, he won't be able to hold her for long. She's too fucking powerful—because of her links to her daughter's essence.

I hear all the knowledge swimming through Serapina's head, how she's realized what Demeter has done to the sacred bond between mother and child, how she's still abusing it now by siphoning energy through Serapina's connection to me.

It's so fucked up and convoluted, an abuse of motherly authority.

Yet it runs deeper than that. It's founded on Demeter's fertility power.

She abused the cycle of life to create Persephone, I realize. *That's… that's how she became pregnant.*

The concept clicks after hearing Serapina's mental analysis depicting *why* Demeter created her own plane and why she feels so responsible for all of Omega kind.

Serapina thought it was out of a responsibility to Persephone, as a result of being gifted with life via Jove.

However, it… it's because of that life—a life she should never have been able to manifest and nurture—that she has this unique link to her daughter. This obsessive, all-encompassing desire to *control* every aspect of Persephone's former and current existence… It's all grounded in the fact that Demeter feels Persephone is *her* creation.

Not a daughter.

Not an Omega.

But a *possession*.

"You're just like all the Alphas locked away in Pandora's Box," I say, stalking toward the treacherous bitch. Her eyes flutter, Morpheus either releasing her from his mental hold or her power coming through. I'm not sure, and I don't fucking care.

I slam my fist into her face, then grab Morpheus by his

dress shirt and haul him toward me. He arches a brow, the only indication of surprise, before he slams his palm against my chest. "On the forearm," he tells me. "I don't fancy wearing your mark on my throat, *Cousin*."

I grunt, then offer him my own arm, and we both bite one another at the same moment.

Heat floods my veins, his power a fucking aphrodisiac to my senses.

Or maybe it's heat from our Omega, because I lock eyes with her and note the way her pupils are dilating.

She's feeling the impact of our bonds, our Omega right at the heart of it all, and it's flooding her with energy, igniting her spirit.

Slick permeates the air, drawing my gaze down her naked body to the sweetness between her thighs.

It's such an intense reaction, one that I know is driven by the need to *mate*.

But we have something else to create first. Something powerful. Something… *spectacular*.

"Distract her," I tell Morpheus, referring to Demeter.

My cousin grins. "Happily."

A piercing scream leaves Demeter, the sound music to my fucking ears. I'm almost tempted to go into Morpheus's mind to see what fresh nightmare he's just sent Demeter into, but I have a more important task to see to.

Glancing at Maliki, I add, "I need you to protect us."

My best friend nods. "Always."

It's a vow, one I take to heart.

Because I believe him.

I believe in all of us.

I believe in this circle, this dynamic, this destiny.

But for us to embrace our future, we need to deal with the past.

A fact that has me walking toward Serapina. I don't

mask my intentions, allowing every member of our circle to hear what I intend to do.

But most especially, our Omega.

Our *heart.*

She reaches for me the moment I'm within arm's length and pulls me in for a kiss. A kiss I indulge. A kiss I *own.*

I heard her thoughts about sacrificing herself, how she thought her soul needed to be reborn, how I may never let Persephone go. But this runs so much deeper than my soul's mate. So much deeper than who I used to be and who I long to become.

This is about *us*—our new bond as Serapina and Hades. She's the mate I never knew I needed. The mate I never knew I desired.

I loved Persephone as an Alpha should, devoted my existence to protecting hers.

But with Serapina, the foundation of my adoration runs impossibly deeper.

She's a strong wind on a cold winter's night, the perfect breeze to stir death from its grave.

I've been living in the shadows for so long that I forgot what it meant to step out into the light. To truly exist again.

She taught me that in a manner I wasn't expecting.

I love that she has memories of my past life with Persephone. I love that she knows the Alpha I used to be. Because it's going to make who I am now—with her—all the more impactful.

I clasp her nape, my opposite arm encircling her waist as I mold us together. Energy hums between us, my Omega knowing exactly what to do. How to weave. How to *create.*

Use me as your conduit, mate, I tell her. *Use all of us.*

She shivers in my arms, her body seeming to vibrate against mine.

Serapina is no longer overthinking or analyzing; she's simply *existing*.

And it's a beautiful fucking sight.

Our own beacon of light.

I hold her with all my strength, ground her as an anchor, and give her all of me.

My death.

My love.

My own fucking soul.

I'm utterly hers. *For etern—*

Pain pierces my midsection, causing my knees to nearly give out.

Morpheus and Maliki both shout, though I can't… I can't hear them.

But as I look down, I realize with horror that I was pierced from the *front*. Not the back.

Which means…

Which means it went *through* Serapina.

Her blue eyes are wide, her lips parted on a silent cry.

And then she goes limp in my arms.

Her life… *extinguished*.

No.

No.

"*No*!" I roar, taking hold of the branch that's connecting us in bloody matrimony, and introduce the limb to *death*.

It dissolves into ash, just like the other one.

Only, Serapina doesn't stir. She collapses into me instead, utterly devoid of movement. Of feeling. Of… of anything at all.

I shake my head, refusing to accept this.

She's not human. I *know* she's immortal.

But Demeter's tricks, her powers, her fucking games…

I'm tired of playing. I'm tired of this ridiculous dance. I'm tired of her insane need to *control.*

"She's no longer yours," I tell the Goddess of Fertility. "She's *ours.*"

I lift Serapina into my arms and slowly face the Alpha who has the audacity to try to take my mate from me. *Again.*

Maliki has Demeter wrapped up in shadows, his expression furious. I'm not sure how her lethal branches got around him, and I don't fucking care.

Because this ends—

Power erupts through the room, the source of it coming from an unexpected source.

From the female in my arms…

A Few Seconds Earlier…

Light.

Creation.

Life.

It's all around me. Swimming through my veins. Flourishing in my soul, my very being, *my heart.* But it's underlined by something cool. Something harsh. Something deadly.

My Hades.

We're weaving together the most unique plane in existence, a manifestation that will serve as a sanctuary for all of Omega kind.

That's not exactly what Hades had in mind when he embraced me. He wanted to dissolve Demeter's world and allow life to re-create itself.

It's what I want, too.

But we need a safe haven to replace Demeter's plane.

A place for the Omega souls to thrive and be reborn at their own pace.

It's a delicate dance, one I'm enjoying when agony rips through my being and yanks me back to the present.

To Demeter's blunt rage.

To her *branch* piercing my sternum and driving into Hades.

To the very real insanity of the moment.

I can't see Demeter, but I can feel her fury. Her betrayal. Her need to annihilate *me*, the entity housing her daughter's soul.

Because she's finally realized we're not the same being.

She's been so blinded by her own ambitions and needs that she never considered trying to get to know *me*—the being born with Persephone's spirit inside of her. She just assumed I was her daughter. Assumed I was the same Omega she ensconced in that prison she called a world.

I played the part once, pretending to be Persephone in that mansion back in the Monsters Night dimension.

Reaper fed me the words I needed to say, ensuring I distracted Demeter.

That won't happen again here.

Because she knows who I truly am now.

I'm not afraid. I'm relieved.

And more than that, I'm *ready*.

I know what I need to do.

So I close my eyes and let death take me. It's what has to happen. I understand that now.

This is all about rebirth.

Resurrection.

The cycle of life.

Darkness descends, but I'm still very aware of myself.

My soul. The tiny bundle of energy pulsing inside me. I stroke it with my mind, whispering contentment. *Everything's going to be okay*, I promise my future child. *Trust me…*

The entity does, implicitly.

I feel that now.

It's a treasured bond, one that begins at conception.

An Omega's purpose is to protect creation.

That's a lesson Demeter will never understand. She's an Alpha. She was never meant to birth Persephone.

I'm going to fix that now.

By finishing what I started with Hades, weaving a new plane of *existence*. One where souls go to thrive. A funnel from the afterlife that feeds resurrection into our current dimension.

I see now that there are already some Omegas who are hidden inside other forms throughout the various realms.

I can't pinpoint them, just sense them.

Demeter has been busy, repopulating the various dimensions with Omega souls. But so many are still trapped in her creation.

Not for much longer.

My new plane—which won't be a world so much as a gentle space that nurtures the restoration of life—will provide them with the freedom they need to choose their fates. Or rather, engage in a second chance at living.

Because that's the point of resurrection, something I fully grasp now that I've tasted Hades's mind and his power.

He's the God of Death, which is so much more than simply overseeing the souls of the world. He manifested an afterlife. The world of the dead. He gives opportunities, as well as creates cycles of his own.

It's so closely tied to fertility in a way that I don't think Demeter ever truly understood.

But I do.

I see the important role he plays in the general life cycle, the need for balance between his gifts and mine.

Only, it's not just us here.

I feel Morpheus's influence, too. His fantasy elements help me manifest even more potential outcomes for the Omega souls. They can dream of who and what they want to be, then perhaps engage in such a life upon resurrection.

It's so much kinder than living in a state of nonexistence.

Freedom is all I care about here.

But I also recognize that some of the souls may prefer to hide.

Or return, I think, considering the Omegas in the various dimensions that have already been reborn beneath Demeter's influence.

I weave a new layer into the world, creating the ability for the affected souls to come and go, making it a sanctuary for Mythos Fae Omega kind.

So I suppose it will be more tangible than I originally intended.

However, it's necessary.

Because if the Alphas are as cruel and as bloodthirsty as Morpheus once said—which I have every reason to believe—then a physical plane may actually need to exist.

It's an intricate process, the manifestation of a new plane. But it's empowering, too. In a beautiful way.

I don't make it large, just… just a safe space. One with trees. Fire lilies. A sun. And an area for snow. It's… it's a combination that's all me and my mates.

A dreamland filled with magic—courtesy of Morpheus.

A place to embrace the afterlife with a direct bridge to Hades's death world.

And I add some sensation elements, too. Like soothing stones and a stream of calming waters. Those enchanted items embody Maliki and his intriguing tattoos.

All of us can be found in this land, and it's powered by our circle. Guarded by our collective essence. Only Omegas will be allowed to pass through or stay. They can make the land into what they desire, or move into the real world once more—as new beings.

Pleased, I pull back to begin dismantling the barriers around Demeter's world. Her power pushes against me, but I simply absorb it—since it should be mine anyway. She used me as her conduit. This is her payment for that betrayal.

Persephone deserved better.

I deserved better.

All of Omega kind did.

Good intentions or not, Demeter is a monster. She has to be stopped. And I… I know how to ensure this never happens again.

What are you doing? she demands into my head, feeling my presence as I create the hole I need to free her trapped souls. *You ungrateful child…*

Oh, I'm grateful, I tell her softly. *Grateful you resurrected your daughter. Grateful that I could help right the wrongs of the past. Grateful for this second chance at life. Grateful for the mate-circle I found.*

I mean every word.

And I inform her of why… *I wouldn't be here or exist if it weren't for you, Demeter. So… yes, I am grateful.* It would be wrong to deny it. *But I'm also going to ensure you can never do this again.*

Because she has to be stopped.

Omegas are not meant to be locked away in a plane of nonexistence, Demeter. Omegas are meant to thrive. To create. Your world—the Mythos Fae Realm—has deteriorated and fallen apart. Because without life, there is only death. And balance is the key to existence.

She says something back to me in a snarl that I can't understand, mostly because I'm not trying to listen. She's been in my head for long enough. Controlled my life for long enough. Made decisions on my behalf for long enough.

It's my turn to choose.

My turn to exude authority.

My turn to *live*.

I pluck away the final block, then wait for the souls to find their new life source—my new plane.

It's all connected now.

Because Demeter's creation is mine. It was built with me as an anchor. And as soon as the last soul leaves, I will release it for good.

The Alpha screeches in my head, her agony almost hurting my heart.

She truly feels this is the only way. But I'll soon put her out of her misery, too.

Come on, Omegas, I think, trying to coax them to leave the dark plane and enter the light.

However, when the first glimmer comes through, it's… it's not what I expect at all.

If I were corporeal, I would blink. But I'm in a weird state of existence, somewhere between soul and Goddess.

I can *see*, just not truly interact.

Though, the soul that just came through looks directly at me.

Because it's *Pip*.

His big blue eyes smile happily, then he does one of his

trademark jigs, and I feel myself weeping inside. *You're okay…*

He executes a bow as though he can hear me, and maybe he can, then he twirls around and raises his hand toward the hole I've made.

For a moment, I think he wants me to go inside, but then I realize he's signaling for someone to come outside.

No, not just someone. *Everyone.*

A string of souls begins to follow him, similar to the geyser I saw shooting upward in the death pits. Except this wave is filled with curiosity and joy, the spirits eagerly leaving their prison and following my Pip to the world I've just created.

It's… it's everything I desired and yet so much more.

You're alive, I think.

Though, I suppose, he's truly not. He's still a spirit. But he's *safe.*

And what's more, he seems to know exactly what to do.

Because he's my familiar, I realize. *This… this is why…*

I still, understanding flooding my mind as I suddenly grasp the purpose of our connection. Fate introduced us for a reason. I would one day need Pip not just to help guide me in the death pits, but also to take the souls to their new state of existence.

Which means he, too, could potentially be resurrected.

Only, I created the world for Omega souls.

Maybe he's a lost Omega spirit?

Or maybe… maybe he can reside there because it's tied to me.

I don't fully know, but I follow him and the others and see them enter my world with ease, the spirits whirling around in happiness just like Pip.

It's unlike anything I thought I could manifest. Yet it all feels so exquisitely right.

However, I'm not done…

Guard them, I think at my familiar.

And he gives me a little nod, suggesting he can definitely hear me.

Then he starts to march around, like he's a guard on duty, and I nearly laugh inside. He's being funny on purpose, trying to lighten the moment.

Maybe because he knows what's coming next.

I blow him a mental kiss, then head back to Demeter's plane. I can no longer hear her, my mind having blocked her entirely when Pip appeared.

There's no reason to listen to her.

She'll be a nonentity soon enough.

I return to the hole I created, aware that the plane of nonexistence is now empty. All that's left to do is demolish it entirely.

Which means… letting go.

To be fully resurrected is to not remember the past. To not know a former life. And to build one anew.

I'll forever be altered by what I've recalled, and the links between my soul and my mates, but I have to see this through. It's the only way to destroy Demeter's manifestation—by releasing the anchor.

I can feel in my mind that I have not just Hades's approval but also his respect. He may not realize what I've done or where I am. However, on some level, his soul is aware.

It's time to say goodbye.

To be officially reborn… as Sera.

I focus on Persephone, her entity inside me, her memories, and her life. *You can finally be at peace*, I think at her. *Your legacy will live on with me. I promise.*

Because a part of me will always be grateful for her existence. She's the reason I have life.

But *I* am the reason I've survived.

And my mates are my anchor now.

As well as the tiny life inside me.

Holding on to my circle with every ounce of my being, I allow myself to be swallowed into the darkness once more and say goodbye to the past.

So I can firmly embrace… *the future.*

MALIKI

Energy ripples through the room, causing my tattoos to writhe as I squeeze them around the Alpha bitch who dared to hurt my mates.

That branch came out of fucking nowhere, infuriating me to my core.

One moment, Demeter seemed to be asleep, and the next, her bloody tree creation speared through Hades and Sera.

If anything happens to her… I can't finish the thought. I felt my own fucking heart break when the scene unfolded, but Sera almost instantly pieced me back together when she burst into a ray of power.

She's alive, I tell myself for the thousandth time. *She's alive and needs me to fucking focus.*

I send another bolt of agony—agony that rivals my

own after watching that tree assault my mates—through my inky ribbons and directly into Demeter.

The bitch doesn't even flinch.

Because she's not *aware.*

She's gone inside her mind to fight a battle none of us can see. But we can feel it.

Because Sera is tugging on our life strands as she weaves some sort of magical haven. Hades has taken the brunt of her need for power, his forehead sheened with sweat. He's still holding Sera in his arms, his dominance and aura cloaking her in a shield of protection.

While Morpheus focuses on Demeter.

Through his mind, I can hear some of what's happening, because he seems to be able to see it through her thoughts. Sort of like a mental escape or a dream, only this is very fucking real.

Our Goddess has created a new state of existence. A sanctuary for Omegas. I can *feel* it. And now—

Demeter roars, the sound echoing through the cavern as everything seems to go still.

The world.

The souls.

The entire fucking kingdom above us.

Even my heart.

Until a whooshing wave follows, the scream of spirits piercing my ears and forcing me to drop to the floor. They swirl in the cavern around us, answering to Hades's power—a power that is furious in nature and marking him as a true God of this world.

He's mending the Netherworld Kingdom, I realize, the sensation of it caressing my skin and raising the hairs along my arms. *Styx…*

I've always known Hades was powerful, but this is on a whole other level.

Because of Sera, I suddenly understand. *Because of our circle.*

He's weaving together a new tapestry of death through his creation, healing the damaged souls and sending them back to where they belong—into an afterlife cycle.

Relief filters through the atmosphere as the spirits find peace, the flows of the death pits restoring order and allowing icy vitality to reenergize the fae of the kingdom.

I feel it running through my veins, healing something deep inside me that I didn't even realize was broken.

Hades has always commented on how the fae don't need to worship him, that referring to him as a lord was a ridiculous formality.

However, he's proving to the kingdom now that he truly is their God. Their source of power. Their *life*.

Typhos Lucifer might be the Hell Fae King and manage the Hell Fae Realm, but the Netherworld Kingdom *thrives* because of their Mythos Fae Alpha God.

It's something I never considered before, mostly because I've never seen Hades use the full extent of his abilities.

I'm absolutely witnessing it now.

And not just his talents, but Sera's as well.

Fucking incredible, I breathe, my tattoos losing their grip on Demeter.

Because she's no longer breathing.

Sera knocked the Alpha out, though I'm not quite sure how. Regardless, I'm fucking proud and wish our Omega would wake up so I could tell her.

And apologize, I think, wincing. *I should have seen that damn tree…*

Impossible, Morpheus replies into my mind, obviously hearing my thoughts. *None of us saw that coming. But our mate is okay, as is the child inside her.*

My focus instantly goes to Sera's belly. "You can sense the baby?" The question spills from my lips, my body vibrating from a very different source than that power around us. "And it's okay?"

"Yes," Morpheus says, answering both of my queries with the single word.

Hades's eyes open and he looks at me, his irises swirling with intensity. "I can sense you in the life energy inside her," he says, then holds Sera out toward me. "Comfort our mate, Maliki. I need to have a word with Demeter."

His choice of demands—*comfort*, not *protect*—makes me wince.

"Voicing a protection command is pointless," Hades remarks, obviously overhearing my insecurity. Or perhaps he just read it in my body language. "You'll always protect her, Maliki. We all will. She's our heart. Now help her heal; she just exuded a lot of effort, and it's going to take her time to recover."

I don't make him ask me a third time, just step forward and take our girl from his arms. She instantly curls into me, her lips parting on a sigh that warms every part of my being.

Sera's alive.

She's safe.

And our child is thriving, too, I think, closing my eyes as I wrap her in my soothing shadows. I don't know if it's actually *my* son or daughter, but it doesn't matter who helped create the life inside Sera. That child will be loved by the circle and treated as our own, regardless of genetics.

Because we're in this together.

As a unit.

Forever.

I press my forehead to Sera's and hum into her mind, letting her hear my adoration and promises of eternity.

My mate. My everything.

I'm only vaguely aware of the energy swirling around us, of Hades approaching Demeter and grabbing her by the throat.

Morpheus joins me in surrounding Sera, his lips pressing a kiss to her temple. "Sleeping beauty," he murmurs. "You are a wondrous Goddess, little dreamer. Your plane for the Omegas is beautiful and perfect."

"Can you see it or just feel it?" I ask him.

Rather than respond, Morpheus pushes a visual into my mind of what he imagines the world looks like. I realize it's not quite that he can *see* it for himself, but he's picked up on the details through Hades's and Sera's minds, his power to fantasize and create visages helpful in painting a picture.

It might not be completely accurate, but I trust his instincts.

Just as I trust that Sera manifested exactly what the Mythos Fae Omegas need to thrive.

Hades releases a low growl, drawing my attention to him for a moment as he rips Demeter's head from her body with his bare hands.

"A bit grotesque," Morpheus murmurs. "But I understand the need."

"She can't die, though, right?" I ask, frowning as the body magically dissolves into a pile of dusty bones. "And how can we even be sure this is real? She's proved to be clever and evasive."

Hades doesn't answer right away, his hand holding her head by the hair as it slowly begins to disintegrate like the rest of her. When whatever spell he's woven reaches her forehead, he finally releases what remains of her form, then watches the rest of her turn to bone-colored ash.

With a wave of his hand, he sends her remains into a

nearby geyser of souls and watches as the particles swirl upward with a scream of sound.

My lips part as a spirit seems to appear in the middle of the chaos, eyes wide and mouth open in an agonized snarl.

Hades cocks his head as he stares at the entity. "Thanks for the tip, Demeter. May your second chance be *fruitful…*" With another gesture of his hand, he sends the soul straight upward, the sound of fury echoing in its wake.

Until silence descends once more, and the other spirits continue to writhe happily in their space.

Order is fully restored.

I can feel it in every ounce of my being… because I feel Hades's peace. Sera's contentment. And Morpheus's… *amusement.*

"That was clever," the God of Dreams remarks. "Using her own *invention* against her."

Hades shrugs. "Seemed a fitting punishment—she forced all the Omegas to go through a form of resurrection, why not send her into the same cycle? At least she won't remember anything she's done."

"Until someone tells her," Morpheus drawls.

"Maybe she'll be reborn as a better God."

"Is there such a thing?"

Hades looks at him. "We can hope, can't we?" His words are serious, his mind telling me he's thinking about all of the fallen Alphas in the Mythos Fae Realm. "Our home world is about to change… perhaps for the better."

"With the return of Omega kind," Morpheus says, his tone a bit more sober now. "It would be nice to be able to return to our palaces someday." He looks around the cavern, his blue-green gaze zeroing in on the flow of souls. "But I fear we're equally needed in this realm. Perhaps *more* needed, actually."

He and Hades lock gazes.

"It would be nice to be able to *visit* the Mythos Fae Realm in the future," Hades finally replies, reiterating Morpheus's words with a twist. "But this is our home now—the Netherworld Kingdom and the Morpheus Kingdom."

"Does that mean you'll consider helping me build a new palace?" Morpheus asks him. "Perhaps on the mountain that stands over the tunnel between our kingdoms?"

Hades considers him. "What's wrong with my palace?"

"Well, for one, it's been destroyed," Morpheus informs him. "Seems the God of this kingdom went on a date with a tree..." He looks at a pile of burnt bark crisps, making me recall how Morpheus and I were wrapped up in roots and branches after falling into this room.

Though, apparently, it was all a mirage.

But Hades was very much tied to whatever Demeter had created down here.

A tree, I guess, based on the mental conversation flowing in our mate-circle.

I shake my head. "This is going to get tiresome," I mutter, already exhausted by all the outward and inward commentary. "Is there a way to turn it off?"

Morpheus, who is still standing close to me and now running his fingers absently through Sera's hair, grins. "No, Enforcer. I'm afraid not."

A sigh escapes me. "Great."

Hades steps up to Morpheus's side and looks at me. "I seem to recall you being in favor of listening to my cousin more," he tells me, referring to the time when I told him that perhaps he should consider working with Morpheus, not against him. "I hope you enjoy headaches, *subordinate*."

"Fuck you, *my lord*," I return in a falsely sweet voice.

The God of Death smiles. "I would prefer to watch you fuck our mate, Maliki."

"After she's done resting," Morpheus inserts before I can reply. "She expended a great deal of energy. We'll play… when she's awake."

"She'll need to eat," I add, thinking of the baby. "I know she's immortal… but…"

"We'll feed her energy while she sleeps," Hades says. "It'll be more than enough."

"Feed her energy?" I echo, my brow furrowing. "How…?"

"We'll teach you," Morpheus promises. "But first, we need a safe place to take our mate." He looks at Hades. "So back to my palace proposal…"

"On the mountain over the tunnel," Hades mutters. Then he shakes his head. "Fine. But no sun. It'll blind my fae."

Morpheus faces him. "We'll need at least one greenhouse for her roses."

"Another for fire lilies."

"And a real fucking garden, Hades. None of that statue crap."

"She liked that garden," Hades mutters. "And my ice."

"Then we'll have to get creative, won't we?" Morpheus tells him. "Good thing you're part of the God of Dreams's mate-circle."

"This is not your fucking mate-circle," Hades bites at him. "It's *mine.*"

"It's ours," I interject. "And stop bickering. Sera is trying to sleep."

They ignore me, the pair of Alphas going into a full negotiation on the palace they want to manifest.

I listen for only a handful of minutes before I shadow

Sera and myself back to Tank's place, tired of the two bantering Gods. Their Alpha energy is fucking suffocating.

I can't believe I'm going to be tied to this for the rest of my life, I think, irritated.

But most of my irritation melts away when I come face-to-face with a panting Ossa. Howl and Mort are panting, too, the giant beast sitting up on the bed and wagging their big black tail.

"Enjoy your nap?" I ask the trio.

Ossa gives me a little growl, but it's less violent than usual. And when she comes forward to lick my face, I still. She's *never* given me a kiss.

"I see you finally won her over," Hades muses, appearing beside me.

Ossa releases a deep bark, then lunges for her master, forcing Mort and Howl to go along with her.

Hades falls beneath the weight of his giant wolf beast, his body disappearing under the mountain of black fluff.

I snort, more than a little amused by the sight of the God of Death being mauled by his familiar. He growls in response, clearly irritated by the show of affection. But I catch sight of his hands scratching the ears within his reach, and I hear the relief in his mind at having found his beast *alive*.

It's clear that while he was technically unconscious, he was still very aware of certain things—like his life force draining those closest to him.

He fought it, trying to protect his familiar, me, and Sera. But Demeter… Well, Demeter won't be a problem anymore, thankfully.

"Can you manifest a new blanket?" I ask him. "For Sera." Because the bedding is currently soiled with fur, something I don't remark on out loud. But Hades must hear that part because he doesn't just manifest a blanket; he replaces the damn bed.

With a much larger one.

"That's ridiculous for this small space," I mutter, but I walk over to tuck Sera into it anyway. "Tank is going to be pissed."

"I'll make him a new hut," Hades says, his voice muffled since he's still being mauled by his pet.

"You can add that to the long list I've already started for you," a deep voice says as Typhos Lucifer materializes in the room. "Welcome back, Hades. We should talk."

The God of Death heaves the largest of sighs from the floor.

And I'm suddenly very glad that I've already put Sera in the bed. Otherwise, her naked body would still be in my arms—something I do *not* want the Hell Fae King to ever see.

He might have his own mate.

However, Sera is *ours*.

"Have you ever heard of knocking?" I demand, irritated by his abrupt presence. King or not, he can't just shadow or mist into any room he chooses.

The Hell Fae King arches a dark brow at me, reminding me very much of Hades.

"You heard me," I tell him, not caring to bow to his dominance today. I've done that before. Kind of, anyway. But I am not in the fucking mood for formalities right now. "It's been a really long fucking… Styx, I don't even know. Month? Year? Regardless, I am not in the mood to pander to your 'royalness' right now."

Both of Typhos's eyebrows shoot upward.

And then my brother appears beside him.

"Great," I mutter, shaking my head. "I see you've taken after your mate's manners."

Az blinks at me, then frowns at Typhos. "What did you say to Maliki?"

"Nothing," the Hell Fae King grinds out. "I was speaking to Hades."

"In *my* space," I tell them. "Where *our* unconscious mate is trying to rest. You can see how that's a problem, yeah?" I cock my head. "Or would you like me to pop over and visit Cami while she sleeps?"

Typhos growls, and Az presses a palm to his chest to stop him from advancing on me. "Point noted, Maliki," my brother says calmly. "Perhaps we can discuss this outside?"

Hades sighs again, then nudges his beast off his body and attempts to move to his feet. But Ossa knocks him right back down with a final kiss before slowly backing off.

The creature jumps up onto the foot of the bed and plops down, the three heads all focused on Typhos. Ossa releases a warning growl, one she usually reserves for me. Only, this one sounds like an actual threat. I reach over and pat her on the head, pleased that she's protecting Sera.

And the beast chomps at my hand.

I release an exhale and shake my head. "I see our bond was short-lived."

She snorts.

But I swear there's a glimmer of amusement in her silver eyes.

At least until she looks at the Hell Fae King again.

"What the fuck happened to you?" Typhos demands, ignoring the creature entirely. He's looking at the dried blood on Hades's torso, as well as his ripped dress pants.

"Got into an argument with my proverbial mother-in-law," Hades responds. Then he vanishes.

Typhos growls.

Which only makes Ossa snarl.

Az looks at me. "Mother-in-law?"

"Demeter." I fold my arms. "We'll handle the cleanup here. There's no need for you to hang around."

"This is still my realm, Maliki," Typhos responds, his voice holding an edge to it. "And I am still *your* king."

"Well, I'm mated to two Gods now," I tell him. "So if you have any feedback you'd like to provide, you're welcome to share it with my Alphas."

Az's expression conveys his amazement. "You joined a mate-circle?"

"Surprised?" I drawl.

"Not really," he admits. "You did open a portal to another world filled with mate games. Seems appropriate."

I roll my eyes. "Another item for you to take up with Hades."

"I have," Typhos cuts in. "He's not the forthcoming type." His ocean-blue eyes dance over me. "Which I suppose is the theme for your *circle*."

My lips curl. "It is. So if you were hoping for a long discussion on what's occurred, that hope is in vain."

"However, I'll provide a swift summary while tending to your *list*," Hades adds as he materializes once more, this time in a fresh all-black suit. Even his hair is combed.

Did you and Morpheus finish the palace already? I ask him mentally, wondering where he changed.

No. He's only just started working on the foundation. It'll take hours, maybe days, Hades replies into my mind. *I just misted into Serapina's old hut to freshen up. I would never leave you to handle the Hell Fae King alone.*

He doesn't scare me.

I know, Hades says, his amusement humming through our bond. *Your inability to fear powerful beings is why we're friends.*

I thought we were best friends, I tell him.

He glances at me, the amusement now showing in his

features. "You make a good subordinate, Enforcer," he says aloud.

I roll my eyes again. "It's like you want me to stab you, *my lord*."

"Sparring can be fun," Hades murmurs. "Perhaps you can practice on Azazel while Typhos and I discuss the state of the kingdom."

My brother arches a brow.

He's always in a fighting mood, his inner Black Phoenix adoring violence.

"I can't," I inform both Hades and Az. "I'm on guard duty."

Hades's lips twitch. "A task I know you'll take very seriously."

"Always," I reply, meaning it. "It's my favorite assignment to date."

"I'll keep that in mind for the future," he muses.

"Don't bother." I sit on the bed beside Sera. "I have a new boss now, remember?"

He just shakes his head, but I hear the humor in his mind.

However, it doesn't show at all as he faces Typhos. "Orcus is waiting outside for a debrief. Shall we?"

The Hell Fae King's jaw ticks. "I've never been fond of Mythos Fae."

"A lie," Hades murmurs. "We're allies for a reason, Hell Fae King."

Typhos doesn't respond, but a flicker of understanding seems to flash in his features. Then he starts toward the door, only to pause and look back at me. "Next time… I'll *knock*."

"Good." I cross one of my ankles over the other. "Because *next time*, I won't be nearly as polite."

Ossa snarls in agreement.

I reach over to pat her head again. This time, she doesn't try to bite me, just leans into my touch as a show of solidarity.

Fleur is going to hate this, I think.

Hades must hear the thought because his lips twitch. *She's asleep on Serapina's old bed, none the wiser.*

Good. And Athena? I wonder at him.

Flying around with Morpheus, I assume, Hades replies.

"What about Pip?" I ask, shifting our conversation to a vocal one rather than a mental one.

"Guarding Omega souls," Hades tells me. "We'll see him again… when Serapina needs him. But for now, he's protecting what our Goddess has built."

With that, he leads Typhos from the hut.

Only my brother lingers for a beat, his gaze flickering between violet and black as his inner beast studies me. "I'm happy for you, little brother," he says, the words sounding belittling, yet his tone reeks of sincerity. "Mateship looks good on you."

He doesn't stay to hear my reply, just slips outside and quietly closes the door behind him.

I look down at the female asleep only a foot away from me and smile. "Yeah," I agree. "Yeah, it does."

SERA

I BLINK, THE FLICKERING BLUE CANDLELIGHT CONFUSING TO my senses.

Where am I? I wonder, taking in the dark decor of the bedroom around me. *Black silk. Bedposts decorated with skulls. A balcony that overlooks twin moons…*

This isn't where I was moments ago.

What happened to the cavern? The death pits?

I roll onto my back and stare up into a pair of beautiful blue-green eyes.

"Hello, little dreamer," Morpheus murmurs, a glass of something clear in his hand. He's sitting beside me on the bed, wearing nothing but a pair of gray sweatpants. "Welcome back to the land of the living."

A snort sounds to my right, drawing my gaze to Maliki, who is seated on my opposite side with one leg bent upward to support his arm. "We're in the Netherworld Kingdom. So, technically, this is the land of the dead."

"True," Morpheus agrees. "It's a figure of speech,

which I hear you're a fan of, especially if they're *humanisms*."

Maliki rolls his eyes. "You've been talking to Hades too much."

"Indeed." The deep voice comes from the foot of the bed, where Hades is standing. He brings a wine glass up to his lips for a drink, his dark eyes holding mine. Then he cants his head. "How are you feeling, Serapina?"

I gape at him, then look at Maliki once more, and Morpheus, too. "I… I don't understand." I refocus on Hades. "How long was I out?"

The God of Death holds my gaze, his expression intense. "A week."

My eyes widen even more. "*A week*?" I sit up and run my hands over my body, then note the gold gown I'm wearing. It's silky and a bit sexy. But it's what I find beneath the gown that I find most interesting. *A pulsing life in my belly*.

My shoulders fall and I close my eyes, relieved to find that everything is as it should be.

But I was out for a week?

"That doesn't make any sense," I whisper. "It felt like minutes."

"You created a world, darling Goddess." The weight on the bed shifts, suggesting Hades has either sat down or placed a knee on the mattress. "That takes supreme effort and intense skill. Not to mention what you did to Demeter…"

My brow furrows. "To Demeter…?" I try to remember, to recall the execution of my plan.

I… I said goodbye to the past.

By releasing an anchor.

Persephone.

However, I don't remember what happened after that.

I shake my head. "All I did was free Persephone's entity… or part of it, anyway." Because, technically, her soul is still within me. Only, it's no longer burdened with the memories of a past life.

Which is very strange.

Because I… I remember certain events that I sifted through before, such as experiences that helped me better understand Hades as well as my general situation.

But the only recollections I possess are officially my own. And the memories of Persephone that I recall… are from my point of view of hearing them, not from her mind.

She's gone.

I'm both grateful for and saddened by that fact.

Hades… My eyes open, and I find him sitting on the bed now, close to my legs, his expression intense.

Yes? he responds into my mind, no doubt hearing me say his name.

Persephone's gone.

I know.

Are you…? Stars, I'm not sure I can even ask.

He arches a brow. *Am I…?*

Are you okay? I force out, suddenly very afraid that I misunderstood his permission before.

Which is asinine.

We were one as we began creating that plane. He was in my mind, and I was in his, our powers melding, our lives mingling, our souls *rejoicing*.

But I still… I have to know…

"Maliki," Hades murmurs, holding out his drink. "Set this on the nightstand, please. I'm going to need both hands for this."

"As you wish, my lord," Maliki replies, earning him a dark glance from Hades as he passes off the glass. Maliki merely seems amused as he sets the drink down, his golden gaze challenging as he stares back at Hades.

The God of Death narrows his eyes even more. "Be a good *subordinate* and take off our mate's dress."

"Shouldn't we explain what's happened first?" Morpheus interjects. "Particularly to Demeter, since Serapina seems to be unaware of her current state?"

"When you dismantled the anchor—by sending Persephone on—you also destroyed Demeter's connection to reality," Hades summarizes, his focus on me once more. "She essentially… fractured."

I frown. "So all the power imploded?" I attempt to translate. "Like, inside of her?"

He considers me for a moment, then reaches out to cup my jaw and pulls me toward him.

I go because I… I want to be near him.

And when he lightly kisses me, I kiss him back.

"Most of her essence—her Alpha energy—was inside that plane," he tells me, his palm sliding to my cheek. "So when you destroyed it, you destroyed her."

"But she's immortal…"

"Mmm," he hums, agreeing with me. "An immortal who mastered the art of removing Mythos Fae Omega souls before placing them in another plane. A fascinating piece of knowledge that we officially possess."

I hear it in his mind now—that knowledge he speaks of.

"You used that information to liberate her soul," I realize, tracing his thoughts. "And sent her on to be resurrected." Because her soul is immortal and she therefore can't die. But she could be given a second chance… in another form. In another life. *Without her memories.*

The way all the Omegas have been reborn or will be reborn.

"That's a fitting punishment," I decide out loud.

"I was only able to accomplish it because you weakened her," he tells me. "And the idea came from your mind—to let go of the past. The best way to do that was to force her soul into a resurrection cycle. She'll never know who she once was, or anyone else for that matter."

"Unless she had a fated mate," Morpheus murmurs.

"Well, yes, that. But with all the Omegas being reborn, too…" Hades shrugs. "There are a lot of second chances in our future." He runs his thumb along my bottom lip. "Including *ours*." He kisses me again, this time with more passion, his mind syncing with mine.

You asked if I'm okay, he whispers gently into my head. *I'm more than okay, Serapina. I'm ecstatic. I'm proud. I'm so fucking in love that I can hardly breathe.* His tongue enters my mouth. *And all I've wanted to do for seven very long days is ravage my mate. My equal. My Omega. So yes, my heart, I'm very fucking* okay.

Tears prick my eyes, his words going straight into my chest. *In love?*

He chuckles and pulls back a bit. "I think it's safe to say that we're all very much in love with you, Serapina."

"After that display of Goddess power?" Maliki asks. "*Love* is a weak word for how I feel."

"Enamored?" Morpheus suggests. "Enchanted? Enslaved?"

"Are you trying to be alliterative?"

"Just suggesting words, *Enforcer*," Morpheus replies. "Obsessed? Possessed? Utterly infatuated?"

"Fucking hard and wanting to claim?" Hades inserts. "Or are you going to keep *chatting*?"

"I do love to talk," Morpheus murmurs. "And if memory serves, our Serapina likes my dirty words."

My cheeks begin to heat.

"Oh, but we should probably feed her first," Morpheus adds, causing me to slowly glance back at him.

"I do not want food," I tell him, the words enunciated clearly for his—*and Maliki's*—benefit.

"You were asleep for seven days," Morpheus reminds me.

"I'm also apparently an immortal Goddess now," I return. "Therefore, I don't need food."

"The baby might," Maliki says.

His words actually do give me pause.

But as I evaluate myself—and the beautiful life inside me—I realize I meant my words. "The baby and I feel fine."

"Then you were right," Morpheus muses, causing me to frown.

However, his words don't appear to be directed at me, but at Hades. "I usually am," the God of Death informs him.

"About what?" I ask, wanting to understand.

"We all fed you energy while you slept," he tells me. "I said it would be enough to sate you and ensure you woke up ready to be claimed."

"Claimed?" I echo, confused. "But I've already been *claimed*."

"By our bites," he agrees. "Yes." His dark eyes glitter with intent. "However, mating bonds inspire a fever-like need to rut—which we've tamed for the last seven days. So, now you'll be claimed by our beasts."

"For hours," Morpheus informs me. "Maybe even days."

"Definitely days," Maliki says, his palm roaming up my arm to my shoulder. "You gave me a task, *my lord*. Shall I proceed?"

"A good *subordinate* wouldn't need to ask," Hades replies.

Maliki smiles, his attention entirely on me. "May I remove your dress, Sera?"

I glance down at the silky gold fabric. "I'm not the one who put this on."

"No, I did that," Morpheus murmurs. "After bathing you earlier."

"We took turns caring for you while you slept," Maliki explains before placing a kiss against my bare shoulder, his lips an inch away from the thin strap of my gown. "It seems Morpheus favors dressing you in gold. I personally find pale rose to be a beautiful color against your skin."

I lock gazes with Hades. "And you?"

"I prefer you naked," he says, utterly unapologetic.

My lips curl. "Then Maliki should probably take off my dress."

"That is what I recommended, yes," Hades murmurs before leaning in to take my mouth again in a heated kiss. His hand moves to my hair, knotting with my strands as he angles my head in the way he prefers.

I sink into him, loving the way he dominates me with his tongue.

Loving even more that Maliki's hand has gently knocked the strap off one of my shoulders.

But it's Morpheus who pulls the other strap down, thus taking some of my gown along with it to expose my breasts.

Hades growls, the sound hungry against my mouth.

He's wearing far too many clothes—a black button-down shirt and pants. Stars, he even has shoes on still.

Actually, *all* of my mates are overdressed.

It's something I fully intend to fix, except Morpheus's mouth against my nipple distracts me from my intentions.

Then Maliki joins on the opposite breast, and I… *Oh.*

Oh, stars…

All three of them have their mouths on me, kissing me, licking me, *sucking*… I swallow, unable to think. Only feel. It's… it's intense.

I…

"We're going to worship you," Hades promises against my mouth. "Show you what it means to be *our* Goddess. Then you're going to take all of us together. And we're going to introduce you to the future, mate."

"A future filled with pleasure," Morpheus murmurs.

"Tenderness," Maliki adds.

"And *love*," Hades whispers. "You're the heart of our existence now, Serapina. Always."

Morpheus's mouth travels up to my neck, his lips hot against my throbbing pulse. "The center of our circle."

"Our very own queen." Maliki sinks his teeth into my nipple, causing me to gasp against Hades's mouth. "Now lie down on the bed so we can pledge our fealty, Goddess Sera."

Hades chuckles. "Yes, be a good girl and do as our Enforcer says."

Morpheus nibbles my earlobe, his palm against my belly as he guides me back. "We're about to make every dream a reality."

"Meet every desire and introduce you to new heights," Hades adds.

"And send you to the fucking stars…" Maliki says, his gold eyes smiling down at me. The world is reflected in that gaze. A world I want to fall headfirst into. A world… that's all mine.

Because I'm finally the woman I've longed to become.

Sera.

An Omega.

A Goddess.

Surrounded by three strong, beautiful mates.

My very own circle of fae.

Existing in a present I no longer fear. Because, for the first time in my life, my future is being crafted by my own choices.

I chose them.

And I choose *this*.

My mates. My circle. *My life…*

"THIS PLACE IS AMAZING," ALINA SAYS, LOOKING AROUND the palace Morpheus and Hades built. "*Wow.*"

It's been a little over a week since I woke up in this new space, and even longer since I last saw my sister. But, for once, she didn't demand to see me.

Because she knew my mates were taking care of me.

She'll always be my big sister, always want to protect me and shield me in her own way. However, I can sense her faith in my mate-circle.

And that makes me happier than I can even articulate.

I'm finally… *me*.

It's a liberating feeling.

One that has me smiling as I take in the surrounding rose garden. It reminds me of the one I used to tend to back in our home world. Only, this one is lit by a purple light that's enchanted to function as sunlight. And there's a faint dusting of snow falling along one row, bringing with it that scent of winter blossoms.

It's perfect.

It's magic.

It's *life*.

"Hades manifested this part for you, didn't he?" my sister asks, her lips curling a little.

"Yes," I murmur. "With some input from Morpheus, though." I glance at the statues decorated with green vines. "They… compromised." I'm not sure that's the right word. From what Maliki told me, it was a week of bickering.

I kind of wish I had been awake to hear it.

But I enjoyed the benefits of waking up to a completed project.

The bedroom they manifested… the giant bed… the even larger bath…

I shiver.

My mates are a fantasy come to life. Which is appropriate, given that one of them is the God of Dreams.

"How is… Death's Palace?" I ask, aware that Orcus rebuilt most of it for his circle.

She smiles. "Less creepy than before."

"Even with Reaper's design choices?"

She considers that for a moment. "Well, there are a few, er, violent updates, I guess." Her brow pinches. "He's been manifesting weapons and hanging them on the walls like art."

"That sounds safe for my niece," I deadpan.

"That's what Flame said!" she exclaims. "Well, not exactly like that, but he… he's trying to talk reason into Reaper. But Reaper feels Thea needs to learn protection skills, especially with the Mythos Fae Omegas being reborn. He's afraid an Alpha is going to mist in and steal her."

"Oh." My nose scrunches. "I can understand that fear." Especially after having visited the Mythos Fae Realm with Maliki and Morpheus. I really don't have any interest in ever returning, though I suspect we will eventually.

Maybe when things calm down.

Or… or to *help* calm some things down.

I don't know yet.

Everything is about to change in that world, which is exciting and terrifying. I just hope the other Omegas are able to find loving mate-circles similar to mine.

Good Alphas are out there. I know it. I have two of them. My sister has another. We can't be the only Omegas who have found our happily-ever-afters, right?

Still, Reaper's concern for Thea is valid.

Fortunately, she has a pack of fathers who will do anything to protect her, and a group of uncles who will fight for her, too.

You'll have that as well, I think, talking to the life blossoming inside me as I palm my belly. *Your fathers won't let anyone touch you. And neither will your mother.*

"Orcus has already created a bunch of wards, similar to that place in Greece we visited, to alert him if any Alphas mist into the palace uninvited," my sister tells me.

I nod. "Hades and Morpheus have done the same here." We don't know yet if we're having an Alpha or an Omega or something else entirely, but it doesn't matter. My mates are all about protection for me and our future little one.

"But I guess ensuring Thea knows how to defend herself makes sense," Alina goes on. "Except she can't even walk yet."

"Which I guess means the weapon art isn't a danger yet either," I point out. "So you have time… to talk some sense into Reaper. Or Flame can maybe knock it into him."

She huffs a laugh. "He's already trying. He actually asked Maliki to help him."

"And what did Maliki say?" I wonder out loud.

"He took Reaper's side," she says, giving me a look. "So. Good luck with that."

I smile. "That sounds like Maliki. He seems to idolize Reaper."

"I don't *idolize* the mad fae," my mate says as he shadows to my side, clearly having overheard his name and taken that as an invitation to join us on our stroll through the garden. "But I respect the Styx out of him."

"As you should," Reaper says, appearing on Alina's other side. "I'm fucking amazing."

"You are," Maliki agrees.

Alina stops walking and faces her mate. "I thought you went to spar with Flame?"

"He did," Flame growls as he also appears in the

courtyard. "But then he heard you thinking about his art and claimed you were calling for him."

"She thought my name," Reaper points out. "Ergo…"

Alina sighs. "That's not…" She trails off and shakes her head. "I was just telling my sister about the renovations at Death's Palace."

"Cupcake Palace," Reaper tells her.

"We are *not* renaming it," Flame growls at him.

"Strawberry Palace?" Reaper replies. "Fuck Palace?"

"*Reaper*," Alina chides.

"What? Thea isn't here." He glances around like he wants to make sure he's right, then looks at her and arches a silver eyebrow. "Nesting Palace? Slick Palace? Pus—"

She puts her fingers over his lips, to which he wraps his hand around her wrist, opens his mouth, and nibbles on her. "You're…" She heaves another long sigh. "Reaper."

"I am," he murmurs against her hand. "*Your* Reaper. And I want to show you some… new renovations."

Her brow furrows. "More renovations?" She sounds exhausted.

"Another nursery," he tells her.

Alina's nose scrunches. "Another one? But Thea already has a room."

"For baby number two," he clarifies, causing my sister's dark eyes to widen.

"*What?*"

"Orcus told him your heat is coming soon, and Reaper's… being proactive in his planning," Flame explains.

Alina looks ready to pass out. She glances at me, her eyes still wide. "I'm going to have to, er, continue this tour later. It seems my mates and I need to… have a talk."

I bite my lip to keep from smiling and instead nod in understanding. "Have a nice, uh, *talk*."

Her cheeks pinken a bit, then she wraps her arms around Reaper and says, "Palace. Now."

His lips curl. "As you wish, pet." They vanish, and Flame goes with them, leaving me alone with Maliki in the garden.

"Why were you spying?" I ask him.

"I wasn't spying," he returns. "I was guarding."

"In our own palace?" I face him. "In the garden?"

He lifts a shoulder in a shrug. "Old habits die hard, trouble. I've been watching you for over a year, and honestly, I don't think I'm ever going to stop watching you."

"Stalking, you mean," I correct him.

"Stalking. Watching. Hunting." He shrugs again. "All the same, yeah?"

I just stare at him.

And he stares back.

"What can I say, sweet mystery?" he murmurs. "I'm fucking obsessed with you." He pulls me into his arms. "And Hades also asked me to come seduce you."

"Seduce me?" I echo.

He nods solemnly. "You know how the lord feels about tasks and assignments."

"I seem to recall you claiming that I'm no longer your boss," Hades says as he walks into the garden. "I also don't remember asking you to seduce our mate."

"Well, I believe you told me to seduce your wife," Maliki drawls. "Something about doing what needs to be done to convince her to marry you and all that. So I asked if that included fucking her, and well, you didn't oppose. In fact, I think you encouraged it."

"So we're talking about an *assignment* from weeks ago?"

"Months ago, really," Maliki corrects him. "But you know me. I like to be thorough. Take my assignments seriously and all that. And I think your wife might finally be ready to marry you, yeah?"

Now it's my turn to give my mates wide eyes. "Uh, what?"

Hades studies me for a moment, then nods slowly. "You know, I think you might be right, Maliki. Do you think she'll be willing now?"

"Only one way to find out, really," Maliki says, taking a step back.

I gape at both of them, confused. "We're already mated."

"We are," Hades agrees, closing the distance between us. "But we would like to be something even more."

"We?" I repeat, my throat going dry.

"We," Morpheus murmurs, appearing at my back.

And suddenly all three of my mates are dropping to one knee, their gazes intently on me as I spin around in a circle between them. "Oh, this... you don't... I mean..." *What are they even doing?*

"Serapina Everheart," Hades begins. "Goddess of our hearts, love of our lives..."

"We would be incredibly honored to be your mated husbands," Morpheus goes on. "For eternity..."

"And whatever exists beyond it," Maliki says. "Will you have us truly? Marry us in front of all of the Netherworld Kingdom?"

"And become our Netherworld Fae Queen?" Hades finishes, holding out a sizable box that contains a beautiful gold crown with a blood-red stone at the center of it.

"I..." Tears spring to my eyes. "Yes. Of course I'll marry you all." I don't know about being a *queen* since this kingdom doesn't actually need one, but I don't care about the title. I just care about them. My mates. *My fae...*

I have no idea when they organized this, or if my sister

even knew it was coming, but I've never felt more loved at any other moment in my life.

Hades stands and places the crown on my head, then kisses me soundly on the lips before releasing me to Morpheus. And finally, Maliki is there, kissing me until I can't breathe.

All three of my fae.

Forming a circle around me.

Spinning me between them.

Touching me on all sides.

Making me feel like the most important woman in all the realms.

"You can update that registry now," Morpheus says conversationally.

"Already done," Hades replies, a hint of emotion in his voice. "But the wedding will make it all very fucking clear."

"Good," Morpheus murmurs. "Thank you for fixing the problem."

"What are you both talking about?" I ask, confused and a bit overwhelmed by the possession rolling off all three of my mates.

"The Netherworld Fae Registry," Hades says, my chin suddenly caught between his fingers as he forces me to stare at him while Maliki hugs my back. "You marked yourself as *single*. And darling *wife*, you are *not* fucking single."

"Not even a little bit," Morpheus agrees.

"You're very much claimed," Maliki murmurs against my ear. "But we want the entire kingdom to know it. No more flirty fae at bars."

"No more rejections at bars either," Hades inserts.

"And no more false notes in a registry," Morpheus concludes. "We want the world to know you are *ours*, just as we need them to know we're yours."

"So I hope you like gold dresses," Maliki says softly. "Because I think Morpheus is already manifesting a dream gown."

I release a startled laugh and shake my head. "I'll wear whatever you want." Because a wedding has never mattered to me. "I already have everything I've ever desired."

"Then we'll introduce you to more possibilities," Morpheus tells me. "Your dreams will forever be endless, sweetheart."

"And we'll fulfill every single fantasy you conceptualize," Hades promises, his nose brushing mine. "Now I want to see you in just the crown, mate. So let's head back to the nest… and play."

I would be a fool to refuse such an offer.

But I can't help replying, "Only if you promise to knot me, Alpha."

He releases a growl, one that vibrates me to my core. "*Always*, Omega. However you want, wherever you want."

"With Morpheus, too," I whisper, shivering at the thought. "While Maliki takes my mouth."

"Our demanding Omega is getting quite good at voicing her wants and needs," Morpheus muses, his lips brushing my shoulder. "Your wish is our command, little dreamer."

The world disappears around me, and I'm suddenly right in the heart of our nest with all three males surrounding me.

It's the perfect conclusion to a perfect day.

An introduction to destiny.

A happily-ever-after… that will go on… *for eternity*.

The End

The Mythos Fae Realm will never be the same. The Omegas are coming. The Alphas are on the hunt. And Pandora's Box is about to implode. Learn more in *Knotty Mythos Fae*, a standalone reverse harem in the upcoming Mythos Fae series.

Not ready to leave the Netherworld yet? Click here for a sexy little bonus scene…

Looking for more standalone books related to this world?
Their Lethal Pet (Alina's story)
Their Royal Pet (Coming October 2026)

USA Today Bestselling Author Lexi C. Foss loves to play in dark worlds, especially the ones that bite. She lives in North Carolina with her family. When not writing, she's busy crossing items off her travel bucket list, or chasing eclipses around the globe. She's quirky, consumes way too much coffee, and loves to swim.

Want access to the most up-to-date information for all of Lexi's books? Sign-up for her newsletter here.

Lexi also likes to hang out with readers on Facebook in her exclusive readers group - Join Here.

Where To Find Lexi:
www.LexiCFoss.com

www.ingramcontent.com/pod-product-compliance
Lightning Source LLC
La Vergne TN
LVHW050917080826
845145LV00001B/116

* 9 7 8 1 6 8 5 3 0 4 1 1 9 *